FACING OFF

TANYA ROSS

Trigger warnings

This book contains romantic interludes only appropriate for ages 14 and above, a sexual predator character, torture, and violence.

*For my daughter, Ashley, whose love, support, and ideas made this book
better than my wildest dreams.*

"The phoenix hope, can wing her way through the desert skies, and still defying fortune's spite; revive from ashes and rise."

—Miguel de Cervantes

____

Recap of Rising Up
BOOK ONE OF THE TRANQUILITY
SERIES

____

At the start of *Rising Up*, Ember Vinata's mother, Talesa, dies. No one answers Ember's questions about her death.

Ember discovers her home has been ransacked and searched. Later, she finds her mom's ring, a token the city grants to outstanding citizens.

Will Verus achieves his dream of a rise to fame and is installed as a Plauditor, an emotional guardian and surveillance officer.

Xander Nobel is labeled a REM (resisting emotional management) and thrown out of the city to The Outside. After walking for miles through extremes, Xander finds other REMs who he begins to organize into a unit.

Will helps Ember with the disaster at her home, is smitten with her, and begins an investigation to determine the cause of Talesa's death.

Will and Ember begin a relationship, but City Hall instructs Will to disassociate with Ember. Later, Will makes a decision to break up with her.

Sciolists take Ember to City Hall for questioning; an examination reveals Ember's super empathic abilities.

Xander and his crew discover a burn site Outside where bodies have been torched.

After the Magistrate discovers Ember's ability, he takes her into his residence for "protection and training." Ember tries to flee unsuccessfully. She is captured, but not before she steals one of the Magistrate's journals.

"Ember and Will discover that the rings are used to poison people whom the Magistrate considers are threats to his power.

Will and Wee decide to rescue Ember at the Plauditorium.

Before it can happen, Xander and his REMs take over the Plauditorium at gunpoint and hold the Plauditors hostage.

Xander shoots Will during the takeover, and Will dies. Ember discovers she can reverse time and then is able to prevent Will from being shot.

Will and Xander agree to team up together with Ember, the REMs, and Plauditors, to lead Phoenix, the rebel group.

Going on the city's public broadcast, the trio reveals the Magistrate's corruption.

Will and his party travel back to the burn site in The Outside. Ember finds numbers of victims' rings etched into tree bark but discovers her mom's ring number is not there.

Ember, Will, Xander, and Wee pledge to begin a revolution.

And that's where *Facing Off* begins!

Soundtrack

Facing Off has a chapter-by-chapter soundtrack! Tanya Ross has chosen music specifically to enhance your reading experience. For the link to the soundtrack, visit www.tanyarossauthor.com and click on the tab for "Facing Off Soundtrack." You will find the link to YouTube and Spotify.
Enjoy!

Facing Off
BOOK TWO OF THE TRANQUILITY SERIES

by
Tanya Ross

1

Will's Loyalty

Will we die today? Will's hands shook, a trembling he'd seldom experienced. He had spent little time in his life thinking about death. Until now.

He and his three companions were criminals. Fugitives. Targets. Enemies of the Magistrate.

They had dared to do the impossible: rebel against Tranquility's revered leader and his Elite. Their plans were raw, tenuous, and risky. They'd been to The Outside, the unforgiving, brutal no-man's-land, and were returning to the danger zone, the heart of the city, to continue the revolution they had set in motion. For this rebellion, they would sacrifice everything, even their lives.

Will and his three companions, Ember, Wee, and Xander, rode in a noiseless, auto-piloted vehicle they'd commandeered the day before.

Their arrival would be met with aggression. They couldn't possibly just float back in through the gates. *If only we were phantoms,* he mused.

"Guys, it stinks so bad in here!" Xander hollered from the front seat.

"Try not to breathe," Ember said, fanning the air in front of her.

"Wee's got the right idea. He fell asleep the minute we got in here." Will gestured to where Wee sat, his body sprawled out and his head lolled to the side.

The van still reeked of corpses carried from Tranquility to The Outside—victims murdered by the city's leader, the Magistrate. The Outside was where they were now, ready for their daring attempt to slip back into the city.

Despite tiny windows and slight ventilation, it thrilled Will to ride in the harsh cargo space. Overjoyed to be anywhere with Ember, his new girlfriend.

Girlfriend. He still couldn't believe they were together. Just looking at her took his breath away. It should be against the law for anyone to be that beautiful. Ember had a smile that electrified him down to his toes. He wanted to be a better man because of her. He wanted to deserve her.

But how did anyone deserve a girl with a superpower? He remembered the first time she'd told him she could both feel and see his energy, all his emotions on display. He had gaped at her in disbelief, feeling stripped down to his soul. When he learned she saw auras around every person, he knew he could never disguise who he really was. The implications were a lot to handle ... He could never hide his feelings. By then, though, he had already committed himself to her. Already fallen in love with her.

And then he flashed back to the most traumatic event in his life, when Ember revealed deeper power. Collecting her own emotions and those of the surrounding people, Ember could stop time. When she did that, she stayed outside the time freeze. Only she was animated. In doing that, she could change what happened moments before.

A shotgun blast had killed him.

He rubbed his chest as he remembered. He had been dead. There was blood everywhere, but Ember had intervened. She had saved his life by erasing five long minutes of utter chaos. It was the first time Ember had ever warped time.

When he'd learned of the entire episode, his love for her intensified. He knew he would never want to live without her. She represented all that was good in a world fraught with lies.

A gear shift from the van jerked him to attention. The vehicle shuddered and made an uncustomary rumble, jarring him out of his memory. Will felt a jolt, then another, followed by a smooth, seamless glide. An abrupt, turbulent stop caused him to fall sideways.

"We must be approaching." Will's voice cracked slightly, and his eyebrows pulled together.

Weeford, Will's best friend, woke as the van came to its rough halt.

"I wonder how far out we are?" He rose from his sitting position on the corrugated metal floor. Standing on his tiptoes, he tried to peer out the abbreviated window above his head but had no success. The window was too high in the twelve-foot-tall van.

"Xander's stopping a good way out," Will said.

"He can do that?" Ember asked, adjusting her position. "I thought this thing was automated."

"Emergency brake. That's why the rough landing." Will chuckled. "You okay?"

Ember rubbed her left hip. "I'm gonna be feeling that for a while."

"Yeah." His body was also stiffer and achier than he thought. The rough ride, with his butt jostled by bumps in the terrain, had taken its toll. Not to mention what they'd been through before the ride—their takeover of the city's Plauditorium, the communications center for the government. All broadcasts originated there. Employees known as Plauditors monitored the city-wide cameras, but they also made sure that the citizens received ongoing positive support. They were the encouragement team, the loyal responders to any citizens' crisis.

Although it went against every humanitarian bone in his body, their rebel group had taken all Plauditors hostage until they'd pledged loyalty to their cause. It was a brazen victory but one that had yet to play itself out. Their rebellion, named Phoenix, had only just begun.

"We won't be visible from the city," Will continued. "Someone will track the transport's GPS, but I figure no one will venture out to find us. It's dangerous and inconvenient. They'll think we'll be stuck Outside and die."

Ember shook her head, doubt etching its signature on her face. "The plan is risky. Leaving the vehicle. Finding a way in. I hope Xander is right about there being a way."

Will didn't care for Xander much. In fact, he'd rather be cuddling up to a porcupine. He often wondered if his alliance with Xander was meant to be. But Xander was the only one in their group of insurgents who had previously been in the transport's garage just inside the city gates. Xander knew what they'd have to avoid. Unfortunately, Will had to trust him.

"Xander's fiery," Ember said with an upbeat tone. "I have confidence in him. His plans and experience are all we have."

And one other thing. Xander complimented Ember too much. Will saw the way Xander looked at her. He had a major thing for her, for sure. Ember was beautiful, so he couldn't blame him, but Xander was dangerously charismatic. He could charm even a concrete statue to life.

"We don't know what we'll be facing out there," Will said, raising his eyebrows. He looked into Ember's innocent eyes, knowing she felt his nervousness as if it were her own. With her empathic ability, she absorbed emotions like a sponge.

Will contemplated all he'd given up to be Ember's confidant. He'd risk his own life any day for her, and he hoped she knew that in her heart and soul. Although Ember could see his every emotion, Will pulled Ember to her feet and kissed her to make sure she understood the depth of his devotion. An aura, no matter how lush, didn't begin to satisfy the way he wanted to pour himself into her. She wrapped her arms around him and deepened the kiss. Her response erased the world around him and sent his circuits surging. He wanted to stay in the moment but resisted the urge. He released her with a sigh, putting his hands on both sides of her face.

"I wanted to make sure I got to do that one more time." His green eyes filled with worry.

"Remember, Will. You're a hero. A Plauditor! Nothing can take that away from you."

"I don't feel like a hero." He dropped his hands from her face. "And I sure don't feel like a Plauditor. Seems like a title from a long time ago."

Will's mind exploded with the memory. He had saved a boy's life, and the act had quickly catapulted him to fame. The city immediately upgraded his Status and appointed him as a Plauditor, the youngest one ever assigned. The position was one of the most desired in the city, and Will loved his job. He'd believed he was perfect for it.

"The hard part will be getting back into the city. Once we do, we can launch our plans." Ember put her hands upon Will's shoulders. "And not to sound like Tranquility propaganda, Will, but we need to be hopeful and positive. Don't forget we have Phoenix. The Plauditors have pledged their loyalty to us."

"I am hopeful. Positive and loyal too. You know that. Never forget it." Will took her hands from his shoulders and squeezed them in his. To his surprise, she dropped hers away before bringing her right hand up in a graceful loop through the air, her thumb and index finger separated. She then laid her hand on her chest, leaving her fingers in the same position. She smiled.

"What was that?" he laughed. "Not the Tranquility salute."

She giggled. "It means 'loyalty.' In sign language."

"I have no idea what that is." To him, it looked like some kind of weird voodoo.

"It's a silent language my mom taught me."

"Teach me."

She laughed. "I can't teach you the whole thing."

"Well, teach me that one, then."

She grinned and grabbed his hand, forcing his fingers into position. Like always, her touch sent his head spinning, but he tried to pay attention. Once she'd manipulated his fingers, she took her hands away.

Ember said, "Now, go like this in the air one time, then let your hand rest on your chest."

He followed along as she did it, a moment of fun bonding before the unknown future swallowed them up. "Loyalty," he said, practicing a second time. "I've got it." He meant it in more ways than one.

2

Will's Sacrifice

Up ahead, the city sparkled, lights reflecting off its translucent dome. The deepening purple sky, streaked with the cotton-candy pink of a setting sun, called like a mythological Siren back to the safe, amiable boundaries of the city. Yet safe, it was not. The Magistrate eliminated citizens if he found them a threat to his power. And the stakes were more extreme for the four of them.

Mere hours ago, they'd stood atop ashes that powdered the arid terrain, ashes of victims ordered executed by the city's Magistrate and Elite Council, in the austere desolation of The Outside. Poisonous honorary rings were the assassin's tools. The bodies were torched. Etched numbers on blackened trees commemorated each life. Will shuddered. His mind seared the image permanently in his memory.

No common citizen of Tranquility had ever been to The Outside and returned alive. But the foursome had done just that. Alive, yes, but emotionally drained. Now, Will felt as if he was looking at the world through a newborn's eyes. So much had changed. None of them were the same people they were only the day before.

They were just inexperienced, sheltered kids. Will felt

ancient after what they'd been through. He was a fresh eighteen-year-old, and Ember was younger than that at sixteen. Once Will and Ember discovered the murders of many of Tranquility's most virtuous citizens, including Ember's mother, they had to take action.

Ember said, "Ready?"

As if she had spoken some secret password, the exterior door to the back slid open with a sassy hiss. Xander and Wee peered into the gloomy interior, and Will and Ember blinked back. Brutal brightness assaulted Will's eyes.

"You okay back here, compatriots?" Xander grinned.

"A bumpy ride," Will replied.

Wee laughed and clapped Will on the shoulder. "Next time, you might want the front seat."

"Yeah. Hope there's no 'next time.'"

Will grabbed Ember's hand, and they jumped onto hard-packed, desiccated earth. Even at this hour, after the sun had gone down, Will wiped his brow. Beads of sweat rolled down his cheeks. Imagining a thermometer, he figured that thing would explode past a hundred and twenty degrees. That's the way The Outside was. You never knew how the environment would be, only that its temperature fluctuated wildly. Up ahead, barely a mile away, the city twinkled like a rainbow.

"So, Xander … You've got a plan for getting back into the city?" Will said, pulling off his yellow and black suede Plauditor's jacket. He sighed with relief.

"Yep. The best way is through the back gate where this transport exits. Where we went out, we'll go back in. We'll just be doing it on foot," Xander replied.

Will's voice lashed out like acid. "Seriously? They'll be looking for us! That's the only way in and out of the city."

"All we need is a distraction and camouflage," Xander explained. "And I've got it figured out." His air of confidence made Will a little bit crazy.

Will's eyes widened. "Is *that* all? A distraction and camouflage? Look around. We got nothin'. What're we gonna use?"

Wee, Will's biggest supporter, glanced at his friend, his eyes clouded with doubt. He wasn't ready to trust Xander, either, by the expression on his face.

"Let's hear it," Ember said, frowning at the two boys. "We have to start somewhere."

Xander flashed Ember a smile before getting down to details. "Okay. We stopped the transport and got out, but no one in the city knows that. And even if they figure that we did get out, it doesn't matter. Because they burned bodies, there's fuel for fire stored in the van. We need to find something we can set on fire and then let it drive into the city—"

"And just what in the heck would that be, something we can set on fire?" Will put his hands on his head. It's not like Will didn't want a plan, but Xander was expecting miracles.

"Well, obviously, genius, we've got to be creative. Any ideas?" Xander looked around the group, his eyes challenging each one in turn.

"Other than burning my clothes, no," Will countered. Their futile position and lack of ideas were starting to tick him off.

"We could fan out. Maybe there's something we could find to burn. There were trees out at the burn site …" Ember's voice bubbled with enthusiasm.

They walked a minute in different directions, meandering back and forth, scrutinizing the horizon. There was nothing to burn in the terrain. A desert without even cactus to ease the bleakness. Will shook his head.

"It's too dangerous and hot to keep looking, Ember," Wee yelled.

Ember's shoulders slumped. Will smiled at her to offer encouragement, knowing she was self-conscious about her naivete. "That could've worked if we'd had more supplies. It was a good idea."

Xander said, "Thanks for trying, Ember." His smile was like a sliver of moonlight but directed only to Ember. "I think we're going with Will's approach."

"My … approach?" Will didn't remember offering any solutions.

Xander turned to Will and raised an eyebrow. "Yeah. You were right. We have clothes to burn."

"What? You're taking off that Tranquility jumpsuit you're wearing, Xander? I know it's ugly, but you're ready to go 'au naturel'?"

"Not me. *I'm* gonna need my clothes. This outfit's all one piece. And this jumpsuit's still an official city uniform of the 'Operation-Move-Dead-Bodies.' If I'm seen, I won't seem suspicious."

Ember gazed at Will with a rueful expression. "True. Xander's not gonna do any good running around naked. But we can make it work. I'll be happy to donate part of what I'm wearing. The Magistrate made me wear this … thing, and it has layers of tulle." She pulled up a layer of the skirt and shook her head. "Ripping these off isn't gonna expose anything. I'll still have the bodysuit on." She began shedding, dropping several petals of her outer skirt onto the soil at her feet until all that was left was the skin-tight, platinum-colored underlayer.

Will watched, totally fascinated, his eyes full of longing. *This isn't something I should be watching.* He turned away.

Xander remarked, "Nice," as he looked her up and down.

"Put your eyes back in, Xander!" Ember said with a hostile tone. Xander just grinned.

Wee looked down at his pink linen shirt. "My shirt can burn, Xan. I can blend in more with only my brown skin. Not a fan of this color anyway." He unzipped the shirt's front, peeling it from his seven-foot frame. "I'm even thinkin' I could grab some of this dirt"—he bent down and grabbed handfuls of the cocoa-colored turf—"and rub it on my pants to make 'em blend in more. We're gonna need to hide in any way we can."

Will sighed. He'd have to do the same. It was the only plausible idea. "Okay. I'm gonna look a lot whiter than Weeford when my shirt goes, but I can get dirty, too." He grinned sheepishly and pulled his knit shirt up over his head.

Xander snickered and shook his head. "We're gonna need more than that for a flame. We need tons of smoke. When that transport barrels through that gate, the fire will be a threat to the bushes around there, but the smoke has to hide us. Will, we're gonna need your jacket."

Wee and Ember reacted in the same way. Their breathing froze.

Feeling lightheaded all of a sudden, Will sensed the blood drain from his face. *His jacket?* The black and yellow suede item was the most important thing he had ever owned. It represented so much of his self-image, his heart and soul. It symbolized achievement, a solid testament to his Status in Tranquility and his role in the city. Although he hadn't been a Plauditor long, that jacket represented both his heroism and his success.

"Uh ... sure." He realized he was trembling and that his eyes were growing moist as he tossed the treasured garment onto the pile. *I can't let anyone see how upset I am.* He concentrated, using his old-school Tranquility teachings of focused breathing and positive thought to quell his misery. He didn't even stop to think about how he still relied on what his schooling had taught.

Xander clapped and gave a mock bow. "Thanks for your *sacrifice*, Will." The remark dripped of sarcasm, and Will gritted his teeth.

"No problem. Got to get this done." Will was proud of how brave he sounded.

Ember stepped to Will's side, her eyes shining with tears,

and hugged him, whispering, "I know. I can barely stomach your loss."

Will felt ashamed. He'd burdened her with his torment. He wasn't always mindful of how Ember's empathic abilities complicated her life.

"No time to waste. Let's get this Burn Wagon through that gate." Weeford moved toward the vehicle but, despite his words, didn't appear to be in a hurry.

Xander raced to the back of the transport. A few moments later, he emerged with a blowtorch. He grinned and held it up in the air. Its metal tubing glinted even in the evening gloom.

"Woo hoo!" Xander called out. The small party converged.

"You were right, Xander. It's perfect," Wee said, his voice feathered with admiration.

"Who's gonna ignite the pile?" Ember asked, her breath coming fast.

"I'll do it," Will answered quickly before Xander could volunteer.

They threw their clothes into the front seat of the van, Will putting his jacket on top at the end, his eyes tearing up. Will pushed the window release button, which would allow the smoke an escape and give the fire more air. When he finally lit it, the flames would combust and flare inside the cab and the smoke would billow out of the windows. An awesome distraction. Kind of like a Trojan Horse, but they wouldn't be inside once it got closer to the gate.

"Okay. Once it's on fire and inside the gate, the smoke should cover us. We slip through. Go different directions, but meet up at the Plauditorium," Xander said. His nervous energy seemed to ignite them all.

"If the cameras in the city are still working, Xander"—Ember's eyes swept the area—"someone could be watching."

Will spoke up. "Remember. The Plauditors oversee the

cameras. And the Plauditors are under control. We hope every camera's immobilized."

Xander tilted his head toward the city gate. "Before we left, I sent a few guys over to the transport garage. Hopefully, they've had success in taking out any guards at the gate. We may just glide right in there with no problem. And don't forget. I still have this rifle." He patted the barrel as it rested on his side. "But I don't have extra ammunition for it." He grimaced.

Ember frowned. "How many bullets?" She eyed the rifle as if she could count what was in the chamber.

Xander ran his hand along the barrel. "Six. And those'll go quick if we use 'em."

"At least they're an option. That comforts me." Ember crossed her arms and squeezed as if it would help her feel more secure.

Will raised his voice for attention. "So … the plan. You all get in the cargo space. I'll light the fire in front and set the vehicle moving with the glide mode on. Xander says regular speed's only twenty miles per hour. Glide mode is less. I'll jump into the van. The smoke will make us choke—hold your breath. With the distraction, slip inside the gate and let the smoke camouflage you. When you're inside, find anything that'll keep you hidden."

"We're separating … We're each on our own to get back to the Plauditorium?" Wee asked, a shred of worry in his tone.

Xander clapped Wee's shoulder. "Yep. Do your best. We can't look out for each other." He wiped his brow with his hand and frowned. The heat was oppressive, its heaviness like an invisible shroud.

Will exhaled. *This could be the last time we see each other.* His heart skipped a beat at the prospect, and his legs felt weak. He motioned to the group to gather, and they put their arms around each other's shoulders, forming a tight circle.

Breaking the circle, Will made the loyalty gesture that

Ember had taught him in the van. "This'll be our new Phoenix salute."

"Yeah!" Wee's enthusiasm was a breath of fresh air. "How's it …? Show me."

Ember laughed, the sound a melody Will loved to hear. "Like this." Ember showed Xander and Wee how to separate the thumb and forefinger and pull them into a position over their hearts.

"I like it. Subtle but strong," Xander's eyes followed Ember's hand as it settled on her chest.

"Together?" Ember said, leading the practice. A silent choreography, followed by grins.

"Okay. We're ready. Any last words?" Will's eyes searched out Ember's.

"You know how I feel, Will," she said, locking his gaze. Then, she looked at each of the others in the tiny circle. "And I know how the rest of you feel. I can sense it all. It's a rainbow of color above our heads." Her head tipped up, her eyes glistening.

"You're able to read our thoughts?" Xander asked, raising his eyebrows.

"Not your thoughts—just your emotions. So, what are you thinking?" Her sight settled on Xander.

Xander locked eyes with Ember. "I'm ready, no matter what. But if we fail—or die—I'll be sorry to lose you all."

Xander's feeling vulnerable. He is human. "I agree. But we cannot fail. We got this."

The group dropped their huddle. Will gave Wee a last bro pat on the shoulder.

Wee said, "We won't fail, die, or succeed 'til we get in there. Roll the dice, and let's go."

3

Ember's Panic

Clothing in place, the group could enter the van. Twenty yards from the entrance, they'd jump from the vehicle. Ember pushed a button to open the back door. It slid open, revealing a dark, caverned interior. Wee jumped in, then Xander, who offered Ember his hand to help her in. She brushed it off. Physical contact would only charge him up in a way she didn't want. Ember pulled herself up by the van's side rivets next to the door and climbed in, leaving the door open.

Outside, Will held the torch to the clothing piled up on the van's front seat. The garments seemed to oppose the fire as if they feared their own extinction. The clothing smoldered for a solid minute before igniting in a feeble flame. As soon as the fire gained strength, Will leaned into the window and pushed the van's "start" button. Without a second's hesitation, its wheels rolled up inside the vehicle and the thing leaped into forward mode, riding on air about two feet off the ground. A fire-breathing machine, it moved ahead, wisps of smoke already snaking their way out the windows.

Will had five seconds to jump into the back before the transport gathered speed. He positioned himself in a flash, grabbed an exterior rivet with one arm, and hopped on, looking a little like a human monkey.

The group broke into laughter, the solemn mood momentarily dispelled.

"Yeah … *thanks* for helping me get on board," Will spat as he sat down just inside.

"You were up to the task," Xander replied, his full-on grin contradicting the obvious mockery in his eyes.

Will shook his head.

Ember felt the stress emanating from the surrounding bodies, but the tension between the two guys was especially heavy. She sighed. Wasn't there enough to worry about?

Her thoughts then focused on her lifelong recurring nightmares. Ember had always dreaded them, but they had been prophecies. She had dreamed of an escape and a pursuit by the Magistrate, Tranquility's leader, the books with the Magistrate's journals, and the "death" of Will. All those cryptic nightmares were warnings of events that came true. She wished for those dreams again with all her heart. Something —anything—to help her know what was to come.

A spongy lurch and a soft air hiss broke her trance. Her eyes met Will's. Ready or not, it was time to launch.

Xander yelled, "Go!"

Ember grabbed Will's hand, and they jumped. Their hands broke apart, their bodies rolling and scraping the ground in a brutal landing. *Get up, get going. Don't worry about anybody else.*

She obeyed her inner voice, chasing the van and tucking herself into an undernourished tuft of gray smoke. Choking, she held her breath. Suck in air and hold … five seconds. Exhale.

Her left side throbbed from impact. Grasping her ribs, she tested for blood. None. She ran on, hope driving her forward.

Her steps propelled her faster than she had expected, and she spied the gate just ahead through the smoke's heavy haze.

Raised voices—yelling—exploded in waves around her. She saw figures of people, but none of them were Xander, Will, or Wee. The silhouettes ran amok, dancing about the fiery van and waving their arms. She fanned out to the side, where thick vegetation formed a lush backdrop for the city's secret entrance.

She slipped inside and hoped the metallic glint of her bodysuit wouldn't make her visible. Pushing through the profusion of vines resting against the interior of the city's dome, she hid herself as deeply as she could and held her breath, a subconscious reaction to the terror that bloomed in her every cell. *I must breathe. Let the stress go.*

She peered out of a tiny space between fragrant vines laden with blossoms. Welcoming the beauty, she took a deliberate deep breath.

She gasped and choked. Clamor around the van gripped her throat like a shrinking rubber band. *Will! This can't be happening … can't be happening …*

Will fought against two Sciolists, who forced his arms behind him. No amount of twisting or kicking granted him a second of freedom. She felt his panic like a force field: desperation … defiance … fear. Her empathic radar picked it up, internalizing each fragment of emotion. She saw Will's aura arc and pop, an explosion of lime green. Sweat glistened on his bare chest, and his golden hair tossed back and forth.

I have to help! But what should I do?

She clenched her fists, her fingernails digging into her palms, as hot tears came to her eyes. *Think.* Was it possible to turn back time again? If she did, would she ruin the advances the others gained? Maybe. Too much risk.

Plus, she still didn't understand exactly what she'd done to make that time warp happen. Her right eye shed a tear, and she brushed it away. *No time for weakness!*

Will writhed like a spider caught in a web. *Someone help!*

Agony ripped her apart at her helplessness and the overwhelming desire to get Will free. To abandon him was like a death. Her heart shattered. She was powerless. No choice but to continue on with the group's plan.

Panic tightened its fingers around her. *Get it together, Ember! Move!*

Will's capture was the ultimate distraction for her own getaway; feral yells pierced the air, as if packs of coyotes had found their kill. Advancing Sciolists materialized out of thin air; a vast sea of red cloaks surrounded Will. Ember took another deep breath and bolted.

4

Xander's Run

It's sheer chaos. Xander's blood rushed in his ears. A convergence of Sciolists flooded the area. He'd never seen so many in one place.

Puffs of white smoke cast crumbled ash into the air, and a scent like burning hair suffused a reluctant breeze. Agitated screams like raging wild beasts shredded the air with jackhammer force.

"Grab him!"

"Where—the others!"

"Don't kill them, just—" were the only intelligible words he heard as bodies dashed back and forth around the deserted van.

The minute Xander broke away from the van, he hustled into the camouflaged alley leading to the transport's garage. The jungle-like foliage there provided instant cover, so he dove in. With a sinking heart, he saw no one he recognized from his band. *Where are they?* He knew it was everyone for themselves, but his isolation was causing the hairs on his arms to stand up. He couldn't stay in the foliage. Even now, he watched wide-eyed as the red-robed Sciolist officers moved along the fence line, a mere hundred yards away, jabbing the shrubbery with long, sharp sticks, their pale faces firm as if cast in stone.

Sheer terror, an emotion Xander had seldom experienced, seized him, threatening to paralyze his thoughts and movement. He continued moving to his left through the outgrowth, toward the transport garage, weaving and sliding along like a satiny, silent snake. His precious last steps into hiding behind the garage's back wall were a literal leap of faith.

The gap between the outer wall and the structure seemed larger than life, but the building welcomed him into its inky shadows. It would offer some cover temporarily until he could view more of the scene they had created and figure out how to get himself in a position to strategize.

He glanced up. A silent camera moved its miniature face from side to side. At least the official Tranquility uniform he wore would discourage questions if its prying lens detected him. He desperately hoped his rebel Phoenix group still controlled the Plauditorium's cameras—that he hadn't given away his immediate location. The thought was a daunting intrusion. He refocused his attention on what he could see from his secluded vantage point.

Holy—! A surge of turbulent activity drew the attention of slews of bush-whacking Sciolists. They streamed from the garage's interior to gather in the center of the transport compound. Additional Sciolists amassed by the second. *Now's my chance.*

But the Sciolists weren't coming for him. Instead, forty feet from where he was, they swarmed like bees around a hive. He saw what drew them. There was no mistake. They had captured Will!

Several red-cloaked Sciolists had Will's arms trussed behind him. Excited, babbling voices and a flurry of movement engulfed Will, but Xander saw no other weapons than the Stingers, the weapons the Sciolists carried. One bashed Will across the back. He heard a yell. Will's voice.

"Shazz!" he cursed. He cringed at his stupidity. His vocalization would betray his whereabouts. He threw his hand across his mouth and then to his forehead.

The rifle on his shoulder suddenly seemed to burn through his clothes. If there was a time to use it, it was now. Would his meager ammo be enough to put down Will's main captors? Should he full-out start shooting? Whatever resentment he had against Will vaporized as he grabbed the rifle and aimed it toward the Sciolists.

If I can shoot one of those Sciolists or create a distraction, will Will have a chance? He shuddered, and his arm quivered. He had no practice with guns. A shot from this far could go anywhere. In fact, he had never seen a gun before he took this very rifle from the hands of a Trank taking bodies to The Outside.

A shot would give away his position. Risky. He'd have to be ready to fly. Then what? Xander lowered the gun and looked around again to measure his situation.

At all costs, I have to get back to the Plauditorium! That's where he had his complete team, the former REMs, now renamed Phoenix. These were the people he'd brought with him back into the city from The Outside to launch a rebellion. Men, women, and teens who, like himself, were REMs, Resisting Emotional Management. They couldn't, or wouldn't, conform to Tranquility's laws for happiness and the Magistrate banished them for their crimes. Without them, and without him to lead the rebellion, there'd be no future.

Okay. No gun. Not yet. His eyes scanned the area. Another idea … The van they'd come in on, their "Burn Wagon," was stolen right out of this very garage by members of his Phoenix team. They somehow got it over to the Plauditorium after the takeover. If they could manage it, so could he.

His mind already racing, one minute ticked by before he dove into action. He felt himself blur into the dash and then shrink to his belly on the ground. He crawled, dragging the rifle with him, each move a stretch, his limbs aching and his heart racing. As he pushed his way across the ground on sweaty palms, he smelled the dirt. He tried to ignore the warlike cries of Sciolists still raging from the center of the quad. Will's voice floated over the top, yelling, its intensity feeling like a sword thrust into Xander's side.

"Good luck, Will," he whispered to himself as he slid into the garage.

A hand reached out and grabbed his shoulder.

5

Will's Struggle

A Sciolist lashed out with his Stinger, an electrified metal pole three feet long, and drove it square across Will's back. Pain shot through him like liquid fire, and his knees buckled. A crushing blow to his side, and Will cried out. He clutched his ribs, the pain making him see white.

"Stop your struggle, Will Verus." The voice, deep and restrained, was commanding.

Will's head jerked up at the mention of his name. His mouth went dry. He met the cavernous eyes of a Sciolist who stood before him and thrashed against the restraints again. He winced, shut his eyes, and gritted his teeth. His back burned.

"It's no use to fight. You're under arrest, *Plauditor*. We'll be taking you to City Hall, where you'll answer to the Magistrate for your crimes."

"Whose crimes? Mine? Or the Magistrate's? Our city leader is a murderer." Will spit the words like bullets.

The Sciolist grabbed his neck. "Our Magistrate keeps Tranquility from becoming a sewer of toxic people. Eliminating anger and sadness is the only way. Our laws are pure. We assign *you of all people* to encourage and help, not to poison the minds of the citizens."

Will froze a moment and looked around. His heart pounded, and his vision blurred as sweat ran into his eyes. This was the moment he had feared. He was without the support of his friends. Sciolists surrounded him. Although the Sciolists looked physically slender, the tight circle and electrified pointed sticks they wielded were daunting. He felt laid bare, as bare as his unprotected chest, vulnerable to whatever they meted out.

He mustered up his courage, blinking away tears. He had to escape. Although it looked bleak, he was determined. Didn't he always find a way? And Weeford, his best friend, would do anything to find him and free him—wouldn't he?

He thought of Ember, and his heart sank again. What was happening with her? Where was she? He closed his eyes and envisioned the worst. If they captured her, he'd never forgive himself. He should be protecting her. Instead, he was helpless and humiliated.

A vehicle Will recognized as Sciolist by its scarlet paint and compact length pulled up soundlessly next to the crowd. The surrounding throng melted away to form a path.

The two Sciolists holding him intensely pressured his arms, jerked him forward, and marched him roughly over to the vehicle. The door opened from the bottom up, almost like it was creating wings. Pushing Will inside, the Sciolist climbed in beside him.

"City Hall," his red-cloaked guard said.

"Right away," the car replied.

Will's limbs ached from the ordeal and the tight restraint. Adrenaline still wired him, but he felt his strength ebbing away.

The Sciolist pulled up the hood on his cloak as if to underscore the seriousness of the matter at hand. "Any words for your defense?" Penetrating Sciolist eyes searched his face, and then he wrapped his hand around the Alt on Will's wrist. His readings had crashed with excessive emotional violations. All that anger. Fear. The Alts readouts blinked like a neon sign.

It can still read my emotions but can't detect a falsehood. Will's thoughts raced. Could a story, an outright lie, maybe save him? If he could make the Magistrate believe he was not *with* the REMs, he might release him. The trip across the city gave him a chance to concoct a narrative. He'd have to hurry. He'd be in front of his nemesis soon.

He squirmed in his seat, uncomfortable with the idea of lying. But City Hall would have no viable way to test him for the truth.

In his mind, he spun a tale. He could claim he was trying to keep the attack on the city from happening. The story was plausible. He could conjure an entire timeline easily.

He immediately regretted his earlier outburst to the Sciolist about the Magistrate being a murderer. That wouldn't help him when he tried to convince them he was still loyal to the city. The denial of it already formed on his tongue.

His personal integrity groaned within him. The lie would be a complete betrayal of his individuality and core values. Of their whole mission. The decision hurt physically, like his heart was breaking. But this one meant his survival.

6

Xander's Flight

A second of frozen terror at the touch of human hands. Caught. He jerked as he turned to face his assailant.

"Xander!" Wee's voice hissed.

"You scared the crap out of me!" Xander whispered back. Relief coursed through him.

"Well, I was brickin' it myself."

Wee was on his belly in the garage under the twin of the transport vehicle they had burned, its sizable, stout steel hulk a perfect hiding place. Xander suddenly repressed the urge to laugh at the way they looked at each other. Their eyes were bugged out, Wee underneath the truck and Xander just a foot away. If it weren't for the life-or-death situation, it would be outright ridiculous, the two guys in the garage, on the floor, Wee's arm firmly on Xander's shoulder.

"Yeah. Got any ideas?" Wee's voice murmured. His hand pushed off Xander's shoulder.

"Of course." Xander pointed up. "Our chariot awaits."

Wee's black eyes seemed to kaleidoscope. "No way."

"Yes way. I've got the suit, got the vehicle. We go."

"We better book it."

"Move over to the passenger side. I'm driving." A wry smile snuck its way onto Xander's lips.

Wee pushed himself like a caterpillar across the slick, concrete floor to the right side of the vehicle. After three feet in forward motion, he hissed, "Where is Will?"

Xander dropped his head. "He didn't make it out. They got him, Wee."

"No! That can't be right. You're messin' with me."

Xander paused, the words refusing to budge from his mouth. "Wish I was. You were spared watching it, at least. Made me sick. He didn't have a chance."

"We gotta get him!"

Impatience and adrenaline shot through Xander's response. "There's no way. We'd be caught just the same. Too much risk. Better we stay safe and get Will later."

"He's my best friend, man. I can't just leave him!" Wee's panicked breath punctuated his words.

"Get a grip. We don't have time. Look at us. You think we're in a position to be superheroes?"

Wee moaned. "I don't like it. But Will's tough. He might be able to find a way out."

"You're absolutely right. Now … On three … into the truck." Xander's skin felt electrified. "And hold on. I'm floorin' it."

"Just don't kill us."

Xander snickered. "One, two, three!"

They jumped up as if on springs and threw themselves into the vehicle. Xander jammed his finger into the ignition button. "Ready?" he demanded. Grabbing an iron bar below the dashboard, he shoved it forward. "Turbo!"

The rig blew forward as if it were a jet plane on takeoff, its wheels immediately elevating up off the ground. Within seconds, it was out in the open, shattering the limits of Tranquility's sleepy speed laws.

"Friiiiiiiiiiiiiik!" Wee screamed. The speed nearly flattened his puff-ball hair.

They streaked past the Sciolist troops still gathered around in a tight circle. Some waved their sticks in the air, as if they craved a fight. Will was in the middle of that mess. Xander felt a twinge of guilt, and then it was gone. He had to worry about the greater good. Will would have to be the sacrifice if that's how it all went.

Xander threw a quick glance at Wee. His eyes still bugged out. His hands gripped the bolt-studded seat. *Poor guy. Not built for this.*

In his rearview camera, Xander watched the resulting chaos of their vehicle's wild ride. The cluster of Sciolists startled by their burst from the garage came alive. One broke away from the group, his screaming a tinny, faraway voice. The mob splintered out and then shrunk back together. One Sciolist shoved another one to the side and began running after their vehicle on foot, yowling and raising a black stick in the air.

How great is this? They had gotten away right under the noses of the stupid security society, and he still had a rifle, a weapon that none of them had. His rifle would come in handy at some point.

They sped through the streets. The city was like a ghost town. Under the cover of night, the only breathing seemed to be theirs.

"Can you see where you're going?" Wee hollered.

"Damn this rain. It doesn't help. This transport's no CommuteCar. It

should be an all-weather vehicle."

The car definitely had a mind of its own, the blinking dashboard warning of the unauthorized top speed and the unfamiliar route. A loud, robotic announcement from the car's dash startled them. "Slow down. Contact City Hall. This vehicle has a route. Slow down. Contact City Hall. This vehicle has a route."

Xander flinched, pounded the steering wheel, and screamed back at it. "Shut up! Shut up!"

Wee just looked at him and rolled his eyes. He pressed his elbows into his sides and shrunk down, making his body as small as possible, which, for Wee, was near to impossible.

The vehicle's voice annoyed Xander, but his lack of experience with driving made his mouth grow dry and his legs shake. Xander felt them skid a few times, the bulky truck throwing them side to side inside the cab like the Scrambler carnival ride he remembered from the Fun Zone. His heart flew into his throat and fluttered there. He clenched his jaw. *C'mon, Xander, you're a badass,* he thought, *so knock it off. This is nothing.*

Wee closed his eyes in abject panic. He only opened them to swivel around to see what was going on behind them. The sweaty sheen on Wee's forehead and his short, shrill screams made Xander pity him a little more with each jerk of the van.

Xander spoke. "They'll be after us soon, but we're miles ahead of anyone. Relax." He pulled back a half-inch on the manual throttle. *For Wee's sake, of course,* he thought.

"Glad to see you're slowing down so we don't die!"

Xander chuckled. "C'mon, Wee. You know you're in expert hands." He took his hands off the wheel and splayed them out.

"Don't—"

"It's fine, Wee. I'm in control." It surprised him to see that his hands no longer shook as they had when he first slid into the driver's seat.

"I know. You're cool, you're cool … How far?" Wee asked.

"Almost there. We're makin' great time. The Plauditorium's less than ten miles away." A tentacle of optimism turned up the corners of his mouth for the first time since they had burst back into the city.

Wee inched his body back up. "Xander ... what do you think's gonna happen to Will?"

Xander glanced at Wee's creased forehead and serious eyes. Wee was worried—beside himself—and Xander didn't have a reassuring answer. For all Xander's bravado, he was smart enough to know that Will's fate wasn't good. Wee was hoping to hear something positive, but encouragement wasn't possible.

"I don't know. But he isn't gonna be with us anytime soon. First, we plot our next move for Phoenix. *Then,* we worry about Will."

Wee's face sagged as if it were a cake left out in the rain. "I'm gonna worry about him *now*. Whatever we do, he's got to be part of the plan."

Xander shook his head. "Better think hard, then. I got nothin'."

"Don't forget. I still have Phenol in my pocket." Wee patted his pants pocket. "It's a weapon we can use. Somehow. Umm, Xander ... careful when you make that turn."

"Whoa! What the—!"

Thick steel pylons. In the road.

Their heavy transport hit the invading pillars like a bomb. He slammed forward in his seat, smashing his head against the vibrating dash. There was a massive crunching sound as the metal of the transport slammed into the metal of the pylons. A ripping of metal. Then, a high-pitched screech. A burnt rubber smell. A tilting roll to the right sent shock waves across his middle, jarring his organs into war with each other. The last thing Xander saw was the shaft of a pylon shatter the windshield into diamond shrapnel. Black smoke blinded him as the truck spun a hundred eighty degrees and rolled off the road.

7

Serpio's Solution

Within fifteen minutes after he received the intoxicating news of Will's capture, Serpio also had learned of the stolen transport van. Common to his proactive nature, Serpio determined what he needed to do in a snap.

He had launched orders to raise up electronic pylons on the streets of the city. The transport van would crash. Reports of it jetting out of the secret garage made him livid, but he had the situation under control now. He clenched his hands and then sprung them open, as if to physically, magically, remove his adversaries. Disposing of the people in the van would bring him great pleasure. Xander had to be in that vehicle. With any luck, he would be dead. He grinned, satisfaction leaking out of every pore.

Pacing, he calculated the space between steps. Waiting for a report was excruciating. Any moment, he would be victorious, and he would never have to deal with Xander again. The Elite would have no decisions to make. And the best part? He could put a positive spin on it for the people of the city. The citizenry would love him. Like a master puzzle solver, he put events and people in place perfectly. He was feeling proud and powerfully lethal.

Serpio walked over to a small, glowing box on his desk. No one else in the city had technology like Lunos. He placed his finger on the screen. A holographic projection materialized before his eyes. He had more than an Alt to communicate. He had virtual reality. A Sciolist's figure outlined in light hovered in the air above the Lunos.

The Magistrate spoke to the figure. "Kennard, what is the status of the van?"

"The pylons were successful. It crashed. As ordered, I sent your medics out."

"Condition of the occupants?"

"Just received. The Medic report from Ava says two deaths, Magistrate. They're … wrapping up the situation. It was bloody."

His plan to kill the occupants of the vehicle had been successful. Giddiness threatened to overcome him, but he leveled his voice. "Yes. Of course. Such a shame it had to come to this. You're sure that the victims weren't just badly injured?"

"Affirmative."

"Names of the victims?"

"Xander Noble is one. No conclusion yet on the second."

Serpio couldn't help but sigh in relief before rushing on to the other critical matter at hand. "Has anyone been able to rewire the Central CitiScreen on Bliss Avenue?"

"Just received word of completion."

"Fully functional?"

"Yes, sir. All connected to your Lunos. Ready to go. If it pleases you, you can put the other plans in motion."

"Excellent." Things were getting better.

8

Will's Story

Less than an hour after being apprehended, Will stood in front of a beastly desk that towered above him.

Serpio Magnus, the Magistrate, unfailingly exuded power, but today, Will shrank from his presence. He'd never witnessed the leader mete out punishment, only heard about it. It was unthinkable that he was facing just that.

Serpio's eyes were like a hawk's, beady and intense. They could drill right through a person. Will kept his gaze steady. He couldn't show any fear.

The Magistrate loomed over him. "Will Verus."

"Yes, sir."

"You are a *traitor* to our city."

"No, sir" He clenched his fists. He could feel his face flush. It was a physical characteristic he'd always hated about himself.

"*Don't* deny it. You have conspired with a group of Emotional Resistors. Those REMs and Ember Vinata have disrupted our city's happiness and spread false propaganda. You are a *disgrace* to the Plauditor community. You have violated your oaths. You have violated the Plauditors' trust. You have held them hostage," the Magistrate continued.

"If you'd let me explain—"

"There is nothing to explain. You are an enemy. Worse than the REMs who have simple minds and no regard for true happiness."

Now was the time. "Magistrate, sir," Will said in a rush. "You're right about the REMs. They're crazy—and hateful. And that's why I've been working as your agent to prevent a disaster for our city." The lie burned in his throat.

"How is that?" The Magistrate's mouth curled in a smirk. "This should be entertaining to hear. Especially since that is *not your job!*" His voice boomed. "You are a Plauditor, not a Sciolist!"

Will kept his delivery calm, steady. "Exactly, but I'm a very loyal, grateful citizen. And Plauditors monitor the people of our city. Right?"

The Magistrate raised his eyebrows and then nodded his head slowly.

So far, so good, Will thought. "Look … I knew something big was going on when I visited Ember Vinata's home. She had a weird break-in after her mother died. We never found anything missing, but it shook her up, as you can imagine. It was a terrible time for her—an emotional situation. That's why I was called. She shared with me afterward that she needed answers. At first, I was just trying to help, but then I realized she was questioning *everything.* Not acceptable. I needed to stay on top of it. Even Austel, my co-worker, encouraged me to keep a watch on her."

The Magistrate replied, "Austel will back you up on this?"

"Of course." Will crumpled inside, realizing that he had taken Austel, his only star witness, away in a van to The Outside. By now, Austel was dead or still wandering around that wretched wilderness in search of salvation. But he couldn't worry about that now. He had to hope that the Magistrate wouldn't try to send for Austel. Pushing his thoughts aside, he continued his campaign. "It was difficult to watch Ember Vinata. Winslow demanded I break off my relationship—"

The Magistrate held up his hands like a physical stop sign. "Winslow made sure you broke off the relationship. You followed the law."

"Yeah. I did follow the law! But I had already heard her plans! I knew you determined she was an asset to the city and needed protecting. You had her best interests at heart. But she was planning an escape from your mansion, sir."

The Magistrate cocked his head, considering. "You knew of those plans?"

"I knew, but because I couldn't see her anymore, I wasn't able to stop her plans to escape."

A muscle twitched in the Magistrate's face. "Why should I believe you? Sciolists caught you reentering the city. That means you left! No one leaves the city unless they are REM."

"I know, but I had to. To convince one of the REMs that I was on their side. You know of Xander?" His tone was bitter. Will's mixed feelings about Xander couldn't have been timelier. "He wanted to meet Ember. I used that as an excuse to get close to him."

The Magistrate's eyes narrowed. "I know all about Xander Noble." The Magistrate slammed his fist on the desk between them. "A REM of the worst kind! Arrogant and contemptible!"

"Agreed, Magistrate! That's why I had to act." Will threw his palms out. "No one knew about their plans for the city but me."

"Your claim to fame—saving a boy from being crushed by the Maglev—is far different from preventing a coup on your own, Will Verus. But you do crave glory, don't you?" A wide, manic grin spread across the Magistrate's face.

He likes that idea, Will realized. *He must relate.* Sick, but he'd play the game.

Will gave his inquisitor a sheepish smile. "I need Alt

points, Magistrate. Look here for yourself." Shackles still bound Will's arms together behind his back. He turned his back to the Magistrate and wiggled his wrists. His Alt showed a descending arrow on a red background. He swiveled around to face his challenger again. "I know it's been registering a downward spiral on the Continuum Spectrum at City Hall. And that's terrible. I admit I've struggled with that lately. It's been a real effort to keep my happiness scores up, although it makes me happy to deceive those evil REMs. And"—he grinned—"I knew once I had a handle on the situation, I'd report it and be a celebrity all over again."

"So … you did all this to keep our city safe? And boost your points?" The Magistrate raised his eyebrows. Will heard the mockery in the man's voice but pressed on.

"Yes! I know it's hard to believe, but I would *never* betray our city. I made a promise to my grandfather and—"

The Magistrate stood up behind the desk. "I have no more patience for this. Your case will go before the Elite. They will make the ultimate decision. If you are lying, you will die."

"I would expect nothing else." Will's insides were jelly, but he projected the confidence of a gladiator. "You'll see that—"

"Enough!" the Magistrate roared. "I order you to a holding cell beneath the city."

A Sciolist materialized out of the shadows behind him and yanked him by the arm. "This way. Now." The man's voice was as abrasive as steel wool.

Will felt relief once they exited the grand room. Wherever they put him, at least the Magistrate wouldn't be there. He could let his guard down and go where he was told. Then he could decide what more he could add to his story.

The Sciolist pushed Will in front of him through a hallway flooded with rainbow lighting. *What a joke*, he thought. *There's nothing rainbow-like about this place.* At the end of the hall, the hallway diverged into two different directions. A sharp turn they took to the right revealed filmy white lighting that seemed to dim as they walked. A black elevator at the end of the corridor opened its doors automatically at their approach, and the Sciolist thrust him inside. Tranquility's anthem played softly through the speakers as they descended at lightning speed.

The elevator opened to a small, square area where two black metallic doors greeted them, each one with a green light blinking over it.

"Door One or Door Two?" Will muttered to himself.

The Sciolist pushed him forward. Door One on the right opened noiselessly, revealing a narrow room with an illuminated "T" on the far wall. The "T," the only light, glowed to a mellow glimmer. No chair. No window.

With the Sciolist giving him one last shove, Will stumbled into the space, and the door came down.

9

Ember's Message

Ember hadn't dared look back when she ran from the scene of Will's capture. She couldn't bear it. Her tears blurred her vision. Somehow, she was to blame for this. She should have been able to do something.

Leaving Will behind was excruciating. This was going far, far worse than she had ever imagined. What were they thinking, trying to take over the city?

She sprinted on, still taking cover where she could. As far as she felt she had run, she knew she was miles away yet. Her upper torso ached from stress, the stiffness in her neck like a vise. Her legs throbbed with exhaustion.

The Sciolist's pursuit terrorized her and drove her to continue running. But no matter how hard she tried to keep her momentum, her energy flagged, and her pace slowed. The nightly rain had begun just as they'd entered the city, its faithful showers gluing her bodysuit tightly to her body. She shoved her dripping wet hair away from her face and surrendered to rest. Behind a bright, tangerine-colored building, she bent over, trying to catch her breath. Once recovered, she looked down the road.

She was approaching the Orange Glen community. Up

ahead, the carrot-colored structures gave her a renewed sense of direction and a glimmer of optimism.

Her eyes darted around, taking in every shadow, every breeze-tipped bush. No one seemed to be pursuing her. *They're probably too involved in rounding up Will.* Her heart tanked, and tears flooded her vision. It wasn't fair! Will didn't deserve to be the sacrificial lamb.

Think. Think. Extending her hands, she gazed down at her fingers. They trembled with adrenaline and fear. Yet these same hands had created magic before, when she'd stopped time and turned it back. She'd created an inexplicable time warp where she'd kept Will from dying. She held up her arms and scrutinized her hands like they belonged to a stranger, beseeching them to perform. She clenched and released her fingers. *What did I do to make them work before?* All she knew was she'd thrown her hands in the air and yelled in exasperation.

Rediscovering the ability could help her now. If she rewound time, she could keep Will from being captured.

She threw them up but then realized she couldn't yell. When the miraculous had happened, emotions within herself and the emotions she'd collected from others in the room had empowered her. But she was alone. The only emotions she had were hers.

Lowering her arms, she took several deep breaths and looked around for the direction she should go. She'd stay on the outskirts of the city until she got closer to the Plauditorium and then work her way across town. She could slow her pace as long as she kept her wits about her. The night offered security; people were sleeping, so no one stirred. Curfew was a respected limit. The government prohibited Tranquility's one hundred thousand people to be out until the sun came up at six a.m.

Thick, glass sidewalks glowed multiple colors from a subterranean lighting system, helping her to see in the dark. She was grateful for its subtle radiance. The path gleamed, but it never illuminated her. She wondered why the city had spent so much money on the sidewalks if no one used them after nightfall.

The city was only twenty miles wide. A hike of ten miles would get her to the center, to the Plauditorium. She smiled as she passed a lit sign for the zoo, a favorite place. Her empathic abilities could perceive the animals' dispositions. It was one of the few times she was content to have her very weird talent. *The animals never need Alts, and yet they're really happy. But they're in cages,* she realized. *The ultimate control.* Her smile faded, and she pressed on.

After a mile, she crept into the center of a large plaza laid with multicolored pavers. The Tranquility Grid was a central building resembling a tiny house. Could it provide a hiding place? She checked for an entrance.

No door. The building had no insides. The front was a semi-open structure and provided no concealment. Regal columns surrounded the outside. *The city spared no expense,* she mused. The pillars were translucent crystal fountains, where water streamed down the sides of them into a ten-foot-wide pool. Displayed across its base was the word "Tranquility." On the top, hidden light fixtures shone beams upward every few feet across a flat fascia, giving it a crown effect. Facing out was a screen, where images flashed one by one upon its surface, showing the "grid," the layout of the city. Buildings were part of the slide show, each one labeled to show its purpose. No point in lingering there. She had no need for a map.

But as she scampered by, an image on the screen startled her. *What?* Her eyes grew wide. She couldn't have seen what she thought she saw … She could have sworn she'd seen a video of her mom standing in front of an art gallery!

Her mother was dead. The city was cruel to have her mother's image on a screen.

Rage and confusion rushed through her like a bulldozer.

She trembled from every strand of her hair to the tips of her toes. *How dare they?* Her entire body flushed with aching loss.

Perhaps exhaustion was taking its toll. *Maybe my imagination's running overtime.* The image had already disappeared from the series. Each display flashed by, only visible for about ten seconds, so she clearly had caught the montage at the end.

To stay so long in an unconcealed location meant peril. But she wanted—needed—to be sure of what she saw. She couldn't let it go. Waiting for the footage to cycle back through was essential to her sanity.

No one could track her since she no longer wore an Alt with its built-in GPS, but cameras were everywhere. Did the Plauditorium remain in the hands of the rebels? Would someone be watching? Regardless, Sciolists would eventually be on the move.

She scanned the area. Where was a good place to hide? A tree with plush benches around it looked inviting but too exposed. To the left of it stood a TrashVac—a black metal box where visitors could insert their rubbish and have it sucked away for recycling at the Envirostation. She scurried over and knelt behind it.

As she waited for the screen to cycle back, she adjusted her bodysuit, still a wet sheath practically grafted to her body from the continuing rain. Her red hair hung in sodden strings, painting her clothes with tear-like beads. She was feeling impatient and tired. Her stomach rumbled and her eyes blinked heavily with exhaustion. If she had to prop them open, though, she would. She watched the screen, determined to find answers.

Finally. Her eyes grew wide. There she was ... Her mother. Goosebumps erupted across her arms. Looking beautiful as ever in a purple gown, Talesa stood in front of Tranquility's art gallery. Ember strained to hear. There was music. The words "Art for the Heart" flashed across the screen, followed by "The Premier Art for Feeling Wonderful. Visit the

Apricus Art Gallery." Ember watched, shocked. It was as if no one had cared to change the city's advertisement after her mother had died. Unbelievable. A tear cascaded down Ember's face.

The animation made her mother seem alive. A bittersweet moment. She had no videos of her mom, and here one was. She could be thankful to Tranquility for *something*. Her heart bloomed with joy, and her eyes misted. How much she missed her.

A second later, she watched her mom's right hand come up. Her fingers moved rapidly in a series of configurations, and then the slide disappeared.

Ember gasped. When she was a little girl, her mom had taught her an ancient dialect. Known as sign language for the deaf, it was now obsolete. Deafness was an affliction of the past. She had taught Will one of the symbols, Loyalty, before they'd re-entered the city.

But there, on the screen, Talesa's right hand spelled out something very different from the word "loyalty." A cryptic message: "Ember, find the golden journal."

<hr>

10

Ember's Resolve

<hr>

Ember stood, rooted to the ground. Her mom on the billboard was one thing, but her mom giving her a message? She couldn't wrap her head around it. And why did the message have to be so cryptic? Having no idea what it even meant or why her mom thought it was important enough to risk a public display made her crazy. Did she actually see what she thought she did? Questioning herself, she watched the billboard ad cycle through again. Her vision confirmed, her hands suddenly trembled, and her legs stiffened further involuntarily. Dizziness overtook her, and she tried to control her breathing to throw off the shock.

When she finally broke free of her body's gridlock, she shook out her legs, scolding herself. She had wasted precious time. Thinking about the message and her mom right now was something she couldn't afford.

What time was it? The overnight rain had slowed to random drops that spotted here and there. It wouldn't be long before the sun came up and her chance to travel in the dark would be ruined. She would be easy prey then.

She darted away from the plaza, frantic, and continued her journey down the street.

~

SHE STILL TIGHTLY HUGGED THE walls of the buildings. Walking through one community at a time, she marked her travels with each one's signature color. She'd just passed Blue Riverfront, the community she'd been assigned to after her mother had passed away. Its trademark royal blue apartments seemed to mock her as she lurked in their shadows, as if they knew that fate had robbed her of a normal life. And the mysterious message from her mother on the billboard about a golden journal felt somehow more urgent here.

Her heart seized. *Will.* For the first time since waking, his absence gnawed at her. She missed his comfort, optimism, and love so terribly. Fear for what he'd be suffering became a gut-wrenching voice. *Is he dead? Is that why I feel this way?*

I can't think of that. I can't think of the dreams. I can't think about Mom. I can't think of my situation. Just hide. Get to the Plauditorium.

Far up ahead, perhaps a half-mile away, she saw a commotion in the street. What was going on? Still too early for people … but people were out! From where she was, she couldn't see exactly what was happening, but when she strained her eyes—a MediCar on the side of the road. An emergency? But it was parked, going nowhere. She'd never seen a MediCar before, a rarity in a safe city like theirs. No doubt, though.

Unlike the CommuteCars in the city, which were painted colors related to Status, this vehicle was powder blue, and a large medical insignia covered its hood and doors. Small windows above each door reflected the dim, emerging rays of the sun.

She couldn't get closer, or someone would see her. *Stay put!*

In a peculiar way, the crash was a gift. The Medics and city officials would allow no one to emerge from their homes until the disaster was cleared.

She squinted to get a better look, taking a few uncertain

steps forward to determine the best direction to go to avoid the area altogether.

Her eyes popped open. Her heart plummeted into her stomach. Was that…? *Shazz!* A transport van. Upside down.

Stay calm, Ember. Can't be the one we used. Our van was a smoking mess when it rolled back into Tranquility. Maybe Sciolists went after Xander in it? But why? Sciolists have their own car …

A question struck her like a slap to the face. Had one of their own crashed this transport van? Xander? Or Wee? *Oh, Shazz!* A hot flush rushed through her veins. The landscape spun, and her breath curled up tightly in her lungs and hung there, as if paralyzed. She had to know if Xander or Wee was a victim. If they were okay. She was quite a distance away, unable to gather any emotions from the scene. Did she dare go closer?

A little further, she could close the distance and get some emotional intel. She would just have to be smart about it. And brave. She had to be brave.

Her eyes traveled back to the scene. If she kept to the walls as she went down the street, she could bridge the gap and still stay hidden. A convenience store for the Blue Riverfront community on the corner became her targeted landing spot.

As she forced herself along, she pushed her terror down. *I have to discard all the "what ifs" like trash. I have to be a leader.*

Her mind conjured up all she'd endured. The death of her mother. Deadly rings. Forced to live with the Magistrate. Will's rejection. A failed escape. Will's near-death. Her unexplained power. So much in a brief time. But she had conquered everything, persevered. *I got through all of that, I can do this.*

She reached the outermost building quickly; now, she was but a hundred and fifty yards away. One victim inside the MediCar who wasn't moving was stretched out horizontally—a giant. *Oh no … Wee? Who else would be that tall?*

Three other people moved around the scene, two Level

Thirteens and … a Level Eighteen. A Level Eighteen! She allowed that to sink in for a moment.

She watched, fascinated, as she tried to tell what they were doing. Too difficult. Her eyesight, unfortunately, was not superpower charged. But the emotions the individuals spawned invaded her consciousness. The auras were dim at this distance but still visible. She homed in.

Clouds of compassion swelled from one of the Level Thirteen Medics. Or was it sympathy? Hard to tell. The aura, a vibrant green, surrounded the orange-clad man. A turquoise blue aura emanated from the other Level Thirteen, a diminutive woman; that color showed calm energy and sensitivity. The Level Eighteen—she couldn't tell if they were a man or woman—generated a dark sapphire essence. But that person was forcibly suppressing emotion. All emotion. Bizarre. Another puzzle.

She watched the Medics remove a second body from the crashed vehicle. A male victim … Some unseen device transferred the person to the MediCar, as if he floated on air.

A flash of black hair and tan clothing confirmed her worst fears. Although there were lots of people with black hair and drab clothes, she knew. Xander! She breathed hard now, struggling to stay calm.

With careful effort, the Medics transferred Xander into the back of the emergency vehicle.

She sucked in her breath. A murky aura of reds and black covered their bodies like a blanket. They were badly hurt. Deep agony came from their emotional fields.

Panic rose within her like an interior tornado. She clenched her hands as if to pull back the pain, whether hers or theirs she couldn't tell. Xander and Wee? She still didn't know for sure. Either dead or close to death. She bit down the urge to scream in rage and frustration. Her hands flew to her head. She felt as if she'd been hollowed out, like someone had cleaned out all her inner parts. *This can't be happening …*

A sharp pang of regret, like an arrow, pierced her heart.

Xander … She'd never even given him a chance. So wrapped up in her own struggles, she'd resented his childhood bullying and shut him out. She'd only wanted him around when he could help them with their plans. What a shallow person she must be!

Her shoulders slumped with the weight of the turn of events. She was alone. How could she carry on without their help? She shivered, her nerves tumbling somersaults. Holding out her hands, she concentrated until the trembling stopped. *I won't give up. I owe it to them to carry on.*

She wiped her tears away and stood up, soldier straight. It was now all up to her.

11

Xander's Salvation

"What … what the hell is going on?" Xander's voice came out in a croak. He lay on a gurney inside some vehicle. He turned his head, grimacing, and saw Wee lying next to him, close enough that their hands were touching. *Wee!* Wee's eyes were shut, and he lay very, very still.

His view of Wee and everything around him was a blurred haze, like someone had thrown white gauze over his eyeballs. He put his hand to his face and felt around. His eyes were swollen for sure. Sore. Probably bruised. The whole left side of his face felt like a water-saturated sponge. He groaned. Pain overwhelmed him. A sharp jab in his side was agony, and he blinked away tears.

In the fuzzy space around him, he noticed several people moving around Wee, rushing equipment to Wee's side. Wires and tubes. A Medic carried a black box-like thing. Two Thirteens laid a blanket with white plastic attachments on top of Wee and then hurried off.

"I *said* what's goin' on? What happened? Somebody talk to me!" His speech was again a rasp. He wanted to yell, but his words came out thin.

"Don't think. Don't worry. We're taking care of you," a female voice said.

Xander nodded and shut his eyes. His head throbbed, and the world around him spun. The dizziness he battled stirred up more than his head. His stomach churned with nausea, and he grabbed his stomach to hold off the vomit.

The voice spoke again. "Rest. Sleep."

Ignoring the command, Xander looked over at Wee's face a second time. This time, he noticed blood streaking down from his cheekbones into his jawline. He fought off a dizzy spell to force words out. "Wee. Wee!"

"He can't hear you."

"What? Why? What's wrong?" he croaked. He moved his right leg and winced. The pain in that leg made him want to cut it off.

"Your friend—Weeford, is it?—he's touch and go. They're … We're … working to stabilize him."

"'Touch and go?' You mean he might *die*?" Xander lifted his head, only to have it fall back again. He wanted to rant and rail, curse and fume, but he didn't have the energy.

The voice became a person at his side. Cool, firm hands touched his arm and then his leg. They stroked his face. *A woman. Level Eighteen.* Her metallic, gold-colored uniform marked her rank, but he didn't care one whit what Status she was. He was helpless. Impossibly useless. He cursed aloud.

"Rest," she said. "Please. Don't fuss. Your pain will soon fade. We're treating it. In just a moment, you'll feel only euphoria. After all, you're in Tranquility." She smiled, and it was as if the sun had been living behind her eyes.

"Who are you?" He worked hard to focus. Her face lingered just above him. He noticed her freckles first, the sprinkling of them across her nose giving her a youthful quality. Yet she wasn't young, probably a good fifteen years older than he. Very short, black hair featured elaborately shaved patterns. Her close-set, light brown eyes gazed at him with warmth. If he had to identify her race, it would be Asian, although race was never a defining description in Tranquility. Only the Samkhats, the black race, were special enough to label.

She leaned over. "My name is Ava. I'm a Medic on Special Assignment." And then, bending over further, she whispered, "I know who you are, and you're in grave danger. Trust me. Completely. Unless you do, you'll be dead by noon."

Xander swallowed hard. "Do I have a choice? Look at me." His weak position made him see red. He wasn't in charge. At this moment, he hated himself.

Ava put her finger to her lips. "For now, don't speak," she said in a murmur. "I don't want the other Medics to know you're even conscious." Her eyes scanned the scene to make sure the others were running diagnostics a few yards away. "Your sedative will take effect, and that will help both of us."

"But I'll be arrested … I can't …"

"Shhh." She squeezed his arm and stepped away.

The medication worked its magic. His arms and legs grew heavy, and a warm, liquid sensation suffused his veins, dulling the pain. He was suddenly happy … content. No anguish. No worries …

He sighed, allowing his breathing to even out, closing his eyes in a brief semblance of sleep. Nothing to do but give in, and he did that gratefully. *Nothing like being in pain to make a person humble,* he thought.

Without the raw torment he'd been feeling, he could finally concentrate on his dilemma. He had to do something, but how? He turned again to Wee, who lay there like a stone. "Hey," he whispered under his breath. "You're gonna be okay, you hear me? I'm gonna find a way out of this."

He lay quietly, watching Ava talking with the other medics nearby. He imagined jumping up and running from the scene. But he knew his body would fail him. Not only that, but he would leave Wee behind. A foolish idea.

Where was his rifle? That was a happy thought. If he could find it, he would look for a chance to use it. He could shoot and kill these Medics and then … His mind raced with possibilities. As the minutes ticked by, he became a bigger hero in his mind.

"Xander!" Ava interrupted his thoughts, her voice still a whisper. "We're leaving now. Don't move *at all*."

He nodded to let her know he understood. Whatever plans he could have put into motion would have to wait.

Ava went around to the other side of the MediCar and slid into the front seat. Without a sound, the vehicle shot away from the scene, leaving the crushed van and the Level Thirteens behind.

"Hey, what about those other medics?" he drawled.

She answered, "I told them that the situation's under control. I told them I'd 'do what was necessary.'"

Do what was necessary? As the car slipped away, he worried about where they were going. Surely a hospital? Or … prison? But he was *alive,* and so was Wee. And Ava had given him hope. Shy optimism, like the rays of the early sun, broke through his apprehension; whether from the drugs or his rugged spirit, he didn't know. He was determined to give himself up to whatever forces were at work.

HAD he been asleep for the whole ride? He sat up with an abrupt jerk in the MediCar, a dull ache making its home in his abdomen. The day was underway, the sun dousing his eyes with its climate-modified shine.

Where were they? A house? Radiant, golden paint on the building's exterior marked it as Elite. Even crazier, he quickly realized that the elegant structure they'd pulled into was the garage. *Holy Shazz.*

Xander shook Wee with a gentle nudge. "Wee. Dude—Wee. Can you wake up?"

"Don't wake him." Ava always seemed to turn up before he realized she was there. "He needs to rest. I'm taking him in first, then you. Be patient."

"In where? This place?" Xander gestured toward the glittery building.

"Yes, this place. My house. That's where you're gonna be. Not safe anywhere else."

"O … kay. I'm a little blown away." His words were slurred.

"Don't get used to it. Temporary. Just 'til you get on your feet."

"Yeah. Good. But you never know. You might like me enough to keep me around. I'm irresistible." He cocked an eyebrow and gave her a drug-induced, lazy smile.

She snorted. "So you say. Jury's out on that one."

A quiet groan ended their conversation. Ava hurried around to Wee's side of the vehicle. "Door down," she said. The entire side of the car lowered from top to bottom, forming a neat, functional table where she efficiently moved her patient out of the interior. "Wee's coming out of it."

"Is that good? That's good, right?"

"Maybe. Too soon to tell. Now, watch the magic." She took a small white box from her pocket and moved it in a rectangular circuit around Wee's body, like an outline. Then, she pulled the box toward her, and Wee's inert body floated off the "table" toward her. Aiming the instrument in front of her and twisting it in a semicircle, she pulled Wee's floating body along like a helium balloon until he hovered right next to her.

Xander's eyes grew enormous. "You weren't kidding."

"Be right back."

"You gonna do that … that magic … for me?"

She moved past the MediCar with Wee, towing him along

with the invisible force field. "If you can't walk, yes. Otherwise, I'll just give you some physical support."

"That sounds like a challenge."

She kept her back to him and called out, "You're on. But don't try anything until I get back. You're worse off than you feel."

He watched her until she was out of sight and haltingly scooted his battered form over to the open side of the Medi-Car. Pain shot through him like a bullet. Blood coursed down his arm from a deep gash slicing his upper bicep. His ribs suddenly seemed diced into pieces, as if their bones were tiny spears hacking him to bits. What used to be the correct movement of his jaw was now jerky, sideways, and disconnected his upper teeth from touching the bottom ones. He couldn't make his left leg move without a crunching noise, like the sound of gravel under tires. The foot he hoped was still joined to that leg had no feeling in it at all.

Buck up, Xander, he said to himself. *Now's your chance!* But leaving without finding the rifle wasn't a good option. He might need it. Definitely needed it. For him. For Wee. He rolled himself to a standing position through the open door and grabbed a metal bar overhead for support. Inching his way along the side of the MediCar to the front, each step an exercise in torture, he peered inside the front cab. There it was. He reached out and closed his fingers around the barrel.

____

12

Xander's Renewal

____

"Stop. Stop *now!*" As Xander's fingers had closed around the rifle's barrel, Ava's yell punched the air. Xander wobbled on his feet, his pain and disappointment making it hard to move. Xander's jaw tightened. He stared at Ava. A scream of frustration in his brain threatened to tumble out his mouth. He wouldn't be going anywhere after all.

Ava rushed over to Xander, her face chiseled by her clenched jaw and flushed cheekbones. "You really don't know what's good for you, do you?"

"That's what they say."

"I asked you to trust me."

"Lots of people ask me that. They all lie."

Ava groaned and shook her head. "You cannot leave. I'm your only hope."

"Yeah? Well, I've gotta get out of here. I'm leading a rebellion … or didn't you know?"

"Small good you're gonna do anybody in the shape you're in! You wouldn't make it fifty yards on foot."

Xander raised one eyebrow and laughed under his breath. "I wasn't planning on walking."

Ava's eyes grew wide. "You'd really take the MediCar? That's even more stupid. It's unmistakable as hell, especially if I'd report it."

Xander was dizzy, though he'd been standing for only a few minutes. He put his hands on his head to stop the spinning.

Ava shook her finger at him. "Look at you, hotshot. I'm getting you inside so I can actually help you, damn it."

"Whoa. You're tough. I'd better follow orders." Sarcasm dripped from his lips.

"Hang on to me. Let's go." Without further permission, she reached out and threaded her arm under Xander's left arm and across his shoulders.

The physical contact not only felt good, but he was surprised at how strong she was. She was a bundle of energy. Although he was a foot taller than her, he wasn't sure he'd be able to take her in a fight.

He wasn't used to being undermined by a woman; it didn't sit well. He cursed under his breath, still averse to all of it.

He was convinced he could walk a mile but realized the door to the house was merely fifteen feet from where the MediCar sat in the garage and Ava had to drag him inside. He sagged a bit but sank deeply into a curved, upholstered chair. He had to admit that the soft, lush cushions felt like heaven. He put his head back and groaned.

"Okay, Xander. Here's the deal. Your friend"—Ava tossed her head in the direction of a room off to the side—"the one you felt you could simply ditch, is in a bed back there. He's not doing well. He's lucky to be alive, but I can fix him."

Xander stared at her, incredulous. "If you can fix him, you can fix me?"

"Yes."

"Why didn't you do it already? At the crash?"

She held up two fingers. "One, I need special equipment we don't carry in the MediCar. We can't treat people for critical injuries on the road. But more importantly, I had to immediately notify the Magistrate that you—both of you— were dead."

Xander looked at Ava as if she had just become the creator of the universe. "You did that? The Magistrate thinks I'm *dead*?"

"Yes. I did that in order to save you. The crash wasn't natural, of course. The Magistrate deliberately raised those pylons to cause the wreck. He came up with a plan to ensure you were killed so there'd be no long pursuit, no capture, no trial. I was hand-picked to make sure your death was absolutely certain."

"But you're Elite! A Level Eighteen. You're a *Medic*. And you're … protecting me? Why?"

"Yes, Xander. I'm Elite. And all Elite members have jobs outside of serving as government officials. I'm the only designated Medic. But don't let my rank fool you. I'm not loyal to the Magistrate."

Xander's jaw dropped. "What? How can that be?" He wondered if he'd lost his mind. Was he was dreaming? Maybe he was in a coma. He scrutinized his body. It looked and felt real.

Ava's voice was soothing, confidential. "It's a story that I promise to tell you. But later. I have to work on your friend, or he'll die. What's his name?"

"Weeford—or Wee. That's his nickname." Xander felt his mouth go dry. Fear wrapped its fingers around his throat. "He's … dying?"

"Close. I'll do my best to heal him. He's bad, but I'm … cautiously optimistic. It'll take a while."

"Do what you need. I'll …rest. And later, if you have food …" His voice faded out.

Exhaustion crept through his bones. He had so much to do, to think about. And yet, here he was, stuck.

He was relieved to hear Ava think Wee would survive.

Xander, fighting the urge to fall asleep, watched with hooded eyes as Ava hustled past him into the adjacent room, leaving him alone.

His head lolled but jerked up. From where Ava worked on Wee in the other room, came a flash of incandescent brilliance. There was no sound, only another flare some thirty seconds later. He was alert, his senses wired.

What the—! I need to see what's going on. What on earth is she doing to Wee?

His body heavy with weariness, he tried to rise. He gritted his teeth, telling himself that only he could prevent disaster if it was happening before his eyes. Yet his legs were a thousand pounds, and pain stabbed him with any tiny movement. Without support, he couldn't do it. He growled and laid himself back down as he tried to accept his failure.

The flashes continued to flicker off and on for the next forty minutes before stopping, the room then becoming bleakly dim. Random fear shot through him. For what seemed an interminable time after that, silence stretched the room. He shifted in his chair, uncomfortable with worry, freaking out. Maybe it hadn't gone well. Maybe Wee was dead after all.

"Xander, do you want to see your friend?" Ava's voice jarred him from his dark fears.

Wee emerged from the room, loping toward him, his typical broad smile blooming across his face. Xander dropped his jaw. Wee was no longer bleeding or … anything. He looked as normal as he had before. Xander exhaled in relief.

"Hey, Xander. I hear you're feeling like you've been run over by a truck?"

Xander grinned with genuine joy for the first time since he'd left The Outside. What he was seeing was a miracle. "Wee. That's not funny," he quipped as he again tried to rise.

"Glad you think you can get up, Xander." Ava approached him, a predatory look in her eyes. "Grab on to me. You're going in next."

Wee cuffed Xander on the shoulder. "I'm good as new, but I probably wasn't as bad off as you. Have you *seen* your face?"

"I haven't, but it feels like raw hamburger."

"Yeah, well that's what it looks like, too."

Ava persisted. "Let's go, Xander."

"Okay, okay. But promise you won't make me look any better than when I started. Girls won't be able to handle it." He managed a painful wink with his swollen eye and a sideways smile.

"You won't have that to worry about, trust me," Ava responded as she braced Xander's body against hers. "I'll be using a machine with light pulses called a Medela. Photons of natural, therapeutic light produce a chemical reaction in the mitochondria of your cells that boost energy production and regeneration."

Xander said with a grimace, "Hope there's no test. Too much information."

Ava laughed as she teased, "I thought you were smart enough to understand, but I guess not."

As he passed Wee on his way to the other room, he called out, "No matter how long it takes, don't go anywhere without me." His smile a little sheepish, he realized he had narrowly missed doing just that to Weeford.

13

Xander's Answers

Sooner than he imagined, Xander was back in Ava's living room, reclining again in his now-favorite chair. Wee sprawled along a sofa, barely long enough to contain his seven-foot frame. Ava had left for the kitchen with a promise to bring back energy-boosting and healing food. She promised to answer all of their questions as they ate. He tapped his foot nervously. He could hardly wait to find out why she was on their side.

Wee threw a gold lamé pillow at Xander, hitting him square in the face. "You trust Ava, Xan?"

"Not at first. But yeah, I do now. Without her, we'd be dead for sure. She even told me the Magistrate sent her to make sure we were dead."

Wee's eyes popped. "She disobeyed an order?"

"Uh-huh. She promised to explain."

Ava entered the room, followed by a self-propelled cart laden with food and drinks. The sweet, smoky aroma made Xander's mouth water. "Ready for a feast?" Ava asked as she smiled.

Xander and Wee bolted upright as the cart parked itself between their two seats. Within moments, their plates were mounded with pieces of steak, juicy blue fruit, Wonder Fries, and Jarnish. A green, carbonated beverage Xander recognized as Ambrosia filled a large pitcher.

Conversation was the last thing Xander wanted. He thought he'd never tasted anything so amazing in his life but realized the food could have been junk and he would have worshipped it. Life on The Outside was cruel, and food was scarce, but he also hadn't eaten for a day or two since they'd been back. Xander noticed Ava laughing at the way they stuffed their mouths, and he grinned back at her. Within minutes, the plates were empty. For the first time since he could remember, Xander's stomach was full. He sighed with satisfaction.

Xander wiped his mouth with his sleeve, still wearing the tan jumpsuit he stole from the van driver before entering the city. He immediately realized the sleeve made a poor napkin. It was filthy and dotted with blood. He reached for a lacy napkin on the tray and rubbed his lips with it.

"Ava, thanks for everything. I still don't know why you're helping us out. We owe you more than we can repay." His eyes misted, and he cleared his throat. He felt small and humbled, a first in his seventeen years.

Ava sat down on the sofa next to Wee. "I'll explain quickly. I disabled the security cameras in here before I brought Wee in. It's only a matter of time before someone notices and reconnects."

"Maybe not—if the Plauditorium is still shut down. Do you know if it is?" Xander asked, hope shining in his eyes.

"Yes, it is. But by now, agents are working to reconnect communications. You know the Magistrate won't tolerate a break in surveillance very long."

"Yet you're ready to put your life on the line?" Wee asked as his eyes examined the cart for any leftover crumbs.

Ava's gaze shifted to Xander. "I am."

"Spin it, then," Xander said as he held her gaze, examining the bright gleam in her eyes. The worst possible thing would be if this was all a sham. He planned to analyze every word out of her mouth.

"I believe in Tranquility's future. I want a place where everyone is happy and kind to one another. It's perfect in so many ways. But the citizens don't understand who the Magistrate really is. He's not what he wants everyone to believe. He's a killer."

Wee inhaled sharply.

Xander jumped from his chair and strode over to Ava. He put his hands on her shoulders in a not-so-gentle grip, his excitement transferring into his squeeze. "You *know* that? Thank the stars! It's not news to us. We know people are being killed. Wee's friend, Will, discovered a conspiracy. Did you know some citizens in higher levels who win the Augur Prize are being poisoned by wearing their rings? And that the bodies are taken to The Outside?"

Ava put her hands over Xander's to settle him down and looked directly into his eyes. "I understand you're upset. I've been upset for … a long time. But I didn't know the Augur Prize murders were happening until I became Elite, and that's only been in the past year. The Elite members don't know. I discovered it myself."

Xander released his hands from Ava's shoulders and paced back and forth in front of her, his energy restored to an almost electric force. He was feeling like his old self—on fire and ready to wreak havoc on the Elite and the Magistrate. He stopped abruptly and looked at Ava, remembering that Ava was part of that institution. It wasn't so black and white after all. "So, how'd the Augur Prize truth emerge? Were you involved?"

"No, no. I only found out because of a personal connection. The city honored one of my dear friends, Bailey, at the last ceremony. I promised I'd have lunch with her to celebrate. The demands of being Elite are high, though, and I got busy.

Time got away from me. I didn't call until a few weeks later. She didn't respond. I left a message. Again, no response. After I tried reaching her a bunch of times, I went to her house in Orange Glen. No one answered the door. When I looked in the windows, the place was empty."

Wee said, "She could have just moved. Moving's really common. How'd ya figure out that she was a victim?"

"I thought at first she'd moved up to a higher level, especially since she was recognized as being the finest citizen of her Status. So, I imagined she became Level Fourteen and was now living in Purple Vale. I set out to find where she had moved. I thought it was strange that she hadn't let me know. We were good friends. It was weird. Because I'm Elite, I was able to get into the central computer at City Hall. But I found no record of her moving to or living in Purple Vale. In fact, I found no record of her name *anywhere*. She was simply gone, like she didn't exist."

"What about her family? Did you get in touch with them? I mean, they had to have known something." Wee's voice increased about a decibel.

"Here's the thing … Bailey didn't associate with her family. She told me once upon a time that it was better for her and them that they weren't connected. It's almost like she wanted to put real space between them." Ava shook her head, her eyes downcast.

"Some people have family problems, Ava. It's not easy to share." Xander thought of his own parents, who had disowned him. His failure to become an acceptable citizen in Tranquility had caused a rift that couldn't be repaired. He shrugged. "Decisions and consequences aren't easy."

"You never figured it out?" Wee said as he leaned in.

"Finally, I looked up 'Health Records.' I saw she was admitted to the hospital, but nothing was listed in the records except for 'Unknown Ailment.' That's as far as I got."

Wee sucked in a breath. "That's what happened to

Ember's mom!" His eyes locked with Xander's. "So, that's the way they make it seem normal."

"Ember? The 'Queen of Hearts' Ember?" Ava asked.

Xander sat down. He was still agitated, but at the mention of Ember's name, he felt his legs grow weak and his heart beat faster. "Yeah. That Ember. She's … a friend. Will first met her trying to discover what happened to Ember's mother because she died. In the hospital."

"Did Ember ever find anything out?" Ava asked.

Wee answered, "Not at first. That's why Will kept investigating. He put his Plauditor career and Status on the line. That's the kind of person he is."

Xander snorted. "C'mon, Wee. He's as human as the rest of us. He only did it because he had the hots for her."

"Where's Will now?" Ava asked as she ignored the jab.

Xander's head jerked around. "You don't know? I thought you'd be in-the-know with the rest of the Magistrate's Elite. Sciolists took Will prisoner as soon as we came into the city. Last time I saw him, they had him surrounded."

Wee's voice took on a new urgency, and he sat up straighter. He almost looked like he was ready to cry. "I'm so worried about him."

"For good reason," Ava said. "If he's in custody, they'll try him as a traitor."

"Can you find out what's going on?" Wee begged.

"I'll make it a priority. But first, there's more to tell."

Xander sat down again and moved closer. "We're listening."

Ava's voice dropped to a low, raspy whisper, as if she was coping with real pain. "My dad, Henry Validus, worked as a Genetic Engineer at Inventum. When I was just a child, only eight years old, Sciolists arrested my dad at the lab. The official word—which I'll never believe—was that my dad and another guy, Drake, intentionally switched vials of DNA, which would have caused severe genetic mutations. I know it was a lie. My father wasn't given a trial or any chance to refute the charges. My dad was banished to The Outside. We weren't able to even say goodbye."

Xander sat back in his chair. He wondered if Ava's dad could still be alive and part of the REMs. But no. There was no one that age as part of his crew. Ava's dad had to be long dead, as most people the city exiled to The Outside. And the Magistrate was responsible.

Xander rose, his face flushed. He clenched his fists. "If I could, I would kill the Magistrate with my bare hands. Just waiting for the opportunity."

Wee's voice was sharp. "Calm down, Xander. Serpio needs to be tried." He turned to Ava, his timbre becoming more plaintive. "Xander's a lil' … passionate. But we're all on the same side. That story, though. I can see why you're not a fan of the Magistrate."

"Not a *fan?* I've worked my whole life to rise up to Level Eighteen, where I can work from the inside to bring him down."

Xander drew himself up as if the information had pumped helium into his lungs. "Then let's do it. We need to get to the Plauditorium, Ava. What do you say you get us there?"

"It's going to be risky. The Magistrate has given the order to take your bodies to the Kelasts. From there, we'll go to the Plauditorium. But first, I'll contact the Magistrate. I'm going to offer humanitarian aid to the Plauditors. That's our plan to get in."

She winked at Xander as she gathered up the plates and dishes left over from lunch. She picked up each item and stacked it carefully back on the self-propelled cart. Her attention to the way she treated each item, from plate to silverware, was careful, deliberate, as if each item was a live creature to be lovingly cared for.

Wee said, "Here … let us help."

Xander picked up the glasses, but Ava put her hand out to stop him. "Please, no. You're my guests."

Once she'd placed the dishes on the cart, she gave it a gentle push. The cart moved away, rolling out of the room toward the kitchen.

In a dramatic gesture, she held up the Alt on her arm and spoke into it, meeting Xander's eyes.

"Magistrate. How are you today?"

"Fine. Everything going well? No delays on the body disposal?"

Ava put the call on speaker mode. Xander could hear everything. His newfound friend wasn't keeping any secrets.

"On my way," she said before hesitating. "Magistrate … you may not know. I have two bodies. Xander had another with him in the transport. His name was Weeford."

"Who is this 'Weeford'?" Xander swore he could hear the frown in the Magistrate's voice.

"I don't know. He was dead at the crash site. I IDed him with his fingerprints—kind of old fashioned, I know, but he had no Alt."

"No Alt? Had to be a REM, then. Two for one."

"I agree, Serpio. You've done an excellent job at terminating these terrorists."

"Remember, we play this issue low-key. The crash was just an *unfortunate accident.*"

"Yes. It's too bad accidents happen. Even Tranquility's superior technology can't prevent those. But I am concerned with something, Serpio. The Plauditors in the building … They're going to need supplies. Food. Water. Maybe even medical help. A hundred Plauditors are in that building."

There was a long pause before Serpio answered, "No. Absolutely not! I don't know if those people are still loyal. And that could work in our favor. We could starve them out. That solves another big problem."

"Will you notify the Elite, then?"

Another pause punctuated the moment.

"The Elite will understand," Serpio said, his voice like iron.

"Are you … sure? The Elite won't approve of starvation, Magistrate. And," she said quickly, "this could benefit your image to all the citizens of Tranquility, bringing help to the Plauditors being held hostage."

The Magistrate sighed and didn't speak for thirty seconds.

Xander paced, throwing his arms up in the air. Wee stood up, glared at him, and whispered, "Settle down."

"Ava, you are the most trusted of my Elite. So, yes … You should drop off some supplies. Make sure you document everything with your personal camera. Surveillance is still down at the Plauditorium."

"Of course. Your act of kindness will be a glorious thing to advertise as soon as the Plauditorium is back in our safe hands. The news anchor can start the show with the words, 'The Magistrate shows unconditional love.'"

"Excellent. I'll look forward to getting footage," the Magistrate said, the remark the last before the call cut off.

"It will take some time to process … everything. Getting the bodies disposed of properly, garnering supplies … I'm planning on tomorrow, with your permission." Xander could tell Ava was choosing her words carefully.

An awkward silence sent Ava into a restless pace.

Ava turned to the guys and said, "Get ready, boys. After you sleep tonight, which is what you need for total healing, you're about to become dead bodies."

———————————————

14

Will's Day In Court

———————————————

Will sat on a rigid, splintery floor in the assigned isolated space, his limbs aching from weariness and his spirit waxing low. He groaned aloud. This had to be the worst thing he'd ever endured. Having to burn his jacket was bad, but being in a cell? What would happen to him?

He felt abandoned. Utterly alone. He stopped his mind from going darker, to thinking his friends didn't care about him. *Wouldn't they be here by now to get me out?* It was easy to feel dcfcated.

Most of all, he yearned for Ember. He imagined her there with him, tucked up next to him, her hand in his. When their relationship began, he had been the one to save her, to help her find out the truth about her mother. To calm her heart, her mind. Now, it was him who needed her. Without her, he fought to breathe. She was like oxygen. Like blood.

But true to his own optimistic nature, over the hours, he buoyed himself up. He began to put the events in perspective. His desperation at his capture gave way to shame at his selfish thoughts. This was bigger than getting help from his friends. He had known what he was getting into. What the risks were.

He still had his Alt. Although it was broken, a winking green icon blinked the time. Almost mesmerized, he'd watched it flash. Over and over and over. It showed him he'd been in prison six hours. Six hours that felt like forever.

He had slept fitfully. His back and ribs still burned with the sting of a viper's venom. The dirt he had dusted on for camouflage felt gritty on his arms or had settled into sweaty lines on his well-defined abs. He put his head in his hands.

A soft whoosh to his right suddenly drew his attention. The electronic door drew up to reveal a Sciolist's silhouette.

"Will Verus. You will come."

"Where? Where are we going?"

The Sciolist didn't answer but shoved him ahead into the hallway, where, once again, the elevator winked its all-seeing eye.

A wave of the Sciolist's hand opened the elevator door. The Tranquility anthem played from the speakers. Its lyrics reminded Will of the hypocrisy of his city.

All common things, each day's events,
That with the hour begin and end,
Our pleasures, not our discontents,
Are rounds by which we may ascend.

Standing on what too long we bore
With shoulders bent and downcast eyes,
We may discern—unseen before—
A path to higher destinies.

Nor deem the hopeless bitter past,

As wholly wasted, wholly vain,
If, rising on its wrecks, at last
To something nobler we attain.

All thoughts of ill; all evil deeds,
That have their root in thoughts of ill;
Whatever hinders or impedes
The action of the nobler will.

THE ELEVATOR WHIZZED UPWARD with the speed of lightning. Whatever fate awaited him, he would know soon. He wondered if the Elite would be merciful, if they were waiting for him. An Elite trial could be devastating. He'd never heard of anyone being sentenced to death, but the Magistrate had been blunt about that possibility. His memory of The Outside made that punishment only a microscopic shade better. He shivered and broke out in a cold sweat, now as familiar as his own skin.

While in the cell, he'd been planning what he'd do if an escape option presented itself, but his mind jumped to the worst-case scenario each time. He couldn't escape physically unless he had some help. His wrists were already almost raw from him trying to get the restraints off. *Please, Weeford, come get me. I don't want to do any of this.*

Will took some deep breaths. He couldn't look like a coward. He was a trained Trank who could sublimate his negative emotions pretty well. One way was to breathe, make small talk, and put on a smile. His story depended on his ability to sell it. And his life depended on his story.

A WALK down the corridor took years. The walls closed in with every beat of his heart, its thud visible on the bare skin of his chest. His pants clung to his damp skin.

Finally, the Sciolist led him into a room through a shiny, gold door. Although he'd never been here, this had to be the Elite's Chambers. He didn't know anyone who had ever been in the chamber before. Even people resisting emotional management wouldn't be there. They'd go first to counseling for Purging, then to the Solace Institute, and then to the Magistrate's inner office. From there, they labeled citizens as REM and sent them to The Outside. His case had to be rare. In that moment, despite his slim odds, the uniqueness of his presence in that almost-holy place made him feel strangely privileged.

The Sciolist pushed him ahead to a small open platform off to the side of the room. He pushed him behind a podium, where he looked out upon rows of gleaming chairs, each seating a member of the Elite. Lustered, burnished furniture and gilded walls were awash in a honey-colored coating. If he hadn't been reeducated, he would have been in awe. As it was, he wanted to vomit from the opulence.

The escorting Sciolist bowed to the Magistrate before exiting.

Serpio Magnus, dressed in a formal black uniform similar to the Plauditors' but trimmed with gold, stood facing the people seated in the chamber. "Are all Elite members present?"

A woman in the front stood. "We are missing one, sir. Ava Validus."

"Ava is on official business," Serpio responded, a vague smile on his face.

Will shuffled a little, his frayed nerves getting the best of him, and then his eyes locked with the Magistrate's. He remembered an ancient saying: "Boldness is a mask for fear, however great." He had learned it in school, and it came to the surface now.

"Sir Magistrate."

"You will not speak. Not yet. The Elite will hear your story." The Magistrate's tone was brisk. "But first, some questions."

Will resisted the urge to argue. He had to be the perfect Tranquilite to pull this off.

"Yes, sir."

"The Elite is aware of your … deeds and wants to know why you not only left the city but re-entered as an enemy."

Don't hesitate. Stay overconfident. "I had to. The only way that the REMs would trust me was if they thought I was on their side. I've followed their plans from the beginning, back when I first met Ember Vinata. I did my job as a Plauditor up to a day ago when Phoenix—that's what the REMs call themselves—stormed the Plauditorium. The only thing I knew was that Ember was asking questions. I didn't know that … that … Xander guy. Never met him."

"So, why didn't you stop the takeover in the Plauditorium?"

"Magistrate, I tried. I went to take down the leaders, but they had guns! Look at the cameras' Docufeed yourself. You'll see it."

"Something deleted the camera's footage."

"Oh. They're crafty, then. But believe me, they attacked me there. I almost died." His chest suddenly hurt, reminding him that that was not a lie at all.

The Magistrate turned to the Elites. "I still do not trust this story. It's way too convenient. Now's the time for you Elite to ask the questions, and then we will decide Will's fate."

"I would be the first to question this Plauditor, Magistrate. May I?" The man speaking wore a suit the color of champagne in a nubby fabric that sparkled in the quartz lights shining from spots on the ceiling. Will noticed that the man's light brown skin was perfectly smooth, as if it had been buffed to a sheen. His gray, wavy hair was a dramatic contrast.

The Magistrate nodded his head. "Please proceed, Harris."

The man stepped forward a pace. He smiled, as if to show how happy he really was, even in the middle of an interrogation. "How did you plan to thwart this coup once you got back inside the city?"

Will squared his shoulders, his green eyes engaging Harris's blue. "Once I was back in the city, I planned to alert everyone to these traitors. I would have concrete information on them. I'd be a *witness*. You'd need proof, right?"

Harris cocked his head as if considering the idea. "Why didn't you immediately alert City Hall with your Alt when you entered through the gate, then? It would have saved you from being arrested."

"I was at a complete disadvantage, Mr. Harris. I broke my Alt." He hung his head, knowing that owning a broken Alt for any length of time without reporting it was a disgrace and a crime.

Harris gasped and shook his head in a slow "no" motion. He looked heartsick, his blue eyes welling up with compassion. Then, as if an invisible force dragged him down, he sat back in his chair without another word.

Will felt his first genuine smile leak briefly from his lips. The Elite seemed freakishly nice. It was easy to see why they were the very top of the Status performance continuum. Did they have hearts of gold to match their rank?

Will's eyes darted to the Magistrate. He had no such look. His chiseled face and high cheekbones glowed as he moved to stand directly under a spotlight.

"Anyone else?" Serpio asked, his arm sweeping the galley.

"I'd like to speak." Another man with fair skin stood. His narrow face, with a pinched nose and squinty brown eyes, had a knowing look about it. His brown, braided hair hung down his back in a perfect line.

"Of course, Thomas. Please begin." Serpio leaned forward and rubbed his hands together.

"Yes, Thomas Nimio here." He cleared his throat. "If you wish for us to capture these traitors, what can you tell us that will allow us to seize them? These rebels, Xander and Ember, are now somewhere in the city! REMs have our Plauditorum locked down. We need information!"

Will looked away and briefly closed his eyes. What would sound believable? He clasped his hands together. *Breathe.* "Well, Xander has a gun, but he told me he was out of ammo. He'll be easy to take if you threaten to harm Ember." *Frak.* That was probably true. "As far as Ember? She's not very strong, either physically or mentally. She … she's in love with me, so she'll be intent on finding me—being with me. She shouldn't be too far from right here at City Hall." A half-truth.

He felt good about feeding them that information. With this, they could look for her where she would never be. Will was confident that Ember would never seek him. At least not until she'd had time to make a plan, which would be unimaginable at this point. She was smarter than that.

Thomas smiled. "Now we're getting somewhere. That's some precious information." He sat with such an air of self-satisfaction that it was like a visible vapor. *Ember could see it for sure,* he mused.

Another Elite rose from his seat. His flaxen, blond hair, tawny eyes, and golden skin made him the living prototype of a Gold. He almost glowed. He left his chair and moved to the front to address the group.

The Magistrate nodded in acknowledgment. "Allston Castus, you may speak."

"Thank you, Magistrate. It occurs to me that we're neglecting a very important strategy for evaluating Mr. Verus. A session with Winslow would tell us a great deal. If we put

Will under the Neuroscope, we'd see everything. We'd hear everything. A mind video such as that would settle the issue."

Will knew nothing about a Neuroscope. It could see and hear everything? In his *brain?*

A murmur rippled through the room, and Will watched as the entire Elite raised their arms with thumbs pointing down.

The Magistrate pounded a gavel for order. Once. Twice. He spoke up. "This motion is being denied. Who would like to speak to it?"

A woman stood, her face pale. She, like all the Elite, was beautiful, her features petite, except for her eyes, which loomed large in her face. She reminded Will of stories he had read as a child about fairies. When she spoke, her voice was soothing but laced with a business-like tone.

"With all due respect to Allston, this cannot happen, Magistrate. We only use the Neuroscope for those with severe emotional management issues. Will Verus has been a model citizen. It would be an insult to force him to undergo a Purging session with Winslow. Will is an officer. A Level Twelve. This unkind action would be completely against our city's philosophy. There must be other ways to determine what we need. The Neuroscope for someone of Will Verus's stature would violate Tranquility's laws."

All around the room, the Elite were shaking their heads in agreement.

"Very well. Thank you, Shalimar. You remind us of our principles," the Magistrate whispered.

Will closed his eyes and exhaled slowly. He would have had no defense if they'd exposed his memories. A feeling of lightness, as if he was an airborne balloon, threatened to carry him away. He nodded his head in thankfulness in Shalimar's direction. But he sensed the interrogation wasn't over yet. Too soon to feel the relief of a "not guilty" verdict.

A lovely brunette woman with hazel eyes and jeweled clothing stood and addressed him from the gallery. He noted not only that she wore a Level Eighteen Augur Prize ring, but that she had several gold medals pinned to her jacket. Her eyes glistened with a sheen that rivaled that of her medals. Of average height, her figure was enviable—perfect proportions. Will estimated her age to be about forty-five, although the only real giveaway was a couple of strands of silver in her hair.

She spoke. "Will, my name is Feren Fiducia. It's very hard for the Elite to imagine that someone as distinguished as you are would be a traitor to our city. But our security here depends on finding out the truth. The cameras' Docufeed of the takeover—destroyed. Everyone in the city saw the broadcast the rebels made. You yourself were on camera, accusing our city leaders of impossible things, along with Ember Vinata, with whom you had a relationship, and Xander Noble, whom you claim not to know. What do you say about that?" Her voice was soft, but the tone was stern.

"Ah. By that time, I was trying to save lives. With a gun pointed at my head, I was told what to say. If I didn't, they said they would kill me and all the Plauditors. It was only for survival that I would ever tell such lies about anyone."

Will counted his heartbeats in the uncomfortable silence that hung in the air. ... *fifteen, sixteen, seventeen* ...

Feren nodded to the Magistrate. "We have enough information. Please escort Will Verus back to his cell."

15

Serpio's Supremacy

The room, instantly under the Magistrate's command, became silent after the Sciolist escorted Will from the chamber. He would take the Elite's decision, but not until his closing words defined the situation.

Serpio looked out upon his audience. A tiny frown knit his brows in what he hoped represented sincere concern as he held his arms out, open, in a welcoming gesture. This was his moment.

"My dear Elite. May I remind you that you are Elite for a reason? You have developed your consciousness and your emotional intelligence to become superior to all those of lower Status. And this is good. They depend on us to ensure their continued bliss in our community. Yet today, we have a decision to make about a popular Plauditor, Will Verus. His story seems to make sense, but we must be very careful. Without a way to determine if he is lying, this is a heavy responsibility for us. Remember that you alone hold the power. You alone have the superior skills for a decision such as this. We follow the rules—the rules that enable us to continue this great society in which we live where there is no famine, no racism, no war. We are all subject to the law—even you, the Elite. It's the dedication and commitment to the laws that keep us human, keep us pure. Emotional Management! Correction! Rules! These are the ways we empower ourselves and our citizens. Will Verus, at the very least, has broken these important laws. He may, as difficult as it is to imagine …" He paused and put his hand over his eyes, as if the grief was just too much, "… be a traitor trying to ruin Tranquility from within."

The Magistrate was proud of his speech. He had delivered it perfectly. He didn't believe Will's story, even though he shivered at what it meant if Will was leading a rebellion. The boy was a born leader. That much was absolute.

The citizens of Tranquility would wait for comfort. When Will, Xander, and Ember took over the Plauditorium, they'd broadcasted their accusations to every household in the city. They'd accused him of *murder*. Even now, citizens would still worry and be distrustful, wondering what all that was about. He could not allow that. Above all, he had a heart for his people. He truly loved them and wanted the best for them. He had to protect them at all costs. They had *families*.

For a moment, his mind slipped into the past, to when he was eleven years old. He'd been getting ready for bed. Uneasy for days, he hadn't been pushing up his Alt readings. He needed to understand his anxiety.

"Mom …"

"Yes, Serpio?"

"Why don't I look like you and Dad?"

His mother had laughed. "You look like us. Two of everything, right? Eyes, hands, legs …" Merriment shone in her face. She was trying to make light of a serious question.

"Mom—you know. In school this week, we studied DNA. I have black hair and black eyes. You and dad have blond hair and blue eyes. That doesn't happen." He looked at her with accusing eyes.

His mother sighed. "Sit down, Serpio. It's time to tell you a story." She patted the bed next to where she sat. "You've also memorized Tranquility's Accords, I know. In those laws, there are safeguards built in for population control. Especially since people live such long lives."

"Yeah … so?"

"Families can only have one child. You were born to a family that already had a child." Her voice, although soft, was matter-of-fact.

"I … was born … to another family? Another mom?"

"Yes, son. Your dad and I had no children. So, when your mom had you, the government placed you with us so we could raise you."

As his eyes became moist, he blinked, trying to hide his shock. He was a transplant? He'd heard about kids like that, never dreaming he was one of them. "Who's my actual mother?"

"Serpio … you're not allowed to know that. It would make things … difficult. We're all happy as a family. No need to upset that."

He shook his head and looked at his "mother" in a new way. Now he understood. Here was the reason he'd never felt a lot of love from his parents. Although they were outstanding citizens and positive thinkers, they'd never given him much physical affection. Hugs were rare, as were other displays of endearment.

The imitation mom spoke again. "We don't love you any less, son. Everything you want, you only need to ask." She patted him on the head. "Now, into bed. An enjoyable sleep will help you process everything. I'll let Dad know that the cat's out of the bag." She laughed, unruffled by his discomfort. He crawled into bed, miserable, and she covered him up, as if to bury everything right there. "Be happy, Serpio. Never let a minute go by without looking at the silver lining. The city chose parents especially for you."

The memory of the conversation and how he'd felt had never faded, although he knew he'd developed coping skills and decision-making abilities because of his unusual upbringing. Since he'd learned he had a biological family somewhere out there that he'd never know, he'd always felt strangely alone.

His attention snapped back to the problem at hand. The thought of families being disrupted because of the threat of a rebellion shook him to his very core. The trouble was that the Plauditorium was still locked down in control of the rebel REMs.

There was no way to get into the building without accessing the secret passageway underneath the Plauditorium. Only he had knowledge of it, and he would never divulge its location. Going back in would be suicide for his Sciolists since Phoenix had guns. Only two, but that would be enough.

A universal broadcast from there would be out of the question. Something would have to happen in order for the citizens to stay happy and calm. In the meantime, his Elite would determine Will's fate.

"You may discuss the evidence, and then I will hear your vote on Will's ultimate future."

At this cue, the Elite stood and mingled with one another. The conversations became a jangle of excited voices until the words seemed to bounce off the walls…

"He didn't …"

"But if he's telling a lie …"

"Our entire city could be in danger …"

The Magistrate smiled. It was sounding like the Elite would vote according to his wish, his will. He chuckled. His *will.*

He glanced up. In 3D lighting on the ceiling, the time of day changed in an array of colors. He watched its pixels flash the minutes passing when finally, at 8:17 a.m., the Elite seated themselves once more.

Feren Fiducia rose. "The Elite have decided."

The Magistrate already felt like celebrating. *Once we remove*

Will Verus or sentence him to death, it will be easy to take down the rebels. The girl is weak, and Xander Noble is just a punk.

"Please, share your decision." The Magistrate smiled.

Feren said, "We can use Will. With some clever management, he can be of great service in taking down the rebels. We'll make him an inside man. Manage him. If he really is on our side, he will have to prove it by taking the REMs down."

The Magistrate took a step back and blinked rapidly. This was the last thing he had expected to hear. *The boy needs to die. And spectacularly!* He lowered his head and pressed his lips together as if to keep his words locked inside.

"Well," he said in a hoarse voice, "this is … unexpected and will require a great deal of planning." He paused. "Which we can do," he added with forced enthusiasm. "Is everyone united in this … decision?"

Feren bowed slightly, her face as serene as a sleeping baby's. "The majority is solid for this plan. Those who are not have promised to look at all the positive possibilities before we meet again so they might return with a purer heart. This plan will tell us if Will Verus is true to his city beyond a reasonable doubt. And if not …" her voice trailed away.

The Magistrate clung to her final words. Will and the REMs could go down all at once. Nothing would make him *happier.*

∾

Down on Bliss Avenue three hours later, a fanfare burst forth. Tranquility's anthem blasted out from gigantic speakers.

The ten-by-ten-foot screen above flickered and illuminated with a flashing rainbow of color. Its pixel morphed into images of various landmarks.

Finally, the screen revealed the building and grounds of City Hall, where a clan of Sciolists marched to the center of the screen, the red of their robes a contrast to the perfect, lush, green carpet of grass beneath their feet.

The flag of Tranquility, its eighteen Status colors standing out against a matchless blue sky, filled the screen next.

The band music faded, replaced by the smooth baritone voice of the Magistrate. The colors blurred away and then came back into focus again. There was a brief blare of trumpets before drums rolled and the heavy banner swept aside to reveal Serpio's tall, slender form approach the camera deliberately. He glanced aside for a moment, then pinned his audience with an intense stare.

"As every citizen of Tranquility knows," Serpio started, "a wave of terrorism swept this city during the past few days. I have directed the Sciolists to search for the terrorists. I am here to bring you the report of the current situation of this unimaginable affair." He paused, drawing a breath.

"This has been a terrible experience for many of our people. And it has been a harrowing time for your public officials. One of our own, a new Plauditor—a man sworn to monitor your city and encourage happiness—has come under suspicion as a prime enemy of the city and of our people. This is a dreadful thing. But that is not all." He held out a hand, his face growing stern. "It involves other dangerous criminals. Despicable REMs. One of them, Xander Noble, formed them into a gang. They took over our beloved Plauditorium. On their illegal broadcast, they planned to stir our citizens to rebel." He nodded and then clasped his hands together. "Please don't worry about this invasion, this assault on our happiness. Rest assured, we have everything under control. But it is with considerable relief that I announce that Will Verus is already in custody, and soon, we will bring down this rebellion." He stepped back, then faded from view.

16

Will's Reinvention

Back in his solitary confinement, Will consoled himself by performing the sign language Ember had taught him. *Loyalty.* Over and over, he looped his hand through the gesture. Then, he paced. Fifteen steps from the front of the cell to the back. He counted the trips in the cell to pass the time and soothe his nerves. Counting was always good. It was something valuable he had learned in school about reducing stress.

For a while, he clenched his fists in anger, and then, once he talked himself down, the shame at his betrayal, both of himself and of his friends, took over. His conscience became a lecturing companion he couldn't shake.

At step 2,093, he watched the door to the cell whoosh upward. Feren, the woman from the Elite, stood in the hallway. The diffused lighting made her appear shadowy. Only her tinseled clothing created a muted, golden halo around her.

Will swallowed, his saliva catching on the lump in his throat.

Feren said, "Will, the Elite has made their decision. It wasn't a unanimous one. You're going to have a difficult situation ahead."

Will felt the blood drain from his face.

This woman would not be brutal with her news. She handled happiness for every person, so her language choices were careful, tactful. *Will they banish me?* he thought. *Kill me?* His body tensed. Muscles contracted. *Get ready.*

She spoke again, her voice soft and warm. "Come with me. You're being given a unique assignment, and you're going to need some new things."

Relief flooded Will as if he'd been resurrected. He swayed a little. Unbelievable news. Not a death sentence. She was giving him an *assignment.* He could handle that. This could be another chance to save his friends, save the city. "I ..." He didn't even know what to say. Thank you? No, thank you? Go stuff yourself?

Feren smiled at him, her white teeth shining even in the dim light as she stepped forward and took his arm. "You'll be on probation, doing a mission. The Elite has decided that if you are telling the truth, you'll have no problem working with us to find the traitors we seek."

Will cringed inwardly. A prickling in his scalp rekindled his unease. What had he done? *Just what you wanted, Will. A directive to betray your friends. You lied, and this is what happened.*

Well, it didn't matter. The Magistrate and the Elite controlled him now, and there was nothing he could do—*until later.* He squared his shoulders, forcing a confidence he didn't feel. But his feet failed to move. They felt rooted in cement.

"Come, Will. We have an urgent situation, and we need to get you ready," Feren pressed. "You're still a Plauditor. Now, though, you'll be a *planted* Plauditor." She led him out of the cell and, with her arm in his, strolled into the hallway, making her way to the elevator.

Still a Plauditor. "And how does that work?"

"The plan isn't complicated. You're getting re-outfitted first." Gazing at his bare, grimy chest and filthy pants, she grimaced, then averted her gaze. "And clean. You need to get clean." She made a show of separating herself from his side about a foot but still held his arm.

"I agree," Will said with a lopsided smile. A chance to get a shower and a fresh set of clothes. He welcomed that news. *A start! A start to an escape strategy,* he thought. *Nothing will keep me from finding Ember and carrying out our plans.*

Ember … His heart ramped up a beat as he thought of his girl. Then, despair crushed in on him. *Where was she? How was she? Certainly scared. Had she made it safely to the Plauditorium? Was she thinking of him, too?*

If the Magistrate and the Elite planned to use him as bait for his friends, he could draw them out but in a way that they'd be protected. He was smart, bold, an alpha male. The city even deemed him a hero, a title he shunned, but it was true; he could rise up no matter the circumstance. A renewed determination fueled his spirit as he waited for the elevator to arrive. A ride to the top mirrored his rise, his revamped resolve. He could beat them at their own game; he was sure of it.

They stepped inside, and the door closed, the Tranquility anthem booming from the speakers as the elevator raced upward. In seconds, they were walking out the door into the City Hall corridor.

Will broke the silence. "So, once I get some clothes, I get to go home?"

"I'm afraid not, Will."

The disappointment hit him like a gale force.

Feren patted his arm. "Now, you're not a prisoner, of course! But you'll be in a chamber nearby to get refreshed, outfitted, and briefed for the job ahead. I imagine you're hungry, too."

"Hungry? That isn't even the word for it," he admitted. "I could eat for a week." He hadn't had food for over two days.

Feren laughed. "You'll have everything you want. What

sounds good to you? We'll have it delivered to you immediately."

A full-on grin lit up his face. "A Geodesic Burger, my favorite … And Jarnish, of course." His eyes became dreamy. "Oh! If you have them … Cheerchips?" he said shyly. His mouth watered. He remembered the first time he'd had those chips, a fresh, new food in the city. The crunchy snack, made using potato stock, starch, and slow-dried gel, dehydrated and then fried, came in different shapes and flavors. Totally transparent, the chips had a rippled texture, and they were to die for. Expensive, though. Only the higher Statuses had access to them.

"Of course, Will. We want you to have the food that makes you happiest." She smiled and suppressed a giggle. "Anything else?"

"I could really use a Limewave Shake, too."

"No problem. You'll earn every bit of those treats. A meal will be the first order of business."

"Is it far?"

"No. Out this door ahead, and we'll be in a courtyard. Just through the back are the guest houses."

So, he was a "guest."

Feren continued, "You're going to be very comfortable, Will."

Keep your guard up. Don't trust this woman. She's Elite. Poison.

They walked apart, Will at her side, without further conversation, along an extensive hallway. A metallic, golden door leading to the outside opened at their approach.

The vast garden that appeared as they stepped through the doorway took his breath away. Flowers and plants here, so delicate and perfect—he imagined they had been born in the lab. Exquisite blooms of all colors formed a rainbow effect, while greenery crawled lushly across the top of the vast arbor.

Floral and earthy scents bombarded his nostrils in a perfumy assault. He inhaled deeply, drinking it all in.

As they journeyed deeper into the arboretum, a profound sense of calm settled on him and gradually grew into a dreamy euphoria. He was so relaxed …

I'm … happy, he reflected. Love and protection hugged his being. Even the blossoms around him appeared to be friendly faces.

"Feeling okay, Will?"

"More than okay," he sighed.

"Good. Good. I told you that you'd be comfortable." She winked.

A final panel of lattice marked the edge of the garden and formed an exit from the pavilion. A lone building stood before them in a grassy clearing. Its yellow paint shone like sunshine itself. The structure, compact but modern, framed large windows in the front. A short, plexiglass deck protruded out from a painted door striped with Tranquility's Status colors. Almost as if Will heard it call his name, a cushioned patio chair suspended in mid-air without a tether invited him to sit down and unwind.

Will grinned, then laughed like a giddy schoolgirl. Hilarious. The house had winked at him.

He was delighted to see that even the lodging's color matched his Level Twelve Status. "You have a … guest house … for every Status?"

"Of course. Why wouldn't we?" Feren replied. "We want you to feel right at home. Let's get you inside."

Will at once felt very much at home. He loved it here. Carefree. Easy. Yet he felt, paradoxically, ultra-awake, reenergized. He turned and gazed at his lovely chaperone. Feren. She was so *kind*. A veritable *angel*. Spontaneously, he reached out and hugged her. Whatever awaited would be wonderful. "I'm ready."

"I'm sure you are. Follow me."

Up the steps to the door and across the narrow deck, Feren ushered Will to the entrance to the cottage, where she waved her Alt to open the door. An electronic voice responded, "Verified," and the door slid to the left.

"You opened that door with your Alt. How am I gonna get in?"

"Your new Alt will open the door."

"New Alt? I'll have one?" Will's mood deflated a little. His stomach suddenly turned over. A wave of nausea washed up his stomach.

"Why wouldn't you? Yours is broken," she said in a sympathetic voice.

"Yeah." He grinned and held up a finger. "You're right. I forgot about that."

"First, the layout here. Bathroom." She pointed to the left. "Kitchen to the back. Bedroom down the hall. And the sitting room here." She moved her arm in an expansive gesture, as if she was creating the room with her hand. "This will be a good place to relax for a few minutes, and I can get to know you a little bit."

That didn't sound so bad. "Sure. But you ordered food, right?"

"Yes, yes. Already on its way. Have a seat."

Will scanned the room and then sauntered over to a yellow, overstuffed chair, where, upon sitting, he felt like he was lounging in a marshmallow cloud. He sank deeper into its depths and sighed with contentment. "I'm sorry. I'm suddenly so tired. Can't wait to just sleep." After all he'd been through, comfort was a glorious gift. His energy level tanked. His eyelids drooped, and he had zero desire to do anything at all.

"Will, it's not time to sleep yet. Can you tell me a little about your family?" Feren prodded.

"Um … yeah. I have a mom and dad. Had a grandpa, but he passed on."

"And your parents?"

"Marina and Jack. They live in White Sands." He hung his head, aware of the stigma of the lower Status level.

"Will, why would your parents be Level One?"

"They chose that."

"I'm sure you've tried to help them, knowing what a caring person you are. Now, your friends …"

"My best friend is Wee. I mean, Weeford. Weeford Amicus."

"And would you like to contact him?"

Will frowned, the creases feeling heavy on his forehead. "I would, but … he's not home. He's somewhere in the city, I don't know where. I'm sure he's busy, though. He's got an important job, so even if he's not home, he's … too busy to come out here." Will knew he was rambling, not making sense, but what was he to say?

"I'm sure he'd love to see you, Will. You have no guesses as to where he might be?"

They've certainly already tried to track him. Did Feren know Wee had been with them? Or was she hoping that his best friend could be an information resource for them? He looked squarely in Feren's eyes, desperately steeling himself not to even blink. "No. Sorry."

"And your other friends? Ember and Xander?"

The room was closing in. His head spun with exhaustion, confusion, and a renewed panic. He couldn't think straight or remember anything very clearly. Feren demanded information, and in his state of mind, he would easily slip. But he didn't know where they were. He could only hope they were safe. "You think I know where they are? How would I if I'm here? I told you they're … not my friends anyway."

"Just double-checking, Will. We need you to be trustworthy."

"Yeah. Well, you can trust what I know. And that's nothing."

"Okay," she said as she touched his arm. "I'll show you your clothes, give you your Alt, and then leave you to rest."

"Yeah. Good. And food is coming?"

"Yes. Don't worry." Out of her pocket, she pulled an Alt.

She gave it a peck with her finger to activate it and extended it, giving him a warm smile.

For a reason he couldn't fathom, the hair on his neck stood up as he took it from Feren and clicked it around his wrist.

Feren crossed the room to a closet, the door sliding open at her approach. "Your clothes."

The news shook him out of his grogginess. New clothes. Will shambled over, his eyes wide. Reaching into the closet, he pulled them out, one by one. Pants. Shirt. Hat. Shoes. Plauditor clothes. *Jacket.* His mind pulled up a painful memory. He had burned his jacket earlier, somehow, some way. He couldn't remember why he'd do such a thing. But everything was all right now. His jacket—inexplicably reborn. He could be, too.

17

Ember's Arrival

Initially, Ember had had the cover of night in her favor. But in the early morning hours just after dawn, the sun was up. The city was coming to life. She had scant time before people would be everywhere. Covering her face with her hands, she hyperventilated before journeying forward.

Trusting her instincts as the day wore on, Ember stayed in the shadows of the buildings, using foliage, alleys, and Tranquility's street-level colorful signage as cover. She trembled every time she saw someone look her way, knowing she was an easily recognized celebrity, thanks to the Magistrate. Her bedraggled appearance, however, would be the last thing any common citizen would expect of the Queen of Hearts. Strangely, her look was the best disguise for her as she folded herself into an origami human wherever she could.

Without an Alt, she had no solid idea how long she'd been running, but as the sun dipped toward the west, her energy dwindled with the sun's rays. Her armpits moist with perspiration from running and fear, she sucked in a breath. There before her, finally. The Plauditorium. Never in all its black-hued majesty had the building looked so comforting, so desirable. She had made it!

As good as home.

Ember paused, breathing hard, wedged behind a thicket spiraling skyward. She was a good twenty-five yards behind the Plauditorium. She'd entered an area thick with trees and foliage, dotted with concrete benches. A tiny park. Hiding behind the bushes benefited her, but she fretted about getting from where she was to inside.

She didn't need her eyes to know there were Sciolists surrounding the place—a guard at every door. Toxic energy invaded her psyche. Only one class of people projected moods like that. *Sciolists. They would still be patrolling outside, watching and waiting for opportunities. Opportunities like this.* Running for any of the doors wasn't safe.

Were the former REMs still in charge? Did they still hold the Plauditorium? No way to know. Not until she was through the door. She hoped with all her soul that her newfound Phoenix allies inside would be expecting them.

She caught herself. It would be only her, not "them." *No Xander. No Wee. No Will!* If only Will were there to welcome her! His absence left a hole, as if she carried an open grave in her spirit. *Failing is not an option,* she reminded herself. *If it's only me, I alone must save the city!* Her heart turned over, remembering their crusade—their sacrifices—the successful takeover of the Plauditorium. A memory burst through her consciousness.

I'd been in the broadcast room with the Magistrate … Xander and his crew stormed the building—right through the front door I ran out of the Plauditorium's interior broadcast room to see what was happening. By that time, the Magistrate had somehow already left—and no one seemed to know how. He'd simply disappeared … But Serpio isn't magical. He had to have had access to an exit. Somewhere.

There was another way in. All she had to do was find it.

She threaded her way through the trees and shrubs to get a better view. The back of the building stared back at her. Gazing up, she saw windows. Go for those? No. They were so far up the wall they might as well be in space. She saw no door

—nothing that could possibly be an exit. But with no doors, no Sciolists patrolled the back area.

She took a few tentative steps out of her hiding place. Nothing moved. Time to make a break for the back of the Plauditorium where she could search.

Her feet flew over engraved square black pavers. Her feet pounded unforgiving flagstones, closing the distance …

She stopped in her tracks. Beneath her feet, the paver had her last name engraved on it. All the stones had names … but her own? *Keep going,* she thought. But her eyes riveted themselves to the name on the paver: "Vinata."

Keep going, her inner voice complained. *Don't stop here. You're wasting precious time.*

She couldn't compel herself to move. It was as if she had no choice whether to stop. A feeling she couldn't shake kept her stuck. The stone drew her like a weird force field. Yet she knew she wasn't in a time warp. It was more like the paver demanded her attention.

Loose dirt covered the first name; it would take but a moment to brush it away. She had to know what it said.

She dropped to her knees atop the stone next to it. *Shazz. On top of everything else, this stupid stone I'm on is so wobbly.*

Quickly scooping the powdery dirt away, Ember saw letters began to emerge V-I-C-T-O-R. Victor Vinata. She gasped. *Victor? That's my dad's name! Why would he have a stone here?*

Sitting back in surprise, she felt the stone on which she knelt shift. The stone had moved half its width out of place, revealing a bizarre abyss. She gasped. Was this why it had called to her? A hole in the ground?

Her head jerked up. Emotions slammed her from every side. In a streaming blur out of the corner of her eye, she glimpsed red. *Shazz!*

No, no, no! Hot, blind fury and panic boiled up, gut to brain. Terror spread through her like liquid fire. Two Sciolists were almost upon her. Others—she couldn't tell how many in the rush—approached from outlying spaces. *I have failed.* In desperation, she balled her hands into fists, preparing to fight, but realized instantly how ridiculous her efforts would be against a horde of Sciolists. Her eyes snapped shut in fear and shame, but her spirit refused to surrender.

She would not go down quietly. Fists in the air, her arms wide, she screamed at the top of her lungs. "Nooooo!"

An instant to prepare for the force of the Sciolist blitz. Hands upon her, roughness. But there was nothing.

She opened her eyes, confused. The world around her was frozen. The pursuing Sciolists were rooted in place, their legs still in running position, their faces angry and contorted. No one moved. Not even the breeze blew. No sounds. Utter silence. It was as if she was the only one alive.

This had happened only once before. In the Plauditorium, when Xander and his REMs took over, Xander had shot Will. And now. Her hands and arms throbbed with electricity. They vibrated with a torrid current pulsing through her veins. She turned her hands over, examining them for a clue to their magic. Yet, other than the feeling that began to slowly subside, they gave her no answers. Something she did or said just now had triggered another miracle, and like before, there was no time to question.

It would be only minutes before regular time resumed. The Sciolists would reappear, angry and violent. She examined where she stood, gazing down into the hole she'd found.

An unnatural glow flickered like a candle from its depths. Using all her strength, she shoved the paver aside.

Barely illuminated, a ladder's steel structure clung to the sides of what appeared to be a tunnel. *Salvation!*

Into the ground, three steps down the ladder, she pushed the heavy stone above her across the opening, inch by inch, with all her might. When the gap closed like a dead man's tomb, she fainted in a heap, and the world went black.

18

Serpio's Revenge

With the new day upon him, Serpio Magnus clenched his fists and paced. The Elite had disappointed him. The Magistrate was certain they would vote to convict Will Verus. But his special Elite Council *believed* Will.

The group rarely voted against the Magistrate's wishes. They were of his mind, selected for that purpose. But this time, they'd betrayed his trust.

He wanted to see Will's head roll. Not literally, but was it too much to ask for a simple guilty verdict?

In his bones, he knew the kid was concealing information. More than that, he was sure Will was deeply involved with the attack on the Plauditorium.

He stroked his chin. He wasn't the Magistrate for nothing. A keen insight with people made him profoundly effective. He knew he was right. He always was. Serpio pounded a fist on a gold-leafed table, his anger so complete and sharp the blow marred the glossy finish. He had to initiate a secret plot.

Serpio's own reflection caught his eye. In the room, a ten-foot-wide mirror spanned the wall opposite him. Softly illuminated around the edges, its luminosity intensified as he looked into it. "Hello, esteemed Magistrate," the mirror intoned with a respectful vibe. "You're looking very regal today."

The Magistrate never tired of the mirror's compliments. Not only did he love the boost they gave him, but he also delighted in his own image, where he could study his superior physical features and pledge to remedy any minor flaws he noticed in the glass. Today, he saw a tiny new wrinkle by his right eye. *I must correct that*, he thought, disturbed that this may have been something he had missed yesterday.

Now, with the mirror as his best friend and confidant, he could develop his most private plans. It was like talking with himself, only better.

He faced the mirror, as if he was before an audience of admirers. "So, Will is in the guest house—that I know. I can't just go get him and do what I want. The Elite made a decision. My hands are tied."

"Are they?" the mirror queried.

The Magistrate turned thoughtful. "I don't have to punish Will directly …"

"No. Good conclusion."

"What better way to penalize Will than to hurt someone or something he loves? And, of course, when he gets his new Alt, he'll have to keep his points up …"

"A brilliant idea, Serpio." The sound of canned applause followed.

Excitement lit up Serpio's voice. "Xander and whoever else was in that transport with him are likely dead. The report will be in soon. I'll have the pleasure of giving Will the news. But that may not be enough to break him. He's more interested in what happens to Ember. Until I find her, I must make Will's life a veritable hell." He paused, never once taking his eyes off his illusionary counterpart.

"How well do you know Will Verus? Look deeper."

An idea exploded in Serpio's mind. "Will's parents. I need to find out more about them."

"Very good, Magistrate."

He rushed to his desk, stabbed his fingerprint into the Lunos, and saw the information he needed materialize. The box glowed with multiple shades of the upper-Status colors, first a pulse of purple, then indigo, followed by the metallic colors.

He activated the screen, pulling up the holographic forms of Will's parents, their images crisp and glowing.

Serpio smiled with satisfaction. "Ah. Marina and Jack, I see. Lunos, tell me about these people."

"Marina and Jack Verus have been married for nineteen years and live in White Sands."

"White Sands? That's odd."

"Yes. Correct. They are an oddity in Tranquility. Happy and positive, but they never move up or down in Status."

"Are you sure?" A waste of words, but the information was mind-boggling.

"Yes. Their son, Will, has excelled and is Level Twelve. He has moved up the ranks of Status quickly. Will's parents have not."

What an opportunity. Manipulation of their Alts, bit by bit, and he could force them into Counseling. A Purging, maybe, for good measure. Just to make things look real. His eyes sparkled with joy at his own genius. If he didn't get more cooperation from Will, he could send Will's parents to The Outside. Perfect.

He'd have to do the Alt engineering himself. Even the Sciolists could not know of his actions, certainly not the Elite. Access to the Continuum Spectrum, the computer at City Hall, was an unquestioned right, as he, himself, meted out the awards and recommendations for every citizen of Tranquility.

He would start immediately on Marina and Jack.

IN HIS GOLD LIMOUSINE, Serpio was on his way to the hall where the Continuum Spectrum hummed its daily analysis. A call from Feren on his wrist device, the OmniCom, interrupted his contemplation of Will's secret punishment.

A regular Alt would never have worked for him. He needed his dark emotions to wield justice in the city. Instead, the OmniCom was loaded with all the apps he needed. "Hello, Feren. How are things going with our young Plauditor?"

"He's in the guest house, safe and sound, relaxed and ready for direction. The garden had the ideal effect."

"Good, good. Any information about Ember? He'll let something slip under the influence."

"That's the problem. With the garden effect, he should have volunteered it. But no. He honestly doesn't know where she is."

Serpio needed that girl—*wanted* her. She was going to belong to him, no matter what. He burned with frustration before remembering that Will would be effective bait for her.

The Magistrate hesitated before replying. For appearances, he should ask about Xander. Xander was dead, according to the report from the crash. The Elite, including Feren, didn't know that, though. Not yet. "And … Xander?"

"Will knows nothing about Xander. And no information about his friend Weeford, either. From what we know, Weeford's not involved in anything. We made the right decision about Will's innocence. He doesn't know a thing." Feren's voice carried its characteristic warmth.

"You'll bring him to City Hall at nine tomorrow after another visit to the garden. He'll need to be open to suggestion when we lay out a plan."

"Yes, Magistrate. I'm taking personal responsibility for him. I'll see you then."

"Looking forward to it, dear Feren."

The rest of the ride allowed him to think about all he had

accomplished in such a short time. His attention to Will, although obsessive, he admitted to himself, would lead to the end of the rebellion and the ultimate capture of Ember. His expert methods of manipulation would work well. He puffed up with pride, all at once more optimistic than he'd been in days.

As he passed the lovely little shops on the street, he indulged himself in some fantasies about Ember. She would ultimately be his again, and he would have her for whatever he desired.

The luxury CommuteCar stopped at his destination, the limousine door gliding open. "Have a lovely day, Magistrate," the car crooned.

Eager to start his plan, Serpio's gold-shoed feet flew across the polished flagstone. He waved his wrist to open a metallic door at Harmony Tower. There, in the confines of the icy room, the Continuum Spectrum computer had never looked so welcoming. He silently thanked the creator of this device and set to work.

19

Will's First Act

"**G**ood morning, Will. Time to rise for a new, marvelous day." The calming voice of his Alt woke Will the next morning. He had spent a restful night in his appointed guest cottage, his physical and mental exhaustion having forced a hard crash. He tried to focus, to recollect where he was. Then he remembered, and his heart sank.

Feren said he wasn't a prisoner, but he knew better. He was just in a more comfortable place now. He swung his feet out of bed. As if it would enable him to see a way out of his situation, he rubbed his eyes.

He had to find out as much information as he could. What was his assignment to be? And where were his friends? He vaguely remembered Feren grilling him about them, but the Magistrate had cameras everywhere. He had to know something.

But first, he needed to get dressed. He hazily remembered being shown new clothes yesterday. It seemed like a dream, but he crossed the room and confirmed it. Yes, there they were in the closet. He grabbed the jacket first, gathering it in his arms and sniffing it. Its dusky smell was comforting and familiar.

Setting the jacket aside, he quickly put on the complete uniform and suddenly felt not only more human but empowered. The Plauditor clothes, especially the jacket, did that to him. He took extra care smoothing the soft suede down on the front of his jacket, fastening the silver rivets on the cuffs, and zipping it up, its characteristic *zzzzzup* noise strangely satisfying. Afterward, he checked himself out in the mirror. He noticed shadowy circles under his eyes, but those imperfections would pass. His blond hair shone like gold, and his clean skin was again smooth and glowing. It gave him confidence he didn't have the day before.

His Alt vibrated, and the initial reminder of the day came up to check in to measure his emotional state. He placed his finger on its face, and the first numbers glowed to life. Points measuring his new self-assurance and positive feelings registered on the Alt's surface. He forced his mind to think positively about what he could accomplish that day. Then, he smiled shyly once more at his image in the mirror.

A tinny, melodic tune, again from his Alt, signaled a call. Feren. He swiped the screen. "Hi, Feren," he said, forced cheerfulness punching through.

"Will, are you dressed?"

"Yep."

"Engage the Alt's live screen so I can see you."

Will adjusted the Alt's screen by blowing his breath across the screen. Feren's image came up. He didn't need to, but Will said, "I'm here."

Feren's pupils showed her appreciation of his appearance. "You're looking better than you did yesterday. Really sharp. It's good to see you back in proper clothes."

"Yes. Thank you. I … appreciate them." *At what cost?* He wondered. Then, a flash of inspiration. "I'm not sure why you want me in Plauditor clothes, unless the Plauditorium has reopened?" He congratulated himself for the way he weaved that question into the conversation.

"No. You won't be going there, at least not yet. Reopening that place will be part of the plans we might make today. That's critical. I'll be by to get you in ten minutes."

"Right. I'll be waiting," he said as he cut the call. He jumped and threw a punch. The REMs were still holding the Plauditorium. Now, all he had to do was get there.

FEREN MADE no pretense of manners when she simply opened Will's door and walked in. He was surprised at her boldness but reminded himself that she was Elite, in control, and she already knew he was dressed. She smiled broadly and greeted him first with the Tranquility arm signal and then with a hug, like they were old friends.

At least she likes me and seems to trust me. I can use that to my advantage, he mused. Already, he was plotting what he could do with that. Whatever they asked of him, he would turn it around and use it against them to help his friends.

"We'll be meeting the Magistrate at City Hall this morning, Will. He's expecting us."

"Will the Elite be there?"

"No. Just the two of us. The Elite Council trusts us to put a plan into place where you help us search out your friends. Or whatever you want to call them," she added quickly.

"A word like 'traitors' would be better, don't you think?" *Play the game.*

"Yes. Henceforth—'traitors.'" Her teeth shined white in a warm grin, her eyes twinkling as if he had just told her a forbidden joke.

Out the door, the sun radiated a dappled design on the grassy area in front of the guest house. Will looked around trying to find the source of the design, finding that Feren's clothing, decorated with gold sequins, played a game with the light. The Elite always impressed.

Will walked next to Feren, unsure, not recalling his trek to the guest house the day before. "I'm glad you're escorting me. I'm usually good at remembering places. For some reason, my sense of direction is off."

"I wouldn't worry. And you would need an escort back into the building anyway. This is a high-level-security area."

Will quickly glanced at Feren's face. She appeared to be telling the truth. It just seemed like overkill. "Of course," he said.

They stepped into an arboretum with a path in the center, where Feren took the lead. Will had a sudden urge to stop and smell the flowers along the path, but his companion urged him along. Like a déjà vu experience, he felt he had been this way before. It had to have been just last evening, and yet it seemed an ancient memory. With every step further, he relaxed. Within moments, he felt on top of the world. He felt his new Alt vibrate with happy points and smiled.

Time fell away as they stepped through a golden door back into a hallway leading to City Hall and its chambers. This was it. His time to shine. His inner hero was ready.

"Good morning, Will," he heard the Magistrate say. The Magistrate extended the Tranquility salute.

"Well … hi." Will put his arm in the air, but the action was weak. It didn't seem to matter.

The Magistrate turned to Feren and whispered, although Will could hear every word. "Will seems a bit too … over-loaded. We need him to be compliant but functional." Serpio spoke into his Alt. "An order of tea brought to my chambers, please."

"Tea? I haven't had tea in a long time. That's nice of you."

The Magistrate smiled and put his hand on Will's shoulder. "Let's sit down over here and discuss some plans for you, dear Will." He gestured to a sturdy table surrounded by three chairs, all so gilded they shone as if dusted by diamonds.

"Sure." He shuffled over, followed by, he realized, the two most powerful people in the city.

An inside door slid open, and a small, dark-haired girl with almond eyes and fair skin in a white dress directed a floating tray to the table. Steam from a golden cup swirled in the air. The girl gave the Tranquility salute before retreating back out the door without a word spoken. Will wondered briefly if she was real or artificial intelligence like A.S.P.E.R., the receptionist at City Hall.

"Please." The Magistrate indicated to Will. "The tea is for you. Drink."

Will smiled but felt stupid about it. Something wasn't right. He didn't want to drink the tea. But what could he do? He grabbed the cup and took a deep swallow. "It's great. Thanks."

"No need to thank us," the Magistrate replied. "We'll soon be thanking you. You're exactly what we need to bring this rebellion to an end and round up your friends."

Feren interrupted. "Not 'friends,' Serpio. Will has agreed to call them traitors."

"Excellent." The Magistrate's face turned serious. "We have plans, Will, and we're going to lay them out. Our first priority is Ember Vinata."

Ember. A warm flush crept up from his thighs to his face. He longed to see her. His Alt's screen brightened with the emotional thrill.

"She's ... been found?"

"Not yet. That's why we need you, Will. You're going to find her."

"I don't know where she is. I've told you!" Will felt the room spin.

"But she's an Empath, as you know. Her emotional radar can find *you* if you're geographically close enough. I'm not sure how strong your bond is ... was ... but if you tour the city, your presence can draw her out. If she considers you an ally, she'll want you working with her and the others."

Will didn't know whether he should be relieved or frightened. This strategy was so hit-or-miss. She wouldn't come to him, would she? But why wouldn't she, if she thought he was somewhere safe? The ultimate goal for their group was indeed to reunite. And how could he swing things his way? His brain felt numb. He could not think.

A shiver ran up his spine, but he was not cold. Instinctively, though, he hugged himself, rubbing his arms over the sleeves of his jacket. *His jacket. That's it.* If Ember were to see him again, the jacket would warn her off. His old jacket was gone. He remembered. He had burned it right in front of her. His mood lifted. His Alt glowed.

The tea he drank had warmed him up inside as well. He was feeling a bit more like himself, whatever that was. He honestly didn't know anymore. All he knew was that he had to make them trust him. "Magistrate, your idea might work."

"We've had Sciolists posted around the Plauditorium. We know she isn't there, or they would have seen her and captured her."

Will nodded. Better to say as little as possible. His mind was still cloudy.

"Would she go to the Plauditorium if she could, Will?" the Magistrate continued, his voice pressing in on him like a physical vice.

"If she knows I'm not there, no," he lied. "Since your Sciolist accosted me as soon as I re-entered the city, like a common criminal, she has to know I was captured, that I wouldn't be there." He thought he sounded a little tipsy but continued with a louder voice to sound confident. "Ember's not strong. She would hide out until she found one of the others. Maybe she went back home, where she feels secure ...?"

The Magistrate's eyes narrowed, as if he was measuring the truth of Will's words with x-ray vision.

Feren, who had been slightly apart, moved closer. "Are the cameras still not working? We would know if she was home if we had surveillance."

The Magistrate shook his head. "With the Plauditorium offline, so are the home cameras. The techs are working to restore them. The Sciolists are on watch at the Plauditorium, but sending them inside, where the REMs have the city's only guns … it's risky. A decision must be made about storming the building. Enough Sciolists can take down whoever's inside with the element of surprise and their Stingers."

Feren's eyes grew wide, and she put a hand on his arm, as if to keep him from charging forward all on his own. "Serpio, you know we can't risk loss of life. There are still Plauditors there loyal to the city. We've no way to ensure they would be safe." Feren's forehead crinkled with concern. "We treat all citizens with love."

"True, Feren." The Magistrate placed his hand on her shoulder to show he would never upset her. "This is why I've not chosen that as the first line of this effort. If we find the perpetrators—-Ember and … Xander, the Plauditorium will easily fall. How long can they hold out for their heroes to arrive? The REMs are ragtag, inept, untrained. They won't hold the place without leadership. They'll surrender."

"That's true," Will said. "What I've seen of them is enough to convince me. They're weak and pathetic. Unsure of what to do. They just took direction from Xander." *Demeaning words, but not far from the truth,* he thought.

"Good to know, Will. In the meantime, we can broadcast to the city through the Jumbotron in the center of town. I did that earlier. That's another tool we will use to alert the city that we're looking for Ember. As far as tracking her down, if she's gone home"—he placed his hand on his shoulder—"Will can physically go there to check it out. If she's at her home—

her *former home*—" He paused to emphasize the words. " — and Will goes to the front door, she'll *feel* him there before she even sees him. She'll readily open the door if she thinks Will's alone. And alone he must be since she'll also feel anyone else within range of that place."

"If she misses me, yes," Will added. "And I think she would." He winked boldly at Feren. There was no chance in hell she would be there. But it would waste plenty of time, and time helped his friends, if they were out there and still alive. He'd have to push for that plan, to convince them that it would be an obvious place of refuge for Ember. He trained his brain on the thought that Ember was safe, and he would see her soon. His Alt points alone depended on it. He had to compensate for being a tool in a madman's hands.

"It looks like your reputation is holding up here. You really are the real deal."

Feren put her right hand on Will's face. Her palm felt soft and warm. He shut his eyes, wishing it were Ember's fingertips on his cheeks.

"Of course," Will replied. "I'm a rising star, didn't you know?" The brag felt dirty but gave weight to his words. "So, when do we start?"

20

Ember's Reunion

Ember stirred, putting a hand to her head. *Oui. What ... happened?* She sat up and groaned; her body ached in every joint, a reminder of the hours she'd spent on the run without respite. She pulled herself up with the help of the ladder next to her, steadying herself and studying her surroundings.

Only about eight feet wide, it was an actual room but damp and uncomfortable, like a cellar. A musty smell pervaded it. Her eyes swept the space. The narrow chamber had no door anywhere. Was it just an underground cellar? There would be no way out other than back up the way she had come. Had she stumbled into a trap?

Although her descent into the space had saved her life, now she was totally closed off. Alone. She glanced around, her eyes adjusting gradually to dim overhead lighting.

This had to be something more than a room. A temporary hiding place would do her no good at all. If it didn't give her access to the Plauditorium, it would be an enormous setback. There'd be nowhere to go but back up, back outside, and then she was doomed. Not only did she escape the Sciolists once, defying the odds, but she didn't understand how she'd caused the time warp that saved her. Beads of sweat gathered on her upper lip, renewed nervousness threatening to overwhelm her.

How long had she been out?

No matter. Her time warp would have dissolved by now. And clearly, no Sciolists had pursued her. All she could imagine was that even the Sciolists knew nothing about this place.

The walls reached upward for ten feet, gray and smooth except for one textured wall, which was rough with bumps and grooves. Ridges there created a rustic piece of art, a large black-and-white image of the city's mascot, the Halcyon. Its eyes, a deep black, gazed down at her with the intensity of a living, breathing bird.

She examined the ceiling. If the Plauditorium was directly above her, there had to be a way to get there. But how? Scrutinizing every inch, she looked for an overhead trapdoor.

As the minutes ticked by, she began to lose hope, the little room feeling more and more like a prison. The walls seemed to close in, and she just wanted to push them back, push them away. A tightness in her chest suffocated her.

Going from wall to wall, she swept her hands across every smooth surface. A hidden door maybe?

No. Nothing.

Finally, she turned to the corrugated wall with the Halcyon on it. Running her fingers over the facade, she gasped. Parts of the ridges lit up wherever her fingers touched. A variety of colors, from mint green to bright pink, glowed to life. Tranquility's colors.

Each area, when lit by her fingertips, created an image. Ridges that turned purple created a dog; the yellow ones, a mountain. Each movement of her hand brought up a new picture that disappeared as she touched another area. Turquoise ... a tree branch.

What an odd discovery.

Her fingers left the tree branch. She touched an area

above it, by now on her tiptoes, reaching her arm far above her head. A circle appeared with a "p" in the center. She gasped and jumped back. The wall opened! Like a door, it revealed another chamber inside. Without hesitation, she stepped in.

With her presence, the nook's interior instantaneously lit up with cornflower-blue beams. She felt an upward force pulling against her body, the sensation oddly comforting, like a weighted blanket.

Within two seconds, she was in another place, pitch dark, surrounded by a black wall or partition. Where was she now? Somewhere worse? The darkness of the space terrified her. She could see nothing, so she stood for a minute, allowing her eyes to adjust.

Feeling along the wall, she discovered the barrier cut off.

She stepped out into a new space, her heart seizing in her chest. Who would be there to greet her?

21

Ember's Entrance

Although the room was dimly lit, Ember recognized where she was. She stood immobile for a moment, dumbfounded. In shock. She was in the broadcast room of the Plauditorium! Relief flooded her, and she blew out a breath. Her body slumped slightly from the offloaded weight of fear and uncertainty.

The interior communication room where she stood was empty of people. The silence in the compact, soundproofed room, usually filled with broadcasters' voices, was eerie. Only the equipment stood vigil.

She dashed from the room, entering the main room of the Plauditorium like a comet.

Early morning sunlight from windows near the ceiling illuminated REMs who paced along the inner wall of the auditorium. Two older REMs occupied each side of the front door of the building. They held fat, steel beams, which looked like amputated table legs. In ninja-like poses, they were in position to fight off any Sciolists forcibly busting through the front doors. Stacked chairs, from floor to ceiling, pushed against the front door, and REMs sat eight-deep across the foyer. At the Plauditorium's two other exit doors, Plauditors flanked each side, but heavy desks turned vertically blocked the entrance. The six-foot-high front windows, designed as portals to view the beautiful, park-like landscaping outside, had their shutters tightly closed except for a slat through which four REMs traded off every other minute, monitoring the probable threats to the building. In the center of the room, a tall, blond-haired, dirt-streaked Outsider stood atop a desk, his rifle trained on the door. Plauditors engaged in active brainstorming sessions or worked at their stations, turning equipment off and on, shouting orders to each other across the room.

A hundred heads turned in Ember's direction. She felt a rush of emotions bombard her. Nervousness, fear, joy, and longing … Then, a dozen members of Phoenix came running toward her, surrounding her in a crush of bodies and tangible hope.

"Holy frazz!"

"You friggin' made it!"

"I don't believe it! How'd you get here?" A pale, thin REM with dark hair and icy blue eyes, the first to reach her side, practically toppled her.

"Umm … from underneath."

His eyes grew wide. "From underneath? How?"

"Yeah … there's a—"

"That story later … Main thing. You're *here*. I'm Bixby, one of Xander's best friends. Is Xander coming, too?" He looked beyond her, his eyes searching the path she had just taken. "Where is he?"

A buzz went up through the room, like a unified question mark.

"Please—please. I'll want to talk to all of you," she said. "I just can't with each of you." She laughed, realizing she hadn't heard herself laugh for days. It felt like forever since she had even smiled.

"Geez, guys. Let her up!" another REM shouted.

The crowd reluctantly parted, and Ember, like a weary but triumphant queen, made her way toward the front of the room, her fan club following her. She turned to face the group.

"I didn't think I'd make it back to you. I escaped Sciolists right outside, even up to a few minutes ago." She looked around at their faces and their multi-colored auras, full of concern, worry, and relief. "You asked about Xander. For safety, we separated the minute we re-entered the city, and … and … I lost him." She paused, her breath catching in her throat before continuing. Should she tell them about the accident? She couldn't be sure it was Xander or Wee. Better not spill her guts. "I also lost Will's friend, Weeford." She took a deep breath, closing her eyes and dropping her head. She looked up. Everyone was staring at her. She choked out her next words. "Will was captured."

The room went silent. Still. Then, a babble of voices rose up, and a flood of despair assailed her from the surrounding bodies. The entire room became a hurricane of sound.

Bixby stepped forward, right to her side. He touched her shoulder and then withdrew his hand. "It's not your fault."

"I'm so upset," Ember said as she squeezed his shoulder. She didn't know if the squeeze was more to comfort herself or Bixby. "I won't believe Will is beyond our help. We have to get him back." Ember exhaled heavily. "One thing I know, Will wouldn't want us to quit. Our distress can't sabotage us. *We're* the ones who have to put together a plan of what to do next. Time's running out."

Bixby looked at her as if he wasn't sure whether to smile or frown. "Yeah. I have hope. I have hope that everyone can come back."

Ember gave Bixby what she thought was her most encouraging smile.

Looking past him, she noticed a stage-like platform under the room's leaderboard. She turned and made her way to it, and stepped up, thinking how bizarre it was that she—not Will or Xander—was the one who'd made it back. Addressing the entire room, her voice was now amplified magically by her body's weight on the dais. She paused but only heard a mumble of voices. "Most of you have been Plauditors a while. You know how things work around here. What plans have you made?"

A Level Twelve Plauditor across the room stood up from his chair. *Still rooted to his station,* Ember thought.

"Is someone in charge?" Ember asked, her eyes scanning the room. "Who's your supervisor?"

An older female Plauditor standing close to Ember said, "It's Banks." She nodded toward someone to the left of her. "But the Chief Plauditor was Tedman Adoravi. Last time we saw him was when you and your friends took over. He and the Magistrate seemed to disappear about the same time."

"The Magistrate went through the secret exit—the one I discovered to get back in here. Tedman must have left with the Magistrate. I'm sorry, your name?"

"I'm Darla. I'm a huge fan of Will's, incidentally."

By the way her face flushed, Ember realized Darla had a special affection for Will. "Good to meet you, Darla. I'm sure Will has good things to say about you, too." Then, she couldn't help adding, smiling, "He is wonderful, isn't he?"

"Yes, he is." A dreamy look came into Darla's eyes, and she shook her head slightly as if to shake herself out of her emotional attachment. "I can tell you Tedman Adoravi's great friends with the Magistrate, so maybe they left together. No one's seen him."

Ember thought about the Plauditors they took to The Outside. She didn't know any of them or their names except for Will's co-worker, Austel. Maybe Tedman was taken with that group.

Ember looked at the sea of people in front of her. "Banks, where are you?"

A slender man with brown hair and olive skin stood and nodded to her. "Miss Vinata, I'm Banks. As Will suggested, we cut the feeds to the surveillance system when you all left. We're almost ready to get these monitoring stations back online. We've debated turning them all back on at once because we decided it would help us to know what's going on in the city. The cameras are our eyes, and they're everywhere."

Ember felt lit up. "That's amazing, Banks! Maybe we'll be able to see Will somehow … or Xander." She wasn't sure if she was strong enough to see what was happening to either one of them. Especially if Xander was … dead. She abruptly stopped her train of thought. The world blurred for a moment before she could tuck her fears away. She looked around at the faces watching her and took a breath. "We can use broadcasts to rally others in the city to our cause. The Magistrate shouldn't be able to stop us from broadcasting if he's not here, right? And, please, I'm just Ember. No one special."

"No, you're special. The Magistrate told the whole city that you have the ability to feel other people's emotions. That's a big deal. Mind-blowing. But I'll call you Ember anyway." Banks smiled. His warmth wrapped around her, and she suddenly did feel special.

Ember smiled back and nodded her approval.

Banks continued as he gestured with one arm to all the stations. "There are advantages to getting everything hooked up again, but there are disadvantages, too. By putting the Plauditorium back online, Sciolists can hack in, if they haven't already. By now, the Magistrate has had to do something about communicating with the citizens, even if it's using the CitiScreens on street corners. We can access those without a connection to the Plauditorium if someone's smart enough. With our screens off and our cameras disabled, we've cut ourselves off from what the Magistrate is doing and saying out there. Reactivating them will get us in the game with an advantage." Banks shifted in his chair multiple times. A slight nervous tic affected his right eye.

"Those are great points, Banks. Sounds like it's better to turn the cameras back on." Ember turned back to address the entire group. "Shall we take a vote?"

"I was thinking that same thing," Banks acknowledged. "All in favor of reactivating cameras, please raise your hand."

Hands went up all over the room.

Ember didn't need the vote. She could feel and see every emotion. She knew the group would vote yes. But Phoenix themselves needed confirmation and solidarity.

Ember gave them a broad smile. "It's almost unanimous. We do it." Spontaneously, she made the Loyalty gesture with her right hand.

A murmur rippled through the group. Confused, everyone looked at each other and at her. "What'd you just do?" a Plauditor called out.

"It means Loyalty." Ember looped through the motion again, most of the room following her movements. "A great way to acknowledge each other. We're all in this together." All at once, she remembered how Will liked it when she made the Loyalty sign. It was as if he was beside her now. Her throat caught as she saw once more his smile. He was the special one.

For the next minute or two, as the group practiced the gesture, they laughed and nodded. Ember suddenly felt a part of something powerful. They could be invincible.

22

Ember's Edict

A Plauditor approached her. The lady, a tall woman with shoulder-length dark hair, hesitated before giving her a weak Tranquility salute.

"Hi …" Ember responded.

"I'm Shawny." The woman had heavy-lidded brown eyes and rosy cheeks. She walked with an assurance that Ember envied. "I'm so happy that you made it back. You probably have quite a story."

Ember touched her arm. This person flared with kindness. "Good to meet you, Shawny. And yeah, I have stories, but I— I don't want to go into detail right now." Ember shivered. The idea of explaining all she'd been through … no. Glossing over it, she continued, "Thanks for being a part of this—part of Phoenix."

Shawny smiled gently as she patted Ember on the shoulder. "I understand. But one thing we absolutely have to do. We need to decide about these." Shawny held up her wrist, her Alt blinking back at Ember. "They're no good to us. And they're sending information second by second to the Magistrate." Shawny's uneasiness slid into Ember's body like a frozen vapor.

"I agree. Let's talk it out …" She addressed the Plauditors again. "Your Alts—they're tracking everything." She held up her wrist. "You have the freedom to take them off. No one should limit you because of what you feel. And, when we rise up together, we'll fight that law."

She looked around at the crowd, hoping her words were making sense. People were shaking their heads in disbelief. She could feel both worry and exultation in the room. They'd never had a life without the Alt on their arm. A few who'd become genuine believers threatened to grind their Alts beneath their feet.

Ember put her hands up, signaling for quiet. "Take it off, but keep it nearby. We may need it later to communicate."

She swayed, her legs suddenly feeling useless. The room spun, and she put her hand to her temples. A murmur rippled through the throng.

"Ember, are you okay?" Bixby cried, worry etched across his forehead.

"I'm just so tired …"

She wobbled again, and this time, Bixby didn't hesitate. He grabbed her around the shoulders.

"You're exhausted, Ember. You need to rest and eat. There's a kitchen here. Jasper!" he called. "Come help me!"

Jasper, his red robe askew, seemed to come out of nowhere. "I gotcha."

The two men supported her, their arms and warm auras wrapping themselves around her. Ember hadn't met them before today, but their REM status somehow made them more human than most people. Their concern was authentic.

"Thanks. I appreciate the help," she said, her voice breathy. "I'll be okay, though. I'm *so* hungry and totally exhausted. But I can walk on my own, guys."

"Well, we have to show you the kitchen, so here we go," Bixby's friend said.

Before she had time to utter one word of protest, Jasper

picked her up. Ember felt lightheaded the entire way down an adjacent hallway to a brightly lit room. Upon arrival, they set her down in a plush, multi-colored, striped chair next to a transparent table. Just being able to sit down without fear was priceless. Xander's friends busied themselves making her comfortable. She sighed, embarrassed, but resigned herself to being cared for. The guys bustled around the kitchen. The table in front of Ember was soon laden with fruit, cheese, and Jarnish.

"Jasper at your service, Ember. You definitely need this." He plunked a tall glass of an apricot-colored beverage on the table. "This is Kasimir. Have you ever had it?"

She looked up at him, taking in his rough appearance. "No. I don't recognize it."

Jasper grinned and stood back, his hands on his hips. "It's delicious, but most of all, it's calming. It's made from apricots, white tea, and a little bit of alcohol." He pinched his thumb and forefinger together to illustrate.

Ember's eyebrows shot up. "Alcohol? I've never had alcohol. Not sure I should, either …"

Jasper laughed as he dropped a straw into the glass. "Believe me, you should. It'll settle you right down."

She picked it up and sniffed it.

Bixby came over to the table and sat down beside her. "Drink and eat. The bathroom's around the corner. Your clothes are filthy." He grinned. "You look like you've been livin' on The Outside. There's a closet of uniforms here. Maybe one'll fit."

"Thanks, guys. But you and your crew … don't you want to take advantage of having a place to bathe?" She felt sorry for them. They looked so scruffy. Their clothes, brown and drab, were the texture of burlap. The red capes they wore were meant to look regal, but they didn't hide the extreme need of sprucing up from head to toe. Both the guys smelled earthy. How did they ever survive on The

Outside without a place to bathe and proper clothes to wear?

Bixby shook his head. "We get along. At some point, yeah, we'd love to have the luxury of a bath. For now, you need it more than we do."

Ember watched his concern for her bloom into a deep blue aura.

Jasper said, "Eat, bathe, change, and rest. We have to find Xander, so you'd better get ready."

Her throat tightened. She needed to tell them about the wreck and Xander. For now, though, it would be something that could wait.

AFTER EMBER HAD BATHED and eaten, she lay down to rest in the lounge just off the kitchen. Although the Plauditors never had a reason to use overnight sleeping quarters, they were there nonetheless. Tranquility's leaders had thought of everything to make the Plauditors happy and productive. She remembered being in this very room before, when she had become ill from carrying her mother's ring in her pocket. Not a memory she wanted to keep alive. It was the beginning of their discovery that the Magistrate was poisoning recipients of the Augur Prize. It had torn her entire world apart.

Her mind drifted to Will. Memories … Bits and pieces of the times she had spent with him lulled her into a soothing contentment. Sleep crept in and stole her away, and she fell into a deep dream state …

"YOU WILL FIGHT TO THE DEATH!" Two dark figures and hazy silhouettes paced back and forth across from each other. Each carried a weapon which sparkled in a strange, unworldly illumination. She cried out and helplessly watched as blood fell like rain from the sky above. The

figures vaporized, as if they were only smoke. Instead, Will stood there. His Plauditor's jacket glowed brightly along its yellow stripe, but his face was unfriendly. Ready to embrace him, she ran to him. She wanted to tell him how much she had missed him. Instead, he put his arms out to stop her, placing his hands on her shoulders. He swiveled her body to where she saw a winding road and a door. Something important was on the other side; she had to get to it! She could feel a presence there, full of love and light …

SHE SUDDENLY SAT UP, wide awake.

A yell. "Outside! A KelastCar! Pulling up to the front!"

What kind of new threat was this? Just when she thought they were safe …

Ember jumped up off the cot and raced down the hallway into the main room.

The guards at the door, one a red-caped REM holding the one rifle they had and another a Level Fourteen Plauditor sprang into action, facing the entrance, ready to attack. The lookouts at the window glued their faces to the adjustable shutters, watching for any movement coming from the KelastCar.

A cry went up. "Move the barrier—fast!"

"What the—!"

"No way—move, move, *move!*"

A flurry of bodies pushed away all the physical barriers reinforcing the locked, bolted door. Human grunts and the scraping of furniture reverberated through the room.

The doors, finally free, opened as if in slow motion. A familiar body pushed through.

"So, how the hell is everybody?"

23

Xander's Arrival

Xander entered the Plauditorium with a large black box in his arms, but he wouldn't let that diminish a dramatic entrance. This was a *moment*, and he intended to savor it. He grinned with the ease of a rock star among adoring fans. His eyes sparkled with devilish delight, knowing he'd managed the ultimate surprise homecoming.

The room erupted, the voices of twelve members of his own crew cheering loudly. Xander's Outsiders pumped their fists in the air or clapped their friends on the back. Some Plauditors simply sat down, shocked to see him. Several applauded respectfully. One guy in the center of the room switched on music, a hard-rock anthem with a repetitive lyric, "good times." After the din became an intolerable roar, a cry of "Quiet!" went up.

Wee entered, pushing a crate on wheels. Wee's innocent face and demure entrance were a sharp contrast to Xander's swagger.

Jasper was the first to run to Xander's side, punching his shoulder lightly. "How'd you get here?" Jasper demanded, his eyes round as a full moon. "There are Sciolists out there!"

Xander laughed. He set down his box and laid a blanket-wrapped rifle next to it. He threw his arm across Jasper's shoulder and clapped him on the back. "Yeah. Long story. We wouldn't be here 'cept for Ava." He turned and threw out his arm behind him in introduction.

Wee, who stood behind Xander, blocked anyone's presence with his seven-foot, two-hundred-pound frame. At Xander's mention of Ava, he stepped aside, revealing Ava to the crowd. She, too, carried a box full of water bottles.

Ava handed off her cargo to a Plauditor, whose smile showed he was eager to help. Plauditor training ran strong and deep.

A staggered gasp rippled through the room as each individual noted Ava's rank. *Elite.* Right there in the middle of a room full of rebels.

"Hello everyone," she said to the crowd with a meek little wave, her dark eyes sparkling.

Bixby, taking giant steps from across the room to get to Xander's side, stopped abruptly, a frozen statue of surprise. He blurted, "She's Elite! What's she doing here? Xander …?"

"Relax. It's okay." Xander freed himself from the mob gathering around him and strode to the front of the room, where he jumped up on the mini stage. "Hey, Phoenix! And yes, that's *all* of you, remember? Please—welcome Ava, the only reason Wee and I are here alive. Not only did she heal us, but she's on our side. History with Serpio brings her to our team."

"You sure we can trust her?" a random voice called out.

"I'd stake my life on it," Xander said with a wink in Ava's direction. "In fact, I have. Yeah, Ava's Elite! That's how she could get us here. She convinced Serpio you needed supplies. But we had to play dead first. Since she was in charge of disposing of our bodies," he grinned. A low hum of sound buzzed through the room.

Xander spoke again, his voice strong and emphatic. "But

we're here, we're *alive*, and we're ready to kick some ..." The words froze on his tongue.

Ember. Across the room. His throat seized up, and an electric jolt rolled through his chest.

"... ass." The word lacked the force he intended, his breath failing to punch it through. His eyes locked with hers, explosive. *She's here. Really here.* A happiness he'd thought was long extinguished came to life.

"Xander! Wee! So glad to see you!" Ember cried. Her enthusiasm bubbling over, she ran over to her friends.

Her face looked like it was full of moonbeams.

"Hey ..." Xander drawled. He'd never been good at controlling his emotional state, but right now, he wanted to more than he ever had. He wanted to look calm, be calm, be in control. After all, he had an audience in the room. He could allow her to see his relief at finding her here, but he didn't want to be over the top. "You're safe. That's ... amazing!" he managed to blurt. He stepped down from the platform, shortening the space between himself and Ember.

When she threw her arms around them in a group hug, words caught in his mouth again, turning him inside out. The act wasn't enough to satisfy Xander, but he realized this was the closest he'd ever been to her. And that was exhilarating.

Wee bounced like a puppy and hugged her tightly. "Girl! You're the best thing I've seen in a looooong time! And look at you! A Plauditor's uniform?"

"Yeah, I know. Weird, but I needed clean clothes. It's okay, though, right?" She looked at the two of them, her eyes full of doubt.

Xander sighed inwardly. She rocked that uniform, its sleek, black silhouette showing off every curve, but he'd save his opinion to share with her later. Privately. He couldn't wait for an opportunity to get her alone.

Instead, he said, "Ember, this is Ava—our angel in disguise."

Ember reached out her hand and grabbed Ava's. "I don't know how you did it, but you have my forever thanks."

Ava laughed. "You're very sweet. I can see why Xander and Wee have such affection for you."

"Shhhh. Don't tell her!" Wee said, chuckling. "She'll get a big head."

Ember smiled and cuffed Wee on the arm.

"I hate to interrupt the reunion," a man's voice interrupted from a ways away, "but I've reconnected the cameras. The monitors are working. We can now send and receive broadcasts."

Xander turned to the voice. "You are …?"

"Banks. Good to see you again, Xander." He gave Xander a nod. "But before you walked in, Ember and, well, all of us decided. We're putting the Plauditorium back online. It's a tool we can use. We were even gonna to use it to track you down. Thank the stars we didn't have to."

Xander looked at Ember, his eyebrows raised. "Well, well. You haven't wasted any time. I *like* that."

Ava nodded in agreement. "It's good. Problem is that the Magistrate will figure out a shortcut to look right back at you. He's already made one city-wide broadcast using the street screens."

Xander allowed the doubt to take hold for a second, but only for a second. "We've gotta get started with communication. We go forward." They were already making progress. He couldn't let anything get in the way.

Xander turned back to Ava. "How long can you stay?"

A frown briefly traced Ava's forehead. "I'd like to stay but gotta go in a few minutes. My Alt'll be clocking my time here. Supplies are delivered. I need to document the situation with my camera, so I can show the footage to Serpio. I'll arrange some convincing photos and video. Then it'll be time to get back to see what Serpio's doing. I'll gather info."

Wee, standing silently by, said, "Info's great. But how can

ya help us? It's not like we can send messages or calls through Alts. Those can be monitored. I don't even have my Alt. I tossed it Outside. Ember and Xander don't either."

Ember said, "All the Plauditors have taken theirs off. I don't know …" She tilted her head thoughtfully before her eyes widened. "We can have a code! Something no one else can see. Or solve."

Xander looked at the three in front of him to gauge a reaction. A code would take time to develop, and they needed a system right now before Ava left. Time to involve everyone in the room. The Plauditors—*former Plauditors*, he thought—could figure it out. He hated to admit it, but they had more experience than he did.

He stepped back up onto the amplified dais. "Phoenix! Who has an idea for a secret code? Before Ava goes, we need a plan. She can help us from inside the Elite, but we've gotta work out a way to send messages."

Groups of Plauditors gathered in groups, their bodies looking like multi-colored, striped, black bugs as they huddled together. They still wore their jackets, as if it were a sin to take them off. He grinned at his own group then, realizing they, too, kept their red capes on. For them—and perhaps for all—the clothes were a source of pride. He noticed that his own crew still separated themselves from the uniforms in the room. He'd strengthen the teamwork later. But his REMs were at work, brainstorming loudly.

Finally, among the clamor, a Level Fifteen made her way to the front of the room. "Hi. I'm Shawny. I've been around a while. As you can probably tell," she said, a brief smile touching her lips. Xander could tell. In spite of all the ways in Tranquility a person could enhance their appearance, especially as they became higher level, this lady had wrinkles. They were soft, but they were there. Time was beating out the efforts of the best interventions at shops that offered Lustrum, an effervescent green solution that helped people appear years younger. *She might be even in her seventies,* Xander thought.

Shawny continued, "There's an old, old code we can use. Maybe the Magistrate will be aware of it, but maybe not. It's worth a try. I read about it in my history class when I was a kid. I was fascinated. Did extra research on it."

"Okay, Shawny. Can Ava learn it fast?" Xander tossed his gaze this way and that, like he had plenty to say but not enough time to say it.

"I've memorized it. I can write it down for us. We only need sounds or light pulses." Shawny appeared unruffled by Xander's frustration.

Ember tilted her head as if listening to music only she could hear. "Sounds too good to be true. What is it?"

"It used to be called 'Morse Code.' It was used in world wars of the past."

"I was thinking … I know another code that my mom taught me. It's no longer used either. Hand motions. It was for deaf people."

"It blows my mind that people didn't have the fix for that." Wee shook his head. "Gotta be thankful we live when we do. But they had their own special language?"

"Yeah. Our hand gesture for Phoenix is 'Loyalty.' It comes from the sign language for the deaf."

Xander made the loop with his hand and smiled. "I didn't know it had a whole language."

"I taught it to Will first …" Ember trailed off, leaving the unspoken implications hanging in the air.

Xander could almost smell the sweetness in Ember's words. He made a pretense of needing to roll up his sleeves to allay the awkwardness he felt.

Weeford reacted by dropping his head. "If it's a whole language, we should give it a shot."

Xander said, "Look, Ember. Get with Ava and Shawny to put that code thing together. You can use one or both. I'm gonna work with the crew here to figure out a broadcast. Citizens need to know what's going on and that we're not some scary enemy."

Ember joked, "I don't know … You're pretty scary." She gave him a wink and a smile. "Good luck." Chuckling, she walked away with Ava and Shawny.

He watched Ember's back, enjoying the view. His pleasure turned sour, though, when he overheard her say, "Ava, do you know *anything* about Will? I'm going crazy…"

He tried to tell himself he cared about what happened to Will. But the truth was, Will would just be in the way. Xander didn't want any competition for leadership, and he hated the thought of Ember being in love with Will.

No sooner did the thought cross his mind that the screens throughout the Plauditorium spluttered to life, winking in and out, before sharpening into a broadcast in progress. And there was Will. *On the screen.*

———————————————

24

Serpio's Scheme

———————————————

As Ember and Shawny began their conversation about a code, CitiScreens all across the city began a special news broadcast. A virtual reality display of Tranquility's mascot, the Halcyon, flew out of the screen, stretched its wings, and turned every color from white to gold. Mood-elevating music that reinforced Tranquility's values played along, synced to the mascot's movements. Finally, the music faded out, and the bird "flew away," revealing the Magistrate. Serpio's face loomed large on the screen, grand enough to ensure the citizens understood his vast importance.

"Dear citizens of Tranquility …We cannot transmit this broadcast directly into your homes due to technical issues at our Plauditorium. So, we're outdoors for this newscast, at Positive Park, enjoying Tranquility's beautiful weather."

The Magistrate threw his arms outward, signaling to the cameraman to pan the area. Multi-hued benches lined the street, and blooming trees provided shade. A fountain sprayed water from an eight-foot bowl to a plantar filled with flowers below. The camera lighted on a golden statue of the Magistrate, spotlighted even in the daylight.

Serpio motioned for the camera to swing back in. "I ask

that you pause to give me your attention for this very important announcement."

The Magistrate, his posture straight as an arrow, nodded. To Serpio's right stood a young, golden-haired Plauditor, his face devoid of emotion, making him appear almost inhuman. His eyes, though, a deep sea-green, were alight, nearly feverish. The boy's physical grace, set off by the camera's exacting lens, made the Magistrate boil under his skin. *How could anyone be that physically perfect?* Any girl, including Ember, would be completely infatuated. Was there no end to Will's negative influence in his life?

The Magistrate cleared his throat and put his hand on Will's shoulder. "You'll remember Will Verus, my guest here today, from a recent newsfeed. Because Will risked his life for a rescue, he's a Level Twelve Plauditor." Serpio patted Will's shoulder. Serpio smiled at the camera, hoping his insincerity didn't show through.

Will's head swiveled to gaze at him curiously, the boy's movements still affected by the earlier pass through the garden.

I need to wrap this up, Serpio thought as he continued his speech. *He's been out of the garden a while.* "Citizens, I broadcast here in this beautiful place because we've had to keep our Plauditorium closed. Unfortunately, Plauditors in the building are still held by terrorists. We will not attack the center, as our very loyal Plauditors could be hurt or killed. I will always put the safety and happiness of our citizens above all." He made a steeple with his fingers and bowed his head toward the camera in a show of subservience. The citizens needed to know he practically worshiped their needs. Once he paused for dramatic effect, he continued. "But be assured. These terrorists are not a threat. The main perpetrator, Xander Noble, has been killed. It was an unfortunate accident, but his death will easily bring all acts of rebellion to a close. In a short time, all will be well."

A yellow-winged butterfly flitted by. It made a loop and returned, landing on Serpio's custom-made, gold tweed suit. He brushed it off, and it landed, wounded, on the ground by his feet.

"We thought initially that Will was part of that rebellion. I was … overprotective, dear citizens. I was worried about our city's safety and looking out for you all. Will is here to set the record straight." He glanced over at Will, scrutinizing his reaction to the news of Xander Noble's death. Will's eyebrows arched in surprise but fell in an instant. His jaw clenched, and his entire face seemed to freeze in a stony facade. Serpio had no way to tell if Will was angry or just shocked at the news. Serpio nudged Will's elbow, as if to bring him back to life. Turning to the Magistrate, Will bit his lip and ran his fingers through his hair.

The camera, a tiny blinking thing, zeroed in on Will's face. *He'd better be ready,* Serpio thought.

"Hello, citizens. I'm Will Verus." He gave a little wave and then stopped speaking for a second or two, causing a moment of panic in the Magistrate's mind. There were multiple risks here, but he needed the people to see that Will was a government man, through and through. When Will continued, Serpio blew out a breath.

"I'm honored to be a Plauditor. My job's to keep you safe and help you be happy. I wouldn't want anything to get in the way of that happiness. *Ever.*" Will paused but continued to look directly into the camera's lens in such an intimate way that Serpio wished he had given him more balancing tea. "That's why I tried to *prevent* the rebellion. Ember Vinata asked too many questions. Classified stuff. I got to know her. Followed her. Discovered her plans."

Serpio pulled out a gold, satin handkerchief and wiped his brow. Luckily, he was off-camera. He watched Will carefully, ready to catch any small error or hint of traitorous speech. He leaned in closer to the boy. An awkward thought forced its way to the forefront of his mind. He suddenly hoped that Will really was sincere. A true-blue Trank. An inspiration to the city. He could, in the end, maybe even be a real help. A right-hand man. The son he never had …

Will glanced over at him as if he could hear his thoughts and then turned back and continued speaking, his voice sounding more urgent. "I'll admit that I was an overeager Plauditor—but I was new. Just wanted to make a name for myself." He paused as if to weigh his words. "I'm from a Level One family. My parents taught me raising Status is important. Therefore, I'm loyal to City Hall. To the Accords. I'll do anything for our Magistrate." Will turned and gazed at his leader, giving him a nod. "And Xander Noble, the real rebel, a worthless REM, was *no* friend of mine." His face remained somber. Only a barely indetectable twitch of his upper lip suggested an emotional strain.

The camera panned back to the Magistrate's face filling the screen. "Thank you, Will. We are *indeed* indebted to your efforts. In the meantime, Ember Vinata, who I recently introduced to you, is missing. We believe she has aligned herself with the rebels." He held Ember's picture up for the camera. "Be on the lookout. If you see her or know of her whereabouts, use the *emergency option* on your Alt. Signing off for today. Be safe, and be happy."

The Tranquility anthem played softly as the broadcast came to a close. The cameraman gave Serpio the Tranquility salute, gathered his equipment, and hurried away.

"You did fine, Will. That's one thing off our list. We can move on to the real need—finding Ember." The Magistrate's eyes twinkled at the thought of the hunt. No matter what Will said, Ember was definitely Will's kryptonite.

25

Ember's Ideas

Ember stood frozen in shock. Her beloved Will was right there on every screen in the Plauditorium. But he might as well be on the moon. She couldn't touch him, reach him, talk to him. Worse, she couldn't feel his mood or see his aura. The image teased her with its counterfeit reality. Her heart seemed determined to run off on its own. Tears welled up, and her breath caught in her throat.

Will's words blasted into their space on full volume, the adjustments for sound being arranged in another place, beyond their control.

The room of Plauditors, so full of its own noise, grew silent. Everyone was listening, transfixed, to Will's announcement.

"I'm honored to be a Plauditor. My job's to keep you safe and help you be happy. I wouldn't want anything to get in the way of that happiness. *Ever.*"

She watched him hesitate for a second or two. Words she expected him to say formulated in her head: *So, that's why you need to know your Magistrate's a murderer.* But when he continued, his words burned her like acid.

He's saying he tried to stop the rebellion? That he followed me because I asked questions? Spied on me?

Murmurs surged throughout the crowd. She couldn't pick out their words, but the Plauditors' voices rumbled in a mesh of surprise and confusion.

Xander yelled out, "Prevent a rebellion! You two-faced—"

"Shhhh! the room hissed like an enormous leaky air hose, collectively shushing him.

"I'll admit that I was an overeager Plauditor—but I was new. Just wanted to make a name for myself." Another brief pause left room for shouts from the twelve REMs, their loyalty to Xander fueling their protests.

Ember could barely hear his speech above the noise. She hollered, "Stop! Listen!" She didn't know what she found more irritating—the whining from the group or the confusion in her mind.

Words about Will's Level One background and loyalty … Loyalty! But to City Hall and the Accords? And to the Magistrate?

Will turned and gazed at his leader, giving him a nod. "And Xander Noble, the real rebel, a worthless REM, was *no* friend of mine."

Oh, Will. What are you saying? Why? She hung on to every word, even though they were hammers pounding nails through her skin. *He has to be lying! Admitting to being a spy?* But it sounded so sincere, the tone of voice so much like the Will she knew. She studied his face. Cool. Innocent. Devoid of emotion. She was beside herself, not being able to feel him.

Then the camera shifted to the Magistrate, her coveted vision of Will gone and replaced by Serpio Magnus. "Thank you, Will. We are *indeed* indebted to your efforts. In the meantime, Ember Vinata is still at large." Her picture! She gasped, her fingers flying to her mouth. She stumbled backward in shock as he pushed the photo forward into the camera. "Please be on the lookout for her, and if you see her or know of her whereabouts, use the *emergency option* on your Alt. Be safe, and be happy."

When the screen went blank, Plauditors shouted. Some of them yelled, "Liar!" while others screamed out curses or pleas to resist. REMs stomped about the chamber, words appearing to fail them. If anger was a real creature, the monster would be thrashing the place. Shawny, who stood next to her, had her hand across her eyes, like she had just been hit.

Ava approached, put her arm around her shoulders, and squeezed. "It's … shocking. But the Magistrate is capable of anything. Remember that. This might not be Will's speech. He may merely be a mouthpiece."

Ember couldn't respond. She gawked at the chaos around her. The speeches had both divided them and torn apart their newly gained peace of mind in less than two minutes. Her gaze settled on Xander across the room. His jaw was clenched, his arms twisted across the front of his body in a straitjacket hold. But his eyes could have set the room on fire. She could feel the heat of his emotions like rays of a desert sun. And she understood. Blood pounded in her temples, too.

Xander mounted the dais again, his arms pushing downward to quiet the crowd. When he appeared satisfied, he spoke. "This—this speech. People, we don't know what to make of it yet. We're ready to judge. But Will is under Serpio's thumb. He could be lying to protect himself." His eyes met Ember's again across the room.

He knows I'm upset. More upset than anyone in here, she thought. *And I wonder what he truly thinks about what Will said.*

Ember turned to Shawny and Ava. "I … I'm good with the code. I'm just … I need to go to the lounge, I think."

Weeford, still hanging with Xander, ran to her side. "Ember, you know that's not Will. He'd never say that stuff unless he had to. You know that, too." His eyes, all brown and soft, comforted her. "You okay? Tell me you're okay." He put his arm around her shoulders.

Ember's eyes flared. "Yeah … I just wasn't expecting to see him. Or hear *that*. You know. And it makes me even more scared about how we're going to get him out of there. He belongs *here* with *us*."

Shawny, Ava, and Wee swooped in with a group hug. Their warmth and compassion flowed in and around her, giving her an emotional boost. In a few ways, being an Empath was helpful. As long as those around her had the right feelings, their emotions bolstered hers. Thank heavens, because her own emotional state was fragile.

Ava said, "We'll figure it out. Remember, I'll be working on the inside. And I'll be there soon."

Ember gave her a weak smile, wishing she could bottle Ava's optimism. Her shock of seeing Will made her feel as if she was drained of life. Ember's heart was spinning. First, she was stunned, then sad. But most of all, she was angry. Whatever was going on, it was wrong. Will, a betrayer? Or was the Magistrate forcing Will to appear loyal to him?

Ember frowned. She'd taught Will sign language that was exclusive, known only to a few of them. Why couldn't he have used his Loyalty gesture on camera? Such a simple communication. Reassurance missing in action.

26

Ember's Experiment

The more Will's words and behaviors came back to her, the more her blood surged. And not just her blood, her heartstrings. And the poor Plauditors, Will's colleagues … Their collective emotions were overwhelming her senses, threatening to eat her alive.

She began to push their feelings away, trying to wring them out like water from a sponge. If only she had the ability to block them …

But … why? Weren't they a source of *power*? All at once, she realized … this was a chance to experiment! She'd been tormented not knowing exactly how to summon her time-altering power. Did she dare try it out?

"Guys, I'm gonna take a break. I'll be in the lounge if you need me." Her voice was strained, her breath tighter. Control … control. Giving them a weak little wave, she backed away, facing them for a few steps before turning her back and hurrying into the break room thirty feet away.

It was a risk. She didn't know what could happen. How far time would retract. All she knew was that the times when her emotions and those around her were at a high pitch, she could pull those feelings in tightly and then release. She glanced around to make sure she was alone. Only the whirr of the KoolKrate and the sound of a spindly branch blowing against a window broke the silence in the lounge. She inhaled, inviting all the collective feelings from the Plauditors in the other room to saturate her. Pulled them together. She closed her eyes, concentrating on her anger over Will's betrayal. Throwing up her hands, she abandoned all her restraint. "STOP HURTING ME!" She opened her eyes. Nothing. The effort had failed. Tears sprang to her eyes, her disappointment turning liquid. Frustration surged through her veins, pooling in balled-up fists.

She bent over, putting her hands on her knees, hyperventilating. The effort had cost her more than she'd imagined. Standing upright again, she felt every beat of her pulse. She wanted to jerk out her own heart. How much could a person endure? Her thoughts scattered into a starburst of directions. Will's betrayal, unimaginable. Her mom, dead. Gone forever. Burning of victims' bodies. Throwing people away Outside. Phoenix's revolution. Serpio's pursuit and "feelings" for her … It all started and ended with *him*, the "benevolent" Magistrate. With each thought, she allowed her hatred for Serpio to course through her, concentrating all her negative emotions to gather like a storm. Her senses reopened to the heightened emotions in the Plauditorium, and she launched a new effort.

As her anger escalated, her heartbeat's rhythm echoed an inner chant: *defeat this man.* She gripped her balled fists with all her strength and released a primal scream.

A surge of electric heat pulsed through her upper limbs and radiated past her elbows into her hands. An intense tingle exploded in her fingers.

Stop!

A pull from inside her body and an otherworldly silence settled around her, as if feathers released their softness onto the world. Yet she was moving and breathing.

She broke from the room and dashed down the hallway to confirm what she hoped was true.

Everything had stopped.

Drawing in a breath, she stood rooted, her body vibrating. Her mind was a thousand butterflies clamoring to get out. She waited for her heart to still.

Ember lapped the room, touching a trembling finger to people to confirm they were frozen. Such a weird way to see people, where touching them resulted in no reaction at all.

They were outside of time. But she was in it, as if she were in space. She counted the seconds until she plummeted back into reality.

A slight tremor traveled down her spine. The tableau before her changed in fluid slow motion.

Shawny, Ava, and Wee were at her side. *Again.* Ava was speaking. "We'll figure it out. Remember, I'll be working on the inside. And I'll be there soon."

Ember gawked at Ava, analyzing any little thing that seemed new. She had heard these words before. Same words. Same Ava. Except she had stepped back in time without missing a beat.

Trying hard to look perfectly normal, Ember knew her face looked flushed. She steadied herself on a chair just within her reach.

"Ember, are you all right?"

"Ummm … yeah. Just … overwhelmed." She put her hand to her head, rubbing it across her forehead. What just happened had pulled out every ounce of energy.

"Ember, you sure?" Wee asked. "You don't look well."

She longed to tell Weeford and the others what miracle had happened. But Will was the only one who would understand. And he wasn't there. Now more than ever, she felt his absence. And, above all, the need to retreat. "Guys, I'm gonna take a break. I'll be in the lounge if you need me." This time, she hurried away without looking back. Feeling weak and shaken, her legs were ready to mutiny. It would only be a moment before they gave out underneath her.

Stumbling through the hallway, she struggled to catch her breath. *If there was a way to host a hurricane in my body, this is it.* She wondered if the use of her power was possibly crippling her, draining her of life whenever she summoned the forces together.

Once in the break room, which was designed for comfort and happiness, she looked for a place to rest. Multi-colored hues throughout the room created a rainbow effect, as if the idea would put anyone's mind to rest. A couple of wide, over-stuffed chairs looked comfy, but the cot against the wall with its soft cotton blankets and fluffy pillow looked more inviting. She flashed back to the time she visited the Plauditorium soon after her mother died. Will had been waiting for her to arrive in their first meeting since he'd been sent to her house to handle her Alt's emotional crash and a break-in. But she became so faint after arriving at the Plauditorium that she had slept in this very cot with Will by her side. Her mother's ring, which she carried in her breast pocket, had then been stolen by Will's coworker, Austel. She had blamed Will for the theft in what was their first major quarrel. She would give anything if he were here with her now.

Lying down, she adjusted her position on the small mattress, planning to do some Tranquility relaxation exercises. If she ever needed them, it would be now. She shut her eyes, and just as she began to unwind, her empathic senses felt a presence.

"Ember."

Her eyes popped open. Xander was standing beside the bed, a soft smile on his face. She instantly sat up.

"Xander … you … scared me." More than that, she felt him. Powerfully. His body resonated with yearning and concern. A silver glimmer tightly outlined his entire body, a phenomenon she'd noticed before and fought against. Its inexplicable, magnetic pull was something she didn't understand. Topped with powdery red and an outer layer of yellow, his aura glowed like a halo. But the angel comparison stopped there. He looked like a devil's warrior, marked with dirt. Streaks of blood decorated his stolen Trank uniform. There'd been no luxury of a shower or any chance for civilized grooming yet. A smell of dampness and sweat exaggerated his disheveled appearance.

"Sorry," he said, with surprising sincerity. "I … I wanted a moment. Before things get crazy."

"A … moment?"

Xander broke eye contact and looked down at the floor. "Yeah. With you, alone. Just wanted to tell you directly … I'm … glad you're here. Glad you made it. I know you were by yourself all this time. Couldn't have been easy."

Ember swung her legs off the bed to the side and gazed up at him, locking his eyes with hers. "Yeah. Awful. Running across town, hiding. And finally, outrunning Sciolists to get into this place. I—I thought I was doomed."

"That takes courage. I … admire that."

"Thanks." She looked at him curiously. She'd never seen this tender side of Xander. In spite of his passion-fueled aura, his eyes were gentle.

Xander's voice grew softer. "Seeing Will on the broadcast. His words … I was shocked and angry. But you … you care for him. That had to hurt worse."

Ember nodded her head, a lump forming in her throat. She couldn't reply to Xander. Will's words washed over her again. A torment. *He'd publicly rejected her.*

"Ember, he could be reading a script. Or his life could be threatened. Until we know the real story, we can't doubt Will's loyalty. It's difficult, I know. But if you need to talk or you want a shoulder to lean on, I'm here."

His sincerity was endearing, all his heart in his eyes.

"Okay, thanks. I'll remember." She started to rise from the

cot, and he grasped her hand, pulling her up, causing her to be mere inches away from him.

"Good. I hope you do." Xander broke his gaze and lowered his eyes but stood there as if he was waiting for something more.

Ember wanted to plug the awkward moment. She sat back down on the cot. "We need to talk about our next steps for Phoenix."

"Agreed. We have a lot to do. But first, I'm getting cleaned up. I can hardly stand myself." He grinned.

She snickered at his admission, the uncomfortable tension broken by his directness and jesting. *At least he realizes what a mess he is.* "It'll be an improvement. But don't put on those same clothes. I mean, ever." She gave him a light shove, separating their proximity to lighten the moment.

"If that's the case, before I tear this place up, you wanna show me where the Plauditor uniforms are?"

"I don't need to show you. Inside the bathroom—the closet to the right of the shower."

"You think I'll find one that'll work?"

"Close enough." The thought of a uniform on Xander either too short or too baggy made her giggle softly.

"Somethin' funny?"

"Yeah. Wondering what color you'll have to put on."

"Doesn't matter. Whatever it is, I'll wear it well." He smiled with the confidence of a king and winked at her.

"Don't flatter yourself."

"I stand by my statement. I'll let you be the judge." He wandered away, his back to her until he turned to throw out a final word. "And by the way, you in *your* uniform? You look frikkin' hot." He shook his hand as if to throw off heat and disappeared into the fully equipped bathroom.

Wow. Conceited as ever. She couldn't deny his charm, though. His larger-than-life presence behind the bathroom door drowned out all other wisps of moods, whims, and energy emanating from the main room. Peeling back layers of emotions, she struggled to find her own. Her heart pounded, and she was strangely breathless. She wanted to beat down the feeling.

Time to go back out to join the others. Especially before he came back. She wasn't taking any chances on exactly how he'd come out of there, either. Since it might be a while until she returned, she grabbed a water bottle from the box Ava had carried in earlier and rushed to find Wee or Ava. Anyone to make her feel less confused.

As if Weeford, Ava, and Shawny had been waiting for her, they met her halfway across the room.

Ava said, "Ember, you doing okay?"

Ember sighed. "More or less."

"Will's your boyfriend, right?" Shawny asked.

"I thought so. Maybe it was all made up." *He wouldn't have made sure we were back together if it weren't real, would he?* Before everything went haywire and they'd been separated, he'd apologized and comforted her. He'd insisted they were a couple. And now, her heart had morphed into something she didn't recognize. She missed Will so terribly. His protection, his trust, and his understanding had disappeared and left something scarred in its place.

Ava put her hand on Ember's shoulder. "You might not like Tranquility's ways. But thinking positive gets you through things like this. Will is loyal until we know for sure otherwise."

"Yeah. I'm sure you're right." She clenched her fists, wishing she could crush something with her bare hands. What made her even more uneasy was that the on-camera Will was wearing a complete Plauditor's uniform. The yellow shirt screamed Level Twelve. With a brand-new jacket. *What did he have to do for that?*

His voice greased with panic, Wee said, "I've been goin' crazy thinkin' about Will. He didn't seem … right. We need to get him out of there, away from the Magistrate."

Ember was glad Weeford understood how Will's actions upset her. "I know. But how?"

"I still have chemicals. The Calcinate and the Phenol." He patted his pocket and bounced up and down on his toes nervously, as if the secret itself threatened to blow up the room.

Ember said, "Those'll definitely help, but it may not be enough. We need a plan. We can't just go charging into City Hall with those."

Wee dropped his head in a hopeless gesture. "No. And we don't want to accidentally blow Will up."

Ember put her hand on Wee's arm. "When Xander's back in here, we'll plan. We have to get Will back. I've never known Will to be untrustworthy. He's totally obsessed with always doing the right thing, and he believes in us and Phoenix. He's already sacrificed a lot for me and for the revolution. We need answers."

"Is that all you need? Just answers?" Wee gave her a wry smile and laid his hand on her head.

She tipped her head back to look up at him. "No. I need him for *me*. Without Will, I'll never be whole."

27

Serpio's Hunt

Immediately after congratulating himself for a successful broadcast, Serpio caught a light sheen of perspiration on Will's forehead. Was he nervous after being on camera? Was he still under the influence too heavily? Or was the pursuit of Ember a problem? Will had seemed quite fluent, but the garden affected every person a little differently. Perhaps he was still tired from his time with the rebels. If what Will claimed was true, he'd been working behind the scenes. He'd accidentally gotten caught up in the Plauditorium raid while he was at work and then been jailed. No matter. Time for action.

As if Will could read his mind, he said, "First to Ember's house?" Will's question sounded strained.

"Yes, that's logical. I have time now. We'll take my CommuteCar, get near Ember's old home. Then, you'll walk alone. I can't be close by, obviously." The last thing he wanted was to tip Ember off. It would ruin everything.

Will fixed his gaze on him. "Ember only feels and sees emotions that are close by. She doesn't recognize the people they're connected to unless she sees them."

"I realize that, Will. I'm counting on the emotional

connection she has with you. You'll be present. She'll feel *you*. Come to *you*. That's the beauty of it."

"Certainly, sir."

The kid was still sweating. Perhaps he really was a traitor and was squirming about the upcoming pursuit. Maybe just excited at the thought of seeing Ember again. *Will's Alt is measuring everything,* he thought. *We'll see what his Alt points show.*

As if the thought triggered Will to act, the young man cocked an eye at his Alt, placed his fingertip on it for a reading, and then glanced back up. He boldly met the Magistrate's eyes. "Looks as if this job still suits me."

Serpio grimaced inwardly, wondering where Will was finding any happiness right now unless … unless he really was innocent and happy to be back where he belonged. It was too hard to speculate. That was the problem with emotions. They were mysterious. Unpredictable.

The Magistrate spoke to his own wrist device. "Car, now."

Serpio never took for granted how advanced in luxury and technology the Level Eighteen vehicles were. His gold CommuteCar pulled up to the curb without any sound at all, the doors opening as a sensor detected people.

Will looked at him, a question in his eyes, as the back seat door opened first.

"Sit in the back, Will. Your level, you know. I'm sure you understand."

"Of course."

The back seat of the Magistrate's car featured a plush, silk sofa. Directly across from it was a built-in monitor for watching any number of a hundred choices.

"Don't touch anything," Serpio said, referring to the entertainment system.

Will settled himself in the back of the vehicle without another word.

Getting in himself, he directed the car. "Abode Twenty-five in Purple Vale." Serpio chuckled to himself as he turned to the back. "Will, you could probably find your way there in your sleep."

"I doubt it, sir. I was only there twice. Took a CommuteCar both times."

Serpio wished he could detect a lie from listening to someone speak. Will had to have been at Ember's more than he confessed. That's one reason why he needed Ember—to detect lies. She didn't have the ability yet, but he was certain she would be able to develop it with the empathic talent she already had.

"Are you excited, Will?"

"Why?"

"She might truly be there. You'll get to see her." He enjoyed baiting the kid.

"I told you. Only Ember had feelings. I kept myself above that."

"Would your Alt readings show that? I can access all the data. Were your points high when you were seeing her?"

A short silence answered him before Will spoke. "Check it all you like, Magistrate. My mood on those days we were together? I was excited."

"Excited … how?"

"Finding out stuff. Helping my city catch a *rebel*."

The Magistrate was secretly impressed with Will's answer. It was true. There was no telling why any person's happiness was connected to any particular cause. Although, he mused, Ember Vinata was beautiful enough to elevate any male's mood, even his own. He had felt it himself, both physically and mentally.

They left the park in midtown and traveled first through Yellow Sunrise. "Ah. Here's your community."

"Yeah."

"Did you enjoy it?"

"Haven't been there long. But it's nice, yeah."

"You know how much work it is? Creating and maintaining all these communities?"

"They're beautiful. All of them."

"I do so many things. No one realizes the effort. Happiness is my mission. A real labor. But of love."

Will suddenly sat up. "We're close. We're in Purple Vale. Ember's place is on the next corner. If you still want to stay back, just drop me here."

"I didn't realize you could read minds, Will. But yes. This is exactly where I'd planned to drop you." He bristled with indignation. He should have been the one to suggest the arrival point. Who did Will think he was anyway?

The car slowed and then stopped at the curb of an intersection—Jubilation Avenue and Glee Glen. Both doors opened, and Will stepped out. Serpio got out too and grabbed Will's arm.

"If Ember's there, assure her she's safe. Give her a hug. Tell her you're reuniting everyone. Then, alert me. Use your Alt. Sciolists are waiting nearby. Understand?" The last question rumbled from his lips.

"Got it."

"You've got a lot at stake here, Will. Your *life*. Remember that," Serpio urged through gritted teeth. "I'll be waiting."

Will turned and walked down Jubilation Avenue, the yellow stripe on his jacket a taunting reminder that, in spite of the Magistrate's desires, Will was still a Level Twelve and a city hero.

28

Will's Visit

Will's heart sank seeing Ember's home again. As he approached, he wished he really was going to be seeing her on the other side of the door, just as he had the first day he had met her. The time he was spending apart from her ripped his soul. He felt he'd let her down. Now, they were both suffering. Was she thinking of him?

He banged on the door with a closed fist. If there was surveillance back in place, he wanted to make sure everything looked legit. He peered in the windows as if to alert an absent Ember that it was him. That he was standing right outside. All he saw was emptiness. A dim, abandoned interior was like his heart without her. He exhaled heavily. He couldn't think of that. Now that he wore an Alt once again, he was forced to fill his mind with positive, buoyant thoughts. With no sign of Ember, genuine relief flooded through him. His happiness depended on believing she was safe. He was never going to betray her. He'd sooner die.

He walked around the house again just for good measure. For appearances. For survival.

"Magistrate," he spoke into his Alt. "There's no one here. Except for a rat. I saw a rat up by the door," he lied. He knew that would disturb the Magistrate even further. Tranquility was way too clean to have rodents.

The Magistrate's voice crackled through. At first, he thought there was something wrong with the Alt's communication mechanism, but then he realized it was the Magistrate's voice itself coming out as a rough stutter.

"You're … sure … no one is there?"

"Yes, Magistrate. It's like a tomb. Except for the rat, of course." He grinned.

"I'll be by to pick you up."

"No hurry. Rat and I are good friends. I think I'll name him …" The Alt went dark before he finished talking.

He watched the limousine slide silkily up the street to where he stood. *What's next?* he wondered as the door opened to let him inside. He didn't dare think of finding Ember during the Magistrate's rounds. And of course, since he didn't know where she was, it could accidentally happen.

The door to the limo opened on cue, and he climbed into the back, keeping his face as neutral as he could.

Without a second's hesitation, Serpio addressed him, turning to look directly into his eyes. "Will, that was disappointing. Do you know anywhere else Ember might've gone?"

"Magistrate, I have no idea. I don't know her that well …" He put his hand to his head to demonstrate frustration at the situation. He was frustrated. Serpio's persistence was getting tiresome.

The Magistrate held a finger up as if to show a new, exciting idea. "How about your parents' house?"

Ember had never met his parents, had no idea where they lived. "No … She doesn't know my parents." *Thank the stars,* he thought. His knee bounced nervously, causing his whole body to vibrate on the plush seat.

"But she could've gone there out of desperation, thinking they would harbor her."

"My parents know nothing about Ember. I haven't talked

to them since … well, since I became a Plauditor. And I wouldn't tell them about some girl who meant nothing to me." The lies were beginning to slide easily out of his mouth.

"Let's just pay them a visit anyway. I'm sure your parents would love to see you." He turned back to face the front, as if everything was settled.

"Look … I could call and ask 'em. It's not like they'd lie to me." He did feel a twinge of guilt at not having called or dropped by since all of this started. He had been so busy with Ember and her mom and … everything. But now? This would be the worst possible time for a call or a visit. He would hardly know how to explain everything that had happened to him, and it wouldn't be safe for them or him to tell the truth. Especially not with the Magistrate right there. Remembering his Alt, he quickly swallowed the guilt, allowing wonderful memories of his parents to sweep through his mind instead.

"I think it's time I met your parents, Will. After all, they raised such a stellar young man. We'll go and chat, and if Ember's there, I know they'd share that with you."

Shazz! This is becoming so bizarre. The only thing is I know is that Ember's not there—would never go there. With the thought, his mood shifted. He could be cheerful after all.

"Magistrate, honestly …"

Serpio gave the command to the limo, and the car took off. "We're on our way. A few minutes, and you'll be at your parents' *humble* abode."

Will felt his face grow warm, his cheeks responding in a light blush. "Yeah. White Sands."

Once more, Serpio turned to speak to Will. He raised one eyebrow. "You've come a long way from your parents' Status level, haven't you, young man?"

This is a good opportunity to impress the Magistrate. The less suspicion directed his way, the more freedom he would have.

"Yeah. I have come a long way, and I'm proud of it. I didn't want to live in White Sands—can't imagine being a

Level One. Ridiculous. I've put a lot of mental work into my rise, including my loyalty to Tranquility."

"So … your parents … *Why* are they still in White Sands? They've had plenty of opportunities, just like everyone else. We don't normally find older people living there. Once you learn how to elevate your moods, you can rise up. It's simple."

Will wondered how to explain his parents to the Magistrate. It was delicate. They believed in an unusual philosophy. It was that philosophy that explained why they stayed in Level One.

Tread carefully. "My mom and dad … They're great people. I've always wanted to help them raise their Status. But they have their own belief system."

"Not a religion, I hope. I'd have to send an intervention team." The Magistrate smirked, looking at him through narrowed eyes.

"No. Nothing like that. Only a philosophy. They believe that when feelings of happiness are your only goal, you'll stop doing the hard things—the challenging things. You'll only do things that bring you pleasure, whether right or wrong. To them, struggle, difficulty, and pain help people really appreciate true happiness."

"There's no happiness in pain."

"Pain? No. But there's a balance. Without the bad, there can be no good. And the idea of gaining more luxuries for themselves? They see that as selfishness."

Serpio cracked his knuckles and sat up straighter. "Nonsense. It's ambition, not selfishness. Ambition makes people work harder, be more productive. It helps Tranquility stay perfect."

"To my parents, the secret of life is to take chances. I guess that's why I take the risks I do, like saving Jesse from being killed. But while I do it to get ahead, they do it to live a simple life."

"They need to carefully balance their Alt points if they're

going to think like that. It's not in harmony with Tranquility's goals for our citizens."

Uh-oh. "They're not behaving outside the limits, though. They're not Resisting Emotional Management. No one's ever recommended counseling. If they're happy where they are …" He realized he was talking too quickly.

"Some people do require less to be happy. Perhaps your parents fit *that type.*"

Will caught the Magistrate's derogatory tone. He looked out the window, using his lack of response to put his mind in the proper attitude for the visit.

Coasting through the gates of White Sands in the Level Eighteen limousine was surreal. People who walked the streets in the community gaped in surprise at an unannounced visit by the Magistrate. His CommuteCar was unmistakable, its very speed an anomaly. While every other vehicle was programmed to move at a low speed to keep Tranquility calm, Serpio's car could reach high speeds in a matter of seconds, assisted by fins in the front and back that extended and changed their shape to zip down the road faster. Lightweight yet sleek, the vehicle sparkled in the sun, its smooth, sculpted body resembling a crouching tiger.

Pulling up to the Verus home, Will wondered how his parents would react. They knew about his "celebrity" status and his promotion to Level Twelve. They had always encouraged him to rise up, so they were proud of him. But to arrive with the Magistrate? He didn't know whether they'd be excited or intimidated.

At the touch of Will's hand on the door of Number 79 Carefree Court, the solid, white door slid open. The severe whiteness inside, illuminated by the room's harsh lighting, played up its intensity. Will blinked to adjust his eyes from the reflective brilliance. But there, just inside at a modest table, sat his parents, their faces beaming with surprise.

"Oh my! Will! Why didn't you tell us you were coming?" Immediately, Will's mother rushed from the table to throw her arms around him.

"Mom." Will hugged her like he would never let go. He smelled her "mom scent," and his eyes teared up. Seeing her fair skin, hazel eyes, and light brown hair, which was always fixed in a perfect bun, conjured up memories of the love and comfort she'd always offered. It had been too long since he had seen his parents. "Dad …" A man with sandy blond hair tinseled with silver strands added himself to the three-way reunion.

Will released the hug. "Um … Mom, Dad … I have … a guest."

The Magistrate stood just inside the entryway, his presence filling the tiny room, gold gleaming off his clothing like vapored breath on a frigid morning.

"Mr. Verus, Mrs. Verus. Now that we're past the lovely reunion, it is a *pleasure* to finally meet the famous Will's parents. Aren't you just the most delightful couple? Will has told me a lot about you. Especially how you enjoy your very simple life here in White Sands." He gave the Tranquility salute, and his parents dutifully returned it.

Will couldn't help but notice how his mother's face had paled.

"If I had known you were coming, Magistrate, I would have planned. I feel so bad," Will's mom said. She looked away but wrung her hands.

She looks sad, Will thought.

"Mom, don't worry. It was a surprise." Will caught the Magistrate's eye. He shuffled his feet. He felt embarrassed for his parents. Their simple, white outfits were looking more threadbare than usual. Even though it was great to see them, he wished with all his might he could be anywhere else. He took some deep breaths.

"Magistrate, please, welcome. I'm Jack, and this is Marina. Really, we're honored you're here."

Will said, "I can get some things from the kitchen, some cookies and tea maybe?" He was trying hard to be a good son.

"Will," his dad replied quietly under his breath, "I'm afraid we have nothing like that to offer."

Will looked at his father. "What? C'mon. Surely you have something—it doesn't have to be fancy …"

"We don't even have bread right now." His father looked briefly at the Magistrate before looking down at the dull alabaster floor.

"You mean, you need a trip to the store. I understand, Dad. Don't worry about it, please." He put his hand on his dad's shoulder and squeezed. "Hey, think positive. Your points'll come up, and you can go get some groceries."

The Magistrate smiled, his lips curling up slightly, like a woman called "Mona Lisa" in a painting from long ago. "You could do the right thing, Will. You could come back later—get some things for them. After all, your main job as a Plauditor is to help people be more positive. We *applaud* our citizens by giving them tools for success."

Marina spoke, her face no longer pale but flushed. "If we could have a word, son? Just a moment in the kitchen here?" She stepped away. A tiny KoolKrate, its motor a low rattle, and a greasy stovetop about ten feet away marked an area as the kitchen. Separating it from the living area was a three-foot-tall wall.

"Sure, Mom."

The two walked away, Will glancing over his shoulder at his dad and the Magistrate standing together. He wanted to be part of whatever conversation might be going on there, too. No telling what the Magistrate would say.

His mom placed her hands on both of Will's arms. "Son,

you know … we're not doing well. Neither your dad nor me. Our Alt numbers … in the past few days … we can't keep them up at all. Not enough to get food. We've been without everything for days. We don't understand it …"

"Mom! Why didn't you call me? I had no idea you were in trouble."

"We tried a couple of times and couldn't reach you, and … and we know you're busy."

Will felt a heaviness on his chest that was so intense it could have been the result of a physical blow. So much had been happening, and he hadn't had any Alt when he was with Phoenix—no communication device. If he were honest with himself, though, he hardly thought about his parents most days at all. But even the lowest of the Level One Tranks should have food. What was happening?

"Oh, Mom. I don't know what's goin' on. I'm gonna figure it out." Will was confused, but he was beginning to wonder if, by visiting his parents, Serpio had a deeper reason than looking for Ember. The Magistrate chose to visit his parents precisely at a time when they were starving.

His mom's voice was warm. "You're so good, Will. I know you'll always do the right thing." She gave him a final squeeze on the arms and then a hug.

"C'mon, Mom," He led her by the arm. "The *Magistrate* is in your house," he said as if he were announcing the Grim Reaper.

No Level One should be suffering like this. And my parents have lived this long without any problems. The Magistrate has to be involved. He's torturing my parents somehow. Is he trying to make me *suffer at their expense? At the very least, he's showing his power … trying to crush my spirit. I can't allow it. Any of it.*

But he still had to maintain the illusion that he served the Magistrate.

He gathered his thoughts as he returned to where his dad and Serpio stood talking. At Will's presence, his dad gushed,

"Son, our Magistrate says that you've worked hard to infiltrate a traitorous group and are helping him find the fugitives." His dad beamed. "That's my boy. And your grandfather would be so proud of your help in keeping our city's Accords."

Will looked from his dad to the Magistrate. Inside, he was ready to blow. *Adjust. Adjust. Breathe. Keep the Alt points steady.*

"Yes, Dad. That's one reason I haven't been in touch lately. I've been a … spy. Self-imposed, of course. I want to help Tranquility stay pure. After all, that's my job."

The Magistrate prompted, "I'm sure Will has a lot to share with you. He's been to *The Outside*. Did you know that?"

His mother gasped. "Oh, Will! Was it as horrible as people say? How did you survive?"

"Mom." He held up his hands. "I was only out there a few hours. I was keeping an eye on the people trying to ruin our lives." *Jeez, but he felt like a jerk.*

"And Ember?" The Magistrate said, his face completely impassive. The Magistrate was baiting him at every turn. Was he passing the test?

The question sounded so innocent, but it was a crafty tease. "Yeah. There was a girl. I had to pretend to be in a relationship with her."

His dad said, "Pretend? I wish it was a real relationship. You need to make time for that, son." He gave Will a wink and cuffed his arm.

If his dad could truly know how committed he was to the relationship. That it was real. That it was the best thing in his life. How she completed him, like his other half …

Will forced what he hoped sounded like an authentic laugh. "The girl was pretty, Dad, but remember, she was a traitor. And she wasn't on my level anyway."

His mom said, "Aww …" Her eyes held a sympathetic, dreamy light.

Serpio said, "Just in case. If you see a beautiful—I mean *beautiful*—young redhead come here—or anywhere—it's probably her. She has to find some place to hide, if she hasn't already. Please report it immediately."

Will's dad responded, "We wouldn't harbor a fugitive, Magistrate. That would be a terrible crime."

"Yes, it would." The Magistrate looked directly at Will rather than at his dad. "And if you do find her, there'd be a reward, of course. It could keep you from starving. But, of course, you'll make sure you get those Alt points up."

"Exactly, Magistrate. Marina and I are pretty optimistic people. I know we'll get them boosted up, especially now that we're seeing Will." He smiled as if he'd just seen a shooting star, and then, as if it were an afterthought, examined his Alt, expecting a surge in points. Confused, he looked away from his Alt and up, his eyes focusing on a plastic white star decoration on the wall.

"I hope so," the Magistrate said, deliberate gentleness oozing from his words. "If you're running out of food and your points don't improve, you'll be summoned for counseling. We don't want that. I'd hate to see our finest Plauditor have parents who end up being REM."

His mom looked at Will, her face suddenly a mask of steely determination. "Will knows we always do our best."

"Well." The Magistrate took a deep breath as if the conversation was becoming an emotional burden. "I think it's time we took our leave. It has been just lovely meeting you both."

Will gave his parents a quick hug and whispered, "I promise I'll be back to help you … as soon as I can."

He turned and stepped outside the door, the Magistrate leading the way.

The Magistrate stopped just before entering the CommuteCar. "As much as you'd love to help your parents, Will, and do the 'right thing,' I'm afraid you're going to be completely tied up. I hope they can pull themselves out of this slump."

Will held a tight leash on his emotions. He gritted his teeth in an effort to push down his anger. "I understand. It's much more important right now helping you find Ember than helping two people who should never have let themselves get into this situation."

And there it was. Totally against his will, his words had hit a new all-time low. He was more of a prisoner than he'd ever been.

29

Xander's Makeover

At long last, Xander could feel human again. Especially with the change of clothes. He had no need for a Plauditor's jacket. Instead, he concentrated on finding an acceptable pair of the typical black pants. Then, he smiled as he sorted through the selection of shirts. Although there was merely a half dozen, a shirt with the perfect color hung on the rack, and it looked like an option size-wise. He held it up. Sure enough, it would come close.

The indigo color couldn't have been more to his liking. Dark, purplish-blue was not only dramatic, but it set off his jet-black hair and fair skin. Although his time Outside had given him an uncharacteristic light tan, the hue enhanced his complexion even more. And though he would have liked a more comfortable fit, the clothes worked. Everything was a size too small, so the length of the pants exposed some ankle, and the shirt, normally designed to be tight fitting anyway, fit snugly enough to make him uncomfortable. But it was better than the tan jumpsuit he'd been wearing, which was not only dirty, but a sloppy fit. The Trank who wore it had a thicker man's physique, something Xander secretly wished he had. This shirt, though, was at least showy.

After washing his hair, he ran a comb through it, doing what he could to make it behave without much luck. No matter how he messed with it and tried to create a statement, the lack of hair products was a problem. Instead, he combed it forward, where part of it fell in front of his right eye. It was annoying, but he'd deal.

Assessing himself in the mirror, Xander decided he looked better than he'd hoped. Handsome, as a matter of fact. With a grin and a final thrust of his fingers through his now glossy hair, Xander emerged from the lounge triumphant, the almost perfect model of a Level Fifteen.

His eyes settled on Ember deep in conversation with Shawny and Ava across the room. Weeford ambled over to where they stood.

They'd better not be making any decisions without him. Unless a strategy was close to ideal, he wanted to be in control of what Phoenix would do next. After all, he'd earned it, hadn't he? He'd been through more trauma than anyone else, except for maybe his fellow REMs.

He observed Ember intently as he entered the room and headed in her direction. In spite of his self-confidence, he had work to do to win her over. He wondered if she could feel how he melted down in her presence. How he could ignite a fire from the way he burned when his eyes met hers. If she did, he could do little about that. It's not like he intended to hide his feelings for her forever anyway. The key was that he had to make her trust him, and he'd have to convince her she should lean on him. The rest would come.

Just as he hoped, her eyes widened at his approach. She looked him up and down before casting her eyes downward. But not before he caught how her pupils dilated and a blush rise in her cheeks. Would it be too much to hope he would make an impression? "Hey there," he said to Ember, Ava, and Wee as he tossed his hair from his eyes. "What's up?"

Wee buzzed with nervousness, as if he'd been consuming

too many energy drinks. His voice crackled with enthusiasm. "We're talkin' about how to get Will out."

"Yeah?" Xander said lazily. He looked at the three faces, trying to keep his face neutral. "Is that wise? It'll be easier if we attack City Hall. Then make the move for Will."

Ember said, "I don't know where Will is. I don't want him hurt if he's at City Hall."

"That's right," Ava said, putting her arm around Ember's shoulders. "If we launch attacks, it has to be when we know Will is elsewhere."

Xander shrugged his shoulders. "Easy enough. We have surveillance."

"And you have me," Ava put her hand on her chest. "If I'm able to find out information, I can pass it along. In fact, I've been here too long. Dropping off supplies is one thing, but staying through the afternoon is another."

Ember's nod felt heavy, final. "If the Magistrate questions you, you were held, too, before you were released with a 'message.' A message to get something we want."

Xander steepled his fingers. "As long as you're not asking to free Will. We don't know enough about Will's state of mind. We don't know if we can trust him." He felt a sharp dip in his heart when he saw Ember's reaction. She dropped her disappointment all over him like a sudden downpour.

Weeford said, "Xander ... we can't leave Will there forever. He belongs with us. Whatever plan we form, we gotta figure him in."

Xander nodded his head, defeated for the moment. "We have to attack City Hall. We have to broadcast a lot. Tomorrow, a newscast from us must go out! We've got to get the citizens on our side. And *then* we get Will."

Jasper yelled from across the room. "Damn! Will Verus is coming up the steps!"

30

Xander's Standoff

Ember gasped, her eyes as round as moons. "Shazz! He got free?" Her body froze in paralysis and then suddenly broke from it. She tore through the space as if her feet were on fire, screaming, "Will!"

Some Plauditors cheered and pounded on their tables as if they were drums. Other Plauditors panicked, as if the Magistrate himself was at the door. A few physical shoves between Plauditors loyal to Will and those who distrusted him were like mini boxing arenas across the room. Yells of frustration flew out over the din.

"Don't trust him!"

"He's a traitor!"

"The broadcast …"

Every REM gathered by the door, a few pacing nervously, not sure if they were welcoming back a hero or admitting a traitor.

"Freeze!" Xander yelled at the top of his lungs. "Keep Ember away from that door!" The hiss and rabble of voices dropped to a subdued hum instantly.

Weeford's face turned stormy. "Xander! Don't! Don't do that. He's ours."

As Ember bolted toward the door, a couple of REMs almost tackled her. Grabbing her by the arms to slow her down, the REMs pulled her back toward the center of the room. "Stop it! Let me go to him!"

Although she continued to yell and thrash, Ember's rebellion wilted under the control of the REMs. Xander ran to the Sector Nine monitor, grateful for the camera there. What could this mean? The Magistrate wouldn't just let Will go …

Although the REMs by the door could see Will through the windows, the surveillance camera would give them sound. Xander spoke with his most controlled tone into the mic. His voice conveyed suspicion. "Will … you're … back."

"Who's at the controls?" Will's voice answered, his voice heavy with demand.

Xander wondered at Will's uncertainty. Surely Will would have recognized his voice? Perhaps not. They hadn't known each other that long. But Xander felt relief. He couldn't betray his identity. The Magistrate, and certainly Will by now, thought him dead. He motioned for Jasper to come over. He'd let Jasper do the talking.

As Jasper advanced over to the workstation, Xander allowed some silence to take shape. He didn't have to answer Will at all … Not yet. Not until he found out more. But he didn't want to lose the chance to get Will back if he was still true to their cause and not being manipulated by the Magistrate.

He watched as Ember argued with the REMs and also Ava across the room. She was like a wild horse, all of her earlier doubts about Will trampled under her excitement.

"This is Jasper speaking. What's the password?"

There was no password, but it would be interesting to see what Will would say.

"I'm … back. No password. It's me … and I'm here for *Phoenix*. To reunite and push the rebellion. Please, let me in. And Ember. Where is she?"

Xander motioned for Ember to come to the monitor. Although he cringed at the thought of Ember pining over Will's presence, especially right on the other side of the door, Ember knew Will. She might be able to determine something from his demeanor. Although Ember was the one with the empathic talent, Xander could practically feel her heartbeat as she approached the station. More than anything, he wanted to wave a magic wand and make all this disappear, Ember's emotions included. Jealousy was like coals of fire in his chest. As Ember approached, Xander put his finger to his lips. He didn't want her to speak, only to observe. Her eyes were bullets.

Xander whispered, "Just check him out."

Jasper said into the mic, "Ember's not here. Tell me the password."

"Ember's … not there?"

Xander picked up on a subtle, strange relief in Will's voice. It was like Will *wanted* a negative answer. He cocked his head, thinking, and pulled Ember by the hand to look. As they watched, Will pulled his Plauditor's jacket tighter, and zipped it up, inch by inch, as he gazed full-on into the camera.

Xander pulled his head back in surprise. The jacket zip up was deliberate. Meant to be seen. If Will had escaped or been set free, he'd never wear that jacket. It was a symbol of his loyalty to Tranquility, not to them. By drawing attention to it, could he be giving them a warning?

Xander looked at Ember's face. She had seen it, too, and seemed just as confused. "He shouldn't be wearing that jacket," she whispered. "And I still don't see our Loyalty gesture."

"Ember, can you read him?"

"No. It's too hard through the monitor." She paused and appeared to concentrate, her brow furrowed, her posture leaning in.

Xander lowered his voice, not so much to stay incognito, but to be sensitive to Ember's feelings. But a crucial decision had to be made. The wrong one could be disastrous. Xander looked around the room. Every person's eyes were on him. The hush became oppressive, heavy on his heart. What to do? Trust Will's loyalty? Open the door and pull him in to rescue him? Or refuse him?

31

Xander's Judgment

"Xander!" Jasper yelled. "Sector Three! Sciolists! I see … at least fifteen."

"Where?"

"Perimeter. Flat against the building. Hard to see 'em, but they're there."

Xander blew out a breath. *This is a trap.*

Xander whispered to Jasper. "Tell him to go away. We're armed, and we'll shoot."

Jasper gave a thumbs-up to Xander before speaking into the mic. "Leave. You have five seconds. If you don't, we kill you."

Xander saw Will close his eyes for a second as if he wanted to shut out the world. Then, he turned and walked down the steps out toward the street. Until he disappeared into copse of trees across the block, Xander didn't take his eyes off him, watching every step.

But there were still Sciolists outside. Were they going to storm the building? Even if they could get in, they'd be outnumbered, and even though Phoenix only had two rifles, they didn't have the advantage of guns like they did. Still, he was uneasy, remembering they could simply come in through the secret passageway like Ember did.

Xander shouted, "I need you REMs with the rifles," pointing to his crew at the door. "Get to the broadcast room! Get to the teleporter." He scanned the room before choosing a group of Plauditors huddled nearby. "You all. Go too." Those guys would be the front lines in case of a breach.

He crossed over to the dais for voice amplification. "All of you … Be ready for attack. We have the numbers. From what we see, even with their weapons, we can smash an assault."

Jasper cried, "Xander! Sciolists heading out … retreating to a troop carrier pulling up."

Xander wiped the beads of sweat off his forehead. He swayed on his feet, the release of his panic making his body weak, as if he'd completed a marathon for which he was not trained. He bent over, putting his hands on his knees before standing back up straight. The bodies in the room echoed his as the collected fear evaporated in what seemed like a massive breath. Arms went around shoulders, and hugs mingled with slaps on the back.

When he finally composed himself and redirected his attention to what was happening around him, he had lost track of Ember.

Ava and Wee stood silently, Weeford twisting his hands and looking shaken. Ava reached out her hand and gently rubbed the middle of Wee's back at the highest spot she could reach, which, on Wee's seven-foot-tall frame, wasn't very high up. Xander knew Wee was more traumatized by their rejection of Will than he was by the imminent attack, and he felt terrible. Wee and Will were like brothers.

Xander's eyes searched the room for Ember. She would be suffering. Would she feel cheated? Sad? Confused? He saw her in the middle of the room, sitting alone in a chair, turtle-in-a-shell style. She stared into space. He hurried over, his pulse quickening the closer he got.

"Ember. Are you okay?" he asked, leaning over her, his hands grabbing the armrests of the chair. *Such a stupid question,* he thought. But he didn't know what else to ask.

"He was *right there,* Xander. I could've touched him and talked to him," she said, avoiding his eyes.

"Not sure he wanted you to. It wasn't safe. He was out there as a lure. What we don't know is if he was okay with that." He waited what felt like eternity for a response. She kept her eyes on the floor. A tear slowly trickled down her cheek. She brushed it off in such a rough manner that it made Xander wonder if she was trying to punish herself or Will.

She finally looked up. "I'm so sad I couldn't get close enough to feel his emotions. I would have been able to tell if he was sincere. He seemed frightened, though. Like he was afraid we'd open the door. The Will I know is assertive, but he's also protective. Maybe he was trying to warn us somehow. I hate this, that we don't know what's really happening. But Will also is strong. He's fully capable—almost invincible. We have to believe Will can take care of himself and move forward."

"I totally agree. We don't know enough. But we have to be on our guard. You understand that, right?" He put his hand on her shoulder.

Ember nodded, finally meeting his eyes.

"Okay, then ..." He pushed away from the chair and stood up.

Xander had no idea where Wee had disappeared to during all the commotion, but he suddenly came running from somewhere. "Ember!" Wee said as he threw his hands in the air. Weeford dropped his head before speaking in a quiet voice, "I feel like we lost Will all over again."

"Yeah." Ember unfolded her legs and sat up in slow motion. "But I ... we ... can't focus on him. And we can't try to save him. We have to move forward. That's what Will would want—at least the Will I know. He wouldn't want us to take risks."

No risks? Then, no matter what, Will shouldn't be threatening them. Ever. Especially not Ember. Xander seethed. The guy should have said something. *Couldn't he have said he was being coerced? He'd be punished, yes, but they would stay safe. It was the least he could do. And, like Ember said, it doesn't take much to use a hand gesture.*

Wee put his hand on his forehead. "Right. You're right. If he's in trouble, we can't make it worse for him."

"Look around, Wee. There are over a hundred people in here. If we'd have let Will know Ember was here, the Magistrate would stop at *nothing* to get to her. We've gotta protect everyone. I don't trust Will. Not at this point. If things change …" Xander shrugged.

Wee looked down at Xander from his giant's vantage point. "Let's get started, then. If we're movin' mountains to get to the truth, get that bulldozer ready."

32

Will's Double Life

Will lowered his head as he left the Plauditorium, every step an emotional struggle. Disappointment mingled with relief at the REMs' refusal to open the door. If they'd opened the door, he could expose Phoenix to catastrophe. The group had to keep the illusion that they were prisoners intact, or the revolution would be over, and they'd be tried as sympathizers. That's why, in spite of his desperate wish to show Phoenix he was still on their side, he didn't dare use his loyalty sign.

Although Serpio sent him there seeking Ember, he'd hoped to learn exactly what was going on in that building. But his visit didn't help. He still didn't know who was in charge. Worse, he didn't know if Ember had safely returned. Missing in action—horrible. His stomach curled. He was failing her! He knew it as well as his own name. His separation from her was like being deprived of oxygen. But if he found her, she'd be in Serpio's hands. He couldn't let that happen.

And where was Wee? His muscles clenched with dread of the unknown.

And Xander? *Dead?* Inconceivable. Xander's boldness and bravery hadn't been enough to save him after all. When Will had heard the news, it was a kick in the gut. Not that he liked Xander, but he didn't want him dead.

His shoulders sagged from the weight on his shoulders. Their rebellion was falling apart. Was he the only person left? If so, their rebellion was completely dead. He was being manipulated like a puppet.

He could justify to Serpio the disappointment he was feeling, registered by his Alt. If he was showing he was loyal to the Magistrate, he'd logically be dejected by not finding the girl. By letting the Magistrate down. It would be excused. What an upside-down existence he had.

A call on his Alt. Serpio. "Will, I heard everything through your Alt. Ember isn't there. Or she won't come out, not even for you." The Magistrate's voice turned bitter for the words, "not even for you." Part of him thought that failure to entice Ember could work in his favor, that Serpio would believe the lies he'd told about their relationship. He sighed. Serpio's final words were, "Standing by down the block."

Will saw the gold limo. Not even a moment of time to himself. Always watched. Always directed. The thought of escape crossed his mind, He could make a run for it. No one but Serpio was around. Even as the idea crossed his mind, he knew it was futile. He couldn't outrun Sciolists if they were called. Better to keep working to safeguard what was left of Phoenix. Readying his acting skills, he entered the vehicle.

"Magistrate … sorry she wasn't there."

"Who did you talk to?"

"I've no idea. Some REM. No voice I recognized."

"You must be concerned. Your colleagues being held hostage? That's a difficult pill to swallow. I know you're hoping for the best, as any good Tranquility citizen would."

"Yeah. I'm worried about their needs. Anyone taking care of food?" Then, as an afterthought, he said eagerly, "I could go in with supplies … help them." His heart leapt at the thought, and he crossed his fingers behind his back. He could even somehow figure out how to get some of the food to his parents.

"Taken care of. A dedicated Elite Medic, Ava, has already been sent."

"Good." He was disappointed that it wouldn't provide another opening for him to get into the building, but at least the people inside weren't going to starve. His chest seized up, though, at the thought of his parents. They would still be without food. *Don't let on that you're upset, Will. Don't be stupid.* He forced a smile and set himself on the task of calming down. Imagining a happy place in his mind …

Serpio interrupted his thoughts. "Ava's Alt still shows her location to be the Plauditorium. You might have crossed paths."

"Didn't see anyone coming or going, but there's a KelastCar out front. She driving the dead?"

Serpio's lips twisted in a sneer. "Something like that. Time to check on her."

Will gave him a sharp look, wondering what made Serpio so confident he could let an Elite into the Plauditorium. "They let her *in*?"

"Yes. They needed supplies. I'm counting the minutes. If she doesn't surface, I've no choice. I'll send Sciolists in, even at great risk to our forces. For her protection, of course," he added hurriedly. "Sometimes, you have to sacrifice some lesser lives for the more important ones." He tapped his head with his index finger.

Will tried not to squirm in his seat. He gritted his teeth and turned his thoughts to ways to fix the situation. Serpio would indeed wait only so long before risking everything to take back the Plauditorium. It was crucial to his putting down the rebellion. Whoever was in there would be killed. And if Ember was there …

His Alt chirped, and Serpio looked at him quizzically. Will's points were dropping.

"Just concerned …" Will said, tapping his Alt as the limo pulled up to City Hall.

Serpio spoke into his Omnicom. "Feren, we're back. Headed in now." He hesitated for a moment before launching another call. "Ava … checking in. What's your ETA?"

There was a heartbeat of silence before Ava's response. "Headed back now. All is well. Meet you in your chambers?"

"Necessary?"

"Absolutely. Trouble. They *held* me. Finally released me with a message," Ava said.

Will's legs stiffened like a wooden soldier's as he walked along by the Magistrate. The hundred feet to the entrance of City Hall gave him time to think. Could things be better than he thought? Play the role. "What can I do, Magistrate? I'm eager to be of service."

Serpio's walk froze. He stared at Will as if he'd caught a bullet in midair. His right hand landed squarely on Will's shoulder. "We will take back the building."

"What? How? You're sending Sciolists in?"

"Not necessary. No need to risk Sciolist lives. We can gas them. Plenty of chemicals in the engineering room. We'll put it through the vents. Kill them all."

Will already knew how deep the darkness went in Serpio. But this? *Killing everyone?* Would the Elite approve of such a thing? But he couldn't protest too much. He'd tip his hand. He had to stop this from his position as an insider. "Great idea, Magistrate. You'll wrap this whole thing up."

Both of them, deep in thought, walked through the doors of City Hall.

33

Ember's Second Letdown

Ember was working hard to hide her misery. While she told Xander that she was okay with letting Will take care of himself, it ate away at her like heat on ice. How much of her would liquefy before she would be only a shell. She remembered days when she could hide herself away before any of these soul-bending events ever happened. When she kept to herself, she avoided pain. Pain like this. If only she could really go back in time, back to when she had Will and his reassurance.

"I'm calling Ava over. We need to make solid plans." Xander motioned to Ava where she stood chatting with some of his REM crew.

"Yeah … okay." Ember forced a smile and watched Ava cross the room to join them.

Xander kept talking, throwing out ideas. "A broadcast first to all households, then a —"

A Plauditor from across the room broke the brainstorming session. "Hey! Got a Will sighting! Sector Fifteen."

"Where's that?" Ember yelled as she tore herself away. Her heart caught in her throat as she sprinted across the room, dodging Plauditors conversing. She tripped on a Plauditor's outstretched legs and then righted herself. She turned her head back to see the guy pulling his legs back in, mumbling, "Sorry."

Xander, too, pivoted so quickly that his shoes squealed on the flooring. "Coming!"

The Plauditor-turned-messenger continued, "Hurry! They're walking from Serpio's limo toward City Hall ..." He turned back to his station to pump up the volume.

One REM responded as well, settling in beside Xander, standing like a soldier to his left. A group of five Plauditors from the stations nearby fled their chairs to join in.

Xander threw his arms out. "Phoenix—there's no space. Stand aside or wait 'til we have the full intel," Xander commanded. The crowd dispersed with disappointed moans, a few Plauditors' faces turning their features into flat lines of irritation, uncommon in previous days. The REM slightly bowed his head and backed away several feet.

Ember scrambled over to Xander's side, her eyes drawn like a magnet to the screen. There was Will, walking along with the Magistrate. They looked ... chummy. The Magistrate even put his hand on Will's shoulder as they stopped to talk.

A ray of perfect sunshine hit Serpio's face before his oily voice slithered into their computer speaker. "We can take back the building."

Will leaned in. "What? How? You're sending Sciolists in?"

"Not necessary. No need to risk Sciolist lives. We can *gas* the Plauditorium. Plenty of chemicals in the engineering room. We put it through the vents ... kill them all."

"Great idea, Magistrate. You'll wrap this whole thing up." He and the Magistrate appeared deep in thought as they walked forward toward City Hall together.

The entire room fell silent as the fifteen-second scene unfolded. Faces drooped in a slow wax melt, sudden fear showing in the flashing of wide eyes.

As the pair disappeared into City Hall, yells rent the Plauditorium. Fists flew up in the air. But then, the anger gave way to panic. People paced and cursed, some crying, others hyperventilating. Many fell into their chairs and sat, just staring. Everyone now knew Will was working with the Magistrate to plan an attack. They were all going to die.

Ember watched in horror as the traitorous words fell from Will's lips as easily as dead flower petals in the wind. She threw her hands over her face before moving them to her ears as if to shut the words out. Her knees threatened to buckle. Will was supporting a chemical extermination? All hope seemed to be sucked from her body, as if she was bleeding out.

Steadying herself before she went into a faint, she leaned against Xander's right shoulder. Within a heartbeat, he drew his arm around her. She heard him curse under his breath, too softly to make out the words. It didn't matter. She had words of her own: *vile traitor.*

Anger surged through her, and she shook herself free from Xander's arm. "So, that's it, then. He's turned. Or he never was with us in the first place."

Xander looked down at her, his brown eyes hot. His emotions engulfed her as they stood inches apart, both of them enveloped in shock and pain. She wondered for a second if she had stopped time again, so frozen was she in the moment.

"Ember. I'm here. For whatever you need."

She paired her eyes with his. "No, I don't *need you*, Xander. I can handle … all this. What I *need* is to move this revolution forward," her voice unusually brittle.

The way Xander's face blanched made her suddenly sorry. She had lashed out, and now, his aura draped itself all over her in a shadowy blanket of pain. Her own confusion and misery didn't make it okay to take it out on other people, especially Xander, who was trying to help. "Hey … sorry. I shouldn't have said that." She reached out and gently touched his arm.

Xander raised his eyebrows as he looked questioningly from her hand on his arm to her face. A thin smile grazed his lips. He kept his eyes, which twinkled in amusement, locked on hers, his hurt slowly dissolving into a half-grin. "I accept that apology. Thank you." His voice dropped to a whisper. "But I say the lady protests too much. You *do* need me, and one of these days, you're not gonna want to live without me."

"Is that right?" Ember shook her head in vehement denial and walked away. As usual, she could feel him watching her as she made her way across the room to Shawny's station. Xander was too cocky for his own good. Even hinting that she'd want to be with him, especially after what she had with Will, was ridiculous. That silver lining within Xander's aura, though, strangely drew her to him against her wishes, and she challenged it with all her being.

Her anger over Will, though, hadn't cooled. She ground her teeth and clenched her jaw so tightly it hurt. Never had she been so emotionally violated. She fought back angry tears. Taking a deep breath, she put her Tranquility training into motion. Clear the mind. Think of something positive …

Phoenix's goal. *Our team is strong. We can prevail. We will win.* As she took deep, cleansing breaths and concentrated, she felt her pulse slow.

Phoenix was in motion. Without Will. And that was okay. Will was firmly in the other camp. The last thing they needed was a worry about loyalty.

But the view of Will and Serpio on camera had soured her.

Xander was already on the dais. "Phoenix … please, get quiet." He put his hands in the air and waited. The cries and wails gradually diminished. "This just happened. It will take Serpio some time to launch the attack he threatened. And knowing the Magistrate, he'll warn us—blackmail us—first. So, we're not dying right now. I hope," he added, putting crossed fingers in the air. His self-assured smile was full of light, as if he were some divine being. When he caught Ember's eye, his lips relaxed and then pressed themselves into a tight, thoughtful line. "We go on the offensive. Make plans now."

Xander left the dais to a heavy round of applause. Giving Ember a nod of acknowledgment, he hurried toward the broadcast room. *There he goes, taking control again,* she thought. But part of her was thankful. While she'd been obsessing over personal stuff, he was taking action. His influence and finger-prints appeared to be everywhere, and what's more, the people in the room responded to him. He had something … some weird charisma. She fought against it herself.

It was past time to be assertive. She was the reason for this entire movement! She'd tell Xander about her time-altering ability. In dire times like this, it might be needed. Only then could he understand how essential and capable she really was. Maybe he'd finally stop trying to be her protector.

34

Ember's Confessions

Ember trailed behind Xander as he crossed the room, wondering how to tell him she had another secret talent. *You don't just dump that kind of thing on someone out of the blue.* And she didn't want other people around. She'd have to wait until she had a chance to do it right—hopefully sooner rather than later.

Ava and Wee stood where Ember and Xander had left them. Each of their faces told a story. Wee rubbed the back of his neck before giving Ember a slight head shake with an open mouth. Ava had pressed her hand to her chest, her frown dressing up pinched eyes as she said, "I'm—I'm speechless. I know Serpio's evil, but I never imagined …"

Wee took a step back as he spoke. "That—that wasn't Will. Couldn't have been. He—he'd never conspire with Serpio. And commit murder? I don't believe it."

Xander made a choking noise in his throat before releasing a small cough. "Hard to swallow, isn't it?"

Wee's emphatic tone showed he wasn't giving up. "It's impossible."

"You're right … I know Will too well. Something must be very, very wrong." Her heart ached. What she just saw made her wonder what parallel universe she was in where the Will she knew would be so dark. What kind of pressure was he under? Could someone as strong as Will be so deeply manipulated?

But she couldn't deny what was there right in front of her. A threat like that, and Will not trying his best to stop it? Her hurt and confusion gave way to anger. Ember's muscles quivered, and her nostrils flared. Fury at the Magistrate and Will threatened to tear her apart. She flexed her arm muscles, praying her anger overload wouldn't trigger an involuntary time warp, and said, "But anything's possible. We just saw Will pandering to the Magistrate, and he's not trying to talk him out of this insanity. All we have to go on is what we see. You can't deny that, Wee. We can't trust Will, especially if he's being controlled." She put her hand on his arm and patted it before inhaling sharply. "We move on. We plan strategy."

"Agreed. Time's short." Xander massaged his temples.

Even Xander's in shock. Ember could barely wrap her head around that. He had put on a good front, but she could see he wasn't good. Ember thrust the conversation into gear. "The best way to fight Serpio is with *information.* We have one of Serpio's journals, but it's not enough. We need more than one to make plans. We use his own words. Not only to broadcast the truth to the people, but we'll learn more about the city. We need names of the Elite to target them. Maybe we'd learn how the citizens' Alts can be switched off. Maps. Banishments. Disciplinary actions. Eliminations. We read them—we can act."

Ava nodded. "The Alts—I know where those are calibrated. But I agree. Every one of those books in the library at City Hall has classified information. That's why no one goes in there but Serpio. Even the Elite members can't read those journals."

Wee said with uncharacteristic sarcasm, "That's *great.* But we'd have to get to them. Is it worth the risk?"

"Ava, you sure they'd be useful?" Xander said.

"The one I stole was useful," Ember said. "Admitting to eliminating people? No wonder he doesn't want anyone in there."

Ava said, "We do need them. Otherwise, it's a shot in the dark trying to take Serpio down. I know a few others who aren't loyal to Serpio, but it's not enough to simply know other resistors. We need to strike where it counts."

Ember said, "My mom sent me a message. We need to look for a gold one."

Wee's eyebrows shot up. "Isn't your mom … dead?"

Ember's eyes misted. "Yeah. But on my journey back here, I saw my mom. On an advertisement billboard."

Their eyes stared back at her in a way that made her uncomfortable. They were looking at her as if she had stated the world was flat. A fluttering sensation in her chest made her want to take back the words.

Ava spoke up. "Ember, are you sure? You were under a lot of stress at the time."

"I didn't imagine it! I watched it over and over. She spoke to me in sign language. I'd be the only one who could decipher it. She said, 'find the gold journal.'"

Xander cocked his head, puzzled. "Do you know why she asked you to find it?"

"No, Xander. Not like we had a conversation. But she risked a lot to do that. There's gotta be something important in there for *me*. And for us. It could be the key to our whole plan."

Ava said, "Your mom … she knew Serpio well?"

"Too well. It's … embarrassing."

Xander said, "Sounds like she was part of our team and you didn't even know it."

Ember dropped her head. "Sounds like there was a lot I didn't know."

"All in favor of a library robbery?" Xander said.

The four of them extended their arms to meet in a group fist grab.

Weeford said, "Nobody's gonna question Ava when she goes back to City Hall, unless maybe to find out what took so long to deliver supplies. But that works in our favor. She can tell them she was held. Threatened. Only released to give the Elite a message—Phoenix gets access to the Magistrate's library."

"Right," Xander said, sarcasm dripping off the word. "And the Magistrate's gonna let us in. *Sure.*"

Ava put her hand on Xander's arm, as if to settle him down. "That's where Weeford comes in. He can get chemicals for explosives in the lab at City Hall. We threaten to bomb places in Tranquility unless Phoenix gets access to Serpio's journals."

Respect dawned on Ember's face. "Wee … you know how to make bombs like that?"

"Easy. And I'll set off one first just to get their attention. Then another. This is gonna be fun!" The destructive light in Wee's eyes made Xander proud.

"Problem is … Wee's 'dead.'" Wee said. "Don't know how I'll get access."

Xander looked Wee directly in the eye. "You got any friends there?"

"No. I don't got nooooo friends." Wee's eyes rolled skyward. "Geez. 'Course I got friends!"

"Tell somebody your Alt's not workin', so you can't get in the door. Nobody needs to know you're 'dead,'" Xander advised.

"Problem. How do I communicate? I got no Alt." Wee held up his wrist and tapped it. "See? Not there. Nope."

"Do you know who's working today in chemicals?" Ava said.

"It woulda been me, but I didn't show up." Wee put his hand over his chest.

"But some other chemical engineer would go there if you didn't come in, right?" Ava looked at Wee with eagerness.

"Yeah … prob'ly Asher. He's the sub."

Ava smiled. "Perfect. You go, Wee. At the door, you're just gonna have to ask Asher to let you in. Say your Alt's broken. He'll be sympathetic—hopefully. Apologize that you weren't there on time and thank him. Then tell him you're going to finish out your shift."

"That's risky," Ember said. "What if Asher says 'no'?"

"I'll make it work!" Wee punched the air. "I'm the key to the whole thing. I'll hafta be a good actor. And if I get arrested, at least I can see Will." He grinned.

"Whatever makes you happy," Xander said.

"Now, who storms the library and does the grab?" Ava asked.

35

Xander's Ideas

"I'm going! I have to find the journal." Ember's eyes blazed with a determined fire.

Xander's head whipped around, his eyebrows shooting up. "No, no, no!"

Ava shook her head several times as she spoke. "No way, Ember. You can't go. You're a wanted fugitive. It'll have to be Phoenix members. Wee's going to set the bombs. A couple of REMs can do the book grab."

Ember agitatedly ran her fingers through her hair. "Won't they be seen and arrested?"

With a flourish, Xander ran his hands down his clothes. "It's gotta be all about disguise …"

Ava gave a thumbs-up. "And transportation. Nothing works if we can't get to and from."

Wee tilted his head. "The Kelast car?"

"Not programmed to go fast. And I can't just pull up at City Hall and let guys out," Ava said. "Unless they're dead."

Xander dropped his idea like a bomb. "I was thinkin' more like a MediCar …"

Wee threw his hands in the air., "And how're you gonna get that?"

Ava's voice was soft but emphatic. "*I* could."

Xander grinned. "Hopin' you would say that."

"You know …" Ava said, her eyes sparkling with mischief, "someone here has been seriously hurt by the takeover—at least, that could be the story."

Ember gave a half shrug. "Would a MediCar come for an injury here?"

"Of course," Ava said. "If a Plauditor's been hurt and I call for one. Remember, I'm not just Elite. I'm a Medic."

Xander did a fist pump. "And when the MediCar comes here to help the injured, we meet those Medics at gunpoint. The REMs wear their clothes and drive to the library, do the grab, and get back in the MediCar. Full sirens blazing. Totally natural after a bombing."

"I'll call the MediCar right now. Can you choose a few guys?" Ava said.

"Jasper for sure. Bixby. He's fast."

Wee said, "Perfect. Which car am I in?"

Ava said, "Wee, first, you need a shirt," she said, looking at his bare chest. "And maybe shower and change. You haven't been here long, but long enough to get cleaned up."

"You think there's somethin' that'll fit me?" Wee looked first at Ava and then searched for answers on Xander and Ember's faces.

Ava nodded, chuckling. "You'll have to dress in whatever we can find."

Xander knew from his visit to the Plauditor's closet that there wouldn't be anything in there for Wee. And he couldn't walk the streets in a Plauditor's uniform anyway. That would draw suspicion. "You need some sort of uniform. Better check out the janitors' lockers."

"Hey, yeah. Maybe. I'll take a look." Wee turned to walk away. "I better not get any kidding about what I find," he warned as a grin creased his face.

"Hope you find something big enough, but anything's

better than those dirty pink pants and bare chest," Ember gave him a head-to-toe appraisal.

Ava said, "You can be in the KelastCar for a little while anyway. I'll drop you a block or two away when I return it. City Hall's only a short walk from there."

"I'll keep out of sight as much as possible," Wee said, ducking down to appear the same size as Xander.

Ember giggled at Wee's theatrics. "You need a shrinking potion."

"Hmmm … Speaking of potion …" Wee dug around in his pocket. "Before I go, I'm givin' you these." In his hands were two vials. "Calcinate and Phenol. You might need 'em. I can always get more."

Xander took them, his face almost reverent. "Calcinate's for putting people to sleep … Phenol is toxic. Right?"

Wee rubbed his chin. "Yeah. Red vial's for Phenol, blue's for knockout slumber. Don't get 'em mixed up. Being dead is a looooong sleep."

"Thanks, Wee." Xander carefully tucked the vials into his pants' pocket. A grin curled around Xander's lips. "Wee, can you be ready in ten?"

"No problem. All right, then. Off to the janitors' lockers." Wee turned and moved toward the lounge, a cheerful expression on his face.

Xander knew finding the right clothes would be a challenge. "I'll help ya look. You might need a second pair of eyes."

As Xander turned to go, Ember grabbed his arm. "And afterward? What happens to Weeford then?"

"Weeford goes home, Ember," Xander said gently. "It's the only assurance he'll be safe. Good news. Serpio thinks he's dead. Hopefully, he'll never realize that the dead guy worked for the city in chemicals of all things."

❧

Xander studied the monitor showing the front of the Plauditorium, his radar alert for the first sign of a MediCar.

The cogs were turning.

Wee had found an extra-large pair of pants and shirt that at least covered him, then retreated to the showers. Ava talked strategy with the soon-to-be Medic imposters. Ember looked to be in some deep discussion with Shawny.

A MediCar pulled up to the front, its horn blaring. The city Medics inside the car jumped from the vehicle with a sense of urgency. Xander chuckled. Their faces were so calm, so serious. You could tell, though, that they were happy to be doing their jobs. The way they held their backs straight, their heads high, spoke volumes about their sense of purpose.

Xander headed for the front entrance to help with the Medic takeover. Several Plauditors waiting by the door opened it without hesitation, allowing the real Medics to enter.

"What's your emergency?" a Level Nine Medic immediately said.

Xander answered, "*You're* the emergency." He held the rifle in his hands, pointing it directly at them. "Get in here and say goodbye to your uniforms." His tone brooked no argument.

"What—what are you doing? We—we're here to *help!*" the other Medic shouted. As he took in the threatening situation, he shook his head as if clearing cobwebs from his mind.

Several red-caped REMs grabbed the Medics by the arms and pulled them into the room, the Medics' resistance requiring extra Phoenix manpower to get them over to the lounge.

"Get their clothes, strip them of their Alts, and put them on. Lock them in the utility closet," Xander said as he watched the Medics being dragged away. "Bixby! Jasper!" he yelled. "Be ready to get Medical."

The guys wasted no time responding to Xander's orders.

Excited, they seemed to slide into Xander as if he was home plate. Xander put one arm on each of the guy's shoulders. "Ninety minutes—you're leaving. That's how long it should take Weeford once he gets to City Hall, enters the lab, makes the bombs, and plants them."

Dressed in lavender janitor's clothes, Wee crossed paths with the Medics being hauled across the room. "I'm set!" he called out.

Ava met him at the front door. "Let's go. Phoenix rises."

36

Ember's Stone

After Wee and Ava left on their mission to bomb the library at City Hall, every Phoenix member watched their cameras' surveillance with obsessive determination. When the explosions hit, Ember wanted to be a witness. She longed to be a part of the action, especially since she was eager to get her hands on the mysterious gold journal her mom had begged her to find.

Unpredictably, her thoughts wandered again to the stone she'd found outside the Plauditorium. Victor Vinata—her dad. She was determined to learn about his life somehow. She would not let Will and his newfound allegiance and betrayal rob her of finding her roots.

At Ember's approach, Shawny turned in her chair, a white aura denoting nervousness. "I'm still shocked about what I heard Will and Serpio say. Poison gas? Inconceivable."

"Worse than bad."

"I understand Ava and Wee are putting a bomb in place …" Shawny's eyes clouded over with concern.

"Yeah. I want to watch the monitors for what's happening. But I—I have to know something. Maybe you can help."

"Shoot."

"Do you happen to know any Tranquility history?"

Shawny grinned and clapped her hands together. "I know a *lot*. I'm not only the historian for the Plauditorium, but I'm a real history buff."

Ember smiled, grateful to find someone who could help her. "When I finally got in here, I came in through a tunnel. Behind the building under a loose stone."

"You got in here from *under* the building?" Shawny asked, her eyes wide.

"Yeah. I take it you didn't know about that?"

Shawny said, "Not a clue. Makes sense, though. Serpio would always want a way out. I'd love to see it."

Ember pointed behind her. "Broadcast room, in the back, behind the curtain. Look for an open space. When you step in, it'll take you down. Go take a look."

Shawny waved off her invitation. "Later. What d'ya want to know?"

"About the stones outside. They're engraved."

Shawny's eyes grew serious. "Yes. All the pavers are engraved. Each is a tribute to a former Plauditor, a special memorial for them. They're important agents."

Ember's brows arched in surprise "The stones are for Plauditors? I ... The one I saw had my last name on it." She hugged her arms around her chest.

Shawny turned to meet Ember's eyes. "Really? Your grandpa's name, maybe?"

"No. My dad's."

"Your dad was a Plauditor, then. You must be proud." Shawny said.

Ember pressed her hand to her throat, and her lips parted in an "o." *My dad was a Plauditor? Like Will.* She took a breath. "I guess he must have been. I never knew him. My mom never talked about him at all. But I know his name was Victor."

Shawny said, "Let's hit up the database." Ember leaned over Shawny's shoulder as she punched a button here and there on the computer system at Shawny's station. "So, why didn't you just ask your mom about your dad?"

"I did. She either didn't answer me or told me that 'some things are better left buried.'"

"Maybe she was protecting you from something she didn't want you to get emotional about."

Ember ran her fingers through her hair in agitation. "I need to *know*. Especially now that she's ... gone."

The screen blinked, and a photo appeared. "There he is ... Victor Vinata."

Ember sucked in a breath. "My dad?"

"Looks like it. Not your grandpa. This picture's dated January 2105. He's ... young. Looks to be thirty-something?"

"I was a year old when he died." She leaned forward to look more closely at the image. Always thinking she looked like her mother, she was struck by her resemblance to the man's face on the screen. His eyes and his smile. His red hair. It was like staring into a mirror.

"Shazz ... Ember. This says he died from an accident."

"An accident? What accident?"

"Doesn't say. Sorry. Just that the stone was made in memory of him. There was a death ceremony ..." She squinted to read smaller print.

"Being a Plauditor is a reasonably safe job. The accident couldn't have been work-related."

"Probably not. But there aren't any details, so only other people who were close to your family would know."

Ember shook her head, her eyes sad. "There isn't anyone. I'm the only one who's left."

With a two-finger pinch, Shawny pulled a transparent holographic "window" off the physical screen, where it hung in the air. "This info's about a gene editing team ... I don't know how that's connected."

Two other pictures. A small group of three women and two men. Underneath were names. The picture was followed by a headline underneath: "Two Arrested for DNA Error."

Ember swallowed, her breathing suspended for a moment. "My dad … he wasn't arrested, was he?"

"No, no … the other men were arrested. Drake Pius, Level Thirteen, and Henry Validus, Level Fourteen. Your dad's picture's here because he discovered something was amiss. He was a Plauditor assigned to oversee that sector of the city."

"So, he exposed the team responsible for making a mess of things at the genetic lab?"

"Exactly," Shawny said. "It says here that 'his careful vigilance is notable and highly acclaimed.'"

"Can you print that? I'd like to read it over myself."

"Sure, but I want to read it, too. Sounds interesting. You want me to print your dad's picture, too?"

"Yeah. Thanks." Within two seconds, two papers flew into the paper tray. Shawny handed them over to her. "Here you go. Hey … isn't Ava's last name 'Validus'? It says here that Henry Validus was one of the two who were arrested."

"Are … are you sure? My dad was the reason Ava's dad was arrested?" Ember was incredulous. "Does Ava know?"

37

Will's Persuasion

Will wondered if Serpio ever slowed down. Or made time to eat. Will was starving, his teenage body needing more fuel than ever with the stress he was under. As he walked from the entrance of City Hall into the Elite chambers, he saw a complete array of food set out. *Nothing too good for the Magistrate,* he thought. But this time, he was glad to be associated with someone so powerful. He followed Serpio's lead, waiting until he seated himself at a round, gilded table. A Level Fourteen servant bustled to their sides, laden with plates of food, before placing them on the table and leaving without a word. Seconds later, Feren walked through the door, her entrance almost regal.

"Do we need a full council, Serpio?"

"Not yet. We must make immediate decisions. Since Will doesn't need to be returned to his chambers right now, he's offered his help. We need to keep him busy."

"What ... decisions?" Will said.

"That depends on what Ava says." Serpio looked at his Omnicom impatiently, his nervous energy obvious in the tapping of his foot. Crossing the room with an agitated gait, he peered out the front window, where his gaze lingered. From there, he could see all the way out to the street.

A pleasant, female voice made Will take his focus off the Magistrate. "Serpio … hope you haven't waited too long."

"Ava, my dear! Just looking for you. Glad you're back safe and sound. Have a seat and enjoy." Serpio greeted her with the Tranquility salute and then made his way back to the table.

Will studied the new Elite carefully. Where Feren was elegant, Ava seemed practical. Earthy even. He guessed her age as mid-thirties. Her golden clothes were simple, just a plain, buttonless shirt and pants. The embroidered Medic insignia, a feather, shone on her shirt pocket. The feather, with dots positioned up its spine, was symbolic of the healing that occurred by the lightness of a person's heart. It also aligned with the mythic bird, the Halcyon, Tranquility's mascot. Unlike her Elite cohort, she exuded a genuine warmth. To Will's amusement, she seemed to appreciate the Ambrosia on the table. She drank deeply before putting it down and nodding for a refill.

Serpio splayed out his hand, gesturing Will's way. "Ava, meet Will."

She gave the customary Tranquility gesture. "Very nice to meet you. I've heard many things about you."

I can imagine, Will thought. He returned the acknowledgment and laughed, hoping to lighten things up. "I'm sure you have."

Serpio got down to business. "The Plauditorium … what's going on there?"

"Terrible," Ava said. "The Plauditors are tied up. They're frantic. And they tied me up, too. Threatened my life if I didn't do what they asked."

Serpio pounded the table with his fist. "This cannot stand."

"It's worse. They only let me go on the condition I give a message to you directly, in person."

"And what is that?"

"They'll destroy your house and city landmarks, including the Plauditorium itself."

"Unless?"

"Unless you agree to allow access to your library."

Serpio scoffed and waved his hand, as if he were battling a fly. "Idle threats. They've no means to do that."

"They assured me they do," Ava said. "And they threatened to retaliate against *me* if I failed to stress the importance of their request."

Feren said, "It's a scare tactic. They're in a weak position now with no escape or working plans. No leadership either."

"It doesn't matter. We're taking action. Will and I have discussed a solution." Serpio, his eyes alight with a noticeable gleam, put his hand once more on Will's shoulder. "We're the ones with the chemicals. Our plan is to leak gas in through the vents. They'll either die or come out crying. We'll have them *all*. The Plauditorium will be back in our hands."

Feren and Ava regarded each other, their faces wary. "Are these measures necessary?" Ava said.

"It goes against the codes," Feren said, her eyes clouding with concern. "The Elite won't be happy with this idea." She turned toward Will, scrutinizing his face like it was a difficult puzzle. "Was this *Will's* suggestion?"

Will grabbed his opportunity. "Partly. Credit really goes to the Magistrate." He bowed his head toward Serpio. "But I have a better idea. We don't want to *kill* them, right? Way too inhumane. All we need is a chemical to put them to sleep. Then Sciolists can go in easily. No one dies."

Ava's lips curved upward and her eyes crinkled. "Perfect. I guess you're all they say you are, Will. Smart *and* loyal to the Accords."

The Magistrate's eyes blinked slowly, as if he was drowsy. A joyless smile crossed his lips. "A company man indeed."

A lonely bead of sweat skittered down Will's spine until it disappeared against his inner waistband. He had stopped a slaughter, for now.

38

Will's Shakedown

---

ill's impression of Ava was that she needed a chair when she first entered the chambers. She had a nervousness about her, as though she'd touched a live wire. Will didn't know what was going on in that place based on what Ava said, but her words carried an urgency. "The REMs have been threatening those poor agents. Their Alts will show duress. Worse than that, when I was in the Plauditorium, many Plauditors no longer wore their Alts."

"They're taking them *off?*" Serpio asked.

Ava bowed her head slightly, her eyes not meeting the Magistrate's. "Either that or they're being taken from them. Serpio ... have you thought about the irregularities the Plauditors' Alts are registering on the Continuum? When they get out of there—which will be soon, of course—their Alts will need to be readjusted."

Serpio let Ava's words hang in the air for a moment. "Another horrifying violation of Tranquility laws! When these REMs come out, death will be too good for them."

Feren's eyes clouded over with concern. "Yes, the REMs need justice. But Ava has an important point. We can't hold the Plauditors responsible for their Alt readings." She turned to Serpio. "That would be unfair. They shouldn't lose points or Status for what they've been through."

A pronounced flinch warped Serpio's face.

Will cringed. *Serpio hasn't considered the Plauditors' Alt readings at all.* Although, this shouldn't have been a surprise. Self-centered and narcissistic, the Magistrate would never be concerned with the well-being of others.

Will spoke up. At last, a chance to defend his people. "Plauditors are respected city agents. Reprogramming their Alts is paramount—the sooner, the better."

Ava nodded. "I agree with Will. Feren?"

"Yes, no question," Feren replied. "Is it possible to reset the Alts with the Continuum Spectrum?"

"Yes …" The Magistrate sighed and paced, a common trait that showed he was thinking deeply. "Yes, but I want to do it personally."

Will mentally scored another point for Phoenix. "Your generosity knows no bounds, sir."

Ava smiled. "This should make our citizens happy. I hope you consider making an announcement about it on your next broadcast."

"I'll do it today. Immediately after our meeting here." Serpio smiled, but the smile never reached his eyes.

"How is it you can reprogram the Alts, Serpio? Or is that classified information?" Ava's voice dropped to whisper.

"Yes, it's classified. But Feren has clearance to know what to do in an emergency."

No sooner had he said the word "emergency," a low-pitched rumble under their feet rippled vibrations that shook the walls. A roar tore through the chamber as if a seven-point earthquake had split the room. Then another. A deafening crack and boom. Plates on the table trembled in place, toppled glasses spreading a liquid map across the tablecloth. Artwork crashed to the floor. Heavy pieces of concrete and sprays of dirt flew up against the window, the impact shattering the panes, showering their once-private room with crystal rain. Will covered his face and head with his arms. He turned away from the source of the blast and dove under the table. He held his breath, his heart pounding in a sick imitation of the series of tremors rippling through the building. Feren's mouth opened in a scream, yet hearing her over the roar was impossible. She, too, dove under the table.

Ava yelled in a voice hot with fright, "They didn't even wait! Take cover, Serpio! They're here!"

The roar dwindled into silence.

Will emerged one limb at a time from his makeshift fortress, unfolding his body, like a snake breaking its coil. He first looked to the window, where a cool breeze drifted playfully in through its open spaces, as if the world had simply gone on.

"Everyone okay?" he asked as he held a hand out to Feren, helping her emerge from beneath the table.

"I'm cut!" Feren said, her voice strained. "A piece of glass flew into my arm." She extracted a shiny, red-stained triangle from her right tricep. Tears came to her eyes.

"You're bleeding!" Will cried, grabbing a napkin from the table and pressed it against Feren's injury, a gouge about four inches long. ·

"Here—let me," Ava said, flying into her Medic persona. She grabbed several more napkins, wrapping them up with ice from the table, applying more pressure as she tied it up. "I'm calling the MediCar." A quick flick of a finger on her Alt sent the request. "You will need the Medela to heal that wound."

Feren cradled her arm with her other. "Yes, okay … b-b-but Serpio? Are you all right?" she cried. She rushed over to his side.

Serpio pushed Feren away with one gentle hand and stood alone. He didn't appear frightened from the explosion, his eyes instead blazing, their blackness burning with fury. His jaw tightened, his face chiseled, stone-like. Locked on a chair, his hands turned pink gripping the outer frame. "How did they do this? Impossible!" At each word, spit flew out.

Will had to admire the man's lack of fear. It was as if the Magistrate thought himself invincible. Will himself was still trembling, the shock of the blast a reminder that death or dismemberment had been mere yards away. Serpio had barely moved during the event, and yet he could have been killed. Puzzling.

Ava finally spoke, her eyes wide. "They must mean what they say." She made her way across the room to the window, her gait stiff and unsure, and looked out. "Magistrate, your limousine was the target. It's ... gone."

Serpio spoke into his Omnicom. "Lock up the chemical labs. Let no one in or out. Look for who might have been there." After putting his arm back down at his side, he still didn't move, his smoldering eyes now directed squarely on Will. "What do you know about this?"

Will cringed. He was getting blamed for this? Not that he wouldn't have been cheering if he were able, but he thought he was making headway gaining the Magistrate's trust. "Sir ... I don't understand. I've been with you the whole time." He attempted his most earnest look.

Serpio's gaze held steady, as if he hoped to see inside Will's head. "You may know nothing," he said carefully, "but *you* will prevent another attack."

"How?"

"You will talk to them. I'm putting you on broadcast again. You will condemn this attack and tell them that no one manipulates Serpio Magnus. If they want war, we'll give it to them. They can threaten, but we can, too. We will use chemicals. They need not know what kind."

"Sir, they won't listen to me." Will pleaded.

Ava said, "And they'll continue to attack. They threatened

your house, other places in the city, and City Hall. If they have explosives …"

Feren wiped her hand across her forehead and then brushed her hands down her jacket, dusting off soot-like particles. "We don't want this to escalate. Think of our citizens, Serpio. It will alarm them. What would they want in the library? Why not give them access?"

"They want my private journals and city business. I classify those. There's no way I'm allowing access to those things. Who knows what these insidious people are capable of?"

At that moment, Serpio's Omnicom interrupted. "No sign of anyone in the chemical room, Magistrate. Locked down now."

"Anything else out of order?"

The tinny voice from Serpio's OmniCom replied, "Yes, sir. I'm sorry to report. City Hall's outer wall … blown to bits."

Serpio's face flushed red, and he clenched his fists. "Which wall?"

"No damage to the main structure. Only the library."

"How much damage?"

"A gigantic hole. It blew out the window and the alarm system. No further damage."

Will held his breath. Was it possible his revolutionaries had gotten into the library? Acutely conscious of his Alt, he couldn't allow his excitement to show up in his points. He'd no idea how closely Serpio was scrutinizing his readings, but if his happiness matched the library breach, his whole masquerade would be in jeopardy. He slowed his breathing and brought concern for his friends into his mind. The sympathy would register as a positive emotion …

"Did they enter the library?" Each word seemed to stand on its own, the Magistrate's voice both sharp and rough as a serrated knife.

"No way to know for sure. Your entire team of Sciolists

arrived almost immediately after the blast. Nothing seen in the smoke. Interior library appears intact."

Ava nodded toward the window. "MediCar's here for Feren. She'll be in excellent hands."

"Good, good." Serpio responded, but he didn't appear to be listening. He continued to look out into space, as if the bomb had splintered his mind into incohesive pieces.

"Serpio?" Ava said, placing her hand on his arm. "With all this, you won't have a moment to change those Alts for the Plauditors. Time's of the essence if the people will come out soon. Feren's injured. If you wish, I'd be happy to recalibrate the Plauditors' Alts."

"What?"

"The Alts, Serpio. You need to recalibrate them."

"Yes, yes. The last thing I need. But … I should do something. I'll grant you emergency access …"

Hope surged in Will's heart. Alts recalibrated? Could Phoenix take advantage of this new situation? Did the REMs find everything they were looking for in the library? Then, worry took over. Serpio demanded that he broadcast again. He'd be forced to tell another lie. And there was no way to tell whatever was left of Phoenix that he was still on their side.

39

Xander's Night

Back at the Plauditorium, a loud yell went up from Sector Eleven's station. The Plauditor there grabbed his mic and spoke into it. "Hey! Bomb went off outside City Hall. Just saw the Mag's limo totally destroyed!"

Plauditors and REMs rushed over, crowding the area until Banks, monitoring Sector Thirteen, called out over his mic. "And there's another! The library wall's blown! Our guys are going in!" The crowd shifted and dispersed from Station Eleven, surrounding Banks's station instead.

Xander raced over the moment a cry went up just in time to see the second bomb blow a hole in the Magistrate's private library. He thought he would split from the grin on his face. Those around him were cheering and congratulating each other with friendly pats and hugs. He did a fist bump with Banks. "Dang! That's the best thing I've seen today!" Xander hollered. As he watched, he began to really *believe*. Before the bombing, believing in their efforts to overthrow Serpio had been a stretch—an enormous leap of faith. But now? His dreams were coming true.

In contrast to his buoyant mood, waning rays of the sun shot through the picture window near the ceiling. The sun was dipping down past the horizon. It would only be another hour before night set in. That, too, was perfect planning. For the investigation, it would be harder for the Sciolists in the deepening twilight. Not that any of their own crew could relax, but they could all go to sleep knowing the day had ended with success. No telling what the stolen journals would reveal or if the marauding Plauditors could get them back here, but his optimism stretched beyond the Plauditorium walls and into the universe.

To tear himself away from the monitors would be hard. He badly wanted to see what would happen next. Unfortunately, seeing and hearing what was happening inside the library, or City Hall for that matter, was impossible. The Plauditorium didn't monitor secret places like that.

It wouldn't be long before a Magistrate-sponsored broadcast would go out. Serpio couldn't cover this up. Word spread quickly. The citizens of Tranquility would know about the bombs. The citizens would be alarmed. Serpio would need to ensure Tranquility's happiness standards and safety were upheld. He would give the citizens words of comfort; an official broadcast was imminent.

Xander rubbed his eyes. He was exhausted and just wanted some time to sleep.

"Xander!" An excited voice rang out. Banks pointed to the screen where the REMs emerged from the rubble, leaping out through a smoky veil. Each carried multiple books of various colors before melting out of sight under a blanket of still-rising dust, away from the camera's lens.

He raced over to the sector where he could see the roadway facing the bomb-torn library. The MediCar idled on the street. Xander held his breath, watching. Clouds of dust trembled in the air, caught up and suffused in a gentle breeze. *The calm meets the storm*, he thought. Waves of earthy powder shrouded the MediCar. Through the haze, he couldn't see much. He squinted his eyes until he realized that wouldn't help clear the smoke. There! Silhouettes. Their guys. He watched them jump into the vehicle, and the car screamed away from the curb.

Xander ran to the Plauditorium's entrance, calling out orders. Once his "Medic" team arrived, they needed an immediate open door. He worried the MediCar would be flagged for its trip back to the Plauditorium. Would someone note it didn't head for the hospital? The advantage of high speed, though, would be in their favor. He paced with an energy he didn't have. Then he heard the sirens. What seemed like forever was merely seconds. The MediCar pulled up. Relief flooded his body, leaving him limp. He wiped a bead of sweat from his forehead. He'd been worried, but now, he felt exhilarated. Success was a new experience, and he embraced it with his whole being.

When the two REMs burst through the door, Xander gathered them up in a huddle. "Jasper … Bixby … good job." He gave each a shoulder pump before letting them go.

Jasper said, "*That* was a rush!" Gripped in his hands were four journals. "Here ya go. A crapshoot. We didn't know what to grab."

"Hope we got stuff we can use." Bixby held three colored volumes in the air.

"Me too. Pass these around. Tell whoever you pick to look for ways to mess up the Alt's Continuum Spectrum." Xander hoped that the more havoc they did, the more Serpio would be busy with trying to fix it all.

"Uh … the Continuum Spectrum?" Jasper had a dumb look on his face.

"Yeah. Master computer that gathers the data. We could shut that down, but we gotta find out how. Find Sciolist sched-ules. Or anything that would destroy Serpio's safety. Ideas for a plan of attack."

Bixby smiled. The open space from his missing front tooth

made him look like a grinning jack-o-lantern. "Yep. Yep. Got it."

As Xander turned away, it dawned on him that he hadn't seen anything resembling a metallic gold book. Ember would be disappointed. His silver lining shrunk a little bit. Now, there'd be no stopping her from starting a new quest. He was for anything that could help them—and Ember had been insistent.

"Guys … thanks. But … no gold journal?" Ember's voice came from behind him. The melancholy wrapping every word was echoed by the way she dropped her head. She hugged herself, as if to physically hold her feelings in.

The guys shook their heads and looked at the floor. "Sorry," they both mumbled under their breaths.

"It's … it's okay. I just hoped …"

Xander's thoughts flew back to Ember's harsh comment earlier when she said she didn't need him. The remark had crushed him more than he let on, his false bravado a shield for his heart. He knew her outburst against him was related to her anger for Will. She admitted that. But with this victory, he felt invincible. She needed him now, and he wasn't passing up the chance to win her over.

"Hey! Chin up." Xander gently lifted Ember's chin until she looked up to his face. "Somewhere, there's a clue. Maybe in those journals. We'll see." He withdrew his hand, tucking away the memory of the soft moment. "Bottom line—we can't just make wild guesses about where it is. And we've got bigger problems, like an escape." He stared into space, thinking, and then turned back to her. "I never had a chance to read the journal we already have, the one you stole from the Magistrate's mansion."

"You're right! You never got to see it. And I've only read half of it myself."

"Where is it?"

"I put it in the lounge cupboard before our trip to The Outside."

"We could read it together," Xander said, his arm gesturing toward the lounge. He cringed inwardly at a fleeting look of apprehension on her face. An instant later, it was gone.

Ember's weak smile wasn't very encouraging, but she surprised him. "Of course. We should both read it. Fully. Who knows what it'll say?"

Elation flowed through him as they walked across the room together, his heart beating more than he wanted it to. It thudded in his ears, drowning out rational thoughts. What's worse was, she *knew.* There was no hiding his desire for her. Talk about the elephant in the room.

40

Serpio's Response

Serpio left the chambers immediately with Will in tow. Although it was a relatively short walk, he would normally have taken his limo. Instead, here he was, waiting for a borrowed Elite vehicle to show up.

His fury was fully on display in his walk from there to the library. He wasn't caring what kind of example he was setting for anyone watching. In fact, he had gone beyond trying to put on a calm facade for the people. Things were not going his way, and he was ready to strike back.

As they approached the exterior of the library, Serpio waited for the Sciolists gathered there to give him the Tranquility salute. He then addressed the Sciolists swarming the scene. "I want a report within the hour. What chemicals and how the bombs were made. Any evidence, no matter how small." His voice sounded like gravel skidding on concrete, even to himself. He and Will stood for a moment, observing the loyal Sciolists, their red robes fluttering in the breeze, working like ants. Bionic scoopers were removing rubble. Chunks of cement were already being cleared away. One Sciolist held a Factive, the computerized unit that described and recorded emergency situations and investigations. Altogether, seven Sciolists were at work, including two that were examining pieces of metal that were part of the bombs used.

As he turned to leave, Serpio tossed out one last question. "Why isn't the building putting itself back together? All our structures have self-repairing bending microfibers."

The Sciolist holding the Factive replied. "That's for hairline fractures only. A self-healing calcium carbonate patch isn't near big enough for this."

"Carry on." Serpio felt as if the bomb had scooped out more than just concrete. It was a blast to his ego and his leadership. He boiled.

He entered the library through its regular door but immediately realized that the blast had opened up a wall big enough for any number of people to go through. And they certainly would have. It would be naive to think they blew the wall and then didn't go in. He cursed softly under his breath.

A remark from Will cut into his wrath. "Magistrate—whoa … They did a number on this place."

"Yes. And these are your so-called 'friends,' Will Verus. Damaging property. Stealing. Making threats. Violating the Accords."

Will rolled his eyes. "Again, not my friends. But enemies of yours for sure."

There were eighteen sections of books, all color-coded to explain the history and incidents of every Status level's citizens. Not only did they have violations recorded, but his own personal observations and thoughts. Serpio strode over to the bookshelves and ran his fingers along the spines marked with dates, examining them. Then, he counted them in his head as he went from one section to another, as if seeing specific volumes missing wasn't enough. He began with the journals for the most sensitive, the higher levels. Those were the Tranks he watched most carefully, as they were the ones who were on track to become Elite.

His worst fears became reality. Level Eighteen had one

journal missing. He cursed again, this time without restraint, his aggravation growing as he moved to the next level down. Level Seventeen … one missing. There were going to be multiple losses, and who knew what those journals would reveal to the thieves? It wouldn't have taken the REMs long to run in amid the smoke and take one book from each area, especially if there was more than one invader.

"Is there something I can do to help?" Will asked. "I can count, too, you know." He gave Serpio an impertinent wink.

The kid was getting on his nerves. Acting like this was a joke. "Yes. Count. There should be fifty of each color."

"Exactly?" Will's eyes opened wide in disbelief.

"Yes. The system's designed that way. Everything needs to be in balance." Serpio watched Will as he began counting Level Fifteen's indigo-colored spines. "Will, check from Level One." That would keep the kid busy and allow Serpio to control the information that needed guarding. He didn't want Will anywhere near the upper levels.

Will shook his head and marched to the other side of the room. "One, two, three, four, five …"

"Silently! Count silently!" Serpio roared. *The stupidity of youth. Ridiculous!*

The tap of fingertips on leather, like the scratching of tiny mouse feet, filled the silence until the mice had danced for a good ten minutes. Will's voice startled Serpio. "So … what's the deal with these?"

"The deal?" Serpio responded.

"Yeah. There are a lot of books here. More than I've ever seen. I didn't know there were real books anymore."

Serpio paused, his fingers reverently caressing a turquoise spine. "Books are timeless. They endure for years. Generations to come will have access to these. History and wisdom must be *written*."

"But can't that all go in a computer?"

He was in no state to be explaining anything to this Plauditor-turned-captive. His agitation was rising further, as he realized that yet another section was missing a journal. He cursed again, this time louder, his control slipping more with each discovery.

Will's head whipped around, his fathomless sea-green eyes narrowing as if he were looking into his very soul. Serpio suddenly wished he had some of the kid's control. Tranquility's rigid requirements for emotional mastery had merit. He should wisely curb his own reactions.

"Before the last World War, every book on Earth was digitized. The experts used one hundred and twenty-four three-terabyte drives to house the entire library of humanity. But technology afterward only allowed for a small number of additions, an electronic book here or there. We're still working on this—expanding the storage capabilities. And we are always concerned about security. We can't have our most classified documents being hacked by evil people, like your friends."

"My 'friends,' as you call them, wouldn't know how to do that."

"Perhaps. But terabyte storage is too uncertain and too informal. Tranquility's Founding Fathers knew this. They first wrote the Accords in a book because the laws were meant to be *permanent*. From there, two former Magistrates have written their wisdom in them. They aren't meant to be shared, but to be cherished."

"Don't you keep *anything* on a drive?" Will seemed to be able to count and talk at the same time.

"Just—" He caught himself, realizing that Will could never know the secrets he had on his very personal data storage device.

"Just …?"

"Did you find any missing?" Serpio demanded. His gaze rested on Will like an earth-to-air missile.

"No. You?"

"Six."

"Not too bad."

Serpio jerked around in Will's direction, his voice like acid. "*Anything* missing is bad."

"Yeah … okay. Uh … sorry."

"And next, we broadcast."

"When?"

"Tonight. Soon. The traitors need to know they'll be punished for what they've done. We broadcast straight to the Plauditorum, one warning. The chemicals coming will cause death."

"But we decided—"

"We tell the REMs they *will be killed*. Do you understand? They'll come out voluntarily."

"Those REMs? No. They'd rather die. And you're gonna frighten the Plauditors."

Serpio shrugged. "They're trained in emotional control. If they can't handle it, they were never good enough to be Plauditors."

41

Serpio's Frustration

As they exited the library through the inner door adjoined to City Hall, Serpio became silent. He was in no mood for small talk with Will. His mind was working overtime.

Like an annoying fly buzzing around him, Will kept bothering him with questions: What will the thieves do with the journals? How will you get them back? Do you think there'll be other bombs? What if—?

He didn't answer Will's questions, just let them drop into silence. Will was becoming both an annoyance and a dead end. All his efforts to break the kid and get information had failed. The trips to Ember's house and to the Plauditorium were both a waste of time. The crush of Will's parents, ineffective. And he still didn't know if Will was on the side of the REMs or if he was loyal to the city. It was time to pull out all the stops. Before he put Will back in front of the rebels, a hardcore mental adjustment was in order.

WILL SURVEYED the six-by-six room they'd entered through a red door at the end of a long corridor in City Hall. At first glance, the room would appear to most as a Level Seventeen chamber because it was bathed in metallic silver. But the walls and floor weren't built for beauty. Instead, they were more like fun house mirrors. The flat, dull "silver" reflected no light. Not even a chair could give it any level of comfort.

"Is *this* where we're broadcasting?" Will looked from his examination of the room to Serpio, his eyebrows arched.

Serpio gave a low chuckle. "No. This, Will, is a therapy room. After all the hard work you've done for us since your return, you deserve a reward." He winked and placed his hand on Will's shoulder. "You're in for a real boost."

Will's focused gaze seemed to dissect Serpio's face. "It's getting late. Shouldn't we broadcast before the end of the day?"

"We'll broadcast after this … energizing treatment."

"Tonight?"

"Of course. We can't wait."

Will shrugged his shoulders. "Whatever. I'm always up for new experiences. Bring it on." A smile threatened to emerge but didn't make it beyond one corner of his mouth.

"Good, good. Strip down."

A look of jagged surprise flared on Will's face. He gasped. "Everything?"

Serpio smiled, a reflection of the thrill he knew was coming. "Everything."

Will's fish-like swallow was practically a gag. "This is *necessary*? Really?"

"You'll be more comfortable. Put your clothes in the pull-out drawer and grab the rubber sandals in there." Serpio pointed to a large rectangular area on the wall. "Touch it. It'll open."

"O … kay."

"Enjoy … I'll see you in fifteen minutes," Serpio said

before walking out through the electronic door, a wave of his hand locking it behind him.

Outside the door, Serpio entered a glass elevator. In a split second, it went to a floor above the room to a narrow loft with two large surveillance windows overlooking the space where he saw Will contemplating the ceiling. *He's seen the lights.* The massive heat lamps made up the entire ceiling, six altogether, each a foot in diameter. He chuckled to himself. *And no escape.* A perfect observation area. He could see both the process and the results of the treatment but also could tailor the specific messages that came over the speaker inside the chamber. Because that's what it was—a place to reprogram people for self-sacrificing service.

Serpio looked at the control board with care before saying, "Option one and two." A purring whir answered, followed by a high-voltage hum. Immediately, the lights above flared and pulsed. First softly, then gaining intensity until they were blinding. Blaring, heavy metal music frayed the silence, a heavy shroud of sound, the guitars amplified to ear-splitting levels. Screaming vocalists shredded the limits of tolerance. But the commands Serpio spoke, weaving their way into the music as subliminal messages, were the most fun. Words of destruction. Words that tore down. Words that held the victim in a hypnotic spell.

"Will Verus … You no longer wish for independence. Your mind is fragile. Physically, you are strong and tough enough to kill another citizen on command. Nothing you have ever known to be true is accurate. Your family has never loved you. None. Of. Your. Friends. Are. Loyal. Going forward, you will remember them as harmful characters in a dream … ghosts in the shadows. The girl named Ember will no longer be attractive to you. Instead, she repels you and is your enemy. The Elite and the Magistrate offer you only help. Leaning on them will heighten your importance. You are made to serve the city. When you broadcast, you will win the hearts of your listeners by telling them your Magistrate knows what is best for them. Everything else in your life is small and unimportant."

Serpio was thrilled at the barrage of sensory ravaging as it rained down on Will. His only regret was that, once recited, he didn't need to repeat the words. They were already in the system.

Will immediately put his hands over his ears to block the onslaught. He bent over as if doubled up in pain, his body stiff. Sweat broke out on his forehead, glistening under the lights like rare diamonds before running down his face in rivulets. Will tried to sit, but his squat never reached the floor. The fiery heat, Serpio knew, would be intolerable and burn through his shoes.

Serpio heard Will scream, "Enough! Let me out! I can't bear this!"

The Magistrate smiled, knowing that ten minutes more would finally bring Will to his knees.

42

Xander's Read

Xander wondered how long they would have before Serpio would formally announce his wicked plans to gas them. By overhearing the conversation, as brutal as it was, it gave them time. Time to pour over the journals for answers. They would need more than evidence to expose Serpio for what he was. They needed a way to get out of their situation. As Xander followed in Ember's footsteps into the lounge, journal in hand, he was a mixed bag of emotions—excited to be with her and desperate to find answers.

Within a minute after entering the lounge, they sat at the table. The journal Ember had stolen when she was held captive by the Magistrate lay between them.

Ember opened the book with care. Some of the pages were rippled from its journey through the rain on the night she grabbed it from the library and ran. Xander was surprised she'd had the foresight to store it at the Plauditorium. It was a chaotic time they'd spent taking over the Plauditorium, identifying the Plauditors who didn't support their cause, and then traveling to The Outside together to exile the uncooperative Plauditors.

"Would you mind if we started close to the end? Say, halfway back? Ember asked, already turning the pages of the journal. I've read the first part already."

"No problem." Xander figured he'd have time to review the first part anytime. He trusted Ember enough if she said that nothing in the beginning would help them.

Ember looked into his face before whispering, "There's an entry about me. I'll show you that first." She flipped through the book.

"Journal Entry #5618. 'I've had my eye on a dear teen lately.'" She stopped and blew air through her nose. "'Unfortunately, her mother, Talesa Vinata, has had to be eliminated. She even made me wonder if I might marry after all, especially since she was very beautiful.'" Ember hesitated. "I never knew they were even seeing each other. That makes my skin crawl."

Xander clenched his jaw. His hatred of Serpio resurfaced in an instant. "I can't imagine having my mom date the Magistrate. I guess restrictions on dating beneath your level don't apply to him. Go figure. But maybe she ended the relationship?"

"Hmm. I don't know." She picked up reading from the page. "The woman's daughter has caught my interest. There is something about her that's different. It's not just her beauty, so much more vibrant than her mother's. Perhaps she is poison as well. Or could she be valuable? I'll be looking deeper.'"

"He was already targeting you. And that's sick, the part about your beauty." His body tensed, as if he was in fight mode. "Not that it isn't true. But he's old enough to be your dad."

"Yeah. He's so ... horrible." She shivered. "There's probably more about me once he discovered my ability. But if it's there, promise me we'll skip it. We already know what happened to me, and we have other things to look for."

"He kidnapped you, right?"

"Yeah." She smiled, a mischievous look in her eyes. "And that's when I stole this book."

They continued to immerse themselves, taking turns reading, until they realized that it had become pitch dark outside, and the evening lights in the Plauditorium gradually lit up the area in a soft, cobalt glow.

Xander began to feel he was glowing himself from Ember's close presence. He grew bolder and edged toward her a little more closely. Then Jasper burst into the room. Both of them flinched at the sudden interruption, but Xander was on his feet in an instant. "Jaz! What's goin' on?"

Jasper worked his jaw back and forth, as if he'd stumbled on an embarrassing situation, before clapping with glee. "You need to see this! It could be our salvation!" He waved an orange journal at them.

"Salvation?" Ember gave Jasper an incredulous look.

Xander's eyes lit on the journal his friend held in his hand. "A new secret?"

"It's a new secret all right. Here …" Jasper held the book out for Xander to take and then, changing his mind, pulled it back and rushed to read himself what he'd found. "'One of the best plans of our city was the building of tunnels underground. If there is fire, the tunnels provide an escape. In the unlikely event we are attacked by an unknown entity, we are protected. All of Tranquility's citizens can retreat. These tunnels are not for public use—or knowledge—otherwise.'"

Ember stood up so abruptly her chair almost toppled. "Tunnels! But where would they be?"

Xander raised his eyebrows, as a realization struck him. "I went through one."

Jasper nodded his head emphatically. "Me too. To The Outside!"

"What?" Ember looked at him, puzzled. "Then why didn't you know?"

Xander splayed his hands out. "We weren't wondering why there was a tunnel. Just figured they built it for sending us out there." Xander hesitated a moment before he raised his eyebrows. And think. When you came into the broadcast room, that was underground, too."

A twitch of Ember's lips turned into an impish smile. "So … there are more. All we have to do is find them. And since they're secret—"

"—no one will think we'd be there." Xander reached out and high-fived both Jasper and Ember. His eyes met hers in the exchange, his heart accelerating.

Voices and heavy movement suddenly rumbled in the main room. People who should have been sleeping or manning the monitors were yelling.

"Something's not good! C'mon!" Xander had already started running.

Ember charged after him into the chaos. Serpio Magnus's image filled the overhead screen. His face was too large for Xander to bear, but his words were worse.

"My dear, loyal Plauditors, and … *detestable* REMs. I'm sure I have your attention." Serpio paused, Xander guessed, to make sure he did indeed have their attention. As if they could ignore an invasion like this. "You are pushing the *limits* of my patience. The REMs' futile attempts at threatening me and destroying public property are worthless. Buildings can be fixed. I remain in power. Nothing you can do will change that. *Nothing.* But here is a threat for *you.* Release the Plauditors. They are innocent of crime. Come out of the building. Surrender your arms and yourselves. If you do, I will be merciful." Serpio took a deep breath, as if the effort to say the word "merciful" was costing him. "You will be sent back to The Outside where you belong. If you continue this ridiculous attempt at a coup, I will stop at nothing to bring you down. You have *one hour.* If you don't exit the building by then, you will be gassed. Poison will come in through the vents. It's surrender or death."

Xander thought his own face must look like he'd been drinking vinegar. His eyes narrowed with hatred, his lips pursed in disgust. If he didn't kill this guy, he hoped he'd die trying. Throwing something would have to be close enough … As his hands clenched into white-knuckled fists, he looked around for some random object to throw at the screen.

But Serpio wasn't finished. "I thought you'd like to see an old friend, too. Will Verus is with me. He's dying to give you a few words of wisdom."

Holy Shazz. Will again! "Dying to give you a few words?" He will be dying if I get my hands on him. Xander despised this final insult, this ultimate slap in the face. As much as he'd hoped Will was true-blue Phoenix, all glimmers of hope had faded earlier that day, and he didn't want to see his stupid face again. Nor did he care what garbage he'd be spewing as the Magistrate's mouthpiece.

The camera panned to Will. "My fellow Plauditors. I am worried about your welfare. The Magistrate has reached this decision after much soul-searching. He doesn't wish to harm you, and neither do I. I know you're … innocent. REMs, take this seriously. You can't want innocent people to die! You don't want to die! Search your souls for some shred of decency. You cannot win this war, but you can spare everyone's lives."

As the screen went dark, Xander thought, *Will looks bad. Especially for a Pretty Boy. He seems exhausted … and stiff. What in the heck is going on with him? Whatever it is, I've no sympathy.*

Xander had little time to reflect. Screams and yells tore the previous silence apart. A few of the Plauditors raced to the front door, hollering to be let out. If it weren't for the group already stationed there with the barricades, the panicked Plauditors would have torn up the area.

All around him people were shouting his name, a nightmarish echo of yowling and yelping. "Xander!" A heavy-set

Level Twelve Plauditor almost toppled him over in his hysteria. "What are we gonna *do*? I don't want to die!"

Xander looked at the man's name badge swinging from his neck. "David, we'll figure it out ..." He tried to reassure the crazed man by speaking softly but authoritatively and asking him to breathe.

More and more people rushed around him, shouting questions. The clashing voices became a roar of gibberish. The scent of twenty sweaty people assailed his nostrils. He wanted to thrust the people across the room as he tried to stem his own tide of dread and helplessness.

He couldn't just walk away. These people needed reassurance, and he was the leader. He reminded himself that this was his calling and he, of all the people there, was the most gifted.

"Let me get through ... yeah ... gotta talk to the whole group now ..." he said as he extricated himself and headed for the dais.

He pounded on the narrow podium for quiet. "Phoenix!" The crowd raged and moved like a supersized amoeba, the people pushing to and fro against one another. "Phoenix!" He pounded the podium again.

A REM from over by the door started a chant. "Let him speak! Let him speak!" Slowly, the mantra swelled and rang out throughout.

"That was bad news you all heard." Xander wiped the sweat off his brow with his hand. "But we will have a strategy. We already have some good information. I promise you we're not gonna die. Instead of panicking, we need to plan. Begin to gather things we'll need as we get out of this place." He stepped down, his heart pumping and his brain whirling with possibilities. One tunnel as a way out—that's all they needed.

He realized he'd been scrunching up his shoulders, but he began to relax, dropping them all at once. Ember's knowledge of the Magistrate's escape hatch could be the key to discovering others. Where exactly was it, and how did it work? Ember would know.

His thoughts flew back to the Magistrate's threat, and he gnashed his teeth over Will's part in the whole thing. And Ember — He suddenly realized she would have seen and heard Will speak, too. She would be hit with another dose of grief and humiliation, and it hurt him to his core.

He scanned the room, looking for her. She had been right behind him during the broadcast but, in the chaos, had disappeared. His eyes darted from one side to the other and came up empty. *Where is she?*

Perhaps she'd gone to the lounge again? Maybe to retreat from seeing Will? Or did she go back for the journal? He raced through the crowd, and his eyes scanned the people with the intensity of a thermal imaging machine. Had he just overlooked her? Although there was little chance of that. She stood out like a brilliant light in any room.

He rounded the corner into the lounge and stopped short. The room was empty save a Level Twelve Plauditor headed to the unoccupied adjoining restroom. Not here! Where then? He stood for a heartbeat in the space, dread beginning to create a force punching into his stomach. Wait … the broadcast room. She could be there …

Entering the dimly lit broadcast room, he saw only one Plauditor. Not Ember. "Hey … you haven't seen Ember, have you?" He tried to keep his voice level.

"Uh … yeah. She was just in here …" The Level Sixteen turned in his chair and shrugged. "Musta left."

Xander exhaled, sweat now greasing his upper lip. At the back of the room, he threw back the curtains where a black wall separated the space. Ducking behind the partition, his heart sank. There stood an open niche. This had to be the escape route. Xander slapped his hand to his head. Ember had left the building.

43

Ava's Activities

The dust had long settled from the bombing, and Ava knew that Serpio was busy. Now was the time to work for Phoenix.

Ava pressed the CommuteCar icon on her Alt. At the curb, she tapped her foot while she waited for her limousine's arrival. Time was of the essence. In the confusion and distractions, she could also pick up Weeford from a prearranged location to allow him safe transportation home. With the cameras being controlled by Phoenix and Sciolists at the bombing scene, getting Wee wouldn't be an insurmountable challenge.

The meet-up location hadn't been an easy decision, but the safest place to rendezvous was under the pedestrian bridge a short way from City Hall. The ornate, golden bridge disguised three-foot-wide sewage pipes that ran under the street. Waste from the government buildings' restrooms went down into those vertical pipes on its way to the treatment facility. In spite of technology to make the system perfect, the very idea of what the camouflaged pipes represented kept anyone from loitering under the bridge. It was the perfect place for Weeford to flee after the bombing. Close enough and intentionally forgotten.

After what seemed like an interminable time, her limo drew up. "Where would you like to go on this fine day?" the car's voice purred.

Ava gave her answer and, within three minutes, reached the bridge. Pulling up as close to the bridge as possible, she ordered the trunk to open, her heart racing with a worry that Tranquility Elite would despise. Breathe … breathe …

Plans were to not exit the car at all. She began to count the seconds; she would not remain if Weeford didn't appear after twenty.

Eight, nine, ten … There. Weeford, his face without its characteristic smile, dashed up from the shadows under the bridge to the vehicle and jumped into the trunk.

Fifteen minutes later, Ava pulled into Weeford's rose-pink garage, remotely opened the trunk, and let Weeford go. The last thing she saw was Wee disappearing into the safety of his home. Her shoulders dropped, and positive feelings lit up her Alt.

Next, she'd head to Harmony Tower, or "HT." The Continuum Spectrum computer had its own building about eight miles away.

Accessing the Alts for the Plauditors would give Phoenix the break they needed. Bringing up the Alt adjustment in the first place was risky. Serpio may not have wanted it, but Feren's approval went a long way.

It was awesome to think the entire Alt system depended on one computer to receive the emotional readings of every citizen. Fine-tuned and perfect, the device was the only artificial intelligence of its kind ever made. Serpio checked the computer daily himself, and he alone ran the numbers. She had no idea if anyone else had ever been in the room. A nervous thrill threatened to send her Alt reading sky high.

Once at the door of HT, she waved her Alt. The access number Serpio awarded her opened the door. Easy. The hard part was yet to come. She'd had no training with the system, and she had never tried to reprogram anything.

She shivered in the vault-like room. Built with various colored bricks on the inside walls, it looked more like a cheery kid's room. Yet, to Ava, no amount of decor would cover up what it was—a wicked method of control.

Serpio insisted that the low temperature kept the computer at its optimum efficiency. The place was more like a KoolKrate for food than a room for humans. The cold suited its purpose. Nothing good was gained by the Continuum Spectrum or the Alts.

In the twelve-by-twelve room, the supercomputer took up half the space. Its steel sides and blocky sections resembled a skyline of buildings, some tall and some short. A steady hum throbbed in surges, as if the artificial intelligence took breaths of air.

At the control panel, she typed in the guest code manually. A set of instructions shot out of the machine. Perfect. She first pulled up the city's entire list of citizens. Alphabetized. No good. She needed only Alts belonging to Plauditors. She examined the choices on the screen:

By household.

By Status Level.

By … job.

She exhaled, not realizing until now that she'd been holding her breath. She chose the "job" option, noting that these were also alphabetized by name. After each name listed were points, along with their Status and Plauditor shift hours. She highlighted all the day-shift agents' names. Standard procedure, according to her instructions. Ready, set…time to manipulate the Alts the way she needed to …

The yellow highlighted names blinked. Several icons appeared next to each: one was an old-fashioned compass.

That one had to be the GPS. According to her instructions, this option was to be left alone. The instructions were emphatic: "Do not touch the GPS function." She was only there to clear the points registering the emotional tracking. Instead, she clicked on each person's, turning the GPS function completely off. She smiled. Phoenix was now untraceable.

Now, the Status points. An orange smiley face represented those. She didn't know the first person listed as a Plauditor, "Davis Decoris." According to the plans, she'd find a green banner reading "Recalibrate" in the upper right corner. She touched the heading, and it flashed. She chose the recalibration option, selecting the orange smiley face in tandem.

Her head jerked back from the screen, shock sending goosebumps down her arms. A prominent arrow appeared on the transparent keyboard. She could move Davis's points up or down however she wished, completely at her whim! Her mind raced with all the ways the Alts could be used to manipulate Status or worse … She blinked in disbelief, her mouth open. The system could be rigged. Easily.

She had to focus. There was work to do. Just as she was allowed, she reset each Plauditor's points to the pre-rebellion level, the legitimate place. If a Plauditor was ever stopped on the street, the Alt would show a normal reading.

Problem was, if a member of Phoenix was questioned, their Alt would still betray their identity. That couldn't happen. She needed to disassociate every Alt from the person wearing it. In fact, she'd have to reassign Alts to Ember, Xander, and all the REMs. She didn't know whether all of the REMs would get Alts, either. Any extras were just those left behind by the Plauditors who were taken to The Outside.

She'd have to remove each person's assigned code. But how? She had no instructions for that. Davis's identification was DBD11272078. The "DBD" were definitely his initials, but the numbers? The last four digits were only slightly different than her own birth year. *Birthdate is part of the code …*

She needed to make each Alt generic. Quickly, she made her way down the list, altering each, typing in fictional names, matching initials, and eight random numbers.

A thought struck her. There was one more important person to take care of—Weeford. He'd had no Alt since the takeover. He needed to be connected to Phoenix. But his situation was more difficult. He was already separated from the group. And he was technically "dead." Wait—maybe she could find an Alt belonging to someone who had really died and reassign it? She'd have to find a list of recently deceased. Then, she'd have to retrieve the Alt at City Hall. Difficult, but doable.

The screen had options, and somewhere, there was a list of Alts that had been disabled. She needed a recently deceased person's name ... and then she saw it. A skull icon. A tap, and a new screen opened. Arranged by date, the list began with a death from today. Ideal. But as an official, she could even go to the person's home and ask for the Alt before it was turned in. She altered the initials and numbers on the screen, feeling the creepiest about this change. Messing with the dead was never a good idea.

She did a mental checklist, making sure she'd done her absolute best to keep everyone safe. Ready to launch, she had a sudden thought. Could she make her own Alt untraceable as well? She weighed the idea. Her comings and goings could be secret with the change ... But if Serpio tried to track her and couldn't, she'd have to have a story.

She pulled up her own name. There in front of her were the same options as she'd seen for the Plauditors. One tweak ... and her GPS became untraceable.

Time to activate the revisions. She sat back in her chair, staring at the screen for what seemed like forever. This was the moment where it all could go horribly wrong. If she pushed the final confirmation button and the computer didn't accept the changes, would an alarm go off? Her fear rising like a surge of heat, she began to sweat. Her pulse thumped against her temples. If the Continuum Spectrum allowed the change, would Serpio discover her duplicity anyway? How well did he know the names of his Plauditors? The questions bombarded her thoughts like well-placed bombs.

Then, she stood and walked away from the computer. Tranquility had trained her well in emotional control. With each slow step, she trembled less. She checked her Alt, noting its downward turn, and breathed. Her points ticked upward. She imagined her fear as a dark phantom. She concentrated, using powerful imagery. Like a tamer with a whip, she forced the wraith back, until it dissipated into nothing. It was now or never.

With one turn of the controls, the monitor went black. She sucked in a breath.

Then, the screen blinked to life once again. A cyber voice spoke. "Your changes have been accepted."

She threw her hands in the air, her head tilted back. "Thank you!" she cried to the silent room. She imagined the Universe smiling back.

44

Serpio's Warning

Beyond the words themselves, Serpio thought Will's message for the Plauditorium seemed sincere, like he was trying to urgently appeal to friends. Serpio beamed with approval as he heard Will's advice: "REMs, please. Nothing is worth the sacrifice here. You're at the Magistrate's mercy. Do the right thing. Abandon your quest. *You don't want to die.* And, my Plauditor colleagues, stay strong. Stay optimistic. Resist the REMs as much as you can."

Serpio nodded to the cameraman to cut, and they made their way from the mobilized communication station to the lawn outside City Hall. That would be the last transmission before Serpio would carry out the poisoning.

He turned to Will. "Good message. You might have convinced them, boy. You sounded very concerned."

Will said, "I don't care about them. But you do, I'm sure," he added promptly. "Not sure they'll respond, though. REMs are ruthless."

"We'll see."

"Could I turn in for the night? It's been a long day."

"Certainly. Feren will escort you to your guest house. She's mended from her injury and feeling fine."

"She doesn't need to bother. I know the way."

"For security reasons, Feren needs to be with you." He talked into his OmniCom. "Feren, please escort Will to his quarters."

A tiny voice responded from the OmniCom's speaker. "Serpio. Are you doing okay? The bombs were frightening, but I'm upbeat as always. Everything will be under control."

"Yes, Feren. A number of journals missing, but I'm confident we'll recover them. Will and I also made a broadcast to the Plauditorium. All will be fine. Now, could you meet me outside City Hall? Will is done for the day."

"I'm sorry, Serpio. I figured you and Will would be working through the night with the investigation. I'm already … in my nightgown. I can contact another Elite for you."

Serpio sighed. He didn't want multiple people looking after Will. But then, like a proper Trank, he looked on the bright side. Maybe Feren was giving him a subtle invitation? The mental image of Feren in her nightgown brought on an inner heat. They'd never been romantic partners, but Feren was beautiful and single. He'd think about this new intriguing idea once he'd taken care of Will …

"Ah … Feren. I'll contact Ava. Thank you. We'll talk again … soon." After terminating the call, he immediately spoke into his OmniCom again. "Ava, Will Verus needs to return to his guest house. Can you escort him?"

Ava's response came quickly. "Certainly. I'll be there shortly. Send me your location." Serpio tapped the screen on his OmniCom. "All set," he said to Will. "You met Ava earlier. She's coming to meet us."

"Great, great. So, tonight …"

"Tonight, we wait for a response from the Plauditorium. I've sent additional Sciolists there already."

"And the plan is still to use the sleeping gas, correct?"

The thin line that was Serpio's mouth curled with sadistic pleasure. "That's what the Elite approves. But there are unfortunate … miscalculations sometimes …" Serpio wanted this to be over. And it would be easier to kill them all than to have to deal with sleeping people who they'd have to drag out of there. Bodies were one thing, but people who would wake up were another.

"Has the Elite approved of the poison?" Will asked.

"Tomorrow morning, we convene for approval. It should be a quick meeting." Serpio sighed, wishing he could dispense with assembling. But the proper procedures had to be in place, even with his underlying subterfuge.

Ava emerged from behind City Hall, her rapid stride making him smile. He thought she seemed especially excited tonight about serving him. Ava was always on top of things, always wanting to please. She held up her hand properly in salute.

"Good evening, Serpio. Hello again, Will. This way," Ava said, throwing her arm in the direction of the path leading behind City Hall. She wasn't wasting any time.

"Are we … are we going through the garden again?" Will asked as he began to follow her lead.

Serpio noted Will's discomfort. The kid was smart. He certainly understood the impairment of the garden. Too bad. That was part of why the guest house was so appropriate. "Ava!" he called out. "You have the necessary protection?"

"Of course, Magistrate," Ava replied as she patted her front pocket. "Always prepared."

Serpio suddenly felt a tide of loneliness wash over him as he watched them walk away.

45

Will's Burden

As curfew passed, the sidewalks began to light up, one area at a time, and the rain would soon begin. Once behind City Hall, Ava peered at her Alt glowing in the now starlit sky. Once the sun disappeared, it didn't take long for the night to fall like spilled ink. Will wondered at her attention to it until she whispered, "Making sure my Alt's closed to calls right now." Her dark eyes seemed to be deepening holes in the blackness around them.

"You can … do that? Block calls?" Will asked. This technology was different from what he had access to on his Alt when every call came through and the conversation was monitored.

Ava's voice dropped to a whisper. "Yes. I'm Elite, remember? We're trusted and can silence our Alts. Now, before we get to your cottage, I have some questions for you."

More interrogation. This time from a distrustful Elite. Did the Magistrate *ever* stop trying to determine where his allegiance lay? "More questions, huh? Serpio making you do his homework?"

"No. But the answers you give me will need to be entirely truthful. Lives depend on it."

Will scoffed, "Yeah? And what makes you think I'd trust you?"

She stopped in the gloom and grabbed him by the arm. Will broke away, alarmed by her serious face. To his surprise, she moved him back into the shadows created by City Hall's columned exterior. "How important are your friends to you?"

He gazed at her warily. He'd been down this road before with the Magistrate. He suddenly didn't care. He had nothing to hide. Shifting his gaze, he stared off into space.

"My friends? You're talking about those Phoenix people. They're missing. At least one is dead," he said. "Enemies of the city. That's the truth."

"Who is dead?"

What was this? This woman … surely, she knew this stuff. "A guy. Named Xander." He felt a momentary unexplained turn in his stomach. A moment of shallow sadness and then it was gone, like a vapor.

Ava studied his face as intently as if he were under a microscope. "Ah. I can see you know Xander."

"Of course. Any loyal agent would know of him. But I did know him … I think." Will shrugged his shoulders.

"Will. Can you just be *honest* with me? I'm not going to tell Serpio what you say. You can drop the lies."

"Look. What do you want me to say? That I hate those people? I do. I've already been through too much because of them." He watched her cringe at his response like he'd slapped her face.

"O … kay. It's just that … people have been wondering where your loyalties are."

Now he was really confused. "Who are 'people'?" he asked accusingly.

"Your … friends. Phoenix." Ava grinned before dropping a bomb. "And Ember." She gazed at him with so much eagerness that he stepped back, uncomfortable.

Ember. The name dropped into his subconscious like a

stone, and he felt rippling effects in his gut. "Yeah … I know the name. She's a wanted fugitive. I'm helping Serpio look for her," he said eagerly before giving her his most reassuring smile. "Don't worry, Ava. We *are* going to find her." The words gave him an inexplicable lift.

"I'm not worried about that, Will." Ava's face looked like a child's when their candy was stolen. "Let's get to your cottage. We're both tired."

Will fell in step with her, his Alt points climbing at the thought of finally lying down. He felt strange, as if he'd been through a soul-flattening event, but he knew it was just the effects of the "relaxation therapy" he'd had earlier. That chamber was powerful enough he didn't even remember putting his clothes back on afterward, only that he was instructed to take them off.

Ava didn't speak to him much after that. She broke the silence only when they got close to the garden leading to the cottage. Right before stepping under the canopy, she reached into her pocket and pulled out a syringe, which she injected into her arm without hesitation.

"What are you doing?"

"The garden has … effects. This drug blocks them. We carry it when escorting … guests to the cottage."

Will sighed. "Could I talk you into giving me one? I'm already pretty relaxed from the therapy today."

"Therapy? What … therapy did you get?" As she spoke, Ava's face suddenly looked pale. But maybe it was the moonlight.

"Serpio gave me a session as a reward. You know … that silver room inside the building?" He gestured with his thumb back the way they had come as drops of rain dotted his face and clothing. He was getting impatient now; he didn't want to stand in the rain.

"I'm not aware of any silver room. If you were getting therapy, Will, you'd be at the Solace Institute."

"I'm telling you … I was in a silver room."

Will examined Ava's face and body language. If she's Elite, she'd know about the room. Why wouldn't she? More confused than ever, he shrugged his shoulders. "Look. It's okay. Serpio's taking care of me. No need to be concerned."

"I'm worried that you're not remembering things well. You realize Serpio's still trying to break you."

Will felt heat rise up in his chest, his eyes narrowing. "*No one breaks me!*" He made a fist with his hand, wanting to strike this woman. What garbage was she speaking? "I am a Plauditor for the city. It's an honor to serve its citizens and the Magistrate. If you say another word against Serpio or me, I will report you as a traitor to him and the Elite. Now, we go back to the cottage. As I said, I'm tired."

46

Ember's Exploration

Immediately after Will spoke his vicious words in the broadcast, Ember boldly stepped into the nook behind the wall in the broadcast room. As when she'd discovered the space-age Lift before, blue lights illuminated her when she stepped inside. Her body felt pressured on all sides, but the feeling lasted for mere seconds. When she scampered out from the nook, there she was—in the secret room below the Plauditorium.

The concealment wall for the Lift closed behind her, and instant claustrophobia set in. She took shallow breaths, trying to remember how to breathe. The walls seemed to close in, and her heartbeat accelerated. The musty smell of neglect and the earthy scent of the subterranean made her wonder if this is how being buried alive felt. Although it was futile, she shook her head to throw off the feeling. Her jitters were ridiculous, but she'd always been afraid of small places. Regardless, she'd have to put up with her nervousness.

She was determined, though. The escape hatch opened outside of the building. Phoenix couldn't just exit the building the same way she'd come in. They'd go pouring out of there and be surrounded … She had to figure out if the room had more than just an exit up the ladder. But unlike when she entered the Plauditorium before, she could take her time searching the room.

If the city had multiple tunnels, could they connect to this escape route?

The Magistrate would have to have a fail-safe escape plan. There *had* to be another way he could go.

The interior's dim lighting made searching frustrating. Yet seeing wasn't as important as feeling. Her fingers were the way to find what she sought. Remembering how she found the lift into Plauditorium before, she explored the wall with her hands, running them back and forth across the surface. This time, she understood. Certain magical images that would light up under her fingertips were triggers.

She watched the same images brighten over and over. So many decoys. After several minutes, she threw her hands up in the air. "Ugh! So frustrating!"

Time was of the essence. She dropped her hands to her sides and stepped back, thinking. Could there be a secondary puzzle to unlock? Or was she wrong and there were no more exits or tunnels?

Unwilling to give up, she ran her palms once more over the surface. One of the illuminations, a sizable Halcyon, about two feet tall and wide, lit up purple and green. She'd illuminated it several times already. Maybe if she pressed the tips of its feathers? She tried that. No luck. *Hmmm ... the eyes?* Her right index finger poked the Halcyon's right eye. Nothing. It felt good, though, to poke its eye. *Take that!* Giggling, she then used two fingers to jab at both of the eyes simultaneously.

Shazz! The eyes lit up bright yellow, and a wall to her left slid open with a low hiss. A tunnel yawned beyond. She danced and yelled, "Yes!"

Unexpected movement on an adjacent wall made her pivot, breathless and startled. Her throat squeezed down on a scream. She put her hand to her chest. Then, she let out a breath. It was merely the Lift's wall that had opened.

Xander burst from the Lift, staggering in like a drunkard, the niche's wall closing tightly behind him.

"Xander! You scared the crap out of me!" she wailed. Her nerves were more frayed than she thought. She hadn't even felt his presence before he was there.

"Ember! Crap! I thought you'd left!" Hot panic radiated from him before he crumpled with relief into a bend, his hands on his knees.

Ember laughed. "I thought about it … then decided you'd miss me too much."

Xander scowled. "Not funny. And yeah, I would."

He put his hands on his head and then forcefully released them upward into the air. "You saw the broadcast?"

"Yeah. Terrifying." She shivered. "Right after Will spoke, I left." She raised her chin in a defiant gesture, sudden anger erupting like a hot bleed.

"You okay? Seeing Will again, I mean?"

"Fine," she said with some venom. "Hard to watch, his telling us to get out or die! But we've got more important things to worry about—like not dying. I've been searching for tunnels. Look!" Ember ran to the wall and activated the Halcyon's illumination. "I found one!"

Xander's eyes lit up, not too unlike the Halcyon's. "How'd you do that?" He hurried over to where the wall had opened and peered in. Stale blackness framed in cobwebs stared back. "Whoa …"

Ember stabbed the Halcyon's eyes again. "See? I can open it … and close it." The tunnel's door, when closed, revealed no trace of its existence.

"After we saw what was in the journal, I thought there might be a tunnel connected to the Plauditorium. While *you* were settling the crowd, *I* found the only way to escape!" Ember almost burst with self-satisfaction.

"But Ember … we don't know where it goes!" Xander began to pace, his full nervousness on display. "It could go straight to the Magistrate's *house* or to City Hall. Or into a horde of Sciolists."

Ember put her hands on her hips and stared at him. "What choice do we have? We *have* to go through it. We're not giving ourselves up."

"You're right. No way we give up! The Magistrate will have to kill me first. But they're panicking like crazy up there."

Ember bounced in place. "But we've found the answer! The tunnel can close after we go through it. We'll be sealed off from the Plauditorium."

Xander's grin got caught up in the dim light. "Yeah? Open that thing. I'm goin' in."

"Into the tunnel *now*?"

"Yeah, I have to. We can't be seeing it for the first time with a hundred people behind us. What if it's a dead end? Or dangerous?" Xander physically posed himself for a dash into the unknown.

Ember sighed, her face scrunched up in worry. "Okay … But we have to be quick." She triggered the mechanism.

The wall slid open, and Xander dove in. "Don't follow me. It might not be safe."

"Too bad. I'm coming." She followed, bumping into him in the dark. He stopped to get his bearings. Her eyes adjusted slowly. She began to see the walls, lined with matte, white tile stretching forward into the gloom. The color gave the tunnel a ghostly quality. "Go, Xander. Hurry up!"

"O … *kay*! I don't want to trip on anything … or set off alarms."

They plodded forward for a yard or two before an overhead light glowed to life. "We can see!" Ember pushed ahead of Xander.

"Yeah!" He grabbed her arm. "But don't go crazy. We go

only another hundred yards, okay? We just gotta make sure it goes *somewhere*. It can't lead us to a dead end."

"Got it."

As they journeyed forward, their movements continued to activate dull ceiling lights along the way. They picked up their pace.

Xander's footfalls, a product of leather Plauditor shoes, echoed through the chamber. "Brings back bad memories."

Ember felt his vexation even before she saw his aura bend. For the first time, she felt sorry for him. "The tunnel to the Outside? It was like this?" Her tone was respectful. Sympathetic.

"Not as nice, believe me. Really dark. Cold. Creepy as hell."

"Sorry. I can't imagine."

"I had a choice. Still don't regret it."

"Weren't you scared?" Ember pulled up beside him and tried to meet his eye.

"No. Well … I just wanted out."

Ember felt time slipping away. "Xander, we should turn back."

A few feet ahead, a spider web dangled from a beam on the ceiling. Xander batted it away. "Let's go a little further … At least we know it's a long tunnel …"

"Look! There's a split!" Ember's breath caught in her throat.

Xander whistled. "So, there's a choice." He stopped walking. "But we don't have time to check that out."

Ember said, "No. I say we choose *now*—hey, what's that?" She pointed to the wall on her right.

"It's just a bunch of boards. Dumb."

"Yeah, but why?" She darted over and placed a hand in the middle of a series of slats.

"Ember, we don't have time for experiments! We need to go back. Now."

"Wait! I feel … air through the cracks." She gestured to Xander to come over. "And this board here is loose."

"What are you thinking?" Xander stared at her as if she was asking for his right arm.

Ember said, "Help me!"

"Seriously? We have to go! We saw what we came for."

"Are you gonna help me, or do I need to do this myself? I'm not leaving." She began to pry a wobbly board apart from the others.

Xander forcibly blew air out his mouth. "Okay! We pull it off. Then we *leave*." He curled his fingers around a jagged section opposite from hers.

Ember said, "One … two … three!" The board gave way in their hands and fell to the ground.

Xander stuck his arm through the opening. "A boarded-up door?"

Ember stepped up behind him and tried to peer in under his arm. "It's got to be an entrance to another tunnel. But why?"

Xander's eyebrows shot up. "I don't know, but if it's never used, it's a way better hiding place for us. I say we go there. When we bring people down, we can easily dismantle the rest of the planks."

"It's risky. It could be the worst thing we do."

Xander nodded. "Yeah. But no time to waste. Let's go up … evacuate everyone. Now."

They turned and sprinted back to their newfound tunnel's entrance.

"Leave the tunnel open." Xander grabbed Ember by the arm. They dashed to the Lift and stepped inside. Close quarters.

"No way more than two people can fit in this," Xander said.

"No kidding. It's tight." Ember felt Xander's emotions heighten even before she saw his face flush. There was no way to avoid being pressed together inside the cavity. *Definitely too close for comfort,* she thought.

~

XANDER DASHED TO THE DAIS. The room vibrated with hysterical, raised voices but quieted as soon as Xander pounded his fist on the podium. "You there!" He pointed to a group of Plauditors over by the lounge. "Grab whatever food and water supplies there are. We're leaving!"

Jasper called out, "Did you find a tunnel?"

"Right beneath us! A Lift to get there. We go by twos. It's the only way. Ember goes first. Then you all follow. Once you're down there, go into the tunnel."

Shawny, standing to Xander's right, asked, "Where's it go?"

Xander grimaced. "No clue. We take our chances that it goes somewhere in the city. It might be a single tunnel or might split off. Our goal is two-fold—escape this building, and come up with a solid plan for what to do next."

Shawny, her voice shaking with nervousness, spoke up again. "That's a huge risk."

Ember felt Shawny's panic and saw her aura quiver. "We don't know, but it's better than here."

Xander raised his voice. "I promised you a plan. This is it. And there is no choice."

One of the Plauditors in the middle of the room yelled out. "What if we get arrested?"

Xander cringed and ran his fingers through his hair. "No guarantee anyone's safe … We have to *hurry.*" His eyes scanned the room for Banks, realizing that the Plauditorium's cameras should be again shut down. "Banks!"

The tech genius called out, "Here, Xander!"

"Pick out a few other Plauditors. Shut down all cameras. Leave nothing on."

"Sure thing. Good call." Banks immediately set to work, commanding a group to follow his lead.

Ember's gaze rested on Darla, whose high-pitched voice sounded like a horse's whinny. "Our Alts! They can track us! The Sciolists will come after us!"

Xander slapped his forehead in frustration. "Leave your Alts behind!"

A murmur went through the crowd. Ember realized that discarding their Alts would be painful. Years of allegiance and their affection for them were ingrained.

Ember said, "I know it's hard, but take them off and leave them at your stations."

To Ember's surprise, Banks stepped up to the podium. In an exaggerated gesture, he removed his Alt and waved it in the air. "We don't need them. I'll be the first to—"

"Wait! Mine's … *flashing*!" A Level Twelve Plauditor held up his arm. "Look!"

Darla yelled, "Hey … mine too! What's goin' on?"

Ember's gaze swept the room. Plauditors were holding their arms in the air, displaying odd sparks and gleams. "Xander?"

Xander smiled so hard the corners of his mouth almost connected with his ears. "Damn! Code?"

Shawny called out, "Yes! It's Morse Code! Ava's at work!"

Ember's mouth dropped open. "What's it say, Shawny?"

Shawny read slowly, agonizing pauses between words. "Alts … reprogrammed … for … communication … Ava."

Nobody could have snatched the smile from Xander's lips. "So, we take 'em! Jasper, collect any extras. Now, *we have to go*!"

Ember called out, "If you have a journal, hold on to it! We leave immediately. No more questions."

"Ember's gonna show you how to get down the Lift." Xander nodded to Ember before grabbing up and brandishing an official Plauditor's hat. "Ember, grab a hat. That hair … it needs to be hidden. See you below after everyone's out." He reached across the workstation and grabbed his rifle.

"Yeah … I'll grab a hat. What about the Medics?" Ember asked. "They're still in the closet! We can't let them be gassed."

Xander chuckled softly. "No one belongs in the closet. They'll go last, with us."

"I've got our journal. Meet you below." She gave him a wink before she wondered what on earth had possessed her to do that. Being less than an hour away from death was definitely changing her. Was navigating hardship better than striving for happiness? She was doing things she had never dreamed of. Squaring her shoulders, she headed for the uniform closet, this time not caring if Xander followed her with his eyes.

47

Xander's Underground

Xander watched the final two Phoenix members descend in the Lift. He sighed with relief. His eyes swept around the broadcast room, and then he mentally revisited the Plauditorium, his mind crowded with images of what had happened there within the last several days. Now the true test would come as they ventured into the unknown.

Pinching the bridge of his nose in weariness, he stepped into the Lift's niche, the lights feeling like a gentle hug. He needed that. He rolled his head stiffly to work out the kinks in his neck.

His shoulders relaxed as he arrived at the space below seconds later. Most of Phoenix was already out of the lower room, headed down the dim corridor. A few waited in the line to move into the tunnel. They were either silent or whispering.

He knew very few of the Plauditors, but the guys at the end of the line suddenly seemed like friends. He put his arm around the last two, and they pushed their way into the tunnel.

Xander had no idea how to close off the tunnel's entrance from the inside. But there had to be a way. He hung back, conscious of time passing. Lights dotting the hallway, a perk they hadn't had before, helped him. He checked the walls on either side … nothing.

About to give up, he turned to join the others. Instead, he tripped, and a curse escaped his lips. An uneven brick on the floor sent him sprawling. He sat for a moment, heat rising to his face, embarrassed, even though no one had been watching. Rising, he gave the traitorous block a kick.

The tunnel's wall moved across. He grinned then, wondering how a wish could be granted so easily.

He hurried down the passage, eager to finally meet back up with Ember. He was more anxious to rejoin her than to discover if the boarded-up opening was a benefit. A hot-footed trek led him again to the end of the line. He craned his neck to see ahead to the split they'd found earlier. But, as they had decided, the crowd had turned off before that and were going into the previously boarded-up area they had found.

"Hurry up, guys!" he bellowed.

"We're going as fast as we can, Xander," a Level Thirteen Plauditor said. "Seems to be moving along better, though."

Within another minute, Xander was where the boards had been pried away. Ember stood there waiting.

"What's—what's in there? Is it safe?" he asked her as he approached.

"You won't believe it. It's a spooky abandoned tunnel with some wooden boards and platforms. Something from a long time ago just left the way it was."

"Everyone's inside?"

"Yeah. It was pretty easy to tear off the boards and go in. The people are freaking out. It's really old. And creepy." She shuddered.

Xander gently grabbed her arm and pulled. "C'mon. Let's get in there and put the barriers back up."

Xander hadn't gone two feet with Ember before he whistled. "Shazz! You're not kidding. I don't know *what* this place is." He switched on his Alt's flashlight feature. Ember already held hers up like a candle in the dark. Stepping in, Xander smelled chalky dust, mildew, and cold stone. The space was constructed entirely of reinforced gray and crumbly concrete. They stood in a thirteen-foot-wide concrete space with parallel boards on the ground, about four feet of space between them, extending in front of him as far as he could see. He gazed up to examine the ceilings. "Wow," he breathed. They looked to be about fifteen feet high. Beside the broad, flat "ditch" in which they stood loomed platforms four feet above them on both sides. Cement columns stood every six feet or so along the platforms.

"Why's this platform here?" Ember's eyes looked like an owl's.

"Have no idea." He peered further into the gloom. Unlike the tunnel they'd just passed through, this tunnel had no lights. Silhouetted members of Phoenix had dispersed throughout, exploring the area. He couldn't see many of them except for their tiny Alt flashlights bobbing around like some fictional fireflies he'd read about. Footfalls along the platforms creaked answers to whispers and muted exclamations.

Ember looked worried. "Serpio can still find us. He's got to know this is here."

"He won't go into the Plauditorium until the poison gas dissipates and is neutralized. It'll buy us time."

Ember's shoulders relaxed. "We need to put the boards back up and close off this entrance with heavy things."

"Jasper! Bixby! Gabriel!" Xander yelled at the top of his lungs. The echo reverberated into a fathomless space. He cringed at the noise, but whispering wouldn't help him now. Every footstep and voice thundered.

Out of the shadows, Jasper came running. "I'm here!" He still carried his assigned rifle crooked in one arm.

"Where are the others?" Xander wondered if they had ventured too far to hear his voice. Jasper simply shrugged.

"Gather some people. Look around for something big we can put in front of this." He gestured to the entrance through which they had come.

"Sure thing. I'll give an order. It'll be like a scavenger hunt," Jasper said with excitement. "With our tribe and this weird place, we'll find stuff."

Meanwhile, Ember had picked up the discarded slats. "We should put these boards up first … somehow. Make it look normal."

Gabriel suddenly appeared behind Xander, carrying two steel poles, each six feet long. "Can we use these for somethin'?"

Xander slapped him on the back. "You bet. If we can find a way to anchor 'em, we can keep these boards in place." Xander motioned to where Ember gathered the boards, ready to lay them across the entrance. "Turn 'em vertical. They're long enough and can span the opening."

Ember quickly set up the boards side by side. She didn't need as many as they'd torn down. "C'mon!" she called out. Bring those poles over here."

Gabe rushed to her side, the poles dragging behind him. As he dropped them at Ember's feet, he cried out, "There! Grooves!"

A couple of guys helped to lift one pole on each end, setting it into carved-out notches on either side of the opening. Although it fit, the pole sat loosely in the ruts. Something else would have to keep it there.

Xander's eyes darted around; there was nothing nearby. Panic began to rise in a wave from his stomach to his throat. His hands trembled, and he shook them out. Maybe this was the worst idea ever. *We should have continued down the regular tunnel to find out where it would go and taken our chances.* He pushed the hair out of his face and stared, as if he could magically secure the pole in place with a concentrated gaze.

"Xan!" Jasper approached from behind him with three

others. They carried an enormous metal thing. Xander figured it was eight feet by ten feet. From the way the guys labored, it was heavy. With some loud, straining breaths, they lifted the object.

"This was on the ground down the way. Some sort of sign …" Jasper said.

"What's it say?" Ember was trying to read the words through the bodies surrounding it.

Gabriel said, "Dunno. Who cares?"

Xander wondered what great thing he'd done to have received a solution so quickly. The sign was perfect. If heavy enough, it would keep the boards in place if they propped it against the pole-supported boards. "Awesome!" Joining the others, he grabbed onto the sign and gestured with his head. "Lean it up against the boards!"

No time to reflect on the windfall it was. The group was on fire as they maneuvered the sign into position. Its broad weightiness sank down with a grating noise, like the rasp on metal on metal, onto the floor.

"It says … Liberty Street Station." Ember ran her hands over the words. "This site is a transportation hub …"

Xander's mouth twisted. "An ironic name, right?"

"Right," Ember replied. "Hope it's a good sign." She gave a thumbs-up.

We could use something else to keep the sign from falling … "What —what the—?" Xander said. A giant cylinder, turned on its side and rusted with age, rolled their direction, pushed by six Plauditors panting in sharp breaths. On the concrete floor, it clanged and crunched with each thrust.

A Level Fourteen in the center of the group grunted and stopped. He wiped the sweat off his brow with his arm before he began to push again. "Some kind of fuel or water tank, I guess. Still might have stuff in it. Heavy son of a gun. Took us a while … Sorry."

Xander could've jumped for joy. He threw his arms in the

air before he ran to assist. The beastly vessel was even heavier than he imagined. "Just glad you found it. Can we set it upright?"

Jasper flew into action, guiding the tank from the front. "Don't think we need to. It'll work just as good the way it is." With thrusts and groans, the team shoved it to its destination.

Xander nodded as he helped to pilot it into the space. "And ... done." No doubt the cistern would hold it all together.

Time to move on. "Ember, guys—we need to find somewhere to gather everybody."

Their job finished, the little group of self-appointed engineers gathered people as they walked along the platforms. In an area where the platform widened out, Xander stopped, doing a mental headcount. Finally, he was sure he had gathered all of Phoenix. Ember stood next to him. Voices buzzed with anticipation and chatter about what might happen next. One thing was certain. They were only safe for now.

Xander tossed his hair off his face. "Phoenix ... listen. I haven't had a chance to explore. Has anyone walked on to see how far this goes?"

One of Xander's REMs called out. "Goes on forever. No end to it."

"We'll go as far as we can. Then check out where the exits are ..." Xander added, "Hopefully." He gestured to the group to move forward where the platforms ended, and Xander and Ember descended a short set of stairs to the wooden track below.

~

"How long do you think we've been walking?" Ember asked.

"Close to two hours I bet." Xander caught the weariness in Ember's voice. She struggled to keep up. Her drooping shoulders, heavy eyelids, and light gray circles under her eyes told him all he needed to know. He was exhausted, too.

"Look. The tunnel splits." Ember glanced at him with an unspoken question.

Xander slowed down, hesitating. A blind choice. "We're taking the tunnel to the right," he called out. "And if there's another turn, we take it. We can't make it easy for anyone to find us."

"How far are we gonna go?" Gabriel spoke from the back, giving voice to the murmurings of the team.

"Until we can reach the furthest point. Then we can stop and talk—make plans." Xander was running on fumes. He couldn't go much longer himself before collapsing in a heap, which would do no one any good. Once plans were made, they would have to rest.

Two more turns and a half-mile later, passing another "station," two staircases appeared. One led down and another led up. Jasper took the upward stairs. "There's some sort of a metal covering here. Could be a way to get to the city."

"An exit. Perfect. Now, we go lower." Xander grinned and led the group down the stairs to find a series of rooms. It reminded him so much of the buildings on The Outside, the ones that had busted up ceilings and broken floors—concrete infrastructures of ruined, abandoned cities. These rooms were better than those Outside but were primitive and empty of everything but ghosts. Xander hammered his fist on a wall's painted words. He read out loud, "'Rapid Transit Subway, Cincinnati.' So, Cincinnati's our headquarters, Phoenix. Sit. We rest for five minutes. Then our planning begins."

The weary fugitives sank down onto the chilly, hard floors. Their voices, muted from fatigue, still echoed in the chamber. Xander never realized how much noise typical movements made … the sound of bodies sitting and shifting. Rustling, scraping, tapping. Some of the group were brave enough to lie down. He simply sat against a wall. Sitting felt good, even in this primitive place. Lying down would just be a tease. He couldn't sleep now. Ember sat down beside him, but the space between them was far wider than he liked. He longed to put his arm around her.

The five-minute rest time was ridiculously short. Xander reluctantly stood and walked to the middle of the room. "Phoenix! Time to make plans. What Ava's done with our Alts will keep our communication safe." He held his arm up, his new Alt's presence still feeling traitorous on his wrist. "But just in case, all communication with your Alts must be Morse Code. Shawny's gonna have to show us."

From the furthest corner of the room, Shawny rose, grinning. "Not that I don't want to teach you guys, but I'm gonna make your life easy. I've tinkered with Morse Code for years, and I finally put it on my Alt as a language and created an app for it."

The group reacted with high fives and cheers. Chanting rang out. "Shaw-ny! Shaw-ny! Shaw-ny!"

As the cheers faded, Shawny said, "I already paired my Alt with Ava's. That's how she messaged us. Now, I just have to pair my Alt with each of yours. Then, you can use the keyboard on your Alt to create messages. Be aware—each letter of the alphabet has a dot or a dash or a combination. Some letters have four pulses. So, your messages will probably be short with just essential words. As you saw with Ava's message, they'll show up as flashes of light, not text."

"If you pair yours with someone else's, can they pair it with another?" Ember asked.

"Let's try it out," Shawny replied. "I'll set yours up first."

Xander never imagined he'd need—or want—an Alt ever again. And now, here he was, hoping he'd be the next one in line.

48

Ember's Realizations

It wasn't as easy as they'd hoped to synch the Alts. Each person, one at a time, had to pair theirs with Shawny's. Ember was the first, and Xander followed. From there, the line at least allowed Phoenix to sit as each person waited his or her turn.

"Ready to do some exploring?" Xander asked Ember.

"In the dark? Not sure I can trust you." Ember purposely made her face as serious as she could.

"Oh … okay. I'll find someone else." Xander's gaze swept the people waiting in line.

Ember gave Xander a little shove on his arm. "Just *kidding*. Of course I'll go with you."

Xander smiled with one side of his mouth. "Good. But … maybe I can't trust *you*. I'm pretty irresistible in the dark."

"I'll try to behave myself." Ember wondered if Xander would ever quit being so cocky.

The two of them left the group and headed up the stairs, back to the platform. Even with the light gleaming from her Alt, Ember stumbled on her way up. "Shazz! You'd think they'd have put some lights in this facility."

Xander reached out to take her arm. "Yeah … careful. If you get hurt, we'll have another problem on our hands."

"Oh, so I'm a problem waiting to happen, huh?" Ember teased.

"Always," Xander replied, laughing.

At the landing, they mounted the upper staircase. It led to some flat, wide, steel plates at the top. They stopped several steps below.

"An entrance to the subway."

"Where do you think it dumps out?" Xander asked. "You know the city better than I do."

"We've walked too far, and I'm turned around. I have no idea. Probably on a street …"

Xander moved closer to Ember. "One way to find out …"

Both of them reached up to push on the road plate. Xander's hand slipped onto Ember's. She felt a quick, hot rush. His gaze solidly locked with hers. In the dark, with only the thin illumination of her Alt, his dark eyes deepened into an endless tunnel of unspoken emotion, intense and limitless. Her breath caught in her throat. This was *Xander*! She'd never cared one whit about him. But something in his eyes and his touch told her that her feelings weren't so simple. And that odd silver nimbus that pulsed at the core of his aura suddenly gripped all her senses. Then, he slowly withdrew his hand, placing it instead, with exaggerated emphasis, next to hers. Xander gave her an awkward half-grin. "Sorry," he said. "Hard not to be on top of each other here."

She wondered if the slip was accidental or intentional. Either way, she was ruffled. "It's … okay," she managed to say.

With a hard shove, they moved the covering enough for them to peer out.

"It's a street. But it's dark—not lit up at all. Like it's not a main one. What do you see?" Ember said.

"Yeah …" He grunted and pushed up on the metal shield,

opening it further. "It makes sense that it'd be somewhere out of sight … It looks like the street leads into an alley."

"Why wouldn't the city planners just close it off completely?"

Xander shrugged. "Maybe they thought it would be useful later?"

"Good for us."

"There are prob'ly more exits like this."

"If we can find those, Phoenix can even go in and out of here if we can throw the Magistrate off our trail," Ember said, the epiphany startling even herself. "It does keep us 'underground.'" Ember chuckled at her feeble joke.

Xander gave her a wry grin, one she found characteristic of Xander's temperament. "The stations we passed on the way … those might be just like this—access to the street if the steel cover is removed. A few REMs can go back to find where those are. We'll need to have more than one exit from here."

"After we confirm plans."

"Absolutely. Let's go back, regroup, and mobilize."

Ember smiled slightly as she walked in front of Xander. She'd been frightened and at her wits' end through all the death-defying hurdles she'd survived, but she suddenly felt like a hero.

As a teen who'd kept to herself, reading had been a great pastime. Her favorite stories were biographies about city founders who'd laid everything on the line. She too was laying everything on the line, but her actions were instead against the law. It made her feel important, empowered. Even more, rebellious.

They walked back down the stairs to the room below, stopping on each of the twelve steps. For every step they took, they brainstormed one idea after another.

EMBER WAS THRILLED to see that only a few more people waited in line to pair their Alts with Shawny's. She and Xander pushed through to the middle of the crowd where Phoenix quietly chattered about the possibilities the Alts would offer them.

Ember tapped Xander on the shoulder. "We should let Ava know what's going on."

"Yeah. I was gonna wait 'til we told her about plans, but we should touch base."

Xander looked over Ember's shoulder as she opened her Morse Code option, painstakingly eking out a brief message. "In … old … subway. Safe." Xander began talking with a few REMs, and the room rang with conversation.

Ember clapped her hands to get the group's attention. Although Xander usually made himself the spokesman, she decided she was perfectly capable of filling the role. To her surprise, the group became silent immediately.

"Xander and I explored the upper stairway. There's an exit." She pointed up. "Now, we must make plans. Our whole purpose is to create a resistance force in the city."

Xander snapped to attention. "We need everyone's ideas. How can we make this happen?"

Sixty voices in a hushed but jumbled chorus generated plan after plan. Some were cheered and others rejected. Teams were formed and abandoned. Risks were outlined and problems solved. After hours of brainstorming, arguing, and concerns for safety, the group hammered out plans for over-turning the city. The discussion went far into the night. Xander and Ember gathered thoughts and lists until they both finally agreed on the best options together.

At last, Xander looked around at the faces in the room and called for attention. "Based on what we discussed, this is the final plan. No one can leave here looking like a Plauditor. You all have to wear something else, and it has to represent a functional city job. Thanks to some very sharp Plauditors"—

Xander gestured in the direction of a group of four—"we have a plan for that."

Ember nodded her head. "A uniform delivery van makes a stop down the street. The service is one of the few businesses allowed to operate before the sun comes up and curfew is lifted. We'll send a team to ambush it an hour before dawn."

"According to Shawny, who helped us find the best location, we'll knock out the van's delivery crew, grab uniforms for Phoenix, and then send you to a new safehouse. The best suggestion was to hole up in the city's emergency food storage warehouses. They're never used and rarely visited."

A murmur of approval swept through the crowd.

Xander chuckled and gave a couple of short claps. "Glad you all approve. Any questions?"

Darla stood up in the center of the room where she'd sat in a circle with five other Plauditors. "Who's goin' on this heist? It's risky."

Ember sighed. Darla was always the one pointing out how dangerous everything was.

"I'll take the team," Xander said. "I'll need three Plauditors to help with location and two other REMs."

Ember turned to stare at him. "*You're* going? How about Jasper? He's capable."

"I could do it!" Jasper yelled out. He raised his fist in the air as a show of power.

Xander threw him a matching power fist. "You'll be part of the team, Jaz." He lightly placed his hand on Ember's shoulder and drew her aside a few feet from the group. Heated exchanges and banter escalated from the group as they stepped away. "Ember, I have to go. I'd be the crappiest leader if I don't."

Xander's jaw was clenched. It was obvious that nothing she said could change his mind. "I'm part of that team, then, too." She wasn't going to take a backseat if she could help.

Who knew if they would need her power to keep them from harm?

Xander dropped his hand from her shoulder. "You have to stay here. The plan's risky. I won't be able to look out for you enough. And you need sleep."

Ember's own determination battled with Xander's answer. "You're not in charge of me."

This time, Xander turned her to face him. "NO. That's the final answer. I need guys, Ember. Strength."

Ember knew she had to stand down. Xander had won this battle. "Okay. I'll sleep. But I want to know when you leave."

"Deal." He pulled her by the hand back to the center of the room.

Ember felt a spark between their palms, something like a warm current. She frowned.

"You two are so adorable," a brunette Plauditor whispered to Ember as they returned to the circle.

"Please," Ember replied, rolling her eyes.

"Uniform team—Jasper, Bixby, and you three Plauditors …" Xander pointed them out like a classroom teacher. "Your names?"

The obvious ringleader, his dishwater blond hair resembling an afro and his broad shoulders carrying a head too small for his body, replied, "Davis here." He put his hand on an adjacent body. "And Colin. Over there," he indicated with a jerk of his thumb, "is Barclay."

The noise in the room escalated again, and Xander waited for quiet. "Just after the uniform heist, everyone puts on a uniform. Take your Plauditor uniform with you somehow. We can't leave it behind in case it's found. Use food bags from here to carry it, or better yet, stuff it in your pants." He paused and grinned at the humor of it. "The team involved in the uniform heist and nine others—once you're in uniform, you'll get back inside the delivery van and ride it to the west warehouse."

Ember chimed in. "Everyone else'll leave the subway a few at a time through different exits, just before dawn. Cameras still won't be working or monitored yet. Go to a food storage warehouse immediately. Plauditors, you know where they are, so divide yourselves up. The uniform heist team'll be west. Ava is sending the code for opening every warehouse door. It's a safe place to hide among the heaps of boxes and make more plans."

Xander waited for the crowd to react before continuing. "Gathering people for the Resistance will have two stages. You have friends and family members. Your uniform is your excuse for whatever fake job takes you there. First, the friend or family member you ultimately visit—recruit them to our side with the facts. Second, that contact has to reach out to others by inviting them to a party or social event in homes. They'll be the hosts. You all eventually will spread out randomly over the city. The only problem is the lower classes. You may not know them. They'll have to be recruited a little at a time."

Ember sensed the concern in the crowd and wanted them to feel confident. "It will be okay. Once you have a group of people assembled, present what you know. Share the Magistrate's journals. That's why we have them. Coordinate your meetings. Keep track of your recruits. Share the Loyalty hand gesture."

Xander looked at Ember before "It's gonna take a while— several weeks—to put an army in position. But we can communicate now. You have an Alt with a personal alias. Abbreviate it for further security. You can't give anyone— other than Phoenix—your identity."

"There are eight journals besides the one I carry." Xander held his copy in the air. "Create four teams right now—two journals for each team. Choose a warehouse for your team. Once you're there, make lists of who you'll contact."

A cry rose from the group. "Good job, Xander!" A swell of soft applause followed.

"Thanks. But if not for all of you, I'd be still a REM—an Outsider. And Ember—if she hadn't started digging for the truth, we'd have no evidence. She's the real revolution."

Ember shook her head. "We all need each other." Up until now, she hadn't realized how alone she'd really been. And then, as she turned to verbally acknowledge Xander, a new truth dawned on her: Xander finally fit in.

49

Ember's Story

By the time it was over, Ember was so exhausted she could barely function. Xander, too, looked like a shadow of himself, his typical energy a long-lost memory. Before the uniform heist could happen, they had to rest. The plans would be nothing without sleep.

Xander still fielded some questions, although the din was softening. Cliques began to form amongst the crowd, becoming teams.

"Ember," she heard Xander say. "We need to crash. Me included. I promise I'll wake you before I go out for Operation Uniform."

The effusion of colored auras in the room resembled a whirling rainbow. Her limbs heavy, Ember sank down on the floor, giving herself some space. She closed her eyes, weary beyond words.

The last thing she heard as she drifted to sleep was Xander directing the REMs to find all the stations and steel road plate exits …

· · ·

WILL! He surfaced out of a fog, first walking toward her with a smile and then putting his arms out in front of him as if to keep her from running to him. He then turned his back and strode into a dark mist. She called after him, but he had completely receded from view, no matter how loudly she yelled his name. The inky cloud in which he disappeared transformed into a field lined with people. They were chanting Will's name. Two figures entered the center space, their bodies and faces looking more like gray steel wool. Blood flowed under their feet, and she could not stop the tide. She tried to scream, but her voice stuck in her throat. Suddenly, a person rose from the audience, followed by other individuals. She felt a powerful force with each person's presence before they dissipated into the air. She felt a deep loss until her gaze fell on a woman nearby. When the woman turned, Ember gasped. It was her mother! Vibrantly alive, and glowing. She approached, and Ember threw her arms around her. They hugged for what seemed a lifetime before Talesa broke their embrace. "You must find the gold journal," she said. "Yes, Mom! I will! Where is it?" Her mother smiled softly and beckoned her to follow. A path lit with purple light stretched out before them. "It's here," she said. A boxy, black building with high, narrow windows appeared at the end of the path. The sign in front read ...

"EMBER! EMBER ... WAKE UP."

Ember felt a gentle shake. She squeezed her eyes and groggily shook her head before realizing her head lay on Xander's shoulder. Around her, other people were stirring, although many were sleeping.

"We've slept a long while. It's almost dawn. I've gotta go soon." He shifted away from her and shook out his right arm. From the looks of it, it had probably fallen asleep.

"Xander!" She sat up and stared into his face, sudden excitement replacing the wooziness of sleep. "I know where the gold journal is!"

"What? How?"

Ember stood up, smoothing her hair, which she knew had

to look like a rats' nest. She gazed down at Xander, some exasperation creeping into her voice. "Just—I … have dreams. They often don't make sense. But—but this time, my mom was in the dream. She told me to find the gold journal, and then she led me down a path to a building. And I know what that building is! It's Inventum Therapeutics."

"Never heard of it." Xander rose, stretching his arms and shaking out his legs.

"It's where the city does all its gene therapies and discoveries."

Suddenly, she had Xander's full attention. "The place that creates things like *Greeloxes*? I'd like to torch it."

"I don't know what Greeloxes are, but I just found out from Shawny that my dad worked at Inventum."

"Who's your dad?"

"I don't know him. He's … dead. But he worked there. And so did Ava's dad."

"Hmm. Your dad worked with Ava's dad … That's a scary coincidence. Ava told me her dad was arrested because of some mistake in his work there. And your mom just up and told you to go to that building." Xander raised his eyebrows and looked at her askance. "But Ember, it was just a dream. You don't know that it means anything at all."

"You have to trust me. My dreams come true. I dreamt of the Plauditorium takeover, although I didn't know what the dream meant until it happened. There was a lot in this dream, too, that I didn't understand—"

"Like what else? If it's so important, we'd better find out before we jump into a risky situation. Like, did your dream have anyone else in it?"

Ember looked away, fixing her gaze on the lifeless, gray wall across the room. "Yeah, there were … other people. Will was there."

Xander groaned. "Can you get that guy out of your head? He's been in there too long."

Ember felt the full array of jealousy emanating from Xander's aura but also a flare of concern for her well-being. He didn't want to see her suffering. "It's hard. It's hard to reconcile what I know about Will with what I've seen. You can understand that, right?" *Maybe not.* Ember understood that Xander had no history with Will. Will was a government agent. She couldn't blame him for his distrust in light of what they'd seen. Will and Xander were perfect strangers only aligned with a common cause.

Not like her history with Will. But when it came right down to it, how long had she really known Will anyway? Only a couple of weeks. They'd fallen hard and fast. Too fast. No doubt his affection for her was real. She could feel that. There were times when the head overruled the heart, though, and if Will had any fault, it would be that. When he'd broken up with her, it hadn't been because he didn't care about her. It was because it wasn't practical and put him too much at risk of losing what he'd worked so hard for.

"I—I don't want to dream about Will. And he—he turned away from me in the dream, which means, I think … that we're not supposed to trust him."

"Ya *think*? Okay. Let's say this *is* some secret message. Why would it come to you?"

Ember hesitated for a minute, thinking. Yet she couldn't put this off much longer. She needed to be fully transparent with Xander. "Because … I'm not like everybody else."

"I already know you feel and see emotions …"

"I think you'd better sit down. I have a lot to tell you."

"And I think we need to leave the room. It's way too crowded in here."

Two rooms away, they sat themselves down in what felt like a secluded sanctuary, and Ember bared her soul.

"… and so, now you know everything," Ember concluded. "I'm a freak. Who else can see auras, feel other people's emotions, dream predictions about the future, and completely take a chunk out of time?"

When she said, "I can rewind time," so matter-of-factly, Xander had shaken his head as if clearing cobwebs from his mind. After that, he hadn't looked away once as she explained what had happened throughout her life as she dealt with all of her odd talents. His feelings were all over the place, from sympathy to complete adoration. "You can change … time. Because …?"

"I don't *know*. It's a mystery. I don't … like these abilities. But they come in handy. I never would have made it here or been able to save Will if it weren't for this 'magic power.'"

"It can't be magic—there's no such thing. There's some other explanation." He grinned then. "I'm glad I didn't end up shooting Will. I remember wanting to, and lately, I still do." He smirked. "I'd better watch my back around you, though." The tease lit up his entire face.

"Uh … thanks. If you stick with me, I promise I won't send you far into the past." She held up two fingers as if it were a pledge.

"So, how much time can you destroy?"

Ember laughed. "Destroy? I don't destroy it. I just get a do-over."

"You realize this is a powerful weapon, right? If we do something wrong—make a wrong decision—we get to make it better."

"Yes … but I still don't know how to control it much or if I can make it work by myself. And I have to pool all the emotions of people around me. The more people, the better."

"So, it doesn't always work."

"No. We can't count on the time thing. But the dreams … the dreams always have truth."

Xander took a deep breath. "We'll go to Inventum."

"You'll go with me?'"

"Who else?" Xander gave her a mock bow.

"Phoenix will be on its own."

"They're ready. But first, I have to go for uniforms." Xander's gaze swept the area before he focused on some powdered dirt in the corner. After a sharp shuffle over, he dipped his fingers into the filth. "We'll smear up our faces for disguise." A few swipes with his hands across his countenance turned him into a brown-faced warrior.

When he returned to Ember, he grinned. "Good enough, ya think?"

"Not … quite." She leaned in and put a finger to his cheek and slid it around. "You missed a spot."

He looked steadily into her eyes, the burn and pulse of his emotions spilling over into her entire being. Her stomach turned over, and her heart fluttered. She put her hand to her heart. Fear? Or …?

What would they do—and how would she feel—if Xander never came back?

50

Xander's Heist

Xander had to wake Jasper and Bixby, but the other part of his new team—Davis, Colin, and Barclay—was already ready to go.

Colin grumbled, "Timing is everything. We can't miss the van's pick-up time. If we do, the vehicle won't be close by."

"We're set," Xander replied, a little miffed at the complaint, "and right on time. Shawny's Plauditorium camera watched this area, so we know for sure. A delivery van stops pretty close by. The exit Ember and I just found up the stairs will work perfectly."

Before heading out, Xander advised the team to take dirt from the subway floor to blacken their faces. His reassurance bolstered by the rifle, he made sure his REMs also had their original bags of rocks. Stones were still his weapon of choice. Damage by those things could kill anyone.

They wound their way up the stairs to where the street connected. Xander fully appreciated the Plauditors' uniforms' black color, especially when their jackets were turned inside out. No definitive stripe showed at all.

At the top, when his fingertips touched the grate, he

paused, momentarily frozen. *We're emerging from safety.* His heart rollicked in his chest, its erratic beat reminding him he was far from invincible. In this moment, with this one decision, he had everyone's lives in his hands.

Jasper, right behind him on the stair, pushed up against him. "Problem?"

"No. No problem." Embarrassed at his atypical weakness, he shoved the plate open a few inches and inspected as much as he could see. Pitch dark. Quiet. No approaching headlights yet. The van would be stopping a half block past them in the alley behind their first business—a delivery company called Divine Drone Delivery that directed UAVs (Unmanned Aerial Vehicles) to drop packages.

Xander never liked the group hug idea, much less being crammed into a tiny space with five other grubby males. In truth, he was also more than a little claustrophobic. Density always led to his discomfort. The air around them was soupy with heavy breathing and the musky scent of the subway's neglect.

"Jasper, this is awkward. Get up on my step and help hold up this road cover." Xander moved over to allow more space on the stair. "It's prob'ly five feet wide and heavy as crap."

"Five feet too much for ya? Yo' mamma could do that," Jasper shot back before he energetically obliged, pushing up the steel cover a few more inches to allow better visibility.

"You know I've got the rifle in one arm. Otherwise, I'd have the guns for it, no problem." Xander's boast caused a ripple of laughter.

"Give me the rifle, then, and let's see," Bixby challenged from beside him.

"This isn't the time ... otherwise ..." Xander said with a half-grin. The thought of handing the weapon over to someone else merely to prove his manhood was a concession he wasn't willing to make.

"Uh huh! I could lift this thing with one finger." Jasper removed one hand from the metal cover and held up his pointer, his brag a dare of the highest order.

"Jaz! Put your hand back up here! You don't need to prove superiority. No question—I've got the buff factor. You only dream of it."

"Yeah? Your muscles couldn't hold Bixby."

The group cracked up, the jabs easing the tension of the moment. Bixby's laughter turned into a jag where he wiped the tears from his eyes.

Jasper nudged Xander with his foot. "There! I see lights!"

"They'll get out and enter the business with some uniforms. That's when we go, right?" Colin confirmed the plan, his vibrating words shellacked with nervous excitement.

The van operators threw open the colorfully banded van's back doors. Within a minute, two women emerged from the interior, loaded down with uniforms. One girl sporting braided pigtails closed the double doors with her backside. Laughing and babbling, they entered the building and disappeared from sight.

"Correct. Get ready." Xander's blood buzzed with energy as he counted down the seconds. "And ... *now!*"

Xander and Jasper thrust the steel road plate up and back, adding their body weight for pressure, and the covering shifted away. Xander winced at the loud scrape and grating noise across the street's surface. Dodging shallow puddles from the night's rain, the six of them sprinted out of the hole and toward the target like madmen. Once at the fifteen-foot van, they jumped inside, closing both doors.

A three-foot aisle inside allowed them plenty of space. The hanging uniforms eked a slight scent of chemical solvents used in cleaning. Xander wrinkled his nose, but it was at least preferable to what used, dirty clothes would smell like.

Multiple dim circular lights along the walls resembled portholes, if not quite as big.

Across the aisle on both sides hung uniforms of all types, sizes, and colors. A definite jackpot. They'd have plenty for Phoenix without leaving the van stripped of its cargo.

The guys moved like wraiths. Jasper and Colin collected six fabric belts from a few uniforms. With the rifle finally necessary in Bixby's hands, he and Barclay served as lookouts in the back.

Xander and Davis positioned themselves in the front of the cargo space, right behind where the workers would sit. Both tore off their jackets and shirts. Then, Xander pulled the key to their success out of his pocket—the Calcinate Wee had given them before he'd left for the bombing. With careful attention, he sprinkled a portion of the bottle's liquid onto each shirt. Wee had warned him to watch the amount. A tablespoon would be enough to put a person to sleep for several hours. Too much …

The young ladies emerged from Divine Drone Delivery, their prattling and conversation a perfect warning to Xander's team. The girls hopped into the front seat and began to buckle their seatbelts when Xander and Davis pounced from behind, shoving the doctored shirts over the women's faces. A muffled scream and flailing arms were the only struggles. Mere seconds ticked by before each of their heads lolled to the side.

With a quick nod to their team, Xander and Davis dragged each woman one at a time out of their seats and into the cargo space. This was the time manpower was vital. Any human body was heavy, but inert ones were real dead weight. With a few curses under their breaths, the team lugged them onto the floor of the van. Using the belts, they tied their wrists and ankles, finally finishing the job with gags. Then, they jostled and pushed each body to different sides of the van under the uniforms to work.

Xander called out a final command. "Jaz! Don't forget to grab uniforms for this delivery service. Two of ya'll have to be decoys later."

With the exception of the lookout, the crew ripped uniforms from their hangers and piled them up. Because they had to cover up their crime, the illusion of an undisturbed van was critical.

"Go! We got this!" Bixby hissed.

Satisfied, Xander monkeyed into the front seat. The dashboard flummoxed Xander for a moment. The van was programmed to move from location to location through the city. How could he make it go backward to where the subway entrance was?

His eyes scanned the options. *Xander, be quick!* he screamed at himself. Everything seemed to be taking way too long. Sweat ran in lines down his face leaving trails in the grimy mask. Webs of perspiration formed on his chest.

There! Beneath his left arm was a two-inch-long yellow switch. He recalled a nearly identical switch on the transport vehicle he and Wee had stolen. It had to be the reverse mechanism. He switched the lever, and the van moved backward. *Hal-le-frikken'-lu-jah!*

The uniform carrier moved at the same speed as every other Tranquility vehicle—slowly and quietly. He wanted to yell with impatience as the vehicle cruised along. The unexpected tinkle of a backup bell put his nerves on edge. Finally, directly next to the subway's street manhole, Xander yanked the emergency brake, and the truck jerked to a stop.

The gang leaped from the van. Davis and Colin stayed inside, tossing calculated armloads of uniforms out. Once loaded down, each guy disappeared down the subway staircase. Davis and Colin grabbed the remainder of the uniforms before they, too, scrambled into the street's abyss.

The final trick would be the piece that held it all together: the truck would have to stay right there in that spot until the entire team of fifteen Phoenix below donned their new uniforms and then returned to the van. That team would travel together to the western warehouse.

The plan meant Jasper and Bixby, dressed in delivery uniforms identical to those of the female victims, would "drive" the uniform truck along its route. They'd deliver a couple of uniforms at each stop using the delivery workers' Alts to open doors to businesses. Nothing would look amiss. If the wrong clothes were delivered—or there weren't enough—they wouldn't be there later to hear the complaints or answer questions.

The ultimate coup would be when they got close to the westside warehouse. They would let their troops out near the west food storage warehouse before continuing on. The ladies on the floor would be going with them. Unfortunately, they'd have to threaten them to get them into the food storage hideout.

Phoenix's final group would have to leave the subway a few at a time immediately before curfew, each tiny sect or individual crossing town to where their assigned warehouse was.

If anyone saw the vehicle was stopped there too long, they'd report it and the city would send out a vehicle repair team or worse, a Sciolist. His nervousness like high voltage, he squirmed in his seat.

Xander had debated with Phoenix whether he should stay with the truck or go down into the subway with the others. If someone came to investigate, staying in the van might arouse more suspicion than his acting as a defensive lookout. He was also the most reviled renegade of the city, next to Ember. It wouldn't take two minutes before he'd be IDed, and the entire jig would be up. Phoenix had made the ultimate decision.

He grabbed his jacket. Checking the area like a human bloodhound, he escaped the front seat, concealing himself as much as possible behind the truck.

The hammering in his chest was a mark of both tension and exhilaration. He was psyched about their success, his mind a garden of pride and elation.

As he descended into the subway staircase below, his

breath caught in his lungs, but not from fear. From electrified anticipation. The girl of his dreams was waiting, only a few steps away, and he was the hero of the day.

280

51

Ember's Quest

Ember's heart had been in her throat the entire time Xander and his team had been gone. Every bone and muscle was taut. Pacing and wringing her hands, she'd stayed right by the staircase. Not because she was missing Xander. No! Only because she wanted to be close by if they needed her powers.

When five of the team climbed down the stairs into the subway, she was able to stop pacing and tugging on her hair. But when she saw Xander descending into the safety of the subway, his bare chest gleaming with the glow of perspiration, she thought she would collapse with relief.

Ember rushed toward him. "You—you're safe," was all she managed to say. She suddenly felt like some sort of fan meeting her music idol. Completely tongue-tied.

"You didn't really doubt me, did ya?" Xander gave her a wink and a light pat on the shoulder. He looked as if he wanted to just stand there with her, gazing at her quivering lips, but then he abruptly broke away and dove back into the room. She trailed after him. Her feelings were overlapping layers of confusion.

Although they were careful about the noise, the minute

Xander came down into the bowels of the subway, Phoenix broke into muted cheers, pumping their fists and patting one another on their backs.

Xander's presence always commanded the attention of the people around him. Ember was beginning to wonder if there was magic after all. Whatever Xander had was spellbinding, especially when he spoke to Phoenix. They gathered around him. "Thanks. Thanks. But we're not safe yet. In five minutes, our team will be ready to leave. And *then* you can celebrate."

It was a sight to behold. Every person in the room worked to take and distribute uniforms. Except for the heist group, who already had secluded themselves for a quick change, the others swapped and commented, each person trying to find the best fit. Most held a uniform in their hands and were ready to duck into another area to disrobe. Modesty was still important to the Tranks, but the REMs threw off their clothes with no restraint.

They had no time to celebrate. The uniform delivery van was still a huge liability.

Ember watched in wonder. It was like watching an origami swan begin to unfold itself.

She would need a uniform, too. She saw a Level Four pink jumpsuit being offered up by a taller guy. "Are you using that one?" she asked.

"No. It's yours." He smiled, obvious admiration crossing his face.

Ember smiled back. "Thanks. I'll try it out." As she took it, she saw Xander following the uniform heist team up the staircase and listened to him wishing them good luck. The rest of the conversation disappeared when they rounded the corner to the upper level.

She hesitated before making the final decision on changing her clothes. If she and Xander were to leave, what should they wear? The new uniforms? She put aside her mental reverie, laid her likely choice behind a concrete partition, and became a wardrobe consultant for everyone else.

Xander bounded back into the room, his energy buzzing from the success of their operation. Then he dove into the fray, helping to match people with uniforms. If they were to leave in small groups just before dawn, a mere twenty minutes from then, time was of the essence.

When the flurry died down enough, Ember sought Xander out. "Should we get in uniforms?"

"Ava said not to. We need to look like Plauditors for her plans to work. Remember, just because Plauditors are here doesn't mean there aren't other Plauditors in the city. There's another entire shift that works nights. When we're with Ava, we'll look legit."

"If you're going to look official, you'd better clean off your face." Ember giggled. "Oh, and maybe get a shirt on?"

As he looked down at his chest as if he'd never seen it before, Xander laughed. "Mmm … yeah."

Xander called out, "I need a shirt, hat, and matching jacket STAT."

A Plauditor behind them tossed them his way.

"Thanks!" Xander took the offered shirt, turned it inside out, and wiped his face with it before climbing into both pieces, finishing with the hat on his head. "Just make sure you tuck your hair into your hat and wear it low on your face."

Ember drew her hair up in a twisted knot and then put her own hat on, pulling it down over her forehead, barely above her eyes.

In record time, everyone had a new suit on, and Xander cried out for their attention. "This revolution … it will test us, hurt us, maybe even defeat us, but no one—*no one*—will destroy us. We were built on ashes—ashes of those who died unjustly—and like the Phoenix, we will always rise. I'm proud of all of you for what we've already accomplished. And this is only the beginning."

Ember stood next to him. "Yes! On behalf of my mother and for others whose lives you are saving, thank you."

"How many of you are ready for the next challenge?" Xander cried, his face alight.

Phoenix responded with yells of agreement, and some made the hand sign of Loyalty. It bloomed across the group until it looked like a choreographed routine. Xander and Ember responded with their own.

"You will leave in the next few minutes, but I have some difficult news." Xander nodded at Ember.

"Some of you know that I was seeking a gold journal. It holds more of the Magistrate's secrets and maybe some solutions—we don't know. But it is important. The team that went into the library didn't find it. I've just learned about its whereabouts. Since I'm dedicated to finding it, I'm striking out on a quest." Then she paused for a moment, knowing that what came next would distress everyone in the room. "Xander has agreed to go with me."

Murmurs went through the crowd. "When?" someone called out.

Xander stepped forward, his hands pushing down for quiet, his face sympathetic. "Immediately. You go, and we go."

Again, the group reacted, their faces stricken, their voices clamoring.

"We aren't deserting you. We're connected." Xander held up his wrist to show his Alt. "We're already communicating with Ava because we need her help. You know the plans, and you're set. Give us five minutes and then you'll leave right behind us." He nodded to Jasper. "You're in charge now, Jaz."

"Got it," Jasper affirmed. "The uniform team left in the van and closed the plate over the opening."

Xander nodded. He grabbed the rifle that had been his constant companion. With a final wave to Phoenix, they left the others, bounding back up the stairs to the upper exit.

With concentrated effort, Jasper, Ember, and Xander

moved the steel road plate aside. Leaving Jasper behind, Xander and Ember emerged into the deserted street.

They moved more easily in the shadows, thankful for the last vestige of darkness. The piney scent of trees and fresh air was a balm to Ember's senses after being cooped up for so long. They didn't hesitate for a minute before melting into the dense trees along the sides of the alley. The area seemed remote, out at the edge of the city. Ember noticed the gleam of the city's dome within fifty yards of where they hid. Confused, Ember pivoted in place to assess where the closest buildings or neighborhood would be.

"I can't see much from here. Can you?" Ember stood on her tiptoes as if that would help. "And we don't dare light our Alts."

"No. Got to move to where we can see something." Xander gestured with his head to his left, away from the dome, and pressed forward.

Ember trailed him by inches, not wanting to admit she found his presence reassuring. This was dangerous, especially if Serpio was able to jerry rig any cameras from a remote location. Pushing through a hedge of thick rose bushes, Xander cursed under his breath as their clothes snagged on thorns. Needle-like barbs clawed at their hands and scratched their faces.

"The city doesn't need any barriers other than these blood-sucking shrubs," he complained.

Ember put a finger in her mouth to stop its bleeding. "No kidding."

A dimly lit street glowed up ahead. Quiet and deserted, the street ran horizontal to where they hid. Across the street loomed the White Sands neighborhood. *That's where Will is from,* Ember thought before striking the thought from her head. "The corner market for White Sands," Ember pointed.

"Yeah! I'll send a message to Ava for a rendezvous." Xander switched his Alt into "dark mode" and hit the icon for the Morse Code device. "N-e-e-d-y-o-u-N-E-m-a-r-k-e-t," he sent. "I don't know the name of that market. I just put NE for North East. She'll find us."

"What if she can't come?" Ember nervously ran her fingers through her hair.

"She will. She'll be here."

"In the meantime, the sun better not come up." Ember glanced at her Alt, noting the time at 5:45 a.m. "We have fifteen minutes …" Her face scrunched with worry.

Xander caught a flash from his Alt. "C-o-m-i-n-g." He smiled and gave Ember's shoulder a quick squeeze.

"Sit, Xander. We'll be less visible."

"Yes, Your Majesty."

Ember shoved him as he sat, pushing him into the rose bush.

"Oww!"

"Oh, c'mon. Are you that much of a wimp?"

Xander laughed. "Just tryin' to make you feel bad. You know, bullying'll get you in trouble around here."

"Yeah. I remember a time when bullying got me in trouble. And you were responsible because you were harassing me!"

Xander's expression turned sheepish, and he gazed out into space, avoiding her eyes. "I … guess I owe you an apology …"

"I'd appreciate it. Even though it's been—what—five *years*?" No matter how long it had been, the memory still stung. She wondered if she'd held a grudge against Xander all this time, poisoned by a traumatic seventh-grade experience.

Xander turned to face her and stared into her eyes. "Ember, I'm sorry. I never fit in. And I'm still tryin' to figure out where I fit. That … infraction … was really what started my journey to The Outside. After that, it was one crap show after another. I was pretty much unstoppable. No one knew what to do with me."

"So, you're saying I'm your ultimate bad-boy turning point? Well, that's quite the honor." She was being rough on him, but she wanted him to suffer at least a little. All she'd done at the time was react, and she'd been punished. The encounter had angered her, so her Alt points dropped, and the school took points from her Alt.

Xander tilted his head back to look at the sky. "You *are* going to forgive me, right?"

"Maybe …" She let the silence linger until he shifted in impatience.

He was so earnest it was kind of comical. A spontaneous smile threatened to break through her pressed lips. It could be fun to toy with him, but she didn't have the heart to drag this out.

"You *have* to—" Xander's eyebrows drew together in a worried frown.

Ember tilted her head as if thoughtful. "Xander. Yes. I forgive you."

He grinned and lifted an eyebrow. "I could *show* you how sorry I am …"

A familiar powder blue MediCar silently drew up to the curb, cutting off anything else Xander could say. They ran to it. Ember hesitated just before approaching the car until she saw Ava in the front. The hydraulic hatchback hissed open, and they jumped inside. Tiny shreds of light eked from the emerging sun. Daylight, unfortunately, had finally found them.

52

Ember's Find

"Ava! Thanks for coming so fast," Ember cried out as the car pulled out.

"I'm just glad you two and Phoenix are safe. Can't wait to hear how you left the Plauditorium." Ava's voice held both relief and excitement.

Ember bit her lip. "Hey, Ava, hope this isn't too dangerous for you, but we really need your help."

Turning onto the main road, Ava said, "Everything's a risk. That's okay. What's going on?"

Ember's voice came out in a rush. "Take us to Inventum Therapeutics. I know the gold journal is there."

"The journal's at the genetic center? How do you know?"

Ember sighed. "It's … complicated. I had a dream. And my dreams give me information. Knowledge about the future."

"Does Serpio know?" Ava asked.

"No. He only knows about my empathic abilities, not the prophecies."

Xander said, "I wish Ember had prophecies about Serpio. But then she wouldn't want to witness what I'd do to him."

Ava chuckled, maneuvering the MediCar down another

street. "Reign it in, kid. You'll get your chance. Now, Ember … you know the book's in the building. Do you know where?"

"No. Hoping I'll get a sixth sense when I'm inside." She doubted it, but saying that out loud would surely make it come true … right?

"Can you get us in, Ava?" Xander said, the realization of impossibility dawning on his face.

"As an Elite, I have a code, yes. Any buildings connected to the city, I can open, unless it's the Harmony Tower. I only got in there when I pressured the Magistrate to do something about the Plauditors' Alts. That's how I was able to rig them."

Xander crawled across the equipment in the back to sit behind Ava. "Thanks for that. We'd be screwed without being able to communicate."

"Have you heard anything from Weeford?" Ember breathed, apprehension in her tone.

"Not yet. I've been planning to go by his place as soon as I can. That's where he's supposed to be. Then I'll give him an Alt. He's important in more ways than just our fondness for him."

Ember let out a breath. She'd been so worried about Weeford. He'd signed on as Will's friend. Now, Will wasn't anyone's friend. She felt like Wee was her responsibility. She'd stirred this whole thing up, and she didn't want him to be a casualty.

"Very far yet?" Xander gazed out the front window from his position in the back.

"Two more streets over. I'm letting you two out behind the building. I'll park down the way, walk back, and then let us in." She glanced at her Alt, noting the time. "It's not open yet. Great for us, but there's no reason for the MediCar to be there, either."

Ember caught Xander's eye and nodded. She wanted to be as brave as Xander seemed. Her nervousness rose. She had to get in there, but if they were stopped … it would be bad.

Deadly even. Xander had the rifle, but it would be a last resort. She counted her heartbeats as they traveled the remaining distance in a taut silence.

She and Xander slid out of the back and dashed behind the bushes along the wall of the Inventum building, only a few feet from the paused MediCar.

"Xander?" Ember whispered.

"Yeah?"

"I'll protect you."

"Right, Ember. It's supposed to be the other way around."

"I'm more powerful."

"We'll see. Shhhh." Xander smiled at her.

Ava let them in the back within minutes and promptly locked the door. Ember saw Ava's aura bend and flare as she looked around the interior of the building. It was obvious that the place had an emotional influence on her.

"You okay, Ava?" Ember reached out and touched the Medic's arm,

"Yes. It's ... hard to be where my dad used to work, knowing ..."

Ember gave her a sympathetic look.

The interior space was a zoo of tables stocked with test tubes, glass beakers, and slender computers. A DNA molecule image hung suspended in the air projected holographically a slight foot from one computer screen, as if someone had left it there in a hurry to get home. An enormous wall listed "Rules for Genetic Discovery," and a scrolling, moving message display blinked in LED.

Xander's eyes swept the room. "We get this done and get out."

Ember said, "Where would records be? We start there. If the gold journal's a log, that is."

"Upstairs," Ava said, moving toward the corner. "I haven't been here in a long time, but there's an elevator ..."

Ember felt a light tingle in her chest, then a feeling like

another person had joined their little group. Yet no one else was there. Just the three of them. She tried to shrug off the feeling, but it persisted. *Mom?* The word popped into her mind unbidden. Was her mom giving her a direction from the grave? She rubbed her arms to soothe a shiver.

Xander looked sharply at Ember. "*You* feeling all right?"

"Yeah. Fine."

As they left the elevator, Ember felt more certain that, somehow, her mother was trying to communicate with her. Impossible as it was, she couldn't shake what felt like a definite shadow.

They emerged into a room with black and white walls, punctuated by a few clear plexiglass desks with matching translucent chairs. It had no books, and Ember's heart dove to her gut. *All this and no books?* Instead, tiny aluminum drawers lined the walls, stacked in rows to the ceiling. The drawers were numbered but didn't seem related to any of Tranquility's Status levels. *They must be holding information on genetic research, and the numbers catalogue it,* Ember mused.

"Shazz! This is … impossible," Xander hissed.

Ava said, "Ember, any thoughts?" She began to move toward the files without waiting for Ember's answer.

Ember put her hand out to hold Ava back, then stepped toward the wall of drawers, willing the odd, persistent feeling to direct her. Her eye was drawn to number 1025. That had been the number inscribed on her mother's Augur Prize ring. That ring had poisoned her mom, killing her. She felt the rush of sadness from the memory. Ember pulled the drawer open. Inside lay a gold, rectangular object the size of Ember's little finger. Engraved on the casing was GJ.

53

Will's Realignment

The morning after Serpio's threat to gas the Plauditorium, Feren came to collect Will early. He had expected it. In fact, he was eager to see what had happened with the threat to the Plauditors and the REMs. Would he find that they had been killed? He had a weird feeling about it, a numbness that seemed to act like a callous on his soul. If the REMs had died, it was a shame, but they had broken the law. As for the Plauditors, he hoped they had walked out the door and been welcomed back into the real world. He was still one of them, and they were influential, critical agents of the city.

Feren had mostly recovered from the injuries she'd sustained in the bombing the day before. She showed him a small mark on her arm where the glass had splayed open her skin. Several inches wide and eight inches long, it had bled with an uncommon fury.

"So, it doesn't still hurt? Doesn't bother you at all?" Will asked.

"No. It hurt terribly when it happened. I felt as if I was dying. Once the Medics began the Medela regimen, I began to feel better. Even an injury as severe as mine can be healed in a day with the proper treatment. The scar will need one more light therapy session for it to disappear."

Will smiled at Feren, happy she was well. His sympathy and concern registered megapoints on his Alt, which buoyed his spirits even more.

Walking through the garden this morning made him loopy again. He made a mental note to ask Serpio if he had proven himself enough to get a preventative injection for it. His loyalty was rock solid. He expected everyone else's to be the same.

As Feren's gold limo glided into the reserved space at the Elite Chambers, he witnessed workmen making repairs to the building. They'd made major progress, but the chambers would be inaccessible for now.

As they entered a nearby conference room, Serpio greeted them from a captain's chair at the end of a marbled table. "Good morning, Feren, Will," Serpio said, giving them the Tranquility salute. Will marveled at the beauty of the stone slab serving as the tabletop. Rainbow colors, arranged from dark to light, melted into one another and swirled, flecked with gold, silver, and copper. Otherwise, the room was plain, the walls lacking any artwork or design.

"Morning, sir," Will said in his most cheerful voice. He assessed Serpio more acutely today, noting a slight weariness in his face he'd not witnessed before. *It must be hard to care for all the citizens in a city like this.*

"Sit. A brief meeting here only. I'm occupied with the Plauditorium today."

"A report, Serpio?" Feren asked. "Did the Plauditors and REMs leave the building? I was expecting to hear late last night—"

"I couldn't open the building until this morning. The ... gas ... unfortunately was not what Will and I discussed. It was a lethal version. Someone must have tinkered with it. Fortunately, I discovered the error before sending good Sciolists into the building."

Feren gasped. "You mean … everyone might have died?"

"Dear Feren, it's quite possible. I'm tracking down whoever may have entered the chemical lab without permission. I'm looking at how this tragedy could have occurred."

Will noted Feren's distress, but the Magistrate didn't look upset. Then he remembered. Serpio had definitely opted for the poison. Yet he wasn't being honest with Feren … Suddenly, he realized that he, Will Verus, alone knew the plan. A surge of pride filled his chest.

"Sir, I understand how difficult this is. Your Elite will need to be informed and given a positive spin. The people of the city, too. I'd be happy to help in any way." Will concentrated on not slurring his words, the full weight of the garden's influence hitting him like a MagLev train.

"Do you know for sure, Serpio?" Feren said, compassion and concern reflected in her eyes. Will could practically see Feren's Alt scores climbing by the second.

"I'm waiting for a report now. Sciolists are opening the building as we speak."

"Surely you should be there?" Feren gently touched the Magistrate's arm.

Serpio gazed down tenderly at Feren's hand. "You know, Feren, how devastating this is. I'll be there just as soon as I'm sure the environment is safe and I've collected some words of sympathy for our city's residents. Relatives of the Plauditors must be carefully informed. I'm having my team of public relations working on something sensitive right now."

Will measured his words. "There's always a silver lining. The rebellion will be *over*. Finally. That will be a relief to everyone."

A chime alerted Serpio to his OmniCom. "Excuse me while I take this. It should be the report." He sighed heavily and spoke into the device as he strode out into the hall.

Feren's eyes seemed suddenly large in her face. "Our Elite will be greatly concerned about the loss of life if this is true. We can be happy, though, as you say. Our city can get back to being the wonderful place it has always been."

"And more good news!" Will continued. "All the Plauditorium's cameras can begin functioning again." He felt a significant lift for the second time that day; his Alt buzzed to let him know the point increase was significant.

Serpio, his face imperceptibly flushed, returned to the room. "Sciolists have opened the Plauditorium and declared it safe. But the situation has changed." Will noted Serpio clenched his fists. "The building is empty."

Will felt exhilaration. No one had died! Again, his points soared. But confusion wove through his mind as well. "What? Where are they?"

"The REMs have no doubt discovered … emergency tunnels designed only for my benefit. And the Elite, of course."

Feren interjected, "I didn't—"

Will felt dizzy on his feet. Whether from shock or garden witchery he didn't know. "Secret … tunnels? How would they find them?"

"Immaterial! Sciolists are descending into them as we speak. It's only a matter of time before we find these traitors." Serpio sounded certain. Overconfident, even.

Will grappled with the idea of underground tunnels but also that Serpio had been outwitted by a ragtag group of REMs who still managed to operate without any leaders. If it had been Xander in charge, he wouldn't have doubted it. The guy had been sharp, fierce, and determined. But he was dead. They had to be relying on someone else. "Who … who would be in charge?"

"*You* wouldn't know, would you?" Serpio reverted to his accusatory persona.

Feren spoke up. "Serpio ... of course Will doesn't know. By now, you should be sure of that."

Will shot her a grateful look. "I wonder, though ... We still don't know the whereabouts of Ember Vinata. *She's* not dead. She's been a ghost."

Serpio's words boiled. "True. She has to be *somewhere*. And she, being a Super Empath, has the power to influence people. Now that we have the Plauditorium back, her picture will be broadcasted night and day on all CitiScreens."

"A Super Empath? What is that?" Will was sincerely puzzled now.

"She doesn't yet know her own strengths. But her diagnosis had four main characteristics. Courage, a strong sense of justice, psychic powers, and an internal locus of control."

"So ... the control. That's what makes her dangerous?" Feren asked.

"The internal locus of control means they don't see themselves as victims. They easily become the victimizers. Now," Serpio said, "I'm leaving to oversee and disperse the Sciolists into the tunnels. Feren, return Will to his cottage."

"Certainly. Then, with your permission, I'll convene the Elite. They need to be informed."

"Yes, yes. Feren. I can trust you to build this up in a *positive way*. Keep me informed."

Will pushed up the small sag in his spirits. He didn't want to go through the garden again. Already, he was woozy and trying to come out of it. And he desperately wanted to be on the front lines and see how the Magistrate would roll everything out from here. "With all due respect, Magistrate ... I know I could be useful. I can help the search or ... whatever you need. I'm completely at your service."

Serpio paced for a few steps, as if the movement turned wheels in his head. "Very well. Better you serve than stay idle. We leave now. Don't lag behind."

It was like déjà vu as Will walked into the Plauditorium. Its emptiness rattled him more than he anticipated. His steps slightly faltered as he checked out the station that Serpio told him used to be his. While Serpio was directing Sciolists, Will was assigned to reconnecting cameras. He hadn't been schooled in it, but he assured Serpio that he could assist the tech crew already busy working at the stations to make sure that all the monitors and cameras were working. Even with the Plauditorium's cameras on, there was no one to monitor them. They were useless. He remembered the responsibility of watching with a shrewd eye and sending a report directly to City Hall about anything amiss. The best of it, though, were the emergencies, where he would go out to help someone having emotional issues. Panic, usually. He loved being the person who could calm a heart and bring a smile back to someone's face. That's when he felt truly alive.

A cheer went up a few minutes later as the tech crew verified that, indeed, every camera was back online. Within the hour, a group of Plauditors would come in and sit at these desks once again. Although the crew who was here had somehow left, the city's second shift of Plauditors had been marking their days without jobs. Will felt a profound sense of security, knowing that the city would be establishing normalcy. He wondered if the Magistrate would allow him to return and simply take his place with the others. He hoped so. As long as Serpio trusted him, he wouldn't see why not.

Sciolists were like red splotches in the vast room, coming and going. Most filed into the broadcast room, where they disappeared. He remembered that the Magistrate had an emergency exit there. He'd been in this room once when Serpio had vanished before his eyes. He couldn't quite recall the details, though …

A Sciolist passed by his workstation, a steel, hot-tipped

weapon in his hands. Will remembered that Sciolists weren't conversationalists, but his curiosity got the best of him. "Hey, there." The Sciolist stopped and turned to look Will up and down. "So, what are Sciolists doing to find the criminals?"

"We're canvassing the tunnels, every one of them under the city. Putting sentries there. Who are you to ask?"

The curt reply didn't faze Will. "Have a little respect. I'm a *Plauditor*. And the Magistrate has asked for my help here. You finding anything?"

The Sciolist seemed to adjust his attitude, his shoulders softening. "The tunnels are extensive. But it's a large group of people we seek. They will be found." With that, the Sciolist headed for the broadcast room. He could see part of the tech crew in the broadcast room, where they seemed to be making adjustments on the system.

Will turned back to his workstation's screen. Already popping up on a twin monitor were pieces of broadcast matter. He had to hand it to the tech wizards—they were fast. Uplifting quotes, sensory-elevating music, and periodic portraits of a warmhearted Magistrate loaded the newly restored airwaves. Will beamed with a smile that could light the world. All peace and happiness were being reestablished.

His smile quickly faded, though. A picture of a beautiful, young redhead flashed onto the screen with a command: "If you see this girl, Ember Vinata, use the emergency option on your Alt. She is still at large and must be apprehended." Inexplicably, his gut wrenched. His heart stopped. And tumbled. Before it began beating again.

54

Ember's Intuition

"Found it!" Ember, beaming, held up a compact object in her fingers.

"That's it? You sure?" Xander strode over to inspect the discovery.

"A drive! I didn't expect that," Ava admitted. "Old school. And I thought for sure we were looking for a book, like an actual journal."

"How did you find that so fast?" Xander asked. "Looked like you were attached to a magnet."

"Well, duh … the number." She pointed to where she had retrieved it. "1025. My mom's number."

Xander grinned. "Genius. Now we need to see what's on it."

Ava shook her head. "Not here. We're outta here. Now. We take it and decipher it elsewhere."

Ember agreed they'd been in the building too long. She watched Xander clench the rifle in his hands. "You getting nervous?" she asked Xander.

"Not afraid for myself. Just for you."

"Do you have the equipment to access this?" Ember

directed her question to Ava as they hurried back to the elevator.

"Tranquility's main tech site's nearby—Novis. State of the art. But decades' old computer equipment is there, too."

At the front entrance, the three left as quickly as they could. Ember noticed a camera at the door, panning the area. A quiver of nerves unleashed themselves as she realized the Phoenix no longer supervised the monitors at the Plauditorium. Would the cameras now be manned? Would the Magistrate see their every move? She swallowed, the saliva catching in her throat.

Xander and Ember flattened themselves again in the shrubs until Ava pulled the MediCar up. They jumped in, the ambulance barely coming to a stop.

"Trying to stay under the radar means the MediCar goes back to the hospital. It's always tracked." Ava's tone was apologetic. "But once I drop it off, we'll grab a Level Twelve CommuteCar, do our job, and then grab another to where you need to go."

"You can take any CommuteCar, Ava?" Ember tilted her head, puzzled.

"Elite advantages give me access to everything. Not that any Elite would ever want Level One privileges." The grimace on Ava's face showed her distaste of the class system.

"Problem is, I don't know where we'll need to go," Xander said. "The info we see on the drive could be useless. We don't have a clue how it can help us."

Ember herself wondered how the information would help Phoenix. She only knew the data was critical. Her mom asked her to find it, but if not that, she felt it in her bones. "It's going to be a turning point," she said with assertiveness. "You might think it doesn't make *sense* to trust a feeling. But feelings are all I've ever known. My body picks up vibrations, and they are more real than facts. And not just for me. The heart, for all of us, is always the best guide. Who can we trust if not ourselves?"

Xander raised his eyebrows. "Ember, I do trust you. And my feelings are why I'm on this crusade. It's important what we feel, and no one should be in charge of that." His voice became vehement. "Or who we love."

Ava's head whipped around, and she looked at Xander, her face registering surprise, as if a realization had struck. "The system is flawed. And I can see"—she grinned—"that Xander has some *definite* feelings."

Ember blushed, the pink heat unwelcome and too obvious to hide. "Are we close to the hospital? If I have to hold this gold journal in my hands one more minute, not knowing what's on it, I'll explode."

Xander looked at her askance.

"I'm not kidding!" she responded.

THE DAY HAD BEGUN in Tranquility. Citizens were emerging from their homes and entering businesses. Transferring into a different car made Ember glad she could stuff her hair into a hat. She pulled the Plauditor's official-looking brim down over her eyes as far as she could. Xander, too, had slicked back his hair, tucking its length underneath his hat and repositioning it. They had to look legit and disguised. Ava reminded them to keep their faces down in case cameras were back up but to smile like any positive-minded citizen would.

They sped off in the yellow CommuteCar, and for once, Ember didn't feel threatened. In her Plauditor's uniform, she "matched" the expected level of their transportation. The car also provided a degree of anonymity with its shaded windows.

The longer Ember held the glinting drive in her hand, the more she knew it had a latent power. The secrets it held made her feel connected to her mother—but also to the Magistrate.

As their journey wore on, she opened her hand to observe the device laying in her palm. She had a feeling that the device was connected like a web to other people. As if the inanimate gadget was trying to reach out. Allowing it to lay exposed somehow seemed right.

As they arrived at Novis, a small colorful building not far from City Hall, Ember closed her hand, trapping the apparatus once again. After all, she would have to carry it.

Xander was still clenching something, too—the rifle. No way could he take that inside. "Is it safe to leave the rifle in the car?"

"I'll close the car to anyone's availability, so yes. We'll need the vehicle again when we come out," Ava answered.

A Level Fifteen sentry at the door to Novis wasn't a good sign. Ember and Xander exchanged nervous glances. Ember watched as Ava, seemingly unconcerned, strode to the door, her two respectful Plauditors in tow. She nodded to the guard and gave the Tranquility salute.

"With all due respect, Elite Medic," the sentry said, "what is your business here today? I have no government orders for an Elite visit." The sentry, all done up in a vibrant, indigo-colored uniform and with an unusual blond afro, bore the typical overdone smile.

"My name is Ava Validus. I'm here to add these two to the official list of today's Plauditors. I'll need them—and their Alts—to do that, as you know. They'll be part of the second shift now. Lucky for them, they were spared from the Plauditorium takeover due to a fortunate short-term vacation."

The sentry responded in a courteous tone. "Novis *employees* do all reassignments. Or, if it's sensitive, the Magistrate."

With controlled impatience, Ava said, "The Magistrate is very busy. He can't be bothered personally with getting these Plauditors reassigned. And you should be aware that the main tech personnel are at the Plauditorium. These are difficult times in our city. What is your name so I may report your excellent guardian work to the Magistrate?"

"I'm Eli Gallus." The sentry smiled bashfully and nodded his head in a respectful manner. "I'd appreciate that, ma'am." He did a quick once-over of Ember and Xander. Ember did her best to straighten her spine and put on the air of a proper city agent. She noticed Xander had no problem. His smile and self-confidence took on a life of their own.

"I just have to verify their Alts and identities before entry," Eli said. "Required, you know."

"Of course," Ava replied. She nodded to Xander and Ember.

Ember happily absorbed Ava's calmness and courage. This was no time to be squeamish. She smiled at the sentry, holding out her arm for inspection.

"Interesting name … Austel," Eli remarked. His gaze lingered on Ember's face, her beauty momentarily dazzling him.

"Yes, it's a family name," Ember lied. She studied the ground, avoiding his eyes.

He examined her Alt's data and moved on to checking out Xander's. "Welcome to Novis, Austel and Danny." Eli Gallus opened the door.

To Ember's relief, there were only a couple of people in Novis due to the early hour. The place had several rows of high-tech devices sitting in the center of the room. Periodic beeps and bells signaled incoming messages.

Ava whispered, "Keep your voices low and your heads down." Caution was paramount. Ava led the way to a door in the back that opened to a sizable inner room where a group of black and chrome boxes sat on an extended counter. She approached a rather bulky, white, antiquated box and plopped down in a modern, translucent chair. Ember eagerly handed over the drive, its sudden absence leaving Ember with a strange sensation of loss.

"Here we go," Ava breathed. She pushed on a button, and the screen lit after an icon that looked like an apple appeared. A white line slowly crawled across the screen. Then, she inserted the gadget into a small, rectangular slit built into the front of the ancient appliance.

"Classified Genetic Therapies," Ava read.

"There has to be more than just DNA experiments on that thing." Xander leaned heavily on the counter with his hands.

Ava hesitated. "My dad's experiments could be on here."

Ember wrung her hands nervously. *Does Ava know her dad's arrest was because my dad reported a problem?* She decided to wait and see what information they'd find. No reason to upset Ava right now.

"It looks like these things recorded here are government-approved therapies. Nothing unique. And it's not written in a scientific way—wait." Ava pointed to the bottom corner. "This is not an Inventum document. This is … Serpio's." Ava put a hand over her mouth.

"What the—? Keep going. Anything with Serpio's name on it is wicked." Xander's voice reflected his bitterness.

Ava could move the information forward with a single click on an oval device sitting in front of the machine. Click after click revealed general notes on gene therapy.

"Ember, are you sure there's something on this thing we need to know?" Ava queried.

"Yes. I'm *sure*."

Ava's forced nod of agreement told Ember she didn't believe her. "Okay …" She scrolled along, picking up her pace.

"Stop!" Xander interrupted. "That's—that's about Greelox." He pointed to the words. One more click, and a photograph came up.

Ava said, "I didn't think those stories were real."

"They're real, all right. I should know. I killed one."

Xander shuddered as though chills were running up and down his spine.

"That's not what we're supposed to find," Ember said, her intuition leading her on. "Although, it sounds horrible, Xan."

"Yeah. That thing still haunts my dreams. I'll have to tell you about it sometime. Keep going, then."

Multiple clicks later had the trio losing faith.

"It's just more info on experiments," Ava conceded. Then a new title flashed up on the screen. "Classified Human Genetic Aberrations." Ava put a strained emphasis on the last word.

"Well, I didn't expect *that*," Xander said.

A long list followed. A list of names.

"Names? Why?" Ember studied the list with piercing scrutiny.

Xander gave a low whistle. "Those are *people*. Labeled *Aberrations*! Why would people—?"

Air suddenly stalled in Ember's lungs. "I should be on that list," Ember said, the words sticking like clay in her throat. "I'm *different*. Maybe they are, too." Shock rolled through her like a chilled, dark wave.

Ava scrolled forward, her mouth slack in disbelief. "This is quite a list. It goes on for several pages."

"Is Ember's name there?" Xander demanded. "C'mon! Maybe that's why we needed to find this!"

"These names have … birth dates. This first page dates back to …" Silence hung in the moment.

"What?" Both Ember and Xander spoke together.

"When … my dad worked there. And that was a long time ago."

"So, your dad was experimenting on *people*?" Xander balled his fists.

"I don't know. I—I can't imagine that …"

"But it's true. Has to be," Xander said harshly.

"The list," Ember urged. She knew this was important. She felt its draw.

"Are these people just walking around in town?" Xander challenged.

Ava winced. "There aren't just birthdates here. Some have other numbers, too."

Ember said, "Please, Ava." She pushed Ava gently and then took Ava's place in the chair. "These are Augur Prize numbers. Not all the names have them, but many do." She scrolled to the next page.

As if set up in lights, a name jumped from the page: Talesa Vinata. Her mother's name! Next to it was number 1025. Her head seemed to float into some alternate universe, its lightness that disconnected thought from her body. Then, dizziness overcame her as her head swirled in an effort to reunify with the rest of her.

"Ember!" Xander leaned in to support her, or she would have fallen out of the chair.

Ava transformed into instant Medic. She knelt and rubbed Ember's hands. "Ember, breathe ... that's right. You're okay. We're here. If you think you might faint, put your head down by your knees."

A sudden flash of inner heat brought Ember stability. She became conscious of her blood coursing through each artery and vein. Strength from thin air seemed to flow into her limbs. Her head settled down, anchored on her shoulders, her thoughts beginning to line up again. "I'm okay. This is what I was meant to find. But this means ... people are dying because they're deviants? But my mom? She couldn't be ... I would have known." Ember finished thoughtfully, agony in her eyes. "And I thought I was the only one."

Ava squeezed Ember's shoulders. "Now we know you're not. But the people on this list ... They're either dead or going to be. We have to find them—warn them. That's why you had to find *this*."

"Yes." Ember felt a missing piece fall into place in her head. And yet … her gut told her there was more. "I … need to find my … name."

A page further, and there it was. Her name. Along with the quick sinking of her heart. No number of course. She'd never been tapped for the Augur Prize. Instead, an asterisk appeared after her name.

"This star has to mean that the Magistrate's targeted me, but obviously not for elimination. For … other things." Ember smirked. "I feel so *special*," she added sarcastically.

"Ember … I noticed your mom's name had a number *and* a star." Xander stroked his chin.

"Yeah? Oh … I didn't see that. Well, we know Serpio thought *she* was special, too. Makes me want to puke," Ember responded.

"Any other notations here? This is our only chance," Ava warned.

Ember clicked the oval tabletop device. What came up on the next page defied reason.

Ember's name was there again, with lengthy notes about the Magistrate's plans for her.

Underneath that … "Talesa Vinata—termination *rescinded*. Sequestered Outside."

55

Xander's Mission

Xander thought he'd have to prop Ember up again. Her face had turned a ghostly white. As if gravity exerted extra force on her body, her arms dropped heavily at her sides.

Ember's reaction wasn't hers alone. The shock of the words "rescinded" and "sequestered Outside," cast a stunned silence over the entire trio. What they'd discovered was simply too much to digest in a single moment.

Xander dove to his knees in front of Ember. He wanted to take her in his arms, but he couldn't—not yet. She wasn't ready to accept such a display of physicality. But the report had turned her life upside down, and he badly wanted to comfort her. Or celebrate with her. He didn't know what she was feeling.

Ember gazed into Xander's face, her eyes enormous with shine. "My mom … she's alive? Xander!" A smile burst onto her face, her body trembling but full of life. She grabbed his arms and squeezed. "That's why I couldn't find her number on a tree Outside! She wasn't killed."

"No wonder you didn't let go of that gut feeling," Ava said.

Xander felt pure joy. Not from Ember's coveted touch on his arms, although that was exciting. For the first time in his life, someone else's happiness was more important than his own. "That's the best news ever! But"—he rose and turned to gape at the screen—"we still don't know where she is."

"Other than The Outside," Ava said.

"And finding something out there is pretty much impossible." Memories and potential dangers flitted through Xander's mind.

Then, Ava said hurriedly, "Is that the last thing on the drive?"

"No ..." Ember drew her eyes back to the screen and clicked. "Oh ... my ..." The group beheld a detailed map of a complex with the label "Resurrection Facility."

"A city site exists Outside?" Xander asked, his grasp on the real world disappearing in a heartbeat.

Ava shook her head in disbelief. "My mind is blown."

"My mom has to be there."

Ava said, "Is there more? We can come back to this map."

The next advance revealed a bird's-eye view photograph. Positioned to the east of the city, the picture captured a vast area of The Outside.

"Shazz!" Ember whispered. "If this is where the place is, you can't see it on the aerial image."

Xander craned his neck to take in the scant details. "Look. There are coordinates."

"Good. Because I'm going," Ember said forcefully. "I have to find my mom."

Xander heard the determination in Ember's voice. It frightened him. "Yeah ... we have the coordinates, but The Outside is *dangerous*. We don't have any way to get out there, either."

Ember returned to the prior page. "The map of the place shows tunnels leading there."

"You think we'll just find that tunnel—out of all those

under the city—and follow it? Not that simple." Xander detested dampening Ember's hopes. "We can't see where that tunnel is connected."

"We need to go. Shelving this discussion for later. I'm printing the map and photo." With that, Ava made several new clicks with the clunky object on the table. Paper flew out of a machine across the room. She rolled it up and tucked it up her sleeve.

As they exited Novis, Ava held up her finger in a "quiet" gesture and then engaged with her Alt. "Serpio," she said. "How's the search going? May I be of assistance?"

Xander strained but couldn't hear Serpio's response.

"So, you're not finding *anyone*? Unbelievable! I'm sure it's just a matter of time ... Are the Plauditorium cameras up yet?" A pause. "Tech crews are taking a while ... In about an hour. Good. Can we expect a broadcast soon?" Ava winked at Ember. "Today? Excellent news, sir." She signed off and addressed Ember and Xander. "The Outside will be the best place for you to hide. Cameras are still not fully restored. If you're committed to finding Ember's mom, now's the time."

"You'll help us? Can we get a vehicle?" Ember said, her excitement an animal thrashing inside of her.

"Not even with my connections, I'm afraid," Ava responded regretfully.

"I know how to get to The Outside," Xander said, "Without a car. The red door in the Magistrate's judicial chambers."

Ava raised an eyebrow. "Yes. I'll bet you never thought you'd want to be there again, Xander."

"It's the only way to get out other than the exit by the transport garage," Xander agreed.

"Won't there be a guard there?" A hushed tone wedged itself between Ember's words.

Ava gave a quick shrug followed by a nervous smile. "As far as I know, probably not. All Sciolists are searching for REMs. But we'll have to hurry. And you need supplies. I can grab survival packs in the storeroom of City Hall. They're never used and won't be missed."

To Xander, Ember looked lit from the inside. He couldn't blame her for being excited about her mom, but this fresh undertaking made the hair on his arms stand up. He was reckless enough to risk danger wherever it called, but this expedition would put Ember's life at stake. "Will our Plauditor uniforms be a good enough disguise going into City Hall?"

"One way to find out," Ava said, holding Xander's gaze.

THIS TIME, there was no leaving the rifle behind in the car. It was their most valuable asset for the journey ahead. Instead, Xander tucked it up his pant leg and held it there with his hand. Heavy and awkward, it gave him an uneven gait and a significant limp, which would serve as an excellent cover story. To have a limp and be with a Medic would avert suspicion and even garner some sympathy if anyone passed their way.

Xander's "handicap" was the only thing that slowed them down. They had to hurry.

A short stop to pick up the survival packs in the closet proved easy. Ava added some extra water canteens and twenty more compact energy bars. As a last-minute thought, she threw some twine into the rucksacks. A check for flashlights was successful.

"Anything else, Xander?" Ava murmured under her breath.

"First aid. Bandages."

Ava chuckled and put her hand to her forehead. "No

kidding. You'd think being a Medic I'd think of that! Guess I'm pretty useless," she added, placing the supplies in the bags.

Ember smiled and put a hand on Ava's shoulder. "You've been wonderful. We would have been sunk without you. Thanks for all you've done."

"One more thing." Ava pulled two items from her pocket. "Before I go, I'm giving you these. Chemicals. Wee passed them to me before the bombing. One vial for each of you."

Xander reached into his pocket and displayed the contents. Two vials, just like Ava's. "Calcinate and Phenol. I used a portion of the Calcinate during the uniform heist."

"Xander, you have two. My two go to Ember." Ava tucked the red and blue vials into the zippered front of Ember's kit.

"Thanks, Ava," Xander said, his usual crooked smiling quirking up one side of his mouth.

"Yeah. Thank you." Ember's face appeared reverent.

As they headed from the storeroom, their feet scuffed along the marble-tiled hallway. To Xander, the gentle echo of three pairs of footsteps seemed to boom in the cavernous corridor. A finger to his lips and a switch to tiptoes united them in a pact for silence.

He'd not noticed the pictures on the wall during his previous singular visit. Portraits of the Elite hung there. The hundred eyes followed every step they took. No real humans in sight, though.

Xander glanced around nervously as Ava's Alt opened the chamber's red door. He heard Ember suck in a breath. His body tensed in a visceral response he couldn't help as he entered the room. Soft lighting gradually glowed, revealing the eighteen steel columns he remembered. In the center of the circular room sat the mysterious crystal globe on its iron stand. Even now, he couldn't fathom its purpose. What drew his eye was the monstrous desk where Serpio sat in judgment of all accused REMs. When Xander had been the accused, the desk dramatically rose up out of the floor. Leave it to the Magistrate to create intimidation and an aura of mystery. The fact that it was on the floor and not below it was curious.

Across the vast space were heavy, red draperies. The door to The Outside lay beyond. Ava threw the curtains aside and grabbed the door's massive handle. "Hurry now," Ava urged.

But the door was locked.

Xander cried out in a soft, agonized wail. "Shazz! There's a key! I remember that."

Ember should have been reacting to his dismay. Instead, she was like a dog with its ears up. "Someone's outside, coming closer. Hide!"

56

Ember's Ploy

The group bolted behind the desk, just in time. Crouched low with Ember in the middle, they waited with mounting fear. Xander patted the rifle he'd laid next to him.

The entrance to the chamber opened, and a presence cruised into the room. Ember couldn't see anything, but the person's emotional state marked his movements as he paced the marble tiles. With her heart thudding at a breakneck pace, Ember's spirits plummeted. They would be found, and it would be all over—no revolution, no rescue of her mother. Anger surged through her.

If there was ever a time for her to use her time control power, it was now.

She'd have to lasso her strength. To pull emotion from her friends. And she'd need luck on her side. The skill was unpredictable.

To the astonishment of her friends, she snatched up Xander's hand with her left and Ava's with her right. "Concentrate! Hard! Anger over fear," she whispered, her tone commanding. She allowed herself barely a moment to fully absorb the vexed energies around her. Then, she closed her eyes and screamed.

Time stopped. She experienced an abrupt jerk, like bumping into a wall at full speed. Then, she wilted with exhaustion, as if the blood had drained from her body.

Yet there wasn't a second to lose. She no idea how long she'd have before everything righted itself. Leaving her immobilized friends, she darted out.

The intruder was a Sciolist! His chin was lifted as if to survey the room, but his body was in a relaxed pose. *He's got to have the key if he's the Sciolist assigned to the room.* Cringing over the very personal invasion, she reached into the side pocket of his pants. Ugh. Nothing. A second try on his right side. Again, no luck. She ran her hands along the interior of his cloak. There —within the folds—a key!

Ember scrambled to the door to The Outside and inserted the key. Perspiration painted the skin above her upper lip. Her chest hummed with breathlessness.

With a click of the lock, she bounded back to the paralyzed Sciolist and swiftly replaced the key. A rebellious urge to stick her tongue out at him was irresistible. Her job done, she prayed for just a few more minutes of safety. *Don't wake up yet. PLEASE!*

A word dropped into her brain like a physical slam. *Calcinate!* The chemical in her kit pocket would induce sleep. She drew it out. All she needed was to put a few drops on the Sciolist's head …

She didn't know how many drops to use, but with a sharp sprinkle, she was done.

Back in position, she waited what seemed like a century. Time seemed stuck. She pondered, incredulous, at what she'd managed to do. She'd gathered enough emotion to save them.

She gazed at Ava, noting the steely resolve frozen on her face, then surveyed Xander. His eyes were closed, black eyelashes stark against his skin. He looked soft and boyish. A few strands of hair lay disobediently across his forehead. His face held a vulnerability coupled with a near-perfect set of features. She smiled, enjoying her private moment.

And then a jolt. Her friends reanimated, and Xander rose to his feet. He reached for her hand to help her up. "Thanks," she said with a sharp inhale at his touch. "The door's open, and our visitor's asleep." She pulled Ava up giving her a quick hug. "Wish us luck."

"How—?" Ava stammered the question. "There's a Sciolist on the floor."

"Just—go, Ava. Be safe." Ember gave Xander a small push. "Out the door. You first." She grinned.

As THE DOOR shut behind them, Xander cleared his throat. "So … you gonna tell me what happened back there?"

"I made it work. The time warp."

"Mmm. I don't remember anything."

"Of course not. I'm the only one who was out of the loop."

"Well … thanks." Then, he added, "But I could've taken him, ya know." Xander caressed the rifle in the crook of his arm.

"Fat chance. We'd be in jail by now."

Xander snickered. "No. Why didn't he … come back?"

"He did. He was just asleep. I had to use the Calcinate." She looked at him apologetically.

Xander raised his eyebrows, and a grin erupted. "Great call. You had to use it. He might even get in trouble, then, if someone finds him sleeping."

"Hope so," Ember said.

Ember ogled the corridor stretching ahead. "You know the way, right? We can't get lost?"

"A one-way ticket. Nowhere else to go but onward." He tossed his head in a forward movement.

"What's the worst part of the tunnel?"

"The walking. It's looooong. Remember, it's miles through the city alone. And it doesn't dump out at the edge of the city. It goes far out."

"Yay," Ember said unenthusiastically.

They slogged along in silence for another hundred feet. Ember realized this was the first time she'd been completely alone with Xander. The thought caused a ripple of anxiety. What if she couldn't handle his rough ways? What if she couldn't trust him? Will intruded on her mind space. Wait. *Will* was the one who couldn't be trusted. She glanced at Xander. "Is it getting darker, or am I just paranoid?"

"Yeah. Sorry. See? The lights are gone." He pointed to the ceiling. "It gets dark. Really dark. That's when the going is slow. But it won't be as bad as when I was here. We have our Alts and flashlights." He smirked and lifted an eyebrow. "You aren't afraid of the dark, are you?"

Ember tossed her head. "I used to be. Not anymore."

Xander gave a low-pitched laugh, the timbre disturbing in the shadows. "If you need to hold my hand ..."

"No. I'm ... I'll be fine, thanks."

"That's good. You might not let go." He winked at her.

Ember shook her head as if to say "unbelievable" and changed the subject. "You ever regret going Outside?"

"No." He paused for an extended beat of silence. "It's a part of me. Changed me."

"How's that?"

"I didn't think I needed anyone. But to survive, I had to be part of a community. The REMs—they were like me. At least, sort of. They became friends, something I'd never had. And even though I felt up to The Outside's challenges, the danger and frequent starvation were ... humbling."

Ember laughed. "You're still not what I would call 'humble.'"

"You didn't really know me before."

"Nor did I *want* to," Ember admitted. "But I wouldn't have been around anyway. It became … difficult … for me in school. As soon as middle school was over, I begged my mom for homeschool. All the emotions hitting me all the time … it was too hard."

"And I went to Panglossian Academy. My parents sent me there so I'd get reformed. We're both oddballs, aren't we? Seems we have that in common. But our paths never crossed again." His voice sounded wistful.

Ember had never thought of her peculiarity as a similarity with anyone, especially not someone like Xander. Yet their self-imposed isolation, determination to change society, and issues with their parents surprisingly tied them together.

"Ready for flashlights?" He paused to dig in his pack. "With the darkness comes more of a descent. As we continue, we go underground."

Grateful for the option, Ember shone her own flashlight around the shaft. Ugly walls of rough brown and gray stucco were brutally drab and, in some places, moldy. The ground was no longer concrete but dirt. It wasn't too different from the old subway, she reflected, but it would be hellish for someone alone with no light and no hope.

"Ember, I hope you're mentally prepared for the way it is out there. It's hard to even breathe sometimes."

"You remember … I've been there. With you." *And Weeford and … Will.*

"Yeah. But we had a vehicle. And we were only there for a short time. Dumping people and checking out trees isn't exactly a full-on experience. We were there for maybe two hours."

"Those trees. I'll never forget how they had numbers on

them. All dead people. But now I know why we couldn't find my mom's number. Her body was never burned."

"And you thought you'd been robbed."

"Yes." *And Will promised to help me …*

"Instead, it was a gift. That's if we can rescue her." The "if" hung in the air.

"We *have* to. My mom and I were super close. I miss her more than anything." A catch in Ember's throat forced her to clear it with a cough.

"I'm sorry, Ember. You and your mom have been through a lot. But I think your mom has a lot of explaining to do. She kept you in the dark over a lot of things."

"I know. It was to protect me, though. I'm sure of it. She didn't want me to be sad or worried. When life is perfect— even if it's not real—it's easier to stay upbeat. She wanted me to be happy and to have the best life."

"But that's what's wrong with Tranquility. You have a right to know. You didn't even know anything about your dad. He's your parent, for crap's sake!"

"Did you know Shawny told me my dad died in an accident?"

"What? What kind of accident?"

"It was supposedly work-related. But he was a Plauditor. Plauditor's lives aren't dangerous. So, I don't know …"

"A Plauditor. You do come from a good family. You never met him?"

"I was just one when he died. And one more thing. He exposed some stuff going on at the genetics lab."

An upward beam of Xander's flashlight caught the way he raised his eyebrows. "Has to be a deep story. With Serpio, you might never know all of it."

"My mom's gonna tell me when I find her. I do need to know this stuff. You're right."

"I'm always right," Xander bragged with an exaggerated tease.

Ember shivered. "It's … cold." She pulled her jacket tighter around her body.

"It'll get colder as we go. Even our Plauditor jackets aren't going to help too much. I made it through the last time with only my REM clothes, so this is a luxury." He flaunted the garment by pulling it apart where it snapped in the front. "I can give you mine, Em."

The way he shortened her name made it sound somehow endearing and personal. For some reason, people always used her full name. And strangely, she'd never questioned it.

"I'm okay. I don't want you to be cold either."

"Like I said, I'll manage." He took off his jacket and threw it over her shoulders. "Anyway, I've got fire inside." He grinned, his smile white in the darkness.

Ember's teeth were chattering as she drew her arms gratefully through the sleeves of Xander's jacket. "Thanks." The temperature had to be less than thirty degrees. If it was going to get colder, she thought she would die of it.

"I'll try to keep your mind off the cold …"

"Good luck." Her whole body convulsed with shivers.

Xander chuckled. "Why should you never trust stairs?"

"What—*stairs*? I trust stairs."

"You shouldn't. They're always up to something."

Ember groaned, then giggled. "How far do we have to go? You have enough jokes to take my mind off twenty degrees?"

"Definitely. What does a house wear?"

"I know this one! Address!"

"You got any?"

"You heard the rumor going around about butter?"

"Butter! No …"

"Never mind. I shouldn't spread it."

"Geez, Ember. Okay … where should you go in the room if you're cold?"

"I wish there was somewhere. C'mon."

"In the corner. It's ninety degrees."

Xander laughed at his own joke, but when Ember shone her flashlight in his face to irritate him, she saw his blue-tinged lips. Hers couldn't be much better. "Xander, i-it-it's r-r-really cold."

"Yeah. But we'll make it."

"Come here." Ember gave him a beckoning wave.

"What?"

"Get over here. We need each other." She held out her arm.

Xander cocked his head and grinned. As they connected, Xander's aura, surging like fire, melted into her. Wrapped arm in arm, they made their way along together, united in body and spirit.

57

Will's Search

In the Plauditorium with Serpio and the Sciolists, Will was finding it difficult to pull himself away from the looping pictures on the newly revived broadcast feed. The picture of that Ember girl bothered him. First of all, wow … she was hot. It was hard to take his eyes off her image. His heart raced, and heat surged through his body.

Yet she was a criminal, one he wished he could take credit for capturing. That would make Serpio's day.

And yet his breath caught in his chest every time her photograph cycled through. His Alt measured his emotions, and they weren't happy ones. Conflicted and tormented.

He struggled with the strange magnetic draw. Analyzing his thoughts and feelings, he decided that the girl was simply evil. What else could unnerve him so much? Once he came to grips with his emotions, he moved away from the screen, intentionally diverting his thoughts.

"Will!"

He heard his name being called. Serpio needed him.

"Cameras are now up. Within the hour, the second shift Plauditors will arrive to man the stations." Serpio approached him, his steps quick.

"The city will be grateful. The Plauditors will work hard to cheer people up from this long ordeal," Will said. Then he added, "I—I miss being at work."

"A few more therapy sessions, and you'll be able to return to your job."

Will wanted to be a Plauditor again in the worst way, but he absolutely did not want any more therapy sessions. He didn't remember much about the one he'd had, but it was horrible. "Being a Plauditor would be awesome, sir."

"For now, you'll leave. Enough Plauditors are coming in." Serpio exhibited an irritating amount of smugness.

A crease appeared between Will's eyebrows. "With only one group, how will you man all the cameras later?"

"They'll work longer hours. They'll cover two stations at night. It's all we can do until we bring the others back."

Will nodded. "Still no sign of 'em?"

Serpio lowered his voice as if imparting a secret. "The tunnels go everywhere under the city. It will take time to find these people. Eventually, they will need food and water. It's only a matter of time."

"Magistrate … I'd like to help in the search," Will begged.

Serpio's eyes narrowed. "And why would I need you when I have a team of Sciolists?"

"I'd be one more person. And I'm motivated. To find the REMs would give me closure."

Will practically saw the wheels turning in the Magistrate's head about whether to grant his request. Serpio seemed to think for a minute, sizing him up, and then said, "I have no other plans for you today. You can search under the command of the Sciolist team. But if you do *anything* out of line, you will be punished. Do you understand?"

"Perfectly."

"If you did find the REMs, Will Verus, you'd secure your future."

Will smiled, his confidence growing. "The Plauditors—

they'll need a warm welcome back. I could be that person, too."

Serpio hesitated again, staring off into space, before finally agreeing. "That could work. In fact, it's a practical idea. I'm leaving for other duties. Make sure you are thorough. We'll be in touch."

Will felt as if he'd won first prize. At long last, he was fitting back into Tranquility's system of leadership. He would not—could not—let Serpio down.

Seconds later, Will met Nikos, the Sciolist in charge. "I'm joining the search team in the tunnels. Anything I should know?" Will was anxious to get started.

"Go below. You'll be an independent scout, but you will check in with me every thirty minutes. Don't get lost."

Not exactly a welcoming message, but Sciolists were trained to be stoic. Will made a beeline for the broadcast room. When he walked in, a twinge in his gut caught him off guard. Excitement, of course. What else could it be? He craved the chance to be useful.

A Sciolist directed him into the nook where the Lift ferried him down. That was an experience in itself, almost magical. Stepping into the secret room below, he paused and looked around. *What a strange little place. Who would ever know this was here?* He felt privileged, though, to be viewing this clandestine basement. His eyes took in the ladder that traveled up the wall to a circle on the ceiling. *That must open up somehow.* To his right loomed a six-foot-wide opening, where beyond was a hallway —or what he now knew was a tunnel.

As he entered the tunnel, he saw Sciolists deeper in. If he caught up, he could hang with them in the search. He picked up his pace, only to see them split off up ahead in two different directions. *Looks like I'm on my own until I can round that corner.* And searching wasn't difficult. Either he came across Plauditors and REMs or not. There were no places to hide.

He halted his progress, his attention caught by an irregular section on the wall. Boards that blended in with the tunnel's wooden trim … Painted an identical color, the spot was easy to miss. *Maintenance? Equipment? Pipes?* He tramped on by, his gaze centered ahead on the split in the tunnel's path. Then, he backtracked. Was it a closet? If that's what it was, it looked secure, but he had to wonder …

He ran his hands across the boards, but they didn't budge. Flat against the inside, even the edges were secured tightly against the wall. With his fist, he pounded against the surface in various spots. Yes, it was solid. He shrugged his shoulders, ready to let it go.

Without warning, Nikos appeared behind him. "What are you doing?" Nikos asked. "You're to be searching, not banging on the walls." Nikos looked pissed.

"Yeah … I mean, yes, sir. But is this … anything weird? What's behind here?"

"Not part of the tunnel system."

"But … shouldn't we check it out?"

Nikos studied Will for a few seconds before scrutinizing the wall. "We can open this. But only to rule out any possibilities." Nikos's tone was impatient.

"Can you spare a few Sciolists? Or tools?" Will said.

Nikos spoke into his Alt, summoning two others. As they arrived, Will realized he was the only one among the group who had no flashlight. On closer inspection, Will noticed that each flashlight was a tool. One end for illumination, and the other end had heavy, curved metal prongs.

Nikos sunk his tool into one of the boards, creating a hole with four forceful hits. A second Sciolist shone his flashlight beam into what should have been an open cavity.

"This is nothing," Nikos hissed. "Probably sealed off from the inside. Clearly a dead end."

Will's shoulders slumped. He thought he had found something to explore. He shrugged his shoulders and turned away.

The light beam from a second flashlight flashed across the area as the Sciolist holding it prepared to put it away.

"Wait —" Will's head swiveled back. The Sciolists were already moving back on their intended trail. Will stuck his fingers into the rupture. He felt an obstruction, yes. But he also felt space. "Hey—come back. I think I've found something," Will said with conviction. "It's not all blocked. You'd better open the whole thing."

Nikos grumbled but reluctantly waved his fellow Sciolists back to the site. "Five minutes—that's it. We won't tolerate nonsense."

"Understood." Will stepped back.

Within a few minutes, they had removed the boards to find a huge metal cylinder blocking the space.

"Just as I thought. Equipment," Nikos said, with a humph.

"Wait. May I?" Will took a flashlight from Nikos and bent his body into a sideways "s," craning his neck to see beyond. "There's … a lot of space back in there. We should move that thing and go in."

"A waste of time," Nikos replied.

Will argued, "It's worth a look. We don't know what's back there."

Nikos addressed him with a stony voice. "We can move the tank. That's all. Then we *move on.*"

"Fair enough," Will said, his patience becoming thin.

After several long minutes of shoving and sweating, the group moved the monstrosity enough to enter. Will pushed through first. "Shazz! Unbelievable …"

The Sciolists stood gaping at a cavernous space. Will wished he could have captured the looks on all their faces. He'd never seen Sciolists so dumbfounded.

Shining the flashlight around, Will gasped as he observed the multiple levels and vast ceilings. More shocking, though … other people had definitely been there. Footprints on concrete from dirty shoes were fresh. The four wandered further where disturbances in the dust-laden platforms were like a trail.

Will had struck gold. *Now the REMs and Plauditors can be found!* All they had to do was go deeper to wherever this bizarre tunnel went.

Nikos spoke into his Alt. "Reporting new findings. Possible hide-out."

"The Magistrate?" Will asked.

"Yes. Also a dozen other Sciolists. They're coming."

"Do we have to wait?" Will asked.

"No. We forge ahead."

They moved together through the dark, their flashlights illuminating the dust motes and mold. Whatever the place was, it wasn't fit for humans.

WILL GREW WEARY. They'd trudged along, checking out every possible new footprint, every single idea. For over six hours, they'd explored, up and down, over and under. The place stretched on and on into miles, and there were no signs of any REMs or Plauditors.

Niko said, his voice gravelly, "We should have found someone or something by now."

"We're not to the end yet," Will replied as he shook his head. "They *have* to be here. Don't you see? It's the perfect place to hole up."

"There's no noise. Nothing. Only dust." Nikos snorted with derision before scrutinizing Will as if he were an alien being. Will squirmed under his gaze, realizing his former understanding of a Sciolist's surly demeanor had been severely underestimated.

"Just—let's get to the end at least. Please." Weariness crawled through his every joint. Dirt had settled into creases on his face, and his discontent bruised his spirit.

Up ahead, they navigated past a wall and into a turn, discovering several rooms. *Empty.* And it was the end of the shaft—or whatever this was.

One by one, each of the group slumped to the floor, bone weary from walking. Other Sciolists would eventually catch up.

Will would have to admit defeat. His vision of restoring the Plauditors and apprehending the REMs faded. A bitter disappointment.

58

Xander's Defense

The journey through the tunnel had been long. With Ember, though, this trip was a pale comparison of his original one when he did it alone. Her company made the experience more of a golden opportunity rather than the horror he had suffered when he'd been exiled.

Even Ember couldn't temper the shock of opening the tunnel's final door to The Outside. Just as Xander remembered, the sun beat down like a demon. The scorching heat was an immediate thaw for the tunnel's deep freeze. It was oppressive, like the very air was dead.

A moon-like landscape surrounded them. Unlike their trip to The Outside in the "death wagon" when they took the uncooperative Plauditors to their fate, there were no trees here —dead or otherwise.

Ember blinked against the glare and shielded her eyes, saying, "We're definitely not in Tranquility anymore."

"Yeah. Fun, huh?" Xander sat on the ground and patted the spot next to him. "We should rest—at least a little."

"We won't melt?" Ember slouched down onto the gray-brown dirt.

"We'll melt whether we rest or not."

"Is it always this hot?"

"No. The temperature changes with the wind. Extremes. When it picks up, it will blow cold. Weirdest thing ever."

"Whichever it is, I need water." Ember pawed her pack, looking for the pull-apart opening.

"You should wait. I know you're thirsty, but we gotta make our water last. Once we're out here a while, you'll need it more." Xander leaned back on his elbows and kept adjusting his position like he was trying but failing to get more relaxed.

Ember set her rucksack aside, resignation on her face. "So, the coordinates … can we use our Alts to find the spot?"

"No. We only have limited function. All we have is a map with a compass app. It'll show the coordinates, but because Ava disabled GPS, it won't show exactly where to go."

"That was so we can't be tracked, but that really bites." Ember wiped her brow. Already, she was sweating. She gazed up at the sun as if to challenge its heat.

"All we know is what Ava told us. *This* tunnel's coordinates are 39° N, -84° W." He examined his Alt to discover more exact information. "Here. We have to find 39.4403° N, 84.3622° W. Should be about twenty miles." Xander held out a hand to help her up. "Shall we?"

"Didn't we just sit down?"

A rivulet of sweat rolled down Xander's face. "Yeah. But we want to get as far as we can. Night'll come, and then we'll want to stop."

"Another few hours, and I'll be totally wiped out. Night or not." Ember already sounded as if every word was an effort.

"Probably. We'll do what we can."

They struck out, keeping to the northwest. A couple of miles seemed like an eternity. The flat, barren landscape made all sense of direction vanish. Oftentimes, they walked in silent misery, but Ember interrupted when she complained about the variation in temperatures and how her skin felt. Finally, at a weedy, skeletal bush, they sat down for a break and some food and water.

"Xander, I don't know how you survived this," Ember said. "How did you find anybody?"

"I saw the smoke. From the burn site. I followed that. Other people—other REMs—must have done that, too. Then, I found the Camp."

"Is that around here?" Ember took a swig of water.

"No. It's east." Xander pointed in the opposite direction. "Not that there's much there. Just some burned-out, collapsed buildings. Scarce food. I'd have been thrilled to have had this." He held up his protein bar before taking a bite.

Xander caught Ember looking at him in wonder before she lowered her eyes. He imagined he saw a deep respect and concern cross her beautiful face. And yes, even in this miserable wilderness where they drew dirt and sunburn to them like magnets, she still looked stunning. Her softly fired hair, shining in the sun, wisped about her face in tiny strands, loosened from a practical, black, elastic band. He slightly smiled as he saw a few freckles being born.

Ember raised her gaze, her eyes softhearted and sympathetic. "It's a wonder you're alive at all."

"Too hard to kill me," Xander joked. But he didn't miss the nuance. She suddenly seemed to appreciate that he was still breathing. He'd take it. But he wanted more.

Ember wrapped a loose tendril of hair around her finger. "I … I want to thank you. You didn't need to come with me. I'm grateful. Whether I find my mom or not, I owe you more than I can repay."

"I didn't think twice. I told you. I'm here for you. Did you think I would let you go alone? Or allow you to give up trying to find your mom?"

"Well, thanks—" The words fell like a stone, Ember's gaze suddenly focused on the horizon.

No more than fifty yards away, a human figure trudged in

their direction. The man—if that is who it seemed—staggered and zigzagged as if drunk. Xander scrambled up from his position and grabbed the rifle, aiming it in the intruder's direction, a scowl on his face. He assumed a militant stance, his feet spread apart, his body tense, unmoving.

"Who—who *is* that?" Ember pressed her fingers to her lips.

"I think we're about to be introduced," Xander said, hoping he'd be able to scare away their unanticipated company.

The person stumbled toward them, drawing closer. The unknown waved, still unsteady on his feet. A voice cried out, but the utterances dropped into the sluggish atmosphere, and Xander couldn't understand the words.

"Get behind me, Em." Xander barked the command.

"Is that really necessary?" Ember responded, but she stood behind Xander all the same.

"Hey! Hey—are you real?" the man approaching them yelled. He kept advancing, his feet picking up the pace as he grew nearer. He stumbled a few steps every couple of yards.

"We're real," Xander called back.

Ember hollered, "We're only passing through."

Finally, the traveler came close enough for Xander to completely see him. No doubt the man was a REM. Xander regarded the man's clothes, the REM uniform, its burlap-like texture and cocoa color designed as a t-shirt and shorts. He knew personally what those clothes felt like, the humiliation of them, the discomfort. The guy's hair, a sandy brown, lay on his head in oily clumps. Reddened skin, burnt by the sun and chafed by the wind, gave him a crispy appearance. The guy wiped tears away as he trudged into their area.

Immediately, Xander felt empathy, but he was also on his guard. As the outcast came to a stop in front of them, he rocked back and forth, his eyes wild. He glanced around furtively, as if expecting something or someone to materialize behind him.

"You're ... REMs?" the guy asked, his glassy eyes shining. "You're—you're not ... dressed ... like REMs." All at once, he turned sharply to his right and yelled, "You—you there! You ... stay away!"

Xander blinked in surprise and clenched his teeth. Was something else out there he hadn't seen? Another person? A threat?

The stranger turned back to address them, now oddly calm. "There's a man ... with big fangs." He used his hands to gesture at his own teeth. "Following me. Gonna kill me." He covered his eyes with his hands. "See? Got to hide."

"Who's this man?" Xander said, a tickle down his spine causing him to jerk. He steadied the rifle, keeping it at the ready. If there was another threat ...

"The man from the moooooon," the Outsider replied in a whisper. "Can't ... let him find me. Or *you*." He laughed, then, under his breath but without mirth.

Scanning the area around them to be sure, Xander realized the ex-Trank was clearly deranged. He wasn't making any sense.

"Tick-tock goes the clock!" The wanderer spun in a circle, his face to the sky. "The numbers lie ..." Coming to a stop, he swayed on his feet. He froze abruptly when he took in their clothes. "You ... are ... Plauditors." A self-satisfied smile lit his face, revealing yellow teeth.

To Xander's irritation, Ember stepped out from behind him. "We're from the city. Not REMs—not Plauditors, either. We're ... Well, we're renegades. Criminals, actually ..."

Xander hadn't yet lowered the rifle. "How long you been out?"

"Don't know ... Can't remember ..." The man's gaze rested on their packs, his expression greedy. He gestured to the black bags. "You got food? Water?" Desperation tightened around his words.

Ember moved closer to Xander. "Yes, but only for our journey. We can spare a little, I'm sure ... right, Xander?"

"What's your name?" Xander asked, his tone softening.

"O-Ogden."

"Well, Ogden. You've been on your own too long. There's a camp out east." Xander lowered the rifle a shade, moving it slightly to his right in a directional gesture. "You can find a few others there. We can't give you much, but a protein bar and a couple of small water bottles will help."

"That's ... that's it? A p-p-protein bar and a couple small waters? You got more than that!" Ogden accused, sounding suddenly sane.

"So sorry, dude. I'd give you more, but we need what we have." Xander was sincere. He really was sorry. But sympathy could only go so far. He had Ember to protect, and they'd not survive their own journey without the supplies they carried.

Ember rummaged in her pack, pulling out the promised items and holding them out. "Here. I hope they help you."

Ogden snatched the protein bar out of Ember's hands and tore into it like a lion eating prey. Guzzling the water so quickly it leaked from his mouth, he emptied the container and hurled the empty bottle across the terrain.

Knowing the man's state of mind, Xander wasn't waiting for a thank you. "Okay, then, Ogden. Go on out east."

Without warning, the man charged. "Food is mine!" He rammed into Xander so hard that Xander lost his footing. The ground met his body with unexpected force, knocking the rifle out of his hands where it flew several feet away. Xander reached out his arms to trip the man, but without success. Ogden swept up Xander's pack before starting to dive for Ember's.

Ember leapt for the rifle. Sliding her hands across it, she yelled, "Stop! Stop right there!"

When Ogden growled and lunged for the other pack, Ember pulled the trigger. The blast echoed across the expanse of empty terrain. It easily missed its mark, but Ogden's face twisted in shock, and he dropped the sack.

"Go! Get!" Ember yelled. Her voice was fierce, her expression dark.

The REM turned away. "Don't forget me … I can do magic." He put his fingers in the air and wiggled them before heading off, humming and mumbling under his breath.

Xander sat up and rose to his feet. "Ember, you okay?" His first thought was of her. Dazed by what she'd done, he realized that, for the second time that day, Ember had saved them from disaster.

Xander approached Ember and threw his arms around her. He captured her smoothly in an almost-desperate hug, immersing his face in her hair. Ember tucked her own into the warmth of his chest. They swayed together, both breathing hard.

Finally, feeling nervous he'd overstepped, he pulled back to meet her eyes. Beneath his gentle smile, he said, "Ya know you told me you owe me? Well, I'd say we're even."

59

Ember's Dependence

With his arms around her, Xander's flaming orange aura, fueled by thankfulness and adoration, burned into her. What she began to label his "chi," the silver lining, vibrated against her like the force of the Maglev train. It was an unwelcome, absolute invasion into her personal space. And yet … when he released her, taking that wave of intensity with him, she felt bereft. A little less whole. Like she'd been robbed of something critical to her ability to breathe.

What really was it that was buoying her up? Self-worth after her heroic gesture? Was it the adrenaline rush? No. What she felt in Xander's arms was nothing like that. Nothing like pride. More like …

Xander shot her a sheepish look. "Ember? I'm sorry I—I overreacted with the hug. Didn't mean to embarrass you."

Ember dropped her eyes, concerned he'd recognize that the blush on her face wasn't from embarrassment. "It's okay. That guy was horrible."

"I should have protected you. I'm sorry. He was out of control." Xander clenched his fists as if trying to crush the whole experience.

"Yeah. Out of his mind. Poor guy. I feel sorry for him."

"Me too. It's … hard out here. I wish we could've helped him more."

Ember's empathic radar had picked up Xander's sympathy for the Outsider, even during the worst of the encounter. With Xander's mental defenses down, it had allowed Ogden to seize a vulnerable moment. She was surprised that Xander of all people was capable of so much concern for another person. He was beginning to look incredibly human and not like the miscreant she'd always thought he was.

Xander reached for the rifle still in Ember's hands. "Maybe *you* should be the one carrying that thing. But undoubtedly, I'm a better aim." He chuckled.

"You sayin' I can't shoot?" Ember said with mock indignation, passing the gun. She was proud and astonished at herself at how she'd stepped up so boldly with the rifle.

"You *can* shoot. And that's more than I imagined you could do." He winked.

"Hmmm. Still underestimating me …" Ember put her hands on her hips.

Xander suddenly got serious. "Never."

"So, let's see what you've got."

"What?"

"Race you." Ember narrowed her eyes, looking ahead into the wilderness. "That direction, right?"

"There's no marker to race to, Em."

"Say we run 'til one of us can't run any further." She challenged him with her stare.

"Not a chance you'll—"

Ember grabbed her rucksack and bolted. "Just try and catch me!" she yelled, the words caught in a sudden icy wind.

After fumbling with the rifle and retrieving his supply bag from where Ogden threw it out of reach, Xander took off after her.

Ember's feet left footprints in the dirt that sent dust into Xander's eyes. "Ember! We shouldn't separate!" he yelled.

She laughed, not worried at all. He probably would catch her easily, although his running with the rifle made it an unfair match. Despite that, he wasn't far behind. A push from a light wind propelled her forward.

"Ember! Stop! We're gonna get too tired!" She heard Xander's voice a few yards behind her. He was closing in fast.

Not ready to give up, she sprinted on harder. She grinned. She was cantering like a gazelle. The run was freeing; she didn't remember a time when she could let herself go, unburdened, to feel the breeze in her hair. The last time she'd run was when she was fleeing the Magistrate, escaping from his mansion, only to be captured like a prisoner and shown off. She shuddered at the memory, pushing it down, and concentrated on the joy of the run. If only she could sprint the whole way to where her mom was, shorten the trip and make it a happy memory. With each stride forward, she dreamed about that moment when they would finally be reunited. And Xander would be there to help her celebrate … The thought made her smile grow wider. Tiring now and not hearing Xander's pleas, she turned her head to see where he was behind her.

In a split second, before she knew what was happening, she tumbled forward. She scrambled to stay on her feet. Balance betrayed her, and she careened into a broad ditch, her hands skidding along in an excruciating slide across the ground. The pain on her forearms and hands screamed before she did. They stung like fiery pins. Hot tears spilled onto her face.

Oww. Oh … She moved an inch at a time to pick herself up. Her regret and chagrin, though, were as intense as her physical suffering.

Xander … he would help …

Sitting up, she dusted off her hands and examined her

wounds. Blood flowed down her arms and into her palms. She shook out her hands before using them gingerly to lift the rest of her body up.

Still unable to stand, she looked around. *Where—?*

Her eyes, cloudy with tears and pain, finally focused on Xander. He was maybe twenty feet away. Why was he just standing there? Was he playing a stupid game? He surely wasn't helping her get up out of the ditch.

Her gaze sharpened as she fully raised her body up, her arms now level with the top of the cursed ravine. She sucked in a breath. First, because she felt stabbing pain in her ankle. And then because of what she saw. Xander was still standing, but he was a statue. His gaze flickered her way, but then, he trained his eyes on the ground. A mammoth red and black snake reared its head, preparing to strike.

Ember screamed, concentrating with all her might, hoping she could rewind to the time before she took off running. Her emotions were running high. It could work. Her heart pounded, her fear and pain mounting.

But nothing happened. She sat firmly, injured; Xander faced the snake. She closed her eyes. *Please, please, don't get attacked, Xander!*

A startling boom tore through the air. Quick and harsh.

Ember jumped, her pulse racing in her temples. Wide-eyed, she gaped at Xander now lowering the rifle. He dropped his head, his shoulders following suit, tension draining from his entire being. He stepped back as if to distance himself from the experience before lifting up the snake in a celebratory gesture to dangle it limply from his fingers. He tossed it away before his eyes lit on Ember. The race was over, but he barreled toward her like his life depended on it.

"What—what—oh ..." Xander moved to her side to pull her up on her feet.

"Xander! You're ... okay? The snake ...?"

"Are you—? Shazz, Ember. You're bleeding everywhere!"

Ember felt his distress collide with her pain. As he tried to lift her, she cried, "I—I'm—My ankle …"

"Shazz. You're really hurt." Worry creased his forehead, and perspiration beaded there. He went for her bag a few feet away.

Ember wasn't sure whether the first aid supplies were in hers or if Ava had chosen his. Luckily, her sack contained medical supplies.

First, he wiped off the blood with a couple wet wipes. Ember cringed in pain, the alcohol burning her wounds. Next, he grabbed the bandages along with some antiseptic lotion. Setting to work, he applied the medicine to her scraped skin and then bandaged her arms with gauze from a roll, taping it gently to her skin. "Sorry," he murmured when she jerked at the pressure.

"I know. At least my right hand is less messed up," she said ruefully. She felt his whole heart in his care. It made her swallow—hard. He was starting to be way too important. And amazing.

Xander gestured back from where he faced off with the snake. "Hold on while I get my bag."

"I'm not goin' anywhere," Ember replied, gesturing to her ankle.

Dashing the distance, Xander snatched up his sack in an instant, turning abruptly to run back. But instead of returning, he lingered there, looking for something in the dirt before he stooped to pick something up.

What are you doing, Xander? Ember was growing impatient. Her pain mounting, she reached down to feel her ankle. Swollen. Definitely swollen. Reaching into the bag to see if she could find a brace or another kind of wrap, she rummaged around. Sure enough, there was a stretchy bandage and a clip.

Ember held up her discovery as Xander approached. "Could you help me wrap my foot?"

As Xander approached, he dropped his bag a couple of feet away. "Of course," he said, kneeling for the task. He looped the binding around her ankle, securing it with the clip. "Now for sure you can't outrun me," he joked, giving her a weak smile. "Can you stand at all?"

"I'll … try." She made a valiant effort while leaning on him for support. A lone tear slid down her cheek.

Grabbing his bag and hers, he propped her up by putting his other around her waist. A few steps forward, and Ember grimaced. "I don't know how I'm gonna do this," she moaned.

"A little at a time, Em. It'll take us longer, but we'll get there."

"Ugh. Why did I *do* that? I'm sorry. I'm such a klutz."

"Shit happens. Not like you meant to do it."

"If …" She took a hobbling step. "If we go this slow, we'll run out of food before we get there." Her face paled at the statement. Inside her head, she was freaking out.

"We'll just have to eat less. Or …" Xander looked at her with mischief in his eyes.

"Or what?" she said, frustrated. "Eat each other?"

He chuckled. "When I went back for my bag, I got the snake to take with us. It's food, baby."

Ember cringed. Because of her stupidity, they'd have to eat reptiles? "Hope you know how to cook that. I draw the line at eating that thing raw."

"Got experience. Master chef here."

Going was sluggish as they hobbled along. Twenty feet seemed forever. More than the real-life slow-mo, it was exhausting. Ember knew how much Xander was suffering, carrying the bags and the rifle under his free arm and also supporting her weight. And not only did she need his support, but as much as she denied it, she enjoyed it.

"If you see anything we can use for a crutch or cane, let

me know," Xander huffed, tossing the sweat off his face with a toss of his head.

"Okay," Ember replied, "but I have to concentrate. It's … painful."

"Wait—did you look for any pain meds in the packs?"

Ember shook her head. "I didn't see any."

"Time to stop for a rest anyway." Xander dropped the bags and gun, then lowered Ember to the ground like she was made of glass. Handing her a container of water, he cautioned her to drink slowly.

Xander peered into his pack and rummaged in it until he held up a small bottle, which he shook. "Painkillers."

"Thank the stars." Ember threw one in her mouth, the psychological effect already helping, and scanned the area around them, hoping to see some sort of makeshift crutch.

Nothing.

"Is there any way to lighten your load?" she asked.

"It's a lot of weight to carry and awkward. I'm wondering …" He measured her with his eyes from head to toe. "We'll go faster if you hold the packs and the rifle and I hold *you*."

A flurry of butterflies flew kamikaze in her stomach. "Carry me? Can you?"

He snapped up his own rucksack and shimmied it onto his back, the cords looped around his arms. "If you hold one pack and the rifle …" He placed the bag on her lap and put the rifle in her hands. "It'll still be slow-going, but"—Xander swooped her up in his arms—"both of us are gonna be a lot more comfortable. And we'll make better time."

"Xander, you'll be—" she protested.

"Shhh," he said, softly. "It's the only way."

Her hundred-and-ten-pound frame rested easily in his arms, and luckily, her pack, compared to his, wasn't too heavy. But she worried about how long they could walk without Xander becoming exhausted.

As they traversed the hostile terrain, she had to admit,

though, that he had been right. They were moving more quickly than the hobbled effort earlier. Talking became a luxury with Xander's effort and Ember's pain, although the tablets had helped take the edge off.

To her relief, the medication was working almost instantaneously. Her thoughts scattered into the past, her mind drifting to the euphoric times she'd had with Will. And they were magical, intoxicating. That first kiss. His restoring her after her mother's 'death.' His smile, unlike any she had ever seen. Her eyes filled with tears, and she frowned. She couldn't let the memories in. As she refocused her thoughts on Xander, she compared the two boys. Total opposites. Will, like an angel, now fallen. Xander, like a sinner, earning redemption. Which attraction was more powerful?

Even though it had only been a few days, her separation from Will seemed like a year. She was already feeling she wasn't the same girl as the one she'd been with him, naïve and afraid. She had been dependent on Will's promises and his purity. Would her heart skip a beat if she saw him again? Would she fall back into his arms if she had the chance? Or was Xander's strength, experience with hard knocks, and blatant sex appeal more what she craved?

At about every half-mile, they rested before journeying on, using the opportunity to chow down some nutrition and drink.

"You feeling any better?" Xander asked, wiping the sweat from his brow.

"Definitely. I'm sure I'll be carrying you in no time." Ember teased.

Xander chuckled, extending his legs out in front of him on the sandy dirt. "I like your spirit."

"I don't know what I'd do without you," Ember said, her

tone serious and warm. She reached her arms up in a stretch. Her appreciation was too intense to meet his gaze.

Out of the corner of her eye, she saw his grin. He seemed to be enjoying her debt of gratitude to him. "Baby, I was made for this," he kidded.

Ember surveyed the changing sky. It was by now late afternoon, the sun dropping its ball of fury on the edge of the horizon. "Won't be long until it's dark. You ready to go again?"

"Yeah. Maybe we can make another mile before night falls." He picked her up, juggling her in his arms. "Oh no," he said suddenly before taking his first step.

"What? What is it?" A touch of panic pushed its way in.

"You definitely gained ten pounds during our stop."

"Shut up!" she said, giving him a playful slap, the banter a welcome distraction.

Leaning into his grasp, she adjusted herself, seeking a more comfortable position. Her curves seemed to suddenly melt into his body in perfect alignment. Tighter up against him than ever before, she felt the ripples in his abdomen as they strained successfully to hold her. His arms, too, contracted around her. Strong and secure, the hard muscles flexed with purpose and toughness. She laid her head against him, this time feeling the beat of his heart, the solidity of his chest. Gazing up at him, she studied the pulse in his throat, quick with effort and a flare of desire. The line of his jaw, determined and yet prey to a quick grin, sharpened a face that, until now, she hadn't realized was so incredibly good-looking.

She gasped, soft and shallow, but held on to the air as if she had dropped into a fathomless pool and feared drowning. An intense yearning lit her up inside until she thought she would explode.

He caught her stare, and she caught his emotions, blazing with sudden heat. He stopped walking, and his eyes penetrated hers, holding and searching them for a long moment.

"Em … if you want to get where we're going, don't look at me that way."

Ember raised an eyebrow, almost as if she issued a provocative challenge before smiling gently and averting her gaze. "Xander …"

"What?" he replied, his voice thick with longing.

"I think … those pills … are working," she said, her words sluggish. She closed her eyes, and sleep stole her away.

60

Ember's Discovery

The shadowy figures were back, facing off, this time carrying weapons with fiery points. Applause and the noise of a crowd grew louder ... Her mother stood off to the side, beckoning her to follow her rather than stay in the place where the two silhouettes shouted at one another. Instead, she tried to run closer to what she knew was a dangerous fight. A loudspeaker blared, but the sound was distorted; the words sounded blurred, a jumble of indecipherable highs and lows. Only one word was clear: Death. She turned in circles, tears streaming down her face, emotional agony, as she struggled to help whoever was in trouble. "Stop! Please stop!" she shrieked at the top of her lungs.

"Em ... Ember." Someone shook her gently. "You're yelling in your sleep. Wake up. Everything's okay."

Tossing back and forth like a rowboat at high sea, she was roused from her dream by the voice. She blinked languidly and attempted to open her eyes a few times, the dream state trying to lure her back. When she finally fully woke, she found Xander crouched next to her, his knees up against her thighs, his hand still on her shoulder. She smiled reassuringly at the look on his face, his brows drawn together in concern, before she sat up. She drew the blanket around her as much for comfort from the dream as protection from the severe chill in the air. Always intense heat or freakish cold.

"You okay? You were really thrashing and hollering." Xander touched her on the arm in an effort to comfort her.

"Sorry I was so crazy." Ember shook her head, almost as if she could shake off the memory.

"Not that you can help it. I was just concerned, that's all. No apology needed." Xander drew his jacket tighter around himself.

Ember took in the situation around them. A tiny fire burned a few yards away. The aroma of cooking food wafted in the air. A survival blanket—a thin, shiny one—lay across her. But she was also resting in a compact, earthy "bed." It was a ravine about the size of the cursed one she'd tumbled into, an incredibly perfect size for her. And, she noticed, this one was even more unique; it had peculiar, smooth sand on the bottom, making it warm and almost soft.

"Wow … practically the comforts of home. How'd you do all this?" Ember said, unable to keep the awe from her voice.

"Trust me—lucky find. The sun went down; it was instant dark. I saw no good place to make camp. At all. So, I kept walking. Not sure I'd made it even a mile more like I'd hoped. Then I couldn't believe it … I saw a few pieces of wood. You were still asleep, so I scouted around for more. No luck, but I had enough to make that." He gestured to the cheery little blaze.

"I thought Ava put some fire starters in our kit."

"She did, but she couldn't pack wood, just a lighter and small kindling. That fire won't last, but it's ours for as long as it does." He walked over and warmed his hands by the fire. "It gets really cold out here during the night, so I didn't want to make it right away. Thought I'd wait 'til midnight—or 'til I thought we'd freeze—before setting it up. Then, I got hungry." He grinned, a sparkle in his eye that mimicked the fire. "Gourmet snake for dinner. Just for you. And don't just jump up," he teased, holding his palms out in a mock "stop" gesture. "I'll bring it to you."

Ember chuckled at his joke, but her stomach growled simultaneously. She was starving! Whatever barbecued snake tasted like, it didn't matter. It had to be better than another protein bar.

With a flourish, he cut a slice of the snake with a knife he'd laid aside on a jagged rock. "Sorry. No plates, ya know. But my hands are clean." He held them up for inspection.

He glided over to her side, gifting her with a couple of wet towelettes. She badly wanted to run the sweet-smelling wipes all over her body from head to toe. She'd been sweaty most of the day and was dirty after the long trek. But for now, with food at hand, she scrubbed her face, neck, and hands before tossing the wipes aside and reaching for the food.

Instead, he held a two-inch piece up to her mouth. "Bite it. But only a small bite—it's chewy."

His fingers brushed her lips, and she felt a thrill, an unanticipated tingle. Didn't they have a supercharged moment mere minutes before she fell asleep?

She looked at him questioningly before obediently tearing off a piece with her teeth. "I kinda thought this would taste better. It's so bland! Like, it doesn't really taste like anything."

"I know," Xander said, watching her chew. "But it'll save our food supplies if you can tolerate it. And watch for the tiny bones. Like with fish, they're in there, and I can't get them out." He fed her another piece, laughing at her reaction as she grudgingly munched on it, making faces.

"I don't think I'm all that hungry after all." Truth was, the snake was really gross.

"At least finish this piece. You have to keep up your strength." He held out another three-inch-long slice.

This time, she snatched it from him. "Okay … I'll eat it. But only because I know you're right. I can't get weak." She was grateful they had the extra food. No matter the taste and texture, it would be the closest thing to a meal. The thought of running out of rations in this place was worse than consuming the yucky fare. "Are you going to eat some or what?"

"I did already. While you were sleeping."

"Sure," she said sarcastically. "For all I know, you ate up all the good stuff."

He smiled, the corners of his mouth creating a small dimple in his lower cheek that she'd not noticed before. "Not sure what you're talkin' about. What's the 'good stuff'? Didn't know we had anything good."

Ember finished the piece of meat—if that's what anyone would call it—and rubbed the leg of her injured ankle with both hands. "In case you'd like to know, I'm beginning to have pain again." She rolled her pant leg up to her knee.

"More pain meds, then?" Xander reached for her bag.

"No. I can't take them yet. And they obviously make me sleepy." She would simply have to do the best she could with the discomfort. Making her way down her leg with her hands, she touched her foot and grimaced.

"Well, it is nighttime, so … you could take more. And we both need to sleep. I'm exhausted." Straightening out his own silver blanket, he looked as if he was ready to crash near the fire. "We have another long, hard day tomorrow."

"Will you stay awake until I can take my next dose?" Ember asked. She didn't want to lie there without anyone to talk to. The whole place was weird and even creepier at night. Snakes and random REMs around them emphasized the illusion that they were truly alone.

"Yeah, sure. As long as you need." He seemed to appraise her ankle as Ember once again rubbed her hands down her leg and started to ineffectively straighten the wrapping, now loosened from her restless sleep. "Here. I can redo that." In spite of the cold, he ditched his jacket and rolled up his sleeves.

Xander moved to the base of her earthy bed and sat. Taking her injured leg in his hands, he laid it in his lap and smoothed his hands lightly over her foot before his fingers brushed her ankle. Appearing to take extra care not to hurt her, he slowly unwound the binding.

To anyone else, he would seem to be the picture of concentration. With particular patience, he wound the bandage back around her heel and painstakingly started up her ankle, his expression one of forced attention. His chest rose and fell forcefully enough that Ember could see the effort. He swallowed hard before a shaky smile trembled on his lips.

That smile made Ember's pulse suddenly forget it had a job to do. *Oh, no. I'm … I'm attracted to him?* She fought every fiber in her body—every mitochondrion—every brain cell for being so attracted to him. Closing her eyes, she summoned a deep breath, holding it in, and then looked skyward, forcing her gaze off his face. Her thoughts wouldn't line up. Every time she tried to align one, it tumbled down, scattering the rest in a beautiful mess. She was slipping, losing the ability to keep what she was feeling repressed.

Xander's fingers began to quiver as he wound the band further up her leg, fastening the clip. His aura flared red, and his emotions flooded out of him, bathing her in a shower of barely restrained desire. When he finally met her eyes, his fingertips lingering and then resting at a point on her skin, she lost control. She reached out and covered his hand with her own.

"Ember …" he breathed, her name both a question and a sound of desperation.

She pulled him forward across her, her eyes never leaving his. He touched her face, and she shuddered. Then, as he drew her closer, her breath seemed to leave her body. With a delicate and deliberate stroke, he traced his fingers down her neck to the dent at its base. She shivered as he traced back up her neck and slowly around her lips.

"Xander, *please*, kiss me." With a brief, languid smile, he opened his mouth against hers. When he kissed her, her heart exploded, revealing a feverish hunger she had unsuccessfully fought and denied. It was the kind of kiss that made her believe she only needed that one thing to survive.

Xander needed no more invitations to kiss her. He kissed her again and again until she could barely catch her breath, his lips hot yet so tender against hers.

Xander whispered, his breath tickling her ears, "You don't know how long I've wanted this. How long I've imagined it."

"And is it what you imagined?" Ember murmured, allowing his aura to leave traces on her body.

"Not even close. Way beyond what I could imagine."

She closed her eyes, falling deeper into each kiss, rediscovering life in her body that she'd buried with her thoughts of Will.

After her lips were puffy from his kisses, he pulled his face away, gazing into her face. His eyes searched hers, so focused and full of light, yet questioning.

She wrapped her arms around his neck and pressed against him tighter. His kisses moved to her neck, sending shivers down her spine. His hand traveled from her thigh to her waist, caressing her almost reverently. A sigh escaped her lips. She drew his hands to her breasts, heard his gasp, and knew he felt her heart pounding out of her chest. He kissed her again, then, more deeply, his tongue wrapping around hers with a sensuality she didn't know existed.

She tilted her head back to more easily grab his shirt, which he helped her pull up over his head. Her fingers rippled across his chest, and then she kissed him where a modest patch of hair lay across his collarbone. She felt a spike in his pulse, his heart hammering in a rush.

He tightly gathered the bottom of her shirt in his hands and raised his eyebrows, waiting for her reaction.

"It's okay," Ember murmured against his neck. "I trust you."

A deep, ragged sigh escaped his lips, as if he was overwhelmed with emotion. Then, he rolled to the side, breathless. "I can't—I can't ..." He sat up and turned away. The flames of the fire illuminated his bare back, his skin glistening with the soft sheen of perspiration.

A gust of icy wind danced across Ember's body, and she shivered. But it wasn't the cold. It was the rampant desire and extraordinary fear. She was frightened out of her mind at how desperately she not only wanted him, but needed him. His confidence. His charisma. His desire for her. He absolutely unraveled her.

And he wanted her. She felt it powerfully. But she knew. The moment had become too hot, and if they didn't slow it down, in the uncertain world in which they lived, she could lose him, and she would never, ever recover.

61

Xander's Confession

Xander composed himself as best he could before he finally stood and walked back to Ember. For a moment he said nothing, just gazed down at her as she sat, her eyes lowered, as if she couldn't bear to look at him.

He dropped to the ground, took Ember's face in his hands, and gently turned her head to engage her with his eyes. The passion still ran wild inside him, but he refused to let it take over.

"Xander, I —" She started to speak, but he shook his head,

"Ember, I had to stop. I could've and would've taken you completely. And believe me, I want nothing more than to do that. Do you have any idea how long I've been waiting? Hoping for your attention? Jealous of Will for having your heart?"

She nodded her head, the shine of repressed tears glossing her eyes. "I know. I do know. I just didn't know or accept what *I* was feeling." Her voice was too quiet in the stillness, the atmosphere suddenly heavy and oppressive.

"And that is?" A smirk lifted the right corner of his mouth.

"I—I— You make me crazy."

He could almost feel the white heat in his eyes, aware his whole face bloomed with his most provocative smile. "I'm excited about that. But …" He stalled.

"What?"

"I want you. But not *only* in that way. I've had … girls. But you … I want you to be *mine*. Mine no matter what happens, not because we're in the middle of some frikkin' desert where we could die."

"Xan …" Ember reached out and touched his face, making him insane again. "Are you telling me you *love* me?"

He grinned and then dropped his head in an uncharacteristic, self-conscious movement. Her hand still on his face, he placed his hand over hers. "Love's a strong word. I feel like we're meant to be together. That we're a perfect combination. And that I care more for you than anyone I ever have." He tried to moderate the intensity in his voice. "But … you? I know you had a relationship with Will, and he hurt you. You saw him change. *I'll* never hurt you. I'll never change." With those words, his voice became vehement.

"What I had with Will was not … like this. He's beautiful. He took my breath away, yeah. I'll admit that. But more than that, he was there for me. Protective. Responsible. He came to my rescue and sacrificed a lot. It was a deep connection, even though it happened quickly. I thought I loved him." Xander noted a catch in her throat. She tilted her head thoughtfully before taking both of Xander's hands in hers. "At least, that's how it seemed … but love's not the same with each person, I guess. It feels different with you—more real. Not like a simple crush at all."

Xander didn't understand whether she was admitting she just wanted him physically or if she felt the way he did. Or if she yet needed more time to get over Will's betrayal. He'd need to take it slow. *If anything happens to mess this up, I'll be ruined.*

He nodded, even though he was confused and out of his mind with this girl, but he wanted to make sure she understood where he was coming from. "So … that's why I couldn't take things to the next level. I respect you, and I—" He wanted to say he loved her, but it wasn't the proper time. And did he? It was the closest thing he knew to it, but he'd not say something he wasn't sure of himself. "When it happens again, it needs to be right."

"Does that mean you won't kiss me again?" Ember asked, a trace of longing in her voice.

He flirtatiously winked at her, aware of the effect. "I will definitely kiss you again. But not today. I have a lot of cooling down to do."

Ember smiled back at him, her face irresistibly alight. "Don't make me wait too long."

A grin escaped from the face he was trying to keep serious. "Right now, we're getting some shut-eye. I—we—need *sleep*. Time for you to pop another pain pill, too." He rummaged in the bag and then sprinkled a pill into her hand. He offered her water and, bowing with mock gallantry and snapping the blanket smooth, covered her up.

To behave himself with her right there would be a feat, but he lay close beside her, knowing the night would only get colder and they would need warmth.

XANDER STARED up at the moon thinking until he drifted off. He didn't know how long he'd been asleep before a snarl woke him. Jerking to full alertness, he grabbed the rifle where it lay at his side. A shiver went up his spine. No question about it. He'd heard it before—a Greelox.

Adrenaline coursed through his body, making his movement to stand almost meteoric. Ember slept on, oblivious to the danger threatening them.

He'd survived an encounter with a Greelox before. But he'd had a team and a giant boulder to shove on top of it. Here, he knew with a sinking heart, it would be only him if the beast came their way. And Ember—she'd be helpless. Sitting prey.

Not that he'd thought he'd been brave last time, but now, there was Ember. He wondered, *should I wake her? Should I try to run with her—get out of here?* But carrying her and running … not a smart idea. Best to hope the beast wouldn't come nearer and then defend themselves if it did.

Again, a roar came. Did he imagine it, or was it closer? Xander stood very still, listening, to best determine where it lurked. The creature sounded like it prowled somewhere within a hundred yards of them, but he could see nothing that far out in the dark. He had his rifle ready.

He paced a few steps back and forth and then leaned forward in the direction of the sound to be proactive. His hands moved down the weapon, almost as if they greased its surface, and then back up to where he positioned the rifle to aim. Truth be told, the weapon was a comfort but also a concern. It wasn't like he'd ever had lessons with a gun.

If his accelerated beating heart had wings, he would be gone, lifted up into the universe and carried away. His very face tingled, his body stiff with the freeze that came from outright terror. Couldn't they have just taken this journey without finding a frikkin' Greelox? Was that too much to ask?

Sweat rolled down his forehead and into his eye. He blinked, the salt a hateful sting as he looked through the scope. His breathing sounded harsh in the night and shrouded his ability to hear the threat.

He stood for what had to be a thousand breaths of panicked anticipation, listening. The sounds hadn't come again. With the fire sputtering nearby, the last of the wood shattering into embers, gray smoke permeated the air. Animals hated flame, he knew. And if there was smoke …

He lowered the rifle and circled around Ember, a good twenty feet in front of where she lay sleeping, oblivious to the world around her. At least he would now be between her and the Greelox if it should come their way.

A deep sigh escaped her mouth, and he spun around to see if she had awakened. But to his relief, she lay sleeping, even adjusting herself ever so slightly to a better position before a delicate snore began. He smiled at the melodic vibration, his heart softening from its fight-or-flight response to tenderness.

Within a split second, though, his heartbeat spiked at the sound of a rumbling "gnarrrrrr." No longer a question. The Greelox was closer, close enough for Xander to see its hulking curves silhouetted in the darkness, now a certain and mere hundred feet from where he stood trembling. The eight-foot-tall mutant, genetically engineered monster cat, was something of a nightmare. Its razor-sharp claws could rip flesh in a millisecond. Its mouth and teeth, bathed in heavy saliva, dripped mucous-like snot from a persistent runny nose. With its tough skin and spiked back, the animal appeared to be a hellish cross between a tiger and a flesh-eating dinosaur.

The creature picked up its pace. Its primal need for food superseded all else, and it would not relent with the scent of humans nearby.

With a quick motion, Xander raised the rifle to his eye, making it ready. A memory of the cat's outer skin flashed through his head. Its skin was tough, not like that of a tiger or lion at the zoo. This was armor-like and hardy. Would bullets even kill it? That was assuming he could hit it, although the Greelox was immense, not like something quick and small that would require extreme precision.

He watched it rapidly approach within a radius of fifty feet. Xander was already able to see its yellow eyes, oddly reflective in the dark. Every cell in his body screamed a mental prayer: *Please let me kill this thing.*

Aiming more carefully and working hard to steady his hand, he pulled the trigger. The smell of gunpowder assaulted his nostrils, satisfying himself that he'd made a difference. But the bullet flew into the air without a hit. If he couldn't aim well enough in the dark … couldn't hit this thing …

He cursed and quickly shot again. The creature keened, and a shrill, snarl-laced scream rent the air. To his great relief and joy, he'd struck the creature's left leg. Roaring with pain and rage, it limped and raised its leg, backing away a few feet. *Maybe he'll retreat.* Hope surged within him. Instead, the Greelox charged forward. Sweat greased his armpits and his hands. He was failing!

Xander heard Ember scream, her frantic sound piercing his heart but fueling his determination. Again, he shot, willing the bullet to hit its mark—anywhere to slow the carnivore down. The blast echoed like a bomb in the night, the gun's recoil setting him off balance. His toes gripping the ground on which he stood, he bent into the moment. Had he—? Yes! It had been a good shot—perfect.

But the Greelox stayed on its feet, advancing with quivering, giant strides. Without one more second's hesitation, save for the indecent curse on his lips, he fired again. The creature careened in a wild circle, blood spilling from a gaping hole in its head next to its ear, before falling inches from where Ember still lay.

"Aye! Oh, help! Xander …" Ember wailed in sheer terror from behind him. Her sobs felt like rain on his soul.

Xander let out a breath, a volume of air he'd trapped inside without realizing it. His first thought was of Ember, but he didn't dare comfort her without being sure the Greelox was dead. In a wary advance, he edged his way, toe by toe, up to the grounded beast, his gun ready in case of the beast's possible second wind—or resurrection. *Movement!* He fell back.

Electrified still, his adrenaline surging, he raised his weapon again. Examining his conquest more closely, he drowned in relief. It was only a gust of wind that gently blew the hair on the Greelox's head into a ghastly illusion of life.

For good measure, he gripped the rifle and pushed his foot into the animal's hoary side. Nothing. Dead for sure.

He dropped the rifle to his side and then to the ground, his tension-knotted shoulders echoing the action of release. He tilted his head back, his body wilting into a rag-doll posture. As he turned to finally acknowledge Ember, who was desperately calling his name, he trembled with spent energy. He only hoped he didn't look to Ember as being as weak as he felt.

When he faced her and ran the distance back, he wiped the sweat off his brow with his sleeve, barely noticing the tear he also brushed away.

As Xander moved toward her, Ember had been trying to rise. She struggled, pushing herself up and turning to use her good leg for the final effort. Successful at last, she limped halfway to him, where he caught her in his arms. She gasped and sobbed a wet spot onto his shirt as she clung to him, her arms tightening until he could scarcely breathe.

"It's okay. It's dead." Xander put his hands around Ember's head, smoothing her hair. He planted small kisses in her hair and on her forehead, holding her until he felt her body relax. The scent of her tresses was comforting. She leaned against him, and he bore her full weight, her injured foot only one reason why she was unsteady.

"You … you saved us. I would've been—*we* would've been …" Ember whispered into his neck. She lifted her head off his chest to gaze up at him, tears glistening. "Thank you." The words sunk deep into the charged atmosphere and into Xander's core.

"You think I wouldn't have sacrificed myself if I needed to —to save you?" He took her face in his hands. For a second, he thought about what could have happened if he'd not had the gun, and a light shiver caused the hair on his arms to stand up.

Ember dropped her head, embarrassed. "I—I don't know. It seems you almost did. Nearly had to. I was scared to death." She hugged him again before she hopped back a step. She took his hands and locked her fingers through his, still depending on him for support.

"But would you miss me?" He raised an eyebrow, the gleam in his eyes mischievous. Xander couldn't miss the opportunity to press her for a reaction. Yet, in his heart, he was serious, hopeful she'd say she could never live without him.

Ember's mouth twitched slightly as if she were holding back her first post-trauma smile. "I would miss you. A lot."

He laid her hand over his heart so she could feel it beating like rapid-fire artillery that had nothing to do with his vanquishing the Greelox. "This much?"

Ember let her smile loose. "Let's see." She took his hand and placed it with exaggerated slow-motion over her heart. They stood together, arm crossing arm, feeling the heartbeat connection.

"Your heart … definitely not beating fast enough." He grinned. "I've gotta be absolutely sure you'd miss me." He kissed her long and deeply, his mouth and everything in him catching fire. Then, he swooped her up in his arms and carried her back to her divot in the ground, where he lay beside her until they both fell asleep until the sun came up again.

62

Will's Conflict

Will and the Sciolist's expedition into the old subway had taken all day and deep into the night. He shook his head, thinking. The abandoned depot had been freakishly full of twists and turns and miles long. He thought this would be his ultimate ticket to win Serpio's favor and put him in good standing at last, especially if it kept him from the therapy room. Will had no way of knowing that the most important leaders of Phoenix were killing mutant creatures and falling into each other's arms.

When he made his way back up into the Plauditorium's main room with the others, he experienced an exquisite, profound sense of loss. If it was disappointment, he understood. But it seemed to be another kind of emotion, more like a disconnection from humanity. Almost grief. He obsessively checked his Alt, making sure he could keep his points at a respectable level, keep positive thoughts and emotions fresher in his mind.

But he hadn't felt right since the treatment in the alienating silver room. He wasn't himself. He knew his mind—no question there. Every step he took, his mind told him it was correct. His allegiance to the Magistrate and the city was absolute. In fact, when he remembered how he became a Plauditor and how he nursed his deep ambition to new levels of Status, it was reassuring. He'd promised his grandfather he would obey the laws and never question them, and he was fulfilling his vow.

Bizarre memories of people and weird circumstances flashed through his brain multiple times, though, fuzzy individuals his gut told him he should know but didn't remember clearly, no matter how he tried; a barren landscape that he was sure was The Outside and that he'd been there; dead trees with numbers; a red-haired girl … The images slipped away so much like a dream that he was beginning to think that's what they were—just pieces of nightmares.

Across the room, the newsfeed advanced across the Plauditors' screens. There—there was that girl again. That red-haired girl. The enemy. He wondered, though, how a girl that young and sweet-looking could ever be considered dangerous.

A message came through his Alt. Feren was waiting outside to take him to his cottage for the night.

"How are you doing, Will? It's past two in the morning. I'm sure you're tired." Feren stood by her limousine and gave him a little pat on the arm. She allowed him to slide into the back of the car first before taking the front seat. Once inside, she commanded the limo, "To the guest cottages."

Feren seemed to make a special effort to make him comfortable, tossing him a small pillow. "When I got word that you had discovered the subway, I thought, 'Will Verus, you've done it. You're the hero of the day.' Almost true. You have keen intelligence and motivation that many don't have."

Will felt his color rise. He'd always been modest, and compliments made him uncomfortable. Will rubbed his hands down his face to show his frustration. "I can't believe—All that time we spent searching, though, and no luck."

"You did your best. You should feel happy about that. Without you, Serpio probably wouldn't have remembered the subway. It's been closed off for multiple decades." She gazed at him with sympathy and respect.

Will brightened with pride. "Yeah, at least we know they were there by what they left behind. Trash and footprints in the dust. I don't understand how they're hanging together. Only a dozen REMs to control a whole staff of Plauditors? They must be threatening them constantly."

"True. But if you're tied up, have no means of communicating, and held at gunpoint, you'd do what you're told."

"Gunpoint … Well, there you have it." Again, an obscure, frightening memory pushed its way to the surface of his brain. Had he been shot at some point? Why did he think he had? He involuntarily reached for his chest.

"Serpio'll be much more open to trusting you, Will, if you continue to help in the search for the REMs and the Plauditors. And if you find the girl … Well, that would be a significant boost for you. You'd never have worry about the Magistrate doubting you ever again."

"I'm curious," Will ventured, hoping he wasn't crossing a line. "The girl Serpio is seeking … Ember? Why is she such a threat? She seems like she's just a silly teenager."

"Ember is dangerous because she can feel people's emotions. She also began spreading lies. But he has great affection for her. His plan, if she's captured, is to install her in his mansion and use her for government work. She won't be punished like the others."

"Hmmm. Maybe all she needs is some therapy." Will looked out the window, the lights of the city blurring by. Somewhere deep down in his soul, a traitorous sympathy emerged for the girl.

"She may need to go to Solace for a while." Feren tilted her head thoughtfully. "After she's found."

"Solace sounds great," Will said. "Better than the therapy room Serpio took me to." He shuddered slightly and hoped

Feren didn't see that. He liked the way she still thought he was a hero.

"What room?" Feren's Alt buzzed with a message that demanded her instant attention. "Yes, Serpio. Oh dear. Thanks for the update." She lowered her arm as if she wanted the news to be as far away from her as possible. "Another bomb has been detonated across town."

"What? How can that be? Who's doing this if not the REMs?" Again, a thought nagged at his mind. Didn't he know someone who worked in chemicals? Yes … his friend Weeford. And Weeford was missing …

Feren seemed genuinely flustered. "Serpio is out for blood. We didn't need this distraction."

"Yeah, it's terrible. I hope no one was killed."

"We're pulling up to the cottage, Will. I'll walk you in."

"Please. Don't you think I know the way by now?" Will's irritation at being shepherded around was on full display. Shocked at this own tone, he added, "Really, Feren. I'll be okay."

To Will's dismay, Feren still walked him to the cottage. By the time he walked in the door, he was dopey again.

With Feren's "goodnight," Will fell into bed.

Then, within minutes, he was already dreaming.

The beautiful redhead was there … a distance away. She called to him., and he ran to her, excited, as if she were the most important being in the universe. Her arms wrapped around him, and warmth bloomed through him. She made him feel secure and … loved. He kissed her deeply, and a flare of brilliant light ignited around her. She took him by the hand, leading him down a path filled with flowers. As she walked, she gazed at him, never taking her eyes off his face. Her bright smile melted him further. He asked her—begged her—*what can I do to make you happy? I'll do anything.* A tear dropped from her eye, and she turned away, letting go of his hand and walking on without him.

"Nooooo!" he screamed out loud, waking himself. Drenched in sweat, he sat up straight. He wiped tears from his eyes, embarrassed. *What was that all about?* He didn't normally dream. If he did, he never remembered. He'd known someone once, someone whose dreams mattered, but his never did. Problem was, the dream had felt real. An undeniable love for this girl seemed rooted deep in his subconscious.

And yet, this hot babe was Ember, enemy of the city—Serpio's project. Emotions surged from his gut. He did *not* know her. She was a threat. A schemer. A *traitor.*

Still … her voice mesmerized him. Her gaze unhinged him. And he badly wanted to touch her. To protect her.

His heart did a somersault. What was real, and what was not? He no longer knew. One thing was sure: the tug of war in his brain had to stop. He'd mark this dream as a fantasy, something like a celebrity crush. Passion stirred from seeing a picture of a beautiful girl had no place in his life. Until morning, only now a couple hours away now, he'd stay awake, on guard.

63

Ember's Insecurity

At the first light of day, as a pink and orange-tinged sky resembled a watercolor painting, the sun's rays began to glow. Ember stirred from her sleep and yawned. Stretching out her arms, her fingers grazing Xander's face, she watched his eyes flutter open a second before a smile lit his lips.

"Morning, beautiful." Xander brushed the hair from Ember's eyes and gave her a light kiss on the forehead before he sat up. He stretched his legs out in front of him to break up the kinks.

Ember gave him a shy smile. Her thoughts quickly raced back to the events of yesterday. Their new romance. The deadly encounter. "It *is* a beautiful morning. We're alive!" She adjusted her jacket, the nighttime forty-degree chill still a companion. Ember ran her hands through her hair in an effort to comb it. She had always been mindful of her appearance, and she imagined she looked like a REM, not beautiful at all.

Xander stood and chuckled. "You got the 'morning beautiful' backward, but yes—we're not Greelox food."

"Speaking of food, I'm starving." Ember gestured to the rucksack. "Protein bar for breakfast?"

Xander rummaged in the pack, removing some items from the bag to dig at the bottom. His eyebrows arched as he pulled out a tubular, paper-wrapped item. Turning it to the side, he read out loud, "Danger. Explosive." He whistled. "Not sure this should be jostled around." He glanced Ember's way. "I'll put it in the outside pocket of the sack. We need to remember it's there."

"What's it for? I mean, I know it's a survival kit, but explosives?"

"Can't hurt," Xander shrugged. "You never know …"

Tucking the hazardous bundle in place, he dug again for the now-unappealing protein bars. He held two out, one in each hand. "Take your pick … both delicious." Grinning, he extended one to her. "Would you like this vanilla flavor?" Then, drawing it back, held out the one in his other hand. "Or *this* vanilla flavor?"

Laughing, Ember said, "I give up. You choose."

"Vanilla it is. Or, we still have some of that snake left. Snake jerky by now." Xander handed her one and then followed up with a bottle of water.

"Thanks. Vanilla over snake."

"Good choice. After this, we roll."

Eating their meager fare didn't take more than five minutes, but it seemed too long to Ember. She was itching to get started on the day. If they made enough headway during the day's trek, they could hopefully reach the coordinates of her mom's location by nightfall. Finding her mom was less than a day away! She was already thinking about hugging her mom, touching her face, sharing laughter. Her eyes misted.

"Xander, I can try walking." She hated the thought of Xander having to carry her again.

But as Xander helped her up and she tried to put weight

on her ankle, she knew it would be impossible for her to walk. Pain shot through her bones and tendons, causing her to gasp. She winced. "I guess not."

"No problem. Carrying you piggyback first, 'kay?" With Ember's nod, Xander fastened the packs together and placed them on Ember's back. He handed her the rifle. "Before we go, I'm morsing Ava. She needs to know we're still alive."

"Morsing?" Ember asked, not concealing her amusement.

"Perfect word for using the Morse Code." He began to tap into his Alt, then frowned. "Not working." He sighed. "We're too far out. I shoulda known we'd have no communication out here."

"I wish we knew how Phoenix was doing too. I worry ..." Ember gazed off into the brightening horizon. "But if Tranquility taught me anything, it's that worry doesn't help anything."

"Yeah ... but it's a bummer that we can't be connected." Xander squatted in front of Ember so she could grab onto him in a piggyback. "Ready?"

"Yep. How far do you think it is now?"

"Look around for landmarks. Then check the map."

Ember pulled up the topographical relief map on her Alt. She highlighted the coordinates of her mom's supposed location. The Outside wasn't a place for many landmarks, but unless they found some things, they wouldn't know where they were. Frustration creased her brow. She saw nothing as they trudged along.

Xander shifted her weight. "So, other than *this*, of course, what do you like to do for fun?"

Ember stayed silent for a few seconds, wondering what she could say that wouldn't sound like she was totally boring. "I haven't done much for fun. I've had to ... isolate myself to stay sane. When I'm in public, I'm picking up everyone's emotions. It can be frightening."

"It's that bad? The empathic stuff?" He quickly brushed the hair off his face.

"Yeah. Being out here is better for my psyche."

"But being out here … it's not life. I could show you so many things." His voice was eager. "We could dine in my favorite restaurant, hit the Fun Zone, go to concerts. Let me show you how life is meant to be lived. You shouldn't live your life hidden."

Ember flashed him a smile. "Someday. If we get through this …"

"We're gonna get through this. Believe it. And then—"

Ember jumped, throwing Xander off balance a little. "Ember!"

"Sorry. Ahead!" She pointed. "A rock formation. It's huge!" She looked at her Alt to verify a location on the virtual map. "It's on here, too."

"Can you see how far that is?"

Ember squinted at her Alt's face. "I don't know. Maybe three miles?"

"And then?"

"No idea."

"Hey! There's a tree over there …"

"So? Why? You want to climb it?" Ember laughed.

"Right," he said sarcastically. "No way. I'm gonna make a litter."

"What's a litter?" The only thing Ember could envision was a box for cat poop.

"It's two poles about six feet long that I can tie together in a triangle. I can put other wood or thatch in between. That way, I can put you in it and pull you along." He sounded excited.

"You saying I'm too heavy for you?" Ember made a face.

"No, just right." He grinned. "I *like* having you wrapped around me. But with the litter, we can go faster."

"Ha! That's your story? Okay. But this is the only time you get to drag me around."

~

AN HOUR LATER, Xander had managed to put together a crude sled from dead tree branches. Blackened and fragile, the limbs made the litter's stability a gamble but one they both agreed they'd need to take. Luckily, the twine in their packs was strong.

Lying on the primitive portable "bed," Ember felt even more helpless, but they were making better time. The landscape was so boring that they began to make up silly games, finally ending up with a "Two Truths and a Lie" competition —a challenge because they didn't know each other that well.

At a tie, Ember tossed out, "I worked at the animal shelter for a year. My favorite color is purple. I can draw just about anything well."

"Hmmm. I'm sure your favorite color is purple. It was your mom's Status color. I don't know about the animal shelter … but you have a big heart, so … that's probably correct. I've never seen you draw—or even talk about drawing. Drawing is the lie."

"Wrong!" Ember laughed. "I can draw anything, even when someone describes it! The lie's the animal shelter. I worked there, but not for a year. *Two* years."

"Seriously? That counts as a lie? Okay. You win, then." Xander slowed down. "Time to take a break." He lowered the litter poles, and plopped down on the ground, wiping sweat off his face with his hands.

"We're almost to the rocks—just a little further."

"Yeah. I just wish it wasn't so frikkin' hot."

"Where's the instant cold wind we had yesterday every mile or so? At least that's a break from the heat."

"The Outside's super unpredictable. That's what makes

Tranquility so great. No change in temperature." Xander gave Ember a bottle of water from a pack on his back, and after she drank half, he drained the rest.

"How much water's left?"

"Probably enough. But we have to be careful."

Ember tried to rise from the litter to test her ankle again. She hadn't needed another pain pill, so she began to hope she was improving.

"What are you doing? If you're gonna get up, you need my help." Xander rushed to her side, pulling her up by the arms.

"I need to stretch a little." She put some weight on her ankle and found it didn't send the sharp pains through her foot like before. She limped a few feet with Xander. "Let go. I want to see if I can walk without you."

Xander released her. "Be careful. Only a few steps."

Ember smiled as she ventured a couple tentative steps. "Getting there. I can't walk the whole way, but maybe a little?"

"Only a little. Just for exercise and strength," he cautioned. "I'll put the stuff on the litter, and you can walk some, but we should get going." Xander followed his own directive, throwing the packs and rifle onto the litter.

They began walking again, Ember limping alongside Xander. "I don't want to slow us down. You think we'll be there before nighttime?"

"No idea. Depends on our speed." Xander put his arm around her. "I can at least help you move."

They hobbled along for fifty yards before Ember stopped. "I can't go any further. Time to get back on that thing."

"You're improving, though. Good job for a cripple." A tiny laugh followed, the tease sounding intimate rather than cruel.

Getting resituated, Ember lay back, content to look at the sky and rest, although the sun was hitting hammer hard even at eleven in the morning. Xander, too, fell into silence, possibly realizing how much effort it had taken for her to walk. She thought about him, his self-sacrifice and passion for her, and sighed. It was a journey in more ways than one.

She stirred, feeling as if she'd dozed off. Xander had stopped walking and was looking at his Alt. "Checking our progress?" she asked.

"Seems we should be closer to those rocks by now. Checking my compass … Frikkin' Shazz. Looks like we've veered somewhat off course."

Ember fought off a wave of guilt. She should have been checking the map. She couldn't expect Xander to drag her and navigate at the same time. "It's my fault. I'm sorry. I think I fell asleep."

"It wouldn't have been long enough to misdirect us. Something's throwin' off the compass."

"How does that happen?"

"Electromagnetic fields and even rocks can do it. Iron under the earth." His eyes swept the landscape.

"Those rocks ahead?"

"Maybe. We're maybe … a mile off course."

"Or more, right?" Ember analyzed Xander's feelings quickly. The dismay was eating him up. "It's okay," she added. "We're not in a hurry."

"We're low on supplies," Xander said, turning to her, his voice flat. "We can't afford mistakes like this."

"Can I help?" she said, her tone soft.

"Not unless you want to tweak time. But we've prob'ly been off course for a while."

"C'mon, Xander. We will get there. March on," she said. "Mush!" Her laughter broke the somber mood.

He grinned then, his smile competing with the glow from the sheen on his face. "Yes, my princess."

After using the stop as a break for food and water, Ember turned her body to face forward. Not only was her foot more elevated, but watching Xander's muscles under his shirt and the way he moved was sigh-worthy.

Xander made a sharp right to change their trajectory. A mile further, filled with banter and citing their most precious wishes, Xander cried out. "Do you see that?"

"I'm looking. Is that … water?"

"Maybe! Not gettin' my hopes up."

"Mirage?"

"We'll see. Heading there. We'll run smack into it the way we're goin'."

As Xander closed the distance and progressed slowly to the top of an unexpected rise, Ember began to lose hope. "We'd see it by now, right?"

At the crest of the hill, Xander let out a whoop. "It *is* water!"

"Woo hoo!" Ember held on tight as Xander flew down the slope. She didn't see much, her mind trying to fill in the details of what the size of it might be.

At the bottom, Xander helped Ember from her crude sled, and together, they shuffled to the edge of a shallow, ten-foot-wide pool, the crystal sparkle on the water more precious than diamonds.

"We have water to drink!" Ember threw Xander a high five.

Xander's face, though, to her surprise, was serious. "You can't trust water out here for drinking. This water sits in one place. It could be contaminated with just about anything radiation, toxins, even poison. But we can fill some bottles and treat them with the tablets in our packs. They'll purify it. Or, if the water turns red, it's not safe no matter what."

Ember's spirits flagged, especially when she felt Xander's concern, his aura a muddy yellow. She held up crossed fingers.

"Give me a sec to fill a bottle with water so I can test it." He jogged over to his rucksack, returning with a bottle. He quickly dipped the bottle into the water until it was full.

"Well?" Ember watched as he sloshed the liquid around.

Xander shook the bottle several more times and squinted at the bubbles in the container. "The water's slightly green." He made a scrunched face as he held it up to show her. "But not red. It's safe enough."

"Yuck. I want to put a tablet in mine before I drink it."

"But first," Xander said, his eyes dancing, "We're getting cleaned up." His jacket long since discarded, he threw off his shirt.

Ember's half-second of admiration suddenly switched to an attack of self-consciousness. To go in the water and get clean, she'd have to not only unbandage her ankle, but shed her clothes. "You first. Then you have to promise … you'll let me bathe in privacy."

Xander put his hands on her shoulders. "Agree," solemnity marking his voice. Then, he raised one eyebrow. "Not that I wouldn't be tempted …"

She gave him a little swat. "Thanks. And I will appreciate knowing you're clean. Keeping my distance hasn't been hard," she kidded.

"I don't blame you. I'm still smokin' hot, though, either way." He winked. "Okay … so, you can turn your back or watch me swim. Regardless, I'm in." With that, he tossed his shoes away.

True to her hope he'd do the same, she turned away, hearing splashes in the water, and his yelps of joy.

She discarded her one shoe and unwrapped her ankle, enjoying its freedom from its binding while he freshened up. She stole a glance at him out of the corner of her eye, catching his backside as he sprang up out of the water—to her senses, almost a slow-motion performance. She turned fully to watch him, appreciating a sight that she'd so far only conjured up in her mind. His skin, shiny in the radiance of the sun, only emphasized his tight, sculpted torso and muscular form. Sleek and strong. Undeniably hot. A storm of internal heat burned her promise into dust. A sigh escaped her lips, her infatuation in high gear. She couldn't tear her gaze away.

When he returned minutes later, he said, "Only about two feet deep, but great. I rinsed my clothes out, too." He ran his fingers through his hair, combing out the water, the droplets falling on the wet uniform he'd put back on. The pants' and shirt's knit fabric stuck to his body like a second skin. And while now completely covered up, Xander seemed unaware of how little his appearance left to the imagination.

. "Be careful with your ankle. Don't move around too fast. I won't be in the water to support you. If you need me for anything, I'll be right over there." He pointed in the direction of where their supplies lay on the litter.

Ember wondered if Xander was better at keeping promises than she was. But she'd grown to trust him. He'd saved her life twice. He'd risked everything to go back to The Outside, a dangerous, horrible place, only for her. And ultimately, he'd been the one to put the brakes on in the middle of a dangerously intense romantic connection. Her concern slipped away.

She slowly dropped each piece of clothing on the gritty bank. The sun warmed her skin, and a light breeze caressed her from head to toe. She sat down in the water, letting it envelop her from the neck down. Warm as a bath, the fluid relaxed her, and she tilted her head back in an almost worshipful gesture. After her first dive under and the glorious feeling of this unexpected miracle caressing her hair, she rose out of the pool, squeezing water from her locks. Sloughing through the wake, she grabbed her clothes and doused them, shaking and turning them until she was sure they were clean —or at least not saturated with perspiration, odor, and dirt.

As she hobbled out to dry land, her eyes sought Xander. A buzz of excitement coursed through her as she thought he might be watching in spite of his promise. If she had been overly tempted, wouldn't he be, too? But true to his word,

Xander sat on the litter beyond, his back to her, shaking water in a bottle to test for safety.

Ember struggled into her wet clothes, her feelings upside down. Deep inside, she wished that Xander hadn't been so trustworthy after all.

64

Will's Fidelity

As Xander and Ember bathed in the water, Will was in the Elite Chambers. All damages had been repaired from the bomb that had struck the chambers days before.

Serpio, Feren, Ava, and Will sat around the room's spacious table. Sunshine beamed into the window, and a lavender essential oil diffuser bathed the room with its relaxing scent.

"We should give congratulations to Will for his finding evidence of where our fugitives were, even though we weren't able to find them," Feren said. "I firmly believe now, without a doubt, that Will has always been on our side."

Why wouldn't I be? Will's internal reaction was instantaneous. Then he remembered his dream, and the dreaded tug of war began again in his mind. "Thank you, Feren."

The Magistrate steepled his fingers in front of him on the table. "Perhaps. I do appreciate your discovery, Will. However,"—he now forcibly opened his palms, throwing them out—"as Feren says, we still haven't found the perpetrators. I'm losing my patience."

Ava sat forward in her chair. "These REMs are smart.

Like rats. A perfect analogy. People think rats are disgusting creatures, but their intelligence, especially in tight situations, is certain."

Serpio nodded, and his voice was grave. "As you know, another bomb went off across town last night. The force was enough to demolish the locker room at the sports complex. With our Sciolists spread so thin on the search, our city's security is at risk."

For some strange reason, at the mention of this new bomb incident, Will felt as if all the air had been sucked from his body.

"I would suggest, Magistrate, that we recruit and train new Sciolists. If we don't contain the threat, we'll need them." Feren spoke gently, sensitively.

Feren has a true Tranquility heart, Will thought. *She's always positive.*

"I suggest a meeting of the Elite to discuss recruitment, Serpio," Ava said.

Serpio gazed into space, as if the answer would suddenly appear in front of him. "I agree. It's time to convene the Elite to make these decisions. I'll send the request for the meeting to be held tomorrow."

"Very good, Serpio." Although Will had seldom seen Feren ruffled, she seemed relieved at the prospect of increasing security. Ava, on the other hand, pressed her lips together and simply nodded.

Will was starting to feel solidly attached to this small group. He didn't know any of them well, but he felt accepted and trusted. When all of them lingered to chat a few minutes about Tranquility's morning broadcasts, he knew his Alt points were soaring. He, too, was happy to know that broadcasts were back, delivering positive news, music, and empowerment strategies to the people of the city. Cameras were up and running efficiently. He sighed with a contentment he hadn't felt for … what? Days? Weeks?

With a final confirmation of the meeting time for the Elite, Feren and Ava gave the Tranquility salute and said their good-byes. Serpio called after them, "In the meantime, stay safe, positive, and vigilant."

Will remained, always dependent on the Magistrate for the day's instructions. Today, Will wanted more than what he'd been given before. He wanted his job back. "Magistrate, sir … as Feren has said, my loyalty should no longer be in question. And … you … suggested that I could join the Plauditors again at work. If the new shift has begun?"

Serpio slowly turned his head to scrutinize him. "We did discuss that, yes. But Feren tells me that you asked her about Ember Vinata."

Will's neck flushed with heat. "I—I only wanted to know why she was a threat. If I'm being honest, she looks … innocent. And I don't know much about her. I thought I should …"

"What do you *think* you know about her?" Serpio's voice was low, but the words hung heavy with distrust.

Will felt himself shrinking inside. Serpio was putting far too much into his inquiry. Just when he was feeling secure … "I only know she's on the run. And Feren told me she's some sort of mind reader or something?"

To his relief, Serpio laughed, but Will couldn't tell whether he thought his question was funny. "She doesn't read minds. She reads hearts." Then, he tapped his OmniCom. "Photo — Ember Vinata." Immediately, her image appeared on the screen, and he extended his wrist to Will so he could more readily see the photo.

Will's pulse spiked, and worse, his face flushed hot. He couldn't help himself. He knew from the buzz on his wrist even his Alt points had surged. Worse, Serpio hadn't missed his reaction.

"You should return as a Plauditor, Will. I'm wasting my time and energy keeping you as a guest of the Elite. But first, I have to be certain of your loyalty. I can't have you asking questions about this girl. Or being so attracted to her. But I keep my promises. As I pledged, you can return to your job after your next therapy session."

"When?" Will's mouth went dry.

"When do you want to return to the Plauditorium?" The Magistrate's face appeared to be a broad, blank slate.

"Today. Take me to therapy, and let's be done with this." Will was frightened of that place, but he had always had enough courage to get through anything. And, he reminded himself, enduring something terrible to get something great was never a sacrifice.

KNOWING what to expect didn't deaden the torture of it. If anything, this was worse than he remembered.

Back in the therapy room, humiliatingly naked as before, Will wilted under the power of inner body heat. The lights above him blazed brightly, but the burn he was experiencing came from the inside of him—as if he'd been put in a microwave and cooked well past when the timer chimed. Every internal organ, each vessel and vein, carried the pulse of an electric current, a web of pain that branched throughout his body. The word "boiling" didn't come close to the temperature that besieged his entire being. Sweat coated him like a second skin before rivulets streamed down his face, his arms, and his legs.

If the rubber shoes he wore would only keep his feet safe. But the shoes, too, melted into soggy flaps, and he could no longer feel his toes.

When the ear-splitting music began, he held his breath in an agonizing attempt to stay human. He desperately wanted to yell above the noise so that his voice would drown the other. Yet he found himself unable to speak.

Covering his ears had no effect; the sound became a laser, sending shockwaves through his shielding hands. If he didn't know better, he'd wonder if his ears were bleeding or if his eardrums would simply collapse from the onslaught. Hearing could only endure so many decibels … A tear slipped out, a tangible fear.

His remaining memories, so dim of late, were being ripped from his head, a physical sensation akin to tooth removal. Agony.

But, unlike the last time, when he wasn't expecting torture, now, he fought. He gritted his teeth. He concentrated with all his might on keeping his thoughts, feelings, and emotions from the hijack. Mentally, he worked every mind trick he knew to reel them back in.

He frantically tried to shut out all access to his mind by reciting the Accords, which he'd committed to memory years ago.

He focused on absolute truths.

Emotions would only make him more vulnerable; he desperately tried to divorce himself from his own heart.

Above all, he would not show fear. He refused to show weakness. And he would not give in.

THIS … it's only a means to an end.

Being a loyal citizen is your only purpose, the subliminal message insisted.

I still have my family, his mind fought back.

Your family lives apart from you. They are disloyal. They have never loved you.

I know I have friends …

Your childhood friend Weeford is dead. You do not remember him. You will not be able to recall any associations with the group known as Phoenix.

I think I love that girl … I want to—

Ember Vinata is your enemy. You do not know her. She will try to hurt you.

I am a great Plauditor ... a city hero ...

Being a loyal citizen is your only purpose.

FINALLY, he screamed, his voice finding its escape from a place deep inside him.

In a final, last-ditch effort to save his soul, a muscle memory reactivated. His hand made a slow circle in the air, his thumb and forefinger creating a letter "L." Loyalty.

The hallucinations began then. Nightmarish scenarios where he faced off against a hardcore enemy and blood ran down the walls.

65

Wee's Connection

Weeford had seldom wondered what it was like to be dead. Being declared dead from the transport crash was one thing. But when Ava gave him a new Alt and explained that it belonged to someone deceased, it seemed downright creepy. Never would he have imagined two months ago that, according to his Alt, he'd be no longer known as Weeford.

He'd been living in his own basement. There, he'd been safe enough because he was "dead." Soon, though, the city would move in to repurpose his home for another Level Five. The government had wasted no time. A team had already placed stickers on the front door.

Since his departure from the Plauditorium and the planting of bombs at the library and in the Magistrate's vehicle, Wee had laid low, waiting for communication and instructions from Phoenix. With being cut off from the world, his happy-go-lucky personality had bounced up and down like an underinflated ball.

The night he finally saw Ava again was when she came by to drop off his new Alt. To get his attention, she'd tapped on the basement window. It was a terrifying moment for him—

he'd thought he'd been discovered. But seeing Ava's face in the window was like Christmas coming early. Her presence was like a beacon of hope, her quick smile reassuring and greatly needed.

After he'd slid the window open, Ava grasped his hand and then fed the Alt through. She cautioned him in a quick whisper, "Very little communication. The essential. Only Morse." Then, she was gone.

When he got back home after planting the bomb at the library, he'd dashed upstairs, grabbing all the food from the fridge. Weeford didn't like too much of it. Frozen-to-microwave Mac and Cheese was a staple for people of his Status, but it got old, especially when he'd eaten all the fresh food before it could spoil.

He had waited for a couple of days without any word from Ava. Each hour that passed, he'd been tempted to fire questions in Morse to someone from his Alt but held his queries back. He didn't want to put anyone in danger, least of all himself.

Then finally! His face lit up when the long-awaited message came through on his Alt. The Morse Code's slow series of dots and dashes rattled his patience, even with the help of the app. "Phoenix left Plauditorium. Most confirmed safe."

Weeford yelled out, "Yes!" Although there was no one there to hear it, the exclamation bubbled out of him, somehow making him feel less alone. With relief, he fell into the chair he'd carried down to the basement. Then the word "most" sunk in. It sounded like some might have met disaster. *Who had been taken?*

He needed instructions—details. Again, a message: "P. to emergency food storage buildings, N, S, E, W." *Locations!* The closest warehouse would be west.

It was time to rejoin the team.

HIS OWN LEVEL Four pink clothing would be easily seen, especially if the cameras were up throughout the city. He'd need black clothing to blend into the night. An old trick came to mind.

Not only was he trained in chemicals for his job, but Weeford had also always loved how you could play around with them. Even as a child, he'd dabbled in fun ways to combine chemicals for mini-explosions or inventions. His parents were indulgent, but he'd pushed their tolerance more than a few times.

Many plants could die fabric, but finding them in his house? Not possible. Nails, though, would work. Covering rusty iron nails or hinges in white vinegar produced a chemical reaction that made black dye.

He'd have to do two chemical processes, though. He had nails, but they weren't rusty. Step one would be to create the rust by combining hydrogen peroxide, vinegar, and salt. A couple of hours would do it. Then, he'd put the rusty nails in vinegar to produce dye. After the change, the rusty items could be removed, and the fabric, dipped. If he had alum, another common chemical, he could make the dye permanent, but at that moment, all he cared about was making his clothes black. Pants and a hoodie. He set to work.

IT WAS two in the morning. In his black outfit, Weeford crept out of his house by the back door. For extra insurance, tucked in his pocket was another vial of Phenol he'd stolen from the chem lab prior to the bombing.

He'd have to keep to the shadows and avoid cameras. He desperately wished he knew if the Magistrate had been able to restore Tranquility's cameras. His Alt had no GPS, so at least he couldn't be tracked. He'd be on foot, but in his area, the westside emergency food building was only four blocks away. Suddenly, he felt like a superhero of lore, like the legendary Spiderman perhaps. If only he had those powers …

He thought of Ember then. He knew she had some weird thing, some ability he didn't fully understand. And Will … always on his mind. Not a possessor of a superpower at all, but a hero all the same. What in the world was happening to his best friend? He'd never stopped believing that Will was on their side. He knew his buddy, and kissing up to Serpio was the last thing Will would ever do after finding out about Ember's mom. He felt it in his bones.

Just outside his place, Weeford crushed himself along the buildings, knowing that if the Plauditors caught him on camera after curfew, a report would be sent and Sciolists would come without delay. He'd be questioned and sent to some higher authority. But staying home was not an option. He would have to do the best he could.

Like an answer from the blue, a message pinged on his Alt. Not Ava's ID. A Phoenix Plauditor had to be sending it. In Morse: "To avoid cameras: E half block to Pleasure Circle's alley between Pink Dreams restaurant and Gaiety Grounds, W quarter block to Delight Drive, under bridge. W half block to Companion Corner's staircase. W half block to Purity Parkway alley. E half block to Cheers bar under street. E half block to Elation Ave underground garage. Basement to back door warehouse." It made sense. Only the Plauditors knew where the city placed all the cameras.

He kept to the buildings, inching along. He decided slow was better, although the urge to run was acute.

So far, after navigating the first couple of blocks, no disaster had befallen him. Even then, relaxing wasn't an option. One false move …

After he descended the staircase at Companion Corner, it

would be a half block yet along buildings to get to Purity Parkway's alley.

Just as he made ready to cross twelve feet of empty space to continue down the block, a flash of light grabbed his eye. A flashlight. *Someone out on patrol is behind the building up ahead.* The one he'd almost dashed to. Then his worst fear: the distinctive red cape, visible even in the dark. The Sciolist stopped and shined his high-powered beam around the area, striking sides of the building and illuminating darkened windows. Weeford shrank back under the staircase, his fright blooming so severely that he thought he'd surely pee his pants. He wasn't cut out for this kind of work.

The flashlight swept around for a second time. *Shazz! He isn't leaving!*

Weeford moved back further into the shadows, hiding himself behind a four-foot-tall TrashVac container, quite a feat for his seven-foot form.

He's coming this way. Only about fifty yards away. If the guy discovered him, Weeford would be an enormous risk to Phoenix. He wondered if he'd be better off dead after all if he were caught.

The Sciolist continued walking in his direction. This wasn't going to end well. He had Phenol, which could produce death if he could get in a position to use it properly. And if the Sciolist was able to alert others when Weeford attacked him, there would be extreme risk.

He quickly scanned the area. No options. He had no weapon. Desperation made Weeford reach into the shielding TrashVac, but his prospects of finding something to use for defense were dim. Rubbish put in the bin was crushed and then sucked efficiently and immediately away to the recycling center.

He closed his eyes, his long arm probing the container's depths. If he were to trigger the vacuum … He didn't want to think about it.

Then his hand bumped up against a long, rounded thing. It felt like a stick but heavier. Whatever it was, it didn't have the correct shape for the TrashVac's intake. Laying crosswise, it had evaded the vac. He carefully drew out a heavy aluminum pipe about a foot long. It could be a good defense, but he'd not want to take his chances against a Sciolist's electrified spear.

Instead, he threw it across the street as hard as he could, away from the Sciolist. Glass shattered. An alarm wailed sickly into the silence. The Sciolist spoke into his Alt and hurried to the source of the threat, leaving Wee to make his getaway.

RIGHT BEFORE WEE made it to Elation Avenue's garage, he sent a message back to whoever sent instructions. "Two slow knocks followed by three short." They'd have to be ready. He wasn't able to just hang around outside the warehouse.

Sure enough, the knock was his code. A wiry, blond male REM whose name he didn't know met him inside.

"Hey. I'm Bixby," the REM drawled. "Ya made it!" Bixby pressed a button to close the electronic door and slapped him on the arm before pulling another set of heavy boxes over in front of the entrance.

"I'm Wee, but I'm guessin' you know that." Wee's gaze swept the warehouse. Stacks upon stacks of shrink-wrapped goods towered their way to the fifty-foot-ceiling. True to a Tranquility class system, even for emergency food stores, the blocks of boxes were color-coded. He stood in front of a box mountain of dried milk marked with mint green wrappings. The giant parcels in Tranquility's eighteen colors sat separate from each other, as if the white ones didn't dare touch the blue.

Small groups of people in distinctive uniforms of plumbers, electricians, food producers, and types of other jobs stood together engaged in conversation. The clothes ... none of them looked like Plauditors or REMs. A few looked at him warily until realizing this seven-foot giant had been amongst them before. Most simply waved at him and smiled, but a few guys he recognized came over to welcome him. With a few introductions, fist bumps, and high fives, he was beginning to feel at home.

"Wee!" Xander's right-hand man suddenly emerged from behind a tower of supplies. Jasper gave him a fist bump and the loyalty hand signal.

"Jasper! Good to see you, man."

"You made it before we could put our new plans into action. We'll have to get ya caught up. Most of our plans were made in the subway. We're just fine-tuning."

"Subway ...?" Weeford's confusion showed up in the lines across his forehead.

"A story for another day," Jasper said, lightly pounding Wee's back.

Weeford gawked at Jasper. "You're ... you have a uniform."

"Yeah!" Jasper grinned with pride.

Wee flicked Jasper's sleeve. "You *scammed* a delivery service uniform? How in the heck?"

"Darkness. Right before curfew got lifted. Plauditors know when and where the vans deliver laundered uniforms. And where cameras are. In the alley was ideal. Half this team lay in wait for 'em."

"That's crazy!" Weeford threw his hands in the air. "I can't believe ya didn't get caught."

"The two female operators were easy to subdue with six of us. We knocked 'em out with some of that magic stuff you gave Xander." Jasper reached up to give Wee a high five. "All of us changed clothes in the subway. Our uniforms are all different. Random Status colors." Jasper chuckled and shrugged. "Now, we're just normal citizens doin' our jobs."

Wee whistled. "No Sciolists anywhere?"

"Most are still hunting for us down below."

"In the … subway, which I still don't get. And how'd you get in here?" Weeford was still struggling to put all the pieces together.

"Ava sent a code for the warehouse door. She's a real miracle worker."

"So, the plan …?"

"We move into the city and gather support. We're starting with people we know. Go to their homes. We're the plumbers, delivery men, electricians—whatever people need, ya know?" Jasper's smile seemed to touch the top of his ears.

"Then …?" Weeford's building enthusiasm made his typical high energy level shoot off the charts.

"Once contact's made, we give 'em pages from Serpio's journals. It's not just our word then. It's proof."

"Ya don't have enough pages for the whole city …"

"Scanning pages with our Alts, 'course. And"—Jasper grin —"it takes just one scan. Hold it over the magic eye on the machine in the back, and we get real-for-real *paper* copies."

"Lemme check that out."

"Yeah. C'mon." Jasper motioned for Wee to follow. "I'll introduce ya to the others here."

"Got one more question."

"Shoot."

"When we all go out to these houses … they'll hide us?"

"If they don't disagree, yeah. There's always a risk that friends or family'll turn us in."

"Anybody from Phoenix get caught yet?" Weeford remembered Ava's coded words. "Ava's message said, '*most* safe.'"

"No. Luck's holding. Ava was prob'ly referring to Xander and Ember."

"Xander and Ember? Where are they?" Wee looked around, as if he expected to suddenly see them stroll out from behind a mountain of stacked boxes.

"They're Outside."

Weeford thought his head would swivel right off his neck. "WHAT?"

"Yeah. Ember found out her mom's alive and out there somewhere. That's why we don't know if they're safe. Their Alts don't work Outside."

"Holy Shazz! No way!" This was the last thing he'd expected to hear. But Weeford knew Xander wouldn't allow Ember to go somewhere like that alone, and there would be nothing stopping Ember. Now, for the first time, he worried more about Xander and Ember than he did about Will.

"The only way they'll survive it is by Xander knowing what to do. And he does. So, we keep holdin' on to that."

Wee's mind raced with "what if they die?" scenarios. But he was here for a purpose, and the rebellion needed him more than ever. "Ya think you have a uniform for me?"

66

Xander's Tactics

After their baths in the shallow water, they'd gathered their things. Ember was back on the litter again, and Xander's euphoric feeling of cleanliness from the mini pond didn't take long to wear off. He was already sweating, the heat continuing its assault. The effort of pulling Ember was becoming more and more tiresome.

Silently chastising himself for going so far off course, he trudged along. The only silver linings were that he was with Ember and she trusted him.

"Em … can you see if there's anything else between here and the rocks we're headed toward?"

"Ah …" Ember was undoubtedly studying her map. "This shows a field of sand ripples."

"Not dunes, I hope. I know for sure I can't pull you through those." His brain almost twisted from the thought of that scenario.

"Doesn't look like dunes. It's labeled Racine Ripples."

"Depending on what you think 'ripples' are. That could be one or the other."

"Yeah. It's still a ways ahead. You're on a direct path to it, though. And beyond that are the rocks we need to find. I'm guessing another five miles?"

"Doable."

He let silence take several minutes of space.

Ember broke it. "Do you think Phoenix got to the warehouses okay?"

"If they didn't, we may never be able to return. We'd be toast for sure. Everyone will eventually be tried and sent Outside or …" His mind spun with dreadful thoughts. How would they even know anyway?

"What—you mean we'd have to stay *here?*"

He felt Ember's eyes bore into his back. "If we get close to the city and we see that things are bad …"

"I can't live out here, Xander. It's crappy enough that we're here temporarily."

"If I thought your life was in danger, we wouldn't go back in."

"My life's in danger either way. So's yours. Is there something about being renegades you don't understand?"

Xander stopped walking and lowered the litter. He turned to look at Ember, a frown altering the shape of his eyebrows. "Oh, *I* understand. It's *you* that doesn't understand. The chances of our making it to your mom, finding a way back, and rejoining Phoenix without being arrested are pretty slim."

"I can't believe you think we're doomed. Have a little faith."

"I have faith, or I wouldn't be here. But the reality is that our food and water are running low. So, if we don't get to where your mom is soon, we're screwed."

"You're being completely negative, even for you."

He cringed, her words a barb to his soul. Was he being so real that she'd change her mind about him? He countered, "I'm real, and I'm reckless. That's what works."

When she didn't respond for a long minute, he turned to face her, dragging the litter with his back against the way forward. He saw that she was trying not to cry, her tears threatening to spill over.

He wanted to stop and comfort her, but they needed to push ahead. "Em … look. We are gonna reach your mom. And then it's a crapshoot. But I will never *ever* put you in certain danger. That's it. The bottom line. I'll do everything I can and then some. That's a promise." He gazed up at the sky, as if he pledged his vow to the Spirit in the Sky.

The sun sent its relentless, burning, steely gaze right back at him.

He was sick of the heat, the sunburn, and the surprises. His eyes suddenly settled on a quirky cloud. A dark purple, it scuttled along as if it was their shadow. He pivoted back to face his path, hoping that the cloud would at least partly obscure the hellish sun.

When he glanced back again, he saw that Ember had drifted off to sleep. That was good. She needed rest to heal.

Sure to what the map revealed, he soon traversed the sand ripples where, he realized, the sand resembled pictures he'd seen of gentle, near-shore ocean waves. No one he knew had ever seen an actual ocean, so his observation of the tiers and jagged lines gave his imagination wings. He dreamed up a scenario where he and Ember laughed as they jumped into real surf …

He toiled along, stopping to drink and eat in a few places. Not knowing exactly where he was, he assumed he'd traveled at least another four miles. He noticed his arms, pink with sunburn. They hurt. He cursed at the sun, realizing it was an enemy as real as the Greelox, the snake, and the crazy REM.

His thoughts darted from his feelings for Ember to his difficult past. When he thought about all that had happened in the last six weeks alone, he wondered if he wasn't on some cosmically predetermined clash with fate. Death and defiance. Doubts and fears. Escape and survival. Love and … hope.

Ah, hope! He realized the rocks he was using to chart his

path were definitely closer. They loomed larger and resembled giant people that beckoned him. And the cloud in the sky … was it three times the size it was? Or was he simply becoming delirious? Without Ember to talk to, he was going crazy.

What was real, though, was a change in the breeze. It had picked up and swirled around him, a typical temperature drop for The Outside. Like now, these capricious changes were often an absolute gift.

Within several minutes, though, the welcomed, cool puff turned bizarrely frigid. Cold cut through his clothing and made him shiver. He stopped walking and covered Ember with his jacket.

She woke, her face lit with surprise. "Oh … I've been sleeping." She sat up. "I'm sorry, Xander."

"I wanted you to sleep. Only rest is gonna heal that ankle. Didn't mean to wake you. But I had to cover you. It's getting cold."

She pulled the jacket up around her with a slight shiver. "Oh … it *is* cold." She hunkered down more, drawing her feet up for warmth. "Brrr." She reached for Xander's hand. "I'm sorry I lashed out earlier."

"Forgiven." He gently smiled before giving her hand a squeeze. "Just remember—I'm always on your side."

"*Why* is it suddenly so cold?" Ember clutched the jacket, her face showing frustration at its lack of cooperation.

"That's The Outside for ya." Xander gazed up at the sky. "It's weird, though. Kinda eerie. I saw one cloud earlier. Now there's a bunch of 'em."

Ember considered the clouds above her head. "Hmmm." Then, she shifted her view to what lay ahead. "You've gone a long way! The rocks don't seem that far."

"Yeah. You should eat and drink while we're stopped."

"Okay. I'm actually starving."

He helped her off the litter to stretch out, and she shrugged her arms into the jacket sleeves. They both sat and shared a protein bar. Grinning, Xander offered her some of the snake, but seeing her adamant shake of her head, only he ate it. The bland flavor didn't bother him, and it helped them conserve food.

When he glanced at Ember and saw her shivering, he drew closer and wrapped his arm around her, dissolving the inches between them. He kissed her then.

"I'm definitely warmer," he said after his lips left hers.

"Not me—not near enough anyway," Ember whispered. She moved her mouth against his again, her kiss the deepest she had given him yet.

When she ended it and looked into his eyes, she shivered. This time, though, he knew it wasn't from the cold. She lay her head against his shoulder. He stroked her arm, wishing desperately he could stay in the moment. Their journey, however, wasn't a thing they could just wish away.

"Not that I want to, but it's time to go, Em. I'm still hoping to make it to your mom before nightfall—only about two hours." Xander felt the wind pick up again, and he worriedly studied the darkening skies. It was almost as if a purple glow illuminated their faces. The cloud's ripe density blotted out the sun.

With Ember back in the litter, the two trekked on, gluing their eyes to the rocks ahead and the clouds above. With every step, Xander felt he was throwing the weather into full tilt. The temperature continued to drop, and the skies closed in.

"Is this normal?" Ember had to raise her voice against the quickening wind.

"No. Never seen it. It might be. I wasn't out here long enough to know for sure." With surprise, he saw his words shadowed by his breath, a light white mist that he'd never experienced.

"It's ridiculous!" Ember sat rigidly in her place, her muscles tense against the cold.

With Ember's judgment, the heavens answered. A lightning bolt forked the horizon, its flickering luminescence producing a freakish strobe effect. Xander's heart quickened. Now they'd be caught in the rain?

"Oh, crimony!" Ember's cry seemed a mix of fury and fear.

"It's only lightning. I'm pretty sure you can't die from that. And there's nothing to do but go forward. If it's rain coming, we'll get wet, yeah, but we can still travel."

A moment later, his thoughts and words imploded. It wasn't rain that was beginning to fall. It was *snow*. What the hell? He quietly cursed. Just what they needed … one more thing.

He heard Ember catch her breath. He turned to see her grinning, her hands outstretched to catch the flakes as they fell. The white crystals stuck in her hair and on her eyelashes, making her appear like a fairy from an enchanted kingdom.

"It's so beautiful!" Ember gushed.

"Yeah." He slowed down and then stopped to take in the experience. He'd never seen snow before, and the wonder of it was magical. Flakes danced before his vision, their glassy whiteness beginning to land like fireflies on his body. He stuck his tongue out and laughed. The feeling of the flakes dissolving when he held them in his mouth was a new sensation. He celebrated it by waving his arms through the flurry and then standing completely still, allowing the miracle of it to engulf him.

As the snow whitened the ground around him, though, he divorced himself from the beauty. He felt the temperature dive again, and' he realized how difficult—if not impossible—it would be to pull Ember the next couple of miles if the snow continued to fall.

Ember was trying to catch, gather, and hold the flakes in her hands. "Is this how you make a snowball?"

"Uh … no. I don't know. We can't think about playing with it. If it doesn't stop, we're gonna have problems."

Realization dawned on Ember's face, her smile quickly gone. "Oh. Yeah. You're right. We're gonna need cover. And … is it me, or is it getting exponentially colder?"

"Not just you." Xander watched the snowfall increase its intensity, and a sharp, bitter wind began a ghostly sounding "woooo." Holy shazz, they were doomed. "We're gonna have to make shelter somehow. We could freeze to death."

"How far are the rocks?" Ember couldn't hide the worry in her voice.

"We might make it if we pick up the pace. We can try." His icy breath seemed to freeze in his chest. Could he push himself hard enough?

Ember put her hand to her head. "We should be running —and then there's me. I've ruined our chances, haven't I?"

"We're *not* thinking that, Em." He pulled foil blankets out of both packs to help Ember stay warmer, picked up the litter handles, and forged ahead, accelerating his pace. His eyes searched the distance. He focused on the boulders, wondering how long it would be until he couldn't even see them anymore through the rain of snowflakes.

"What can I do, Xander?"

"Use your Alt compass. Help me go in the right direction. And keep encouraging me. I need your positive thinking right now." He began hoping for more lightning. It would at least light their way.

"You're doing great. Aim to your right … that's it."

He concentrated, her reassuring words caressing him as he pushed on.

67

Xander's Survival 101

The snow continued to increase along with the wind. Before it reached a point where they couldn't see anything at all, they had reached the rocks. Xander was colder than he'd ever been in his life, his hair frozen to spiky peaks, his lips freakishly blue. His hands were stiff, and his fingers felt brittle. Ember was worse off. Unlike him, her lack of movement caused her to finally just curl up on the litter in misery. By now, the snowfall and wind were a blizzard. The snow wasn't so magical anymore. It felt like needles, the wind pushing each particle into places he didn't know he had.

At the first outcropping of boulders, he halted. They'd reached a stopping place none too soon. He was exhausted, his every bone sending out an SOS.

But they'd made it. He sunk down into the snow for a long minute, his first rest in what seemed like a thousand years. He couldn't rest long. The next challenge was to make a shelter.

"Em, we're stopping for the night."

"Oh … What?" She stirred from her hunkered-down position on the litter. "Oh my gosh. It's too cold!" She sat up and squeezed her eyes shut again.

His hands frozen into five-pronged popsicles and his eyes

blinking back snowflakes, Xander scooped snow from an area next to the face of a giant stone to make a wide dugout. Scrounging in his bag, he pulled out the other survival blanket and laid it in the dugout.

He pulled Ember to her feet, leaving her foil coverings behind. He half-carried her to where he laid her down in the hollow he'd constructed. The ground would still be cold, but they wouldn't be lying in snow. "We're go-gonna have to g-get creative," he said, his teeth chattering.

"I'm so … c-cold … I'll do anything. What're … you thinking?" Her words broke in the wind and with the trembling of her mouth.

He didn't answer. He took the litter and tilted it over her, connecting the broad part to the stone and resting its handles in the snow. It resembled a half teepee, the other half formed by the side of a monstrous boulder. He covered the outside of the device with both of the wet blankets, tying one to the top of the litter and packing snow around the other to keep it in place.

Then, he ducked his head into the makeshift tent. "I n-need your jacket."

"Wh-what?" Ember's tone sounded as if he'd just told her that pigs absolutely did fly.

"Just do it." He rubbed his hands together. It didn't help to thaw them out.

She took off her jacket and handed it to him, her eyes now wide with worry.

He discarded his own with a proper shiver and tied them to the open spaces on either side to block the wind and snow. With longing, he thought of a fire, but it would never stay lit. He collected their rucksacks. They would go into the shelter with them.

He crouched down to enter the tiny space. "Trust me?"

"Yes."

"We have to take off our clothes."

Her face displayed the shock he was expecting, but she nodded, still shivering uncontrollably. "Wh-what? Everything?"

"Leave your underwear on." With some effort, he managed a half-smile, but he was already removing his own clothes. "It's Survival 101. Body heat. And our clothes are wet. No good. We'll freeze in 'em." He busied himself with making sure their fragile structure was embedded enough in the snow and dirt to stay stable. And, out of respect for Ember, he didn't want to watch her disrobe right in front of his eyes.

After she handed him her pants and shirt, he gathered their clothes in his arms and wedged the fabric around them as insulation against the snow. Then, he sandwiched himself behind her, his front to her back in a spoon. With an effort to cement himself to her, he pulled her tightly against him and wrapped his arms around her waist.

"Now, we warm up." He laid his head on her shoulder, his mouth against her neck. He entwined his legs with hers, forming a sort of human braid.

Darkness set in, not only from the steel wool clouds, but because the sun had set. Their own bodies became pale forms enveloped in shadows.

They lay for a long time, not speaking at all, just holding each other, watching their breath make clouds, listening and watching the brutal wind whip by. The two of them shivered together, their teeth chattering and their body heat seeming to evaporate into the chill. The blizzard raged around them, their lean-to roof sounding like a series of baseballs hitting targets before bouncing off. Xander's jacket blew off the side and was gone.

The force of the wind terrified him. He'd never experienced anything even close. If they didn't get warmer, they would get hypothermia. After all this—all they'd survived—they could easily die. He watched the snow hit the ground outside the tiny shelter and begin to pile up. A thought traipsed through his mind: would the snow pile up so much they'd be trapped?

Yet holding Ember in his embrace, his body her only real protection, was a little piece of heaven.

He loved feeling her breathing, in and out, her ribcage surrounded by his arms. And even though it made sense under the circumstances that her breath emerged as a frosty, ghostly white mist, it hardly seemed possible. Not from Ember. She was too warm inside, too alive.

As Xander lay with her body up against him, warmth pulsed through him, a welcome but provocative heat flushing him from his chest to his toes. He whispered, "I—I'm trying not to … react."

"Don't worry. Remember … your feelings are already coursing in and around me like blood. I feel everything that you're feeling, and if it's physical, just know I'm … responding, too. You can't see my reaction, but it's there."

Her words made him groan out loud. *Keep it together, Xander,* he chided himself.

Her hair lay around her shoulders, damp from snow, its sparks of fiery color a stark contrast to the weather outside. Impulsively, he lifted a strand away from her face, winding it on one finger and then letting it go to observe the way it fell so perfectly back into place. "Your hair is so beautiful. It's one of the things I love the most about you."

She gently touched his fingers before they returned to their place around her waist. "Is it your *favorite* thing?"

"My favorite thing? No." Turning his face into her neck, he inhaled her scent. He felt slightly dizzy, as if he'd stood up too quickly. "It's how you smell like sunshine."

"Mmm." She sighed. "You haven't been close enough to me that often to decide it's your favorite thing."

"It's a very recent discovery. But an amazing one." He smiled tenderly and tightened his arms around her.

"What else do you like?" She snuggled in and turned her face in the direction of his.

He hesitated for a long moment before responding. "You make me feel things I've never felt before. I've always loved girls. But you—you make me want to be a better person. You stir things deep inside me that I didn't even know were there. And I'm attracted to you like no girl I've ever met." If it was possible for a heart to swell, his felt close to bursting with devotion.

She twisted her upper torso and tilted her head back to look into his eyes. He thought he would drown in their depths, her gaze starry-eyed and intense. She allowed her head to drop backward, her face totally upturned, her neck open in an invitation.

Those eyes, her lips, her warmth … He gritted his teeth, now not so concerned about their chattering as a help with physical resolve, and fought against the torrid tide sweeping him away. He had asked her to trust him. That the removal of their clothes was a survival tactic. And now, what was he thinking?

He walked a tightrope of indecision. He cared so deeply for her that he couldn't risk any kind of betrayal. Yet, as if echoing his own, he felt the wild vibration of her heartbeat buzz through him.

Xander brought her hand to his mouth, his breath warming her fingertips. He kissed her fingers and allowed his lips to trail across her palm and then to the back of her wrist.

Ember turned her head toward him, her cheek flat against his chest. "You … make me h-happy."

He smiled then, feeling his cheeks stretch the stiffness of his face.

In a delicate graze with his fingers, he touched her cheek. He ran his tongue along his own lips to warm and moisten them in readiness for the kiss he knew he wouldn't and couldn't resist. Then, Xander bent his head, running his lips across hers, feathery, as if deciding whether he was ready to commit.

Ember laced her hands behind his neck and tugged in a blatant demand for greater pressure, and she sighed and arched her back. He drew his mouth away instead for a full moment, bestowing on her his most smoldering gaze. Then, he dipped again, barely running the tip of his tongue across her upper lip.

She cried out in an agonized whimper, then whispered low and thick, "Xander ... why are you holding back?" She defiantly changed her position, sitting up, before possessively slipping her arm around his head and pulling him to her to force a kiss.

"No ... I want it this way." Xander put his arm around her and lowered her to the ground, her body on its back laid out before him. He rolled over on top of her, one arm on either side of her, propping himself up. He again stared into her eyes, his pulse a throb he knew she could see reflected in his own eyes.

He finally kissed her, gently nuzzling and pushing her lips open. Again, he lingered, softly, barely parting them, but as he eased away, he tenderly tugged at her upper lip with his teeth in a sensual tease. As always, the very moment their mouths met, emotions flooded him—commitment, desire, and heart.

When he broke the kiss, Ember's voice caressed him. "You're amazing," Ember murmured. "I want ..."

"Yeah ..." He growled low.

"I want to be a *lot* warmer."

"You're not warm enough yet? That's too bad ..." His slow smile and raised eyebrow were deliberate hooks. He was losing the ability to think clearly. A profound, accelerated stir of desire drove him.

"I'm still freezing." Ember pulled him down on top of her, and her hands dropped to his back, where her fingers caressed and gripped him as far as she was able to reach. Ember pushed herself more tightly against him and whispered, "I want you to feel me like I feel you."

Her breathing quickened, the bodily pressure between them an explosion of ecstasy. He moaned, his resolve totally gone to ash. His desire for her was getting more dangerous by the moment. When she said things like that about him and what she wanted, she was opening the door. He completely lost the control he was seeking.

His mouth came down on her neck, his tongue licking the bare curves down to her shoulder and invading the upper swell of her breasts on her chest.

She gasped, the sharp intake of breath a sign she was either surprised or aroused. Then, she tilted her head to give him free rein. His one arm held her tightly as he lifted her hair from her neck, his open mouth continuing to devour her before he turned her head and kissed her slowly all along her neck.

She murmured his name, and he hesitated, wanting to make sure she wasn't admonishing him to stop. "Xander …" she said again with tenderness. He lightly stroked her shoulders, dragging his fingers down to where he felt the rise of her breasts.

Again, he stopped, wanting to draw out the experience, the anticipation.

"You make me insane," he groaned roughly.

Ember languidly slid her arms around his neck to kiss him in a gradation of intensity that forever made her his deepest anchor in an insane, unforgiving world. Her insistent mouth parted his lips over and over, sending tremors coursing along his nerves. He'd never known he could be capable of feeling like this—like it was opening his soul, like tasting every color of the rainbow.

When she stopped to breathe, panting, he took her chin in his hand, cocking her face to kiss her as deeply as he could, his tongue looping around hers in urgent discovery. He kissed her with everything in him, letting her know that he was there, that he wasn't going anywhere, that he was hers.

His hands drifted down, this time not hesitating, to cup her breasts. "Oh," she whispered, her breath still misting around her. She arched her body against him, further inflaming his need. Keeping his mouth on her neck, he gently squeezed her breasts, kissing her until she cried out.

"Xander …" Ember panted. In a slow move, she eased one leg over his.

Xander pulled her on top of him, allowing Ember's hands to stroke his chest.

In only a moment, he would be beyond the point of no return. Her body on his, their eyes locked … It would take superhuman restraint to stop himself from doing what his mind and body craved. He wanted it.

Instead, he pulled his head forward and held her in a rigid hold. "Em—don't … move." Xander put his arms on hers, and he gripped her. Her body was hot to the touch.

"Don't *move*? Xander …" she breathed. "Please … don't ask me to stop, not again." Her pupils were dilated, her desire like a Pandora's box he badly wanted to open.

When she leaned down, he kissed her in response but with less ardor, his heart threatening to blow apart. "Ember … stopping is not what I want. But it's what's right." The words mocked him, but he got them out.

"Right for who?" she whispered, her eyes wide.

"For you. For us." He gave her a soft kiss before murmuring, "You're a dream. My dream." His hands then immersed themselves in her hair, pulling her tenderly to his side.

Her head on his chest, he lay with her for several minutes, his eyes closed, his heart pounding. The heaving in his chest seemed to suffocate the words he wanted to say.

She, too, kept her eyes closed, but he finally opened his and gazed down at her, taking in the way her eyelashes lay against her face, her nose still pink from cold, and her flawless skin flushed with exertion. Her face was aglow, a sweet smile on her lips. She opened her eyes to gaze up at him with an adoration he could barely fathom.

He finally whispered, "You've dazzled me beyond what I should have allowed. You're just so beautiful that I get carried away."

She sat up and turned her head fully to meet his eyes. Her gaze held a fire that positively melted him. Her voice dropped to a purr. "Xander … don't be sorry."

He held her face in his hands and planted a kiss on her forehead. "If you ever feel like I'm pressuring you, you need to be blunt."

"Pressuring me? I'm right here, with you—where I *want* to be. And I'm absorbing all your emotions. I'm having a harder time than you. I have twice the heat."

"I seriously doubt that," he argued. "But when we got here, I asked you to trust me …"

"And I'd call Survival 101 a huge success. I'm definitely not cold anymore."

He grinned. "Yeah. I'm hot as hell." He pulled her tighter to him. "But you and I … we're not finishing this here. We're not making love in a place like this. You're too important to me." He remembered when he told her he would protect her. But he never realized he'd have to protect her from himself. "You're—we're too young. And I don't have any protection. It's not like I have what we'd need in our survival kits."

She laughed, her eyes bright. "I think we're old enough to know what we're doing *and* what it means." Ember stroked his arm, her eyes lowered.

"Yeah. I know what it means. It means this, Ember—once I completely have you, I could never let you go. It would kill me."

A slow smile opened Ember's lips. She tilted her head back and looked deeply into his eyes. "Well, then. My heart, at least, is yours."

68

Ember's Wake Up

Sometime during their romantic interlude, the wind slowly petered out, but their attention on each other put them in another world—a place that, for the moment, would be an escape, a dreamy refuge. For the remainder of the night, not even aware that the storm gradually decreased in strength to light snow flurries, they slept soundly in each other's arms.

Ember woke first, opening her eyes to a patch of sunshine illuminating her face from the holes in the litter that had miraculously sheltered them. The little splash of warmth was something she wanted to bottle up in case she'd ever wonder in the future if the sun would shine again.

"The sun is out!" She sat up, stirring Xander, who rubbed the sleep from his face with his hands. She smiled, both at the sun shining in and at Xander, whose mere presence now made her heart skip a beat.

"We made it, Xander," she said, caressing his arm with her hand.

He laughed slightly. "There's no way that storm could have frozen us last night. It was no match for us."

"True," she said, stretching her legs. "No regrets, then?"

"Oh, I have regrets. Just not ones that I can do anything about."

She glanced his way, a little nervous about how things ended up. *He probably thinks I'm wild.* Then, she frowned. She was sitting there in all her glory, still in her underwear. She looked around for her clothes. The crinkly pile was luckily within her reach. She shook out her shirt and threw it on, its dampness uncomfortable. But that was okay. She had clothes, and they would dry.

As Ember slowly stood up, she toppled the litter. It fell over, making an impression in the dirt still decorated with small patches of remaining snow. With one hand on the boulder next to her, she put on her pants. Realizing the ease of her effort, her spirits soared. "Hey … my ankle isn't hurting today."

"Really? Thank the stars," Xander said, exaggerating his words the way he often did. "You can walk?" He got to his feet, his hand reaching out to help stabilize Ember.

"I … I think I can." She stepped forward, her move tentative. "No pain!"

"But can you walk a distance? I don't want to leave the litter here if you're going to need it."

"Either way, the litter comes with us. We can both pull it, and it'll hold our stuff." To prove herself fit and able, she picked up her rucksack and laid it on the litter. "Hand me yours?"

"I've got it." Xander placed his pack on before pulling their thin blankets and her jacket from the litter where they were still barely attached. The last thing on was the rifle.

"Think you might want your clothes?" Ember admired his bare chest for a moment before tossing his things to him.

"Thanks. Eww—they're still wet. Maybe I'll—"

"No, Xander. Put them on." Ember laughed. "You didn't mind it yesterday after your bath. Even if it gets hot, you need to be protected."

He grunted and then threw on his clothes, back to looking like a respectable Plauditor, if not a little wrinkled and wet one.

They pulled the last two protein bars from each of their sacks. Their lack of food last night made Ember ravenous, but they had to make these stretch. They should be at their destination today, but if not, they'd have to conserve. The snake was getting gamey, so Xander tossed it aside. To her disappointment, their water was frozen.

They each grabbed a handle on the litter and began walking.

"We should make it today if you can walk it," Xander said. "It should only be a few miles."

"I'm counting on it." She was more than done with this journey and ready to be on her feet again.

"Remember … we don't know what we'll find or even if we'll be able to find your mom."

"I had another dream." Ember had dreamed twice—one last night and one during the day right before the storm hit them. The dream she'd had in the daytime as Xander pulled her in the litter was the familiar one. As always, it made her fearful. She wasn't ready to share that with Xander.

The one she'd dreamed last night would help them today.

"And?" He pressed her.

"We're going to find her. She's … underground."

Xander's face was inscrutable, but she felt his alarm before he spoke. "You mean, like, in a bunker? We won't even be able to see a building?"

"No, but I saw what the access door looks like. I think I'll be able to recognize it when we search for it. And my mom's not suffering. At least not from torture or lack of food. It's just lonely. She told me that in the dream. That's a relief." Ember felt her mom more keenly than she'd yet experienced, like a powerful lure was pulling her forward. It was similar to what she'd experienced with the gold journal, but it was her mom herself drawing her.

"Check your Alt map and compass. If we can locate the area, you think you can find where it is?"

"I'm certain," Ember replied, her eyes on her Alt. "I think two more miles." She grinned, her excitement rising.

"If you're right, we'll be there in less than an hour." Xander spontaneously grabbed her hand. "I'm happy for you, Ember."

Her breathing suddenly felt oxygenated, her heart lighter than it had been in the many long weeks since her mother's death. "I'm so anxious to see her. But I wonder … how am I going to explain who you are?" She threw him a look of mock mystification.

"Ah … After all this, you're still confused? I'm your *boyfriend,* Ember." Then, with his signature sarcasm, he continued, "Or is that just too much for you to handle?" He squeezed her hand but gave her a somewhat serious appraisal.

Ember played the game. She tossed her hair. "Hmmm. I might have to think about that. Sounds like a pretty heavy commitment." Her smile became flirty. This was one of the things she loved most about Xander—the back and forth, the kidding, the cat and mouse. With Will— She caught herself. What in the world was that thought for?

"Oh, you're committed, baby. You just might not know how much I've yet to rock your world." He raised an eyebrow and then chuckled.

She gave him her sweetest smile. "You don't think you have anything left to prove?"

He abruptly stopped, all of a sudden dead serious. "I'll prove whatever you need. Whatever it takes."

"I look forward to it." She swung her hand in his and winked at him. But inside, she shivered, realizing that her dreams had yet to play out.

$$\overline{}$$

69

Ember's Reunion

$$\overline{}$$

Ember was starting to tire. Her ankle supported her, but it began to slightly ache again, reminding her she wasn't yet a hundred percent. She trudged along, though, refusing to accept Xander's suggestion to get back in the litter.

An hour later, after the sun began its indecent aggression, they found themselves walking to and fro across a broad field. Here and there were tiny tufts of grass, a bizarre accent on the landscape. There was no wind or dips anywhere. The ground was curiously and perfectly flat.

For all they could tell, they'd found where the coordinates should be. For Ember, it was a giddy accomplishment, her emotions in full bloom. Xander's aura flared yellow, his expectancy and spirit of adventure on display.

The two dropped the litter to strike out and took turns crisscrossing the area, then walking in circles. Ember could feel her mother's presence. She was close, but where?

"Em, let's branch out a little. You go south; I'll go north for, say, one hundred yards. Then, we can go east and west. It's not like we have an exact line in the dirt."

"Okay. I'm going on gut feeling …" She lassoed her mind

and consciously opened herself to whatever power she could access.

As she trudged in her assigned direction with careful, measured steps, her heartbeat began to dance in an irregular way, each beat seeming to push the next one to greater speed.

It could only mean one thing: she was incredibly near to where her mom was.

She scrutinized the ground, all her focus on finding the hatch she'd seen in her dream. There … there! "Xander!"

"Yeah?" he called back.

"I found it!" She jumped up and down, a silly childhood gesture but one that completely fit the moment.

Xander came running. When he drew up and saw the black metal circle in the dirt, he threw Ember a high five. "What are you waiting for? Open it!" He leaned over it with Ember, grabbing and pulling a protruding tab on one side. "Ahhh! It's not budging!"

They looked at each other, stymied.

"Wait! The explosives in my rucksack!" Xander darted away before Ember could even process what he said.

Thank you, Ava! Ember hoped her thoughts would find their way to the city.

Xander returned without running. His countenance showed concern. "I hope the snowstorm didn't damage this. It wasn't very well protected."

"One way to find out. You know what to do?" A nervous tic began on her lower eyelid.

"Do you doubt it? Of course," he bragged. He pulled a pink-colored tube from the round packet he held in his hand, then extracted a lighter from his pocket. His eyes held a hint of mischief as he squatted down to lay the narrow, pipe-like device on the side of the hatch. "You need to go over there." He gestured. "Far out of the way."

"Xander, you … you'll be in danger. How can you light

this and be safe?" Ember felt his bravery and determination, but under it all was a tiny spark of fear.

He gazed at her. "You're not forcing me to do this. And I would do it for anyone in this situation. But most of all, I'm doing it for you. I'll be fine. Just—just get some space—at least fifty yards."

She gave him a concerned face but scuttled to where she thought fifty yards would be. Watching him set the explosive was making her as nervous as a steer in a butcher shop.

He appeared to check that he'd positioned the apparatus properly, and then he glanced her way. With a thumbs-up, he put the lighter to the stuff before he ran, throwing his body as far away as he could. He lay on the ground, his hands covering his head.

Two seconds later, the device exploded. Clods of dirt, filaments of grass, and sharp grains of sand rocketed up and outward in a vertical spray, then showered the area like sharp, coarse rain. Reddish-brown smoke swirled around in a sulphuric cloud, its smell a combination of overcooked eggs and sweet transmission oil. The lid of the hatch clanged and scraped as it barreled off its hinges, its displaced force making it a dangerous projectile.

Ember raced to the site, her nerves in a frenzy. *Please let Xander be okay.* She choked and blinked her eyes to defray the burn of the smoke storm. She could see somewhat, but it was like looking at everything through a dream.

"Xander?" She waved her arms through the vapor, as if by doing so she could push it away. No answer. "Xander! Where are you?"

"Here ... I'm here."

She beelined for his voice. He was still lying on the ground but beginning to sit up when she almost stumbled into him.

"Oh! Are you okay?" She knelt next to him, her worried mind racing to bad possibilities, like having a piece of his arm blown off.

"Yeah." He sat up completely, his face streaked with dirt and his hair in total disarray.

Ember gripped his shoulders to look at his face. She ran her fingers down his arms to his hands. "You … you really are okay? No missing parts?"

"There better not be." He grinned, his sideways smile the perfect affirmation of well-being.

She wrapped her arms around him in a tight hug. "That was … frightening."

"More like exhilarating," he countered. "A real adrenaline rush."

"Oh, stop it." In this moment, his bravado simply shook her up. She let him go, witnessing the smoke begin to clear.

She stood first and tried to assess the area. He rose and sauntered over to where their target was.

He gestured to her. "It's open."

Ember shot over and looked down into the portal where she knew her mother would be waiting. All she saw was a concrete wall. "There's what looks like part of a ladder. I'm going in!"

"No. I will first. We prob'ly blew off the top of the ladder. But it's attached to a wall …" He lowered himself down into the hatch's space, where his feet dangled for a minute. "Pretty primitive."

"Don't—don't fall!"

"I'm on some steps." It took about thirty seconds before he spoke again. "Now I'm down—on a floor. Come on. I'll help you. Watch your ankle."

She descended, and Xander supported her as she got off. They stood in a small, eight-foot-wide circular, concrete area with walls all around. Facing them was a heavy, gray door. It didn't look to be electronic but rather oddly made of wood. There was no door handle or knob.

Ember accosted the door, knocking as hard as she could. "She had to have heard the explosion."

"Of course. But she doesn't know who's out here. It could be someone bad."

Ember focused her mind, clearing her thoughts and allowing her senses to be open to communication. She could feel her mom, but could her mom feel her?

Xander pounded on the door. "It could be soundproof."

Ember stepped in front of Xander. "Shhh … stop. I'm gonna try something." She rested her palm on the door and stood there, quietly waiting. A minute ticked by.

"We might have to use explosives on the door."

She shook her head and closed her eyes, concentrating again. "Wait."

Ember and Xander jumped back as someone from the other side pushed the door open. With a shudder and a groan, the door eased out. As the opening grew wider, Ember's breath caught in her chest.

Then, she cried out as her mom's face appeared. As Talesa emerged, Ember sprung forward. She threw her arms around her mom, returned by a fervent embrace.

"Ember!" Talesa began to cry. "You really did find me! Oh my …! Ohhh!"

"Mom! I'm—I'm so happy you're *alive*! I'm—oh, it's been terrible." Ember was crying, too, her tears blurring her vision. She wiped them away, wanting to see her mom clearly, and stepped back, keeping her hands on her mom's shoulders. Talesa looked thin but as beautiful as Ember remembered. Her violet eyes sparkled. Shiny, dark brown hair fell slightly curled around her chin. Ember pressed her face against her mom's, feeling the softness of the skin that she had so missed.

Talesa drew back but put her hands on both sides of Ember's face. "I can't believe you got here!" She turned to Xander, taking in his disheveled appearance but smiling as if he was a long-lost friend. "And who's this? Someone you must really trust."

"I'm Xander. So good to meet you. I'm Ember's body-guard." Xander winked and chuckled.

"No, he isn't! Mom … Xander's my boyfriend. And without him, I wouldn't be here, or maybe even be alive." Ember gazed at Xander with blatant adoration.

Talesa reached out to grasp Xander's hand. "I'm grateful to you, then. Especially if you've come all this way with her."

Sarcasm lacing his words, Xander said, "I'm just a *little* familiar with what's out here."

Talesa's eyebrows lifted. "Oh, that's a story to hear, then." As if she was still struggling with the reality of their arrival, she grabbed Ember in a hug again and rocked back and forth with her. When they separated and Talesa looked into Ember's face, she said, "No one knows you're here?"

Ember said, "Only one person. Her name's Ava. She helped us."

Xander's gaze swept the cemented cylindrical anteroom in which they stood. "Are there alarms here? Cameras? If so, we're already screwed."

Talesa shook her head. "No cameras or alarms. Serpio has nothing to worry about. There's no way for me to get out. No one even knows I'm here. But are you sure you weren't followed?"

Xander said, "I'm sure. No one is looking for us here. They think Ember's in the city. And they think I'm dead."

Ember's mom studied Xander's face. "Oh. How did you even get out of the city?"

Ember answered, "It's a long story. We'll have to fill you in. But first, we need to make plans to get us out of here."

"I'm looking for another way besides up through that hole," Xander said. "We could do it, but then it's miles back to the city through The Outside. We're short on supplies and patience."

Talesa opened the door and gestured. "Come in, come in!

I'll give you the guided tour. You can rest and eat. Then, we'll talk and plan."

Entering the interior, Ember was stunned to see a comfortable living space. When someone was a prisoner, weren't they in a type of jail?

The bunker was quite large. Ember imagined it was maybe six hundred square feet. The walls were a pale lavender, and the furnishings plush and exquisite, each piece designed to complement the others. A velvet upholstered sofa in a solid lilac fabric held pillows with bright, optimistic sayings in shades of purple and the palest gray. A striped armchair sat in front of what looked like a window, but of course, it was just an illusion. To their right was a tiny kitchen with a white table, an old-style microwave, a KoolKrate, and a sink. On the other side of the room, through an arch in a wall, Ember could see a bed. A bathroom was likely attached. Her eyes drifted to a panel to the left of the window. Although it had no distinctive characteristics of a door, it had to be a separate way in and out of the bunker.

The beauty and elegance of the place was the last thing she expected. "Mom, it's so nice! I mean, not like home, but not at all what I expected."

"I know. There's a reason. But no stories yet. First, a drink, food, and maybe showers?"

Ember felt as if she'd hit life's jackpot. Her mother was alive. She and Xander could get food and water. And to get in a shower with *soap*? "Yes! Thanks!" She gave her mom another big hug, still scarcely able to believe she could put her arms around her. She breathed in her mother's scent, the same as ever. It just smelled sweeter now.

Talesa hugged Ember again, this time even more tightly. "Oh, Ember. I don't want to let you go ever again!"

"Never." Ember thought she would explode with joy. Her mom—the most important person in her life—was here and *real*. No more sorrow or separation!

Talesa did let her go and went to rustle in a kitchen cupboard for three glasses and ice-cold water. She said, "I don't have much on hand. My food's delivered daily. I keep a few leftovers in case I need them for emergencies but never need them. Everything I need gets delivered right on time. Same time, every day."

Ember and Xander accepted the water and gulped it down. Talesa refilled their glasses before offering them a couple of cookies, a half sandwich each, and a few pieces of cheese. Regardless of the odd combination, it was the best thing Ember had tasted for days. A bottle of orange liquid labeled Sunshine's Sugar finished off their meal. Talesa explained that it had vitamins and electrolytes in it to make sure she stayed healthy.

The three chattered about how they'd set the explosive to open the hatch, and Talesa listened with owlish eyes. She confirmed Xander's guess: the bunker was heavily insulated and soundproof. The only thing she'd felt was a mild vibration and then Ember's presence outside the door.

"Ember, go take a shower. I have a limit on water, but if you keep it to less than ten minutes, Xander'll be able to shower, too."

Ember's face budded with a smile. "Okay. Just don't interrogate Xander while I'm in there," she joked.

"And help yourself to what's in my closet," Talesa called after her.

As she skipped off, Ember listened as Talesa thanked Xander again for helping her daughter come for her.

"I'd do anything for her," she heard Xander say.

70

Ember's Renewal

Ember spritzed herself with her mother's signature fragrance. Simply called "Happy," the perfume was flowery, with a hint of grapefruit, mimosa, and bergamot. She brushed her hair, tying it back in a high ponytail, then stopped suddenly, gazing at herself in the mirror.

There stood a girl who was reborn. Not only had her shower cleaned off the muck from her journey, but the face that stared back at her wasn't the same one as the girl from only a month ago. Her eyes, once drowning in doubt and fear, were now wise and strong. They had witnessed what evil could do but also seen a completely different, fresh life. The success and acceptance of her hidden talents translated to a posture that oozed confidence. And while her skin showed the brutal pink of sunburn, it was also the blush of discovered, raw passion. Rough scrapes on her arms marked her as a battle-scarred warrior who had prevailed over uncommon hardships. Fingers that had quivered from the cold could heal broken hearts with a loving touch. Most of all, her smile was transformed. Where it was often false in the city, it was now alive with true happiness.

With a sigh of contentment, Ember emerged from the

bathroom, dressed in a soft, knit, short-to-the-knee jumpsuit that buttoned up the front. There wasn't any choice on the color. Purple had been her mother's Status, and it seemed that assignment had continued into the bunker. Talesa was a shade taller than Ember, but the clothes otherwise fit her as if they were made for her.

Xander remained seated at the small table in the kitchen, appearing to be having some laughter and conversation with Talesa. When Ember re-entered the room, he stood, his smile practically splitting his face in two.

Xander's eyes didn't leave her as Ember walked over to the table. "You look beautiful. But you always do, even traveling through The Outside, dirty and tired." Xander gave a shoulder tilt to Talesa with a side smile. "She comes by beauty naturally, though, I see."

Talesa laughed and put up a hand in protest. "I don't hold a candle to her. But thanks. Now go see what you can do with yourself."

Xander chuckled as he shoved his hair away from his face. "I'll do my best."

"Xander—you can take something from the closet, too."

He grinned. "No offense, but your clothes won't be right for me."

"Not my clothes." Talesa paused and looked down at her glass. "Serpio keeps a few things here …"

There was a stunned silence where Xander and Ember exchanged looks of horror, their mouths open and eyebrows raised.

"I know, I know. Part of the story I have yet to tell you later. Now, go to it."

An inhale from Xander was audible. With tight lips, he said no more. He merely nodded and exited the room.

"You have quite the young man," Talesa said.

Ember smiled and lowered her eyes, suddenly shy about discussing her relationship with her mom. "Yeah … I didn't think he would ever be anyone special. But I'm head over heels. He's been a beautiful surprise."

"He's got confidence and courage. When did you meet and how?"

"I met him first in middle school." Ember smiled, the memory now tender in a different way than then. "But he—he's a REM."

"An emotional resistor. No wonder I like him!"

Ember flashed a smile, but it was a rueful one. "I—I guess you would. You've been through the worst. From sick to dead to a prisoner!"

"I was able to hold on, Ember, because I needed to come back to you. I wouldn't ever want to leave you alone."

"But, Mom, how did you survive? You were dying. Then you weren't there. And no one wanted to tell me where your body was. I was sick with grief!"

"You see why they couldn't tell you where my body was! How awful for you. And then you had to keep your Alt points up ..." Shallow tears gathered in her eyes. "I was trying to communicate with you, but I was way too weak."

"Your ring ... it was poisoned."

"I didn't realize it until long after we'd already gone to the hospital. Then, I tried to tell you, but it was too late. I couldn't get the words out." Talesa wiped a tear from the corner of her eye.

"You tried. I just couldn't get the meaning of it. I was so upset! Nothing made sense."

"My poor, sweet daughter. I was hoping you could understand, but I didn't have the strength to explain. Then, as hard as I tried, I couldn't fight anymore. I knew I was dying.

But I ended up here. I was as surprised as you are. Happy to be alive, but in such a bad place."

"You were suddenly just gone from your bed. I couldn't find you. The medics wouldn't help me ..."

"The bed had a large headboard, remember?"

"Yeah?"

"It had a door in it that opened, and a device moved me into another room. I guess that's what they do after someone dies to remove the body. I only know because a medic told me when he fixed me up with a Medela healing machine. It took several days and a recirculating flushing of my blood. There was no way I could reach out to you." She put her head down, and Ember saw her tears splash onto the table.

Ember took her mother's hand. "It's okay. You couldn't do anything. And I was lost. I didn't know who to turn to."

Talesa wiped her tears again and lifted her chin. "And that's when you met Xander?"

"No." She paused. "I met … someone else first—a Plauditor. He helped me learn about the ring."

"And he's in the city? Is he someone I should thank?"

Ember looked down at the table, as if the table could suddenly become a shield. "Umm … it's complicated." Her desire to change the subject was overwhelming. She raised her eyes to her mom's teary face. "So much has happened. I'm sure I won't have time to tell you everything, but we have an entire team of resistors now. We're plotting to overthrow the Magistrate. There are over a hundred of us. I'm in it with Xander. We call ourselves Phoenix."

"Did I hear someone say my name?" Xander strode into the room in the way he always made an entrance and moved over to where the two sat.

Ember checked out Xander's appearance. He wore all black, having kept his drowned, resurrected Plauditor's pants, but he'd borrowed the rest from Serpio—a smooth dress shirt he left half unbuttoned down his chest, the sleeves rolled up to his elbows. Ember knew what muscles lay beneath that shirt. But he was leaner and younger than Serpio, so the shirt fit somewhat loosely around him. Even then, her infatuation caused her to blush.

"You heard right. Ember was starting to explain Phoenix and your connection."

Xander's face shone with pride. "Ah. Phoenix … Born from a group of REMs I recruited. Their emotional resistance was perfect for our cause. When we grabbed an opportunity to get back into the city, we took over the Plauditorium and converted them."

Talesa's jaw dropped, and her brows shot up. "You did that?"

Xander answered, "Yeah, I started the ball rolling, but Ember has been a leader, too."

"Ember! You've been doing all this?" Talesa looked at Ember as if she'd just seen a ghost. "I'm so proud of you!"

Ember's chest grew tight with pride. "Thanks, Mom … but we should get started making plans. Any idea how we can leave without returning to the city through The Outside? I'm not sure we'd make it."

Talesa pointed overhead. "You got in here with an explosive. Do you have more?"

"Yeah. A few in our rucksacks up top," Xander said.

"Good. I have an idea, yes. Let me show you what's outside my window." Talesa led them over to where the striped armchair sat facing a pane. She voiced a command. "Open for delivery."

A light turned on beyond the glass. Ember took a step back. Instantly illuminated was a narrow tunnel with a single track.

Talesa explained, "This is where my deliveries come."

"How?" Ember ogled the unexpected accommodation. She hadn't had an earlier opportunity to ponder how the delivery of food and supplies would work.

"A small car comes on that track. It stops outside, and a mechanical arm conveys my supplies." Talesa pointed out a rectangular eight-inch cutout in the glass. "This window within a window opens, a large tray flips up, and the stuff is put through. Then, the carrier returns to the city."

Xander stroked his chin. "Your idea for the explosives is to blow this wall and we can ride the car back?"

Talesa tapped her head. "That's my thinking."

"But where does the delivery car go when it returns to the city?" Ember had questions explode like popcorn.

"I don't know. I've been asking Serpio questions. But I have to be careful what I ask."

"Wait. Serpio *comes*?" Xander sneered.

"Yes. That's why his clothes are here."

"Oh no, Mom. What does he want?" Ember put her hand to her forehead.

Talesa locked eyes with Ember and sighed. "It's time you sat down and learned the whole story."

"Mom, yeah. I have a lot of questions. So many things I don't know!"

Xander's tone was apologetic. "We can't talk much. We've gotta be ready to go soon. About getting out … How does that door work?" Xander gestured to the electronic panel on the wall.

Talesa took a deep swig of water, running beads condensing on the glass. "Only Serpio's OmniCom or someone with a passcode can open and close it. And only Serpio ever comes."

"What time does the delivery car come?" Xander eagerly pressed his questioning.

Talesa gave him a quick reply. "Six every day."

Xander said, more quietly, "Does Serpio ever come then?"

"No. If he comes, it's at night. After dark."

Ember wandered over to the window, as if to gaze out. "How does he get here?"

Talesa joined Ember and put her hand on her shoulder. "In a different car. It also comes through that same tunnel, but it's bigger with a couple of seats. He can come and go whenever he needs to."

Xander rubbed the nape of his neck. "The delivery cart. Is it big enough for all of us if we'd ride in it?"

"Hmmm. It would be really tight. It's like an extreme mini car, maybe eight feet long by three feet? A robotic arm's attached to the top and moves back and forth on a track. Two electronic doors open immediately upon arrival. One person could fit in each cubby. Ember and I could do that. But you, Xander. You'd have to ride on top somehow. And we'll have to work fast. It doesn't stay here long."

"Hmmm. On the top? How fast does it go?" Xander looked as if he was trying to imagine the situation in his head.

Talesa gave Xander a crooked smile. "Not fast. Maybe ten miles an hour?"

"I hope there's a way to hold on. Does it have a bumper?"

"No, but it has a curved, raised structure for a light on top. You should be able to ride on top and lie flat on your belly and hold on with that."

Xander paced. "Wherever that thing goes, we're not going to be able to ride it all the way to its port. We'll have to bail out before it gets there."

Ember felt Xander's concern. They were riding into the unknown.

Xander glanced at his Alt. "My Alt's got no signal. What time is it?"

"Four," Talesa replied, glancing at a panel on the wall.

Xander stopped pacing and put his hands on his hips. "About two hours 'til we bust outta here, then. We have to be ready. In the meantime, a short nap, Ember? We're gonna need it."

As much as sleep called her name, Ember had too many questions for her mom. She wasn't going anywhere without answers.

71

Ember's Answers

Ember moved to the sofa, where Xander sat on one side of her. Her mom pulled the striped armchair over to sit across from them.

Talesa's violet eyes seemed particularly luminous. "Sweetheart, I'm so sorry. I've kept a great deal from you. To protect you. But now you need to know everything. It's a lot to handle, but I can see you're ready." Ember felt her mother's pain at having to finally divulge uncomfortable secrets. Her mom forced a weak smile and then reached over to put her hand briefly on Ember's knees, almost as if she was begging for forgiveness.

"I'm more than ready," Ember asserted.

Xander put his arm around Ember and looked at her in support, his eyes steady and warm.

"Serpio and I were in a ... weird relationship." Talesa wrung her hands and averted her eyes.

Ember slowly nodded. "Believe it or not, I stole a journal from Serpio's library. It said that he was dating you. That he wanted to marry you! I—I couldn't believe it."

Talesa let out a short gasp. "You *stole* a journal?"

Ember grinned for a brief moment at her mom's shock.

"Had to. It's a big deal, too. We have that journal for Phoenix. Among others. Too much of a story for now."

"Evidence," Talesa confirmed.

"Yeah. Tons of things. But I did read Serpio's thoughts about you." Ember couldn't help a slight shiver.

Talesa said, "*He* thought we were in a relationship. Just one of the few things that are … off about him. He's delusional—narcissistic."

"And other things." Ember didn't want to tell her mom how Serpio constantly had pawed her body and overpraised her when he took her into the mansion. "But how did this all start?"

"We met over a year ago when I was a guest on the morning broadcast."

"Were you promoting something?" Xander scoffed.

Talesa answered Xander with a smile that faded as she explained. "I'm—I was—the spokesperson for the city's art gallery."

"Cool." Xander sat back, as if preparing himself to listen to an extended story.

"After the broadcast, Serpio saw me and almost immediately drew me aside. We chatted a bit. Nothing much. Just about my job and how I was doing. Then he told me that I was beautiful! I was flattered, of course. I'd never met him personally before, and then to have *the Magistrate himself* tell me I was beautiful? I could hardly believe it. Who wouldn't want to be with someone so amazing and powerful? After he left, probably within the hour, he called to ask me out for dinner."

"And you went." Ember searched her mind for when that date would have happened and came up empty. She would have been fifteen.

Talesa shifted in her chair before folding her hands together and twisting them slightly. "As soon as I got there, I was uncomfortable. He asked a lot of really personal questions. I felt more like I was being interrogated. I had to think positive, though, and I used a lot of Tranquility stress-relieving strategies. Finally, I told Serpio I had to leave to get home to you, Ember."

Xander had thrown his head back and was looking at the ceiling. "But he didn't 'get it,' right?"

"That should've been it … but it wasn't." Ember tugged on her ponytail to transfer her nervous energy.

Talesa put her hands on either side of her face, pulling her cheeks down. "He wouldn't take no for an answer. He'd stop by my work and call multiple times a day. A Sciolist tracked me for a while. I knew he was watching me at home, too, through the cameras, because he'd tell me things he couldn't know. Like what I had for dinner or what my bedroom looked like. My Alt points were dropping …"

"He *stalked* you." Xander clenched his jaw.

"He kept telling me that he was in love with me. It was disturbing." Talesa took a deep breath before fully focusing on Ember. "Finally, he asked me to marry him. And I told him 'no.'"

"So, he poisoned you with a ring." Xander growled. "That's rich."

Words tumbled from Ember's lips in a rush. "But then you didn't die. Someone saved you. Serpio?"

"The Medics used an antidote first. Then, they treated me with the Medela and blood flushing. It was over a week of treatment because I was so close to death. Serpio told me he couldn't kill me. He said he loved me too much to do it. That's why I'm here. And he comes to visit me … to 'love me.'" The way Talesa put emphasis on the last two words left no doubt about their meaning.

"Oh, Mom." Ember's bottom lip quivered, and she reached out and hugged her.

"I didn't know what he was doing with the rings until after I was a victim and Serpio told me." Talesa's words fell dead and brittle like fall leaves.

Scowling, Xander pushed his chair back as if to get up. "He's pure evil. Someday, I'm going to kill him."

"I understand your hatred, Xander, but you're young. You can't take on that responsibility."

Xander balled his fists. "Being young has nothing to do with it."

Talesa's vehemence came out. "Yes, it does! You're the leader of a revolution! You *cannot* be a martyr! Serpio needs to be stopped, though. Exposed. When I get out of here, I'll be part of Phoenix and help you do it."

Fear flushed through Ember. "Mom, you'll need to go somewhere safe! Not in harm's way."

"No. I'm part of the solution. I have … powers."

Ember froze for a moment before reacting. She squeaked, "You … have powers?"

Talesa looked down at the floor for a moment before saying, "I'm telepathic. I can send thoughts to people—people like us."

"Like … us?" The degree of Ember's astonishment could melt iron. "You know I'm an Empath?"

"Yes, Ember. I've known since several years after you were born. I know about your dreams and your ability to warp time." Talesa reached out and took Ember's hand. "*You* were born with powers because I have altered DNA. I have a high aptitude for empathy, but my power isn't the same as yours. Mine's not as strong, either."

Ember drew in a deep breath and looked from her mom to Xander. "That's why my name's in the gold journal! And that's why you wanted me to find it."

"So, you saw my message on the billboard?" Talesa leaned in, her aura flickering into a new color.

"Yeah. I was so confused. But I got it, and we found it! How—why—did you put that up? When?" Ember realized she'd been gripping her hands together so tightly they were turning pink.

"When Serpio kept trying to pursue me, I got worried. I knew if something happened, you'd need to know about the others. It was my insurance plan."

"Couldn't you have just *told* me? Or left me a *note*?" Ember released her hands from their vice-like grip and splayed them out.

Talesa sat forward, her body tight, and placed her hands on Ember's knees. "That would have been too risky at the time. Notes can be found. I didn't want to expose anyone like us if I didn't have to."

"Did you know the gold journal led us here? I wouldn't have known you were alive without it." When Ember said the words aloud, she shuddered. Her mom might never have been found.

"I didn't know what was going to happen to me. And, no, I didn't know you found this bunker because of it. Serpio included that on the drive?"

Ember nodded mutely.

Talesa reached out and rubbed Ember's arm. "If something did happen to me, I needed you to find the gold journal with all those names—names of people like us. I wanted you to know about your connection in case you needed it."

"But that list … all those people … They're all empathic? They can loop time?"

"As far as I know, only you can alter time, Ember. The others have different talents. There are many more of these people in the city than there are names on the gold journal list. But they're in hiding."

"They're all in danger?" Ember was feeling more and more surprised. A wave of panic rushed through her as she thought about how vulnerable the people on the list were.

"Yes. When Serpio discovers that people have these abilities, he finds ways to get rid of them. They're a threat. We'll need to keep their identities secret."

"Shazz!" Xander's slapped a hand to his head. "That

explains a crapload of stuff. These people are in hiding. So, if they suddenly get sick or die, their families and friends don't ask questions. They don't dare. It would expose them and their network."

"That's right, Xander. That's why they self-isolate to the greatest degree possible. They don't even stay connected with family because of the risks. And they frequently don't have friends. They're held captive by their fears of discovery. But they can also help us if we can recruit them for Phoenix. They may not want to, but it's my hope that they'd take a risk if they thought we could change the current state of affairs."

"But how can they help us if we don't have the whole list?" Ember thought back to the list of names she'd seen on the drive. It was quite short.

"I know who they are." Talesa dropped the information like a bomb.

"You … how?" Ember stammered.

"I have to be careful, but one of my abilities is a mental connection to other people like us. I can communicate with them fairly easily. It could be that Serpio suspects this. With your help, I can pull them into Phoenix."

"Unless they've been killed already …" Ember thought of all the trees on The Outside marked with numbers.

Xander said thoughtfully, "But Serpio has to move slowly. Carefully. That's why the Augur Prize rings work. He can't let anyone discover what he's doing."

"How and when did Serpio find out about all … of us?" Ember asked.

"That's where your dad's story is, Ember."

72

Ember's Dad

"My dad! Mom, you could have at least told me about him." Ember felt a talon of resentment open a scar inside her. Seeing her dad's name on the stone behind the Plauditorium was burned into her memory: Victor Vinata.

Talesa gave Ember a sharp look. "Ember, the less you knew, the better. I had to keep all this information from you for your own protection! Now that you know that people like us are in *danger*, you can understand why I needed to go to great lengths to protect you."

Ember shook her head in disbelief. "Did my dad know about our powers?"

"Of course. I couldn't hide mine from him. We were married and deeply in love. You and I were both born with these mutations. Your dad never knew about yours. I suspected, but you were too young for us to know if your DNA was affected. Victor didn't live long enough to know." Talesa's eyes began to grow teary.

"Yeah. An accident. I found out ..." Ember remembered Shawny's investigation.

"It was no accident. He was eliminated." Talesa spat the words as if they left a bad taste in her mouth.

Ember exhaled and rubbed her face. Xander put his arm around her shoulders and squeezed.

Talesa rose from her chair, her emotions a deep maroon flare. "Your dad was a hero. Since he knew about my powers, he tried to protect me. As a Level Seventeen Plauditor, he had the means to do that, but he got tangled up in a ... situation—"

"Because he was a Plauditor? I don't understand." Ember knew she had to be patient, but none of this was making any sense at all.

"First, you need to know how some people came to have these powers. CRISPR technology, what our scientists use, is a tool for editing genomes. DNA sequences can be easily altered. Gene functions can be changed with a 'cut and paste' process. With this, they can correct all genetic defects. No one's born with any diseases. Disease can be corrected either before birth or shortly afterward. Our technology and gene-based inoculations take care of all that. This is why our population is so healthy. We even use CRISPR on our food—all genetically engineered."

"I know all that. What does it have to do with my dad?" Ember was bouncing her knees, unable to keep her feet still.

"Around thirty years ago, parents could request characteristics they wanted their children to have. The government approved those on a case-by-case basis. Eye and skin color, sex, talents ... you know. When the program started, it was safe. Then, they began experimenting further with animals and radiation."

"The Greelox," Xander said in a rush of breath.

"Animal experiments were and are necessary. And they were able to change animals' traits. They blended DNA with radiation and got unusual results."

"No kidding." Xander's sarcasm hit a new high.

Talesa leaned toward Xander. "Some animals were released to The Outside." Talesa lowered her voice. "I can see by the look on your face that you might know what those animals are like?"

Xander appeared ready to boil over. "What they're *like?* More like—"

Ember squeezed Xander's hand. "No time for that story now, Mom."

Talesa nodded. "Right. But they ventured into using radiation on humans to see if they could enhance certain characteristics. The people they experimented on also exhibited extraordinary superpowers. And because the mutations were genetic, they could be passed down. The Elite closed the program because the scientists couldn't control the results. Our government determined that it was dangerous and immoral."

Ember said, "That explains a lot."

Talesa continued. "These human mutations were done long before Serpio. At the time the project was shut down, the city documented all the affected people. Names were kept private in data at the genetics lab. Laws forbade anyone who had unnatural abilities to use them, and people made pledges —just like they do when they agree to all the Accords. Problem solved."

"Not," Ember replied.

"It worked very well—until Serpio came to power."

"No surprise there." Xander bit off each word.

"The Inventum lab was in your dad's sector to watch. He noticed that Serpio visited Inventum daily. Victor found it odd. Your dad began watching more closely, and then he, too, began frequent visits to the lab. Under the guise of caring for his designated sector, Victor would go and give them simple encouragement, do what Plauditors do to inspire their assigned people. Victor encouraged the lab workers to voice their concerns to him."

"But that opened a can of worms," Ember said.

"A can of worms? No. An avalanche! One day, when your dad stopped by, he asked the scientists—Drake Pius and Henry Validus—why Serpio was spending so much time at the lab. Because your dad was so well respected, the scientists risked everything. Drake and Henry revealed how much they distrusted the Magistrate. At first, Victor thought that was odd. Then, they really confided in your dad, telling him that Serpio demanded the names of people with abilities. Names that were *sealed*. They didn't dare say 'no.' And of course, Serpio assured Drake and Henry he was only issuing more protection for the people and needed to know who they were. He cited some problems that were going on. They knew that wasn't true. No one had ever revealed their identities, so Serpio's reasons were questionable. Although Drake and Henry didn't want to do it, they thought the best thing they could do—the only 'save'—was to give Serpio an abbreviated list."

"How awful for them. They were up against it." Ember grabbed the back of her neck and frowned. "Drake and Henry's Alt points had to be impacted, too."

"Horrible for them! Can you imagine the guilt? But more than that, your dad was terrified that my name might be on that list."

"But it wasn't, was it? Not then."

"No. But my name was on the longer list—the one they didn't give to Serpio. It would be just a matter of time ..."

"So, Victor had to act." Xander's mouth formed a straight, tight line.

"Victor went back to the lab. They decided there was only one thing to do. He, Drake, and Henry set out to destroy all the data on the other people. They began to first purge the list of names, but just after they'd finished, Serpio marched in with two Sciolists. By then, he had seen the list they'd given him and knew it was incomplete. There weren't enough names on it—not for all the years of CRISPR. Nor was there any information about what their mutations were. And during that confrontation, your dad was there."

Ember's stomach dropped. "He wasn't arrested, though, right?"

"He wasn't, no. That's because ..." Talesa paused and clenched her teeth. "He didn't stand up for Drake and Henry. He told Serpio that he'd seen what the scientists were doing on his shift at the Plauditorium and had been checking on them—only to catch them trying to wipe out the data."

Ember's eyes grew wide, and she looked at Xander. Shock traveled in waves down her body.

"Mom ... you're saying he *lied?*"

"To protect *us*. You and I wouldn't be safe. And to protect himself. He knew if he were arrested, so many terrible things would happen! And if he could stay in Serpio's confidence, he could maybe do something about the leak ... find out Serpio's real agenda and protect the people."

"He tried to do the right thing in the worst way." Ember swallowed, a lump forming in her throat. Everything was beginning to be too overwhelming, too convoluted. "This is ... a lot to process."

"Now you know why I never shared this with you. Victor was questioned, yes. But Serpio never publicly doubted his story. Your dad was even on *Tranquility News* a day later as having uncovered a problem at the lab."

Xander grimaced. "Henry and Drake. They were arrested, though, right?"

"Yes. Serpio made up a story about them, and they were punished." Talesa's eyes filled with tears.

Ember bit her lip, her whole past coming apart at the seams. Innocent people were arrested. And her dad was partly responsible! How could she believe anything anymore?

Xander jumped up from the sofa. "Our friend, Ava ... Henry Validus was *her* dad. Ava told me that her dad was sent to The Outside because there was 'an error'"—Xander made the quotes with his fingers—"at the DNA lab—a mix-up in chemicals for vaccines! That must have been the story they made up."

"But Dad—what happened to him? If he was not under suspicion ..."

"It could be that Drake or Henry betrayed him. I don't really know. All I can tell you is that one night, on his way home, he—he fell off the Bird's Eye Pass Bridge. And you know that couldn't have been an accident. He wasn't even found until the next day, even though I sent the emergency message through my Alt when he didn't return home."

Ember felt as if a knife had stabbed her in the heart. The Bird's Eye Pass Bridge? That was where Will had saved a kid's life. The irony of it all hit her like a blow across the face. Two men she loved ... each a disappointment. Her own emotions were on fire, and the intense feelings from her mom and Xander blew into her like a storm. She swayed in her chair, dizzy, wondering if she was going to faint.

Xander dashed to her side. "Em! Are you okay?" He sat down next to her and flung his arm around her.

"Yeah ... Yeah. I'm okay. Just ... overwhelmed." She was more than overwhelmed. She was devastated.

Xander's fingers smoothed her hair away from her face. "I can get you water ..."

"No. No, Xander. It's okay."

Talesa pinched her nose with her fingers and then reached out to take Ember's hand. "I know. It's terrible. And you know I couldn't grieve for him ..."

"Oh, Mom. I know how that feels."

"Ember, you see why I couldn't tell you all these things? Even now, I know it's hard." Talesa's face was worried.

"I understand. And yeah, it's hard. But I'm glad I finally know."

Talesa suddenly jerked, her eyes on the wall. "We'd better get ready. The delivery cart comes in a half-hour."

"I'm ready to ride," Xander said, his eyes alight.

"To do what we came to do," Ember responded. "Punish Serpio for all the pain he's caused!"

"And we'll have help you didn't even know existed," Talesa said, a tentative smile back on her face.

Ember used to feel she was the only one in the world with bizarre abilities. But now that she had found her mother, she was determined to meet the rest.

73

Xander's Ride

Xander's legs trembled on his way down from retrieving all their gear from up top. His trauma and lack of sleep and food were beginning to take their toll. He tried to shake off a relentless buzz in his brain. If they could pull this off, the possibilities would be incredible. Yet the tenseness of his shoulders magnified how the risks knotted him up; his fear flared knowing their entire operation would be jeopardized with one mistake. He never wanted to show anyone his fear. Problem was, Ember could feel it. Ironically, he'd have to practice some Tranquility techniques after all.

Xander pulled the remaining explosives from his rucksack as he gave his directive. "Go into the bedroom as far back as you can. The explosives I used above here threw a lot of dirt around, so we need to move stuff out of the way."

Ember was gathering small objects that could become deadly projectiles. "Help me. This furniture should be pushed back, too."

In less than five minutes, they'd accomplished their goal of emptying the room.

"I'm setting the explosive to blow the wall before the cart comes. Don't wanna blow up our transportation."

Xander's nervous energy made him feel almost as potent as the explosives. "Okay. Go get safe. I'm gonna set this, and then I'm gonna be right behind you."

"Be careful!" Talesa and Ember chorused the words simultaneously.

Xander grinned. "No ... I'm ready to blow myself up." He put his bent arm over his eyes in a melodramatic gesture, like someone in an old-timey vaudeville production.

"You're impossible," Ember said, laughing.

Xander laid the explosive on the convenience counter underneath the delivery window, checked the bomb's position, and adjusted it. He checked it again twice. It was ready, and he was too. He glanced around him. Girls in the bedroom. Furniture ... confirmed where it sat. He pulled the lighter from his pocket.

Taking a breath, he ignited the two-inch string and bolted, scrambling as far as the arch to the bedroom. The thundering blast sent him rocketing the few remaining feet through the doorway.

He shook himself. His ears rang, and a heavy white fog drifted his way. Jarred but safe. He lifted his torso from where he lay on his back. "Ember! You all right?" She was always his first thought.

Already running toward him, Ember called out, "We're okay!"

Talesa ran over to him from the bathroom. "How 'bout you?"

"Yeah," he said as he wiped a trickle of blood from his forehead. Some glass or small object had made its mark.

"What—? Oh, Xan. You're hurt." Ember ran back to the bathroom to grab a wet towel, which she pressed to his head. "Here ..."

Talesa said, "I'll get some first aid. Is that your only injury?"

Xander nodded. "I'm fine! Just—I need pressure to stop the bleeding, that's all. We need to bounce." He stood up, wanting to see the effects of the blast.

He moved forward through the smoke, fanning it away with his hands where he whooped in triumph. "Perfect! Some debris, but we can easily clear the track."

Talesa and Ember began to throw chunks of the plexiglass window and small pieces of wall. The electronic door had toppled over into the room in one piece.

"Not bad for an amateur," Xander bragged as he threw rubble aside.

Ember gazed down the tunnel for the oncoming delivery. "No harm to the track ..."

"Yeah? I'm glad it worked. If the track got damaged, we'd be in trouble." Xander pulled the towel from his head and tossed it aside before walking further into the tunnel. "Let's get our stuff and be ready. It can't be long."

Talesa wandered into the dissipating smoke. "Only twenty minutes before our chariot arrives."

THEY STOOD READY, as if they were simply waiting for a normal CommuteCar to show up. Xander's impatience and adrenaline made for an emotional hurricane. He put his arm around Ember and hugged her to him. Talesa stepped several feet away, seeming to recognize a private moment brewing.

Xander whispered, "Ember ... if anything happens to me ... if things go bad ... I want you to know that these days with you were the most amazing of my life. If I die tomorrow, I can say I had the most incredible girl in the world as my partner in crime."

Ember gazed up at him, her face awash with tender

concern. "Don't … don't even think those things. We're gonna make it and be together."

"I just needed to tell you."

"Xander, no matter what happens, you're *completely* mine."

Xander laid his head against Ember's. "Totally." Her words set his heart spinning.

A half beat later, the delivery cart came into sight. If it hadn't been such weird circumstances, Xander would have found the transfer of goods fascinating. He watched as the curious car's doors opened automatically and the long-arm mechanism unloaded the items and, with no window or counter, dropped them where they normally would have landed in a matter of a minute.

Ember hugged her mom, then threw a kiss to Xander before climbing into the open hatch of the mobilized cart. She sat with her knees drawn up and her arms around her legs. Talesa hopped in afterward, immediately folding herself down into the other compartment. The doors whooshed closed.

Grabbing a molded bar similar to a sports car's spoiler, Xander hiked himself up onto the top of the car, wrapping his arms underneath and through the nine-inch, upside-down U-shape on its roof. Barely in place, Xander felt the car begin to move. It reversed its direction and shuddered in a mechanical shimmy before it properly engaged with the track. He only hoped their combined weight wouldn't cause the thing to stall. The conveyance journeyed for about fifty feet before sharply turning and heading up a ramp.

Xander felt a slight bump before the cart leveled out. He relaxed a little. He held on easily, as the souped-up cart traveled forward, smoothly navigating its automated journey.

The cart's speed gradually increased, becoming a thrilling, ten-mile-an-hour ride. Xander held on tighter as it rounded periodic multiple curves, his body slipping side to side on its polished surface. *I might as well enjoy this,* he thought. *It's definitely something I'll never get to do again.*

With his eyes and hands, he examined the cool, steel curves of the roof and sides, knowing he'd need to spring the doors before the contraption made it to its final landing place. There had to be a panel there with buttons. If not, they'd be in trouble.

Sure enough, down the right side, his hand encountered a small, flat window. With merely three buttons, these had to be the emergency options for doors and brakes. The trick would be in the timing. He didn't know how long the trip would be before they'd have to bail out.

He figured his journey with Ember to the bunker had been a good twenty miles. This trip was a straighter shot. He figured they'd be, at most, on a two-hour ride.

He glanced at his Alt. Still nonfunctional. No way to tell time. He cursed and sighed heavily. How would he estimate the hours? Counting? Too hard.

But music would work—a song by his favorite band. He began to sing, knowing he'd be pretty tired of it after forty long renditions.

As he sang, he noted where emergency doors were built into the tunnel's wall. With no lighting in the shaft, he'd have to pay particular attention to their placement along the way.

He anticipated when the next door would come into sight. Wherever they were, it would be a crapshoot. But they weren't to the city yet, so even if they had to walk a longer distance, he felt optimistic. He made his move, thrusting an eager finger to activate all three buttons on the vehicle's emergency panel. The car jerked and vibrated before coming to an awkward stop. He slid off, damp with perspiration, just as the hatch doors sprung open. Ember arose from her cavity with the rifle, followed by Talesa with the rest of their belongings.

"Ugh! So cramped! I thought we'd never stop!" Ember stretched her arms and shook out her legs.

"It was long! Better than walking, though." Talesa looked to Xander. "You okay? No worse for the wear?"

Xander tried to smile, but the truth was, his body ached, and his brain felt like scrambled eggs. Even his eyes burned. "I'm good. Let's get outta here." He pointed ahead. "Should be an exit door up ahead in the next hundred feet. I hope. It's narrow in this tunnel … and I have to restart the vehicle so it gets back to its destination."

Xander pressed the buttons again, and the car closed its doors and took off. He didn't know why a sense of relief caused his shoulders to drop. They were far from safety.

Talesa blinked her eyes as if she could part the gloom. "It's dark but can't be past curfew. We have no idea where that door leads. It could open into a building. I wonder if it's better to wait 'til curfew or try to blend in."

"We need to see what's behind that door." Xander led the group, their footsteps a soft clatter in the tomblike shaft. With the dark gray walls and no ventilation, the place gave him acute claustrophobia. He reached for Ember's hand. Her fingers wrapped around his were the perfect comfort.

Before looking for a trigger for the automatic door, he pushed on its center. No luck. Then, he noticed a switch on the wall. "Ready?" he breathed.

"No, but—Hey, my Alt lit up!" Ember's face caught the glow. "It's almost eight."

"Can we send for help?" Talesa asked, a nervous eagerness in her voice.

"Yeah." Xander's smile stood out in the dark, now also illuminated by his Alt. "But we've still got no GPS, so no one can find us."

"Flip the switch," Ember urged. "We can't stay in here."

The resulting release revealed a grassy area shrouded by trees. Xander heard and saw nothing else but a dim streetlight. The rifle was out of ammo, but he aimed it in front of him and leaned his head out the doorway.

It appeared the tunnel was above ground. The outer stone walls stretched along in two directions. He looked around in hopes of finding a landmark.

"Shazz! There's the sign for City Hall," Xander's voice cracked uncomfortably. He slid back in and hit the switch, leaning back behind the wall as the door closed. "And the street … gotta be Angel Avenue. I saw the donut shop."

"That's the best news! I'm morsing Ava!" Ember's eyes looked bright even in the murky space. She hugged her mom before punching her message in.

Ten minutes later, Ember's Alt chimed. "Ava's here!"

Xander flipped the switch, and the automatic door slid up. Two Sciolists stared back at them.

74

Ember's News

Ember gasped before swaying on her feet. She leaned into Xander.

"Go back inside," one of the Sciolists commanded, pushing Talesa back.

Xander stepped in front of Ember, his rifle trained on the Sciolist who spoke. "I *will* kill you."

"You're not in danger," the other Sciolist said crisply. "Ava sent us. We're retrieving you. But first, here. You'll need different clothes. For disguise." The tall, dark-haired man, his face inscrutable, held up a cloth bag.

The three looked at each other before nearly collapsing with reassurance.

"Get inside. You can't be out." The shorter Sciolist of the two, a black man of Samkhat race like Wee, clenched his teeth. "You're putting us all at risk."

This time, the little band followed orders and retreated back into the tunnel.

"Change. Now. Time's wasting."

Xander took the bag, pulling out pieces of clothing and handing them to Ember and Talesa. "Level One clothes?"

"You won't be scrutinized in those. No one will care who you are."

"Huh." Xander held up a large knit turtleneck shirt in one hand and a simple blazer in the other. "No worries. I can rock these."

Ember snickered but, in her mind, agreed. Xander seemed to make a statement in whatever he put on. She sorted through the bag for herself, finding a long, white straight shift loose enough to dwarf her. A second later, a cheap tie belt came to her rescue. She slid a pair of pearl-colored, flat sandals onto her feet. Stripping down in front of Sciolists was not going to happen. She ran down the tunnel to where it made a bend. In a minute, she was dressed, a quick change that surprised even her.

Talesa crossed her path on the way back, waving an elastic-waisted woven skirt and linen blouse.

Returning, Ember grinned as she watched Xander finish changing into the shirt and throwing on the jacket.

When Talesa returned, the tall Sciolist collected their other clothes, putting them into the sack.

"Let's go." The black Sciolist waved them forward and opened the door.

Outside on the street was a waiting van. Ember didn't know what she'd expected—that Ava's limo would be there? But the vehicle was Sciolist.

In the backseat, Ember shivered slightly. What if this was a trap?

Xander, though, was undeniably calm, his aura a soft green. "What are your names?" he asked the two men.

"No names. We stay anonymous. Better for all," the left-seated Sciolist said without turning around. "We're part of the revolution."

Ember wanted answers to a ton of questions. What? How? Why? Instead, she asked, "Where are we going?" Ember continually evaluated the Sciolists' emotional states. They exuded only a thin self-assurance.

"West emergency food warehouse." The reply, like all Sciolist conversation, was clipped.

Ember sighed, her entire being exhausted. She couldn't fight off one more thing, even if they'd said she was going to visit Serpio.

~

AFTER A BRIEF FAILURE TO stay awake, Ember lifted her head from where it had lolled against her mom's shoulder.

"Em! We're at the warehouse." Xander jostled his hand on her knee.

"We'll escort you in. Make sure there's no suspicion." The Samkhat rummaged in a different cloth sack and handed them each a unique hat. "Put those on."

Ember's felt hat was rounded and closely fitted her head even with her hair tucked up inside, with a plain, wide brim she pulled down to shade her face.

"Xander, won't the team freak if Sciolists are here?" Ember feared a total heart attack from someone inside.

Of course, Xander had thought of everything. "Already Morsed the warning," Xander said, donning a Panama-style hat.

At the door, Xander knocked in Morse Code: "Loyalty."

When the door opened, Ember was the first in. Her eyes lit on Wee waiting just inside. He caught her in a bear hug, lifting her off the floor and knocking her hat to the ground.

"You're safe! So glad to see you, girl!" Wee cried.

"Same!" Ember added "Woohoo!" She hadn't known Weeford long. But he was so completely lovable. His loyalty to Will was still unshakable; a friend to the end, Ember knew he'd stay true always.

Xander exchanged a bro handshake with him. "How're ya doin'?"

"Good. I'm good. This must be Ember's mom?" Wee gave Talesa a wide smile.

"Yes. I'm Talesa." She walked forward and extended her hand.

"Wee. Actually Weeford. But just call me Wee. So glad you're alive!"

"Me too." Talesa laughed. "It's been a surreal experience."

Xander turned to Ember. "Now that introductions have been made, it's time to go to sleep. I'm done."

Ember's eyes swept the room. "Wee, is there any good place to get halfway comfortable?"

"Most of Phoenix is already sleeping. They're bushed too. But it's a big room. You can find space. No blankets or anything, though." Wee's aura flared lavender. Sympathy.

"It's okay. We'll just make do." Ember reached for Xander's hand and flirtatiously said, "C'mon. I'm not sleeping without you."

Xander took her hand, raised one eyebrow, and grinned. "Say no more, baby."

Ember realized too late that her new relationship with Xander would be a shock to Wee. Indeed, Wee shuffled his feet and scratched behind his ear to cope with the sudden awkwardness.

"Umm … what's goin' on here?" Wee looked from one face to another.

Ember blushed, at a loss for words. How could she explain this total one-eighty to Wee?

"Ember and I are *together*." Xander spoke with a boldness that lacked any sensitivity. Even his eyes, tired as they were, carried a passionate and prideful spark.

"Well, isn't that somethin'?" Wee's words were rushed, as if he just wanted to get saying them over with. "Yeah … So, take a look around, then. Plenty of room for the two of you." He coughed.

Talesa, easily sensing an awkward moment but not understanding it, tried to smooth things over. "I'll let you two find your own space. Wee, how 'bout a quick tour?"

"Sure." Wee offered Talesa his arm, and they walked away. "Hope you get some good rest," Wee called out over his shoulder.

75

Ember's Introduction

Ember's eyes fluttered open, taking in Xander, still asleep. In spite of the lack of any creature comforts where they lay on the floor in a corner, Ember slept like she'd been drugged. She was snuggled up against Xander, her arm over his waist. Taking a moment to enjoy his measured breathing and the way his hair fell across his face, she sighed. Then her dream came back to her, and she frowned.

SHE WAS WRAPPED *in red cords, which tightened across her middle little by little. Sirens wailed from somewhere far away. Then, suddenly, she was surrounded by a sea of people crushing in on her and shouting. Her eyes were closed tight, and she couldn't open them, no matter how hard she tried. Her mother's voice cooed, but she couldn't see her. "Your eyes are shut for a reason. You don't want to see what's coming." Will appeared in front of her and forced her eyes open with his fingers. He disappeared, replaced by Xander, who spoke to her, his eyes sad. "This is goodbye, Ember ..." He turned and disappeared into the crowd, and she struggled against the ties that bound her. She couldn't free herself. Two hazy figures appeared a distance away. They were both shadowy, but she called out to them. "Help me, please ..." The cords around her disintegrated. Each figure spun away, and she ran after them. She almost caught up before she slipped on blood under her feet ...*

SHE SQUEEZED her eyes shut again, trying to erase vestiges of her confusing and disturbing dream. Ember heard people's voices, a soft chatter that gave her reassurance. Someone sneezed, and laughter followed. Some rustling and calls for food. "Canned pears anyone?" was answered by a chorus of yays and boos.

"Xander ... wake up. I think it's morning."

"Hmmm. Morning already?" he murmured. He opened one eye before drawing her to him for a quick but tender kiss.

Ember's stomach growled in a persistent plea. She sat up, wondering if she could get a can of pears. Leaving Xander to fully wake up, she wandered out to where the action was.

"Hey—Ember!" Jasper greeted her with the Phoenix hand gesture. "You brought Xander back with ya, I hope!"

She chuckled. "I considered leaving him behind, but yeah, I brought him."

"I'll introduce you around." Jasper spent a minute assigning names to the people helping themselves to the food stores.

Talesa emerged from behind a stack of boxes of dried cereal. "Good morning, sweet daughter! Sleep okay?"

"Like a dead weight."

Talesa gave Ember a bear hug. "Still so good to have you with me."

Then, turning to the people she'd just met, Ember made introductions of her own. "This is my mom, Talesa. We're lucky she's still alive. She was on Serpio's death list, so it's a miracle she's here. And she's the reason I became part of Phoenix."

Applause and a few "Yeahs" answered her comments, but

Jasper seemed to express the group's feelings. "It's great you're here, Talesa. You of all people should be our spokesperson, telling everyone in Tranquility what you've been through."

"If it were safe, I would be," Talesa said. "But I can help in other ways. Can we have a short meeting?"

Xander burst out from where they'd slept. "Food!" He helped himself to several cans of what was marked "ERMS." He read out loud the small lettering beneath—"Emergency Ration Meat Source"—before handing off some to Talesa, Ember, and the others gathered around. "Sounds gross, but hey—" He wasted no time tearing off the lid and diving in with his fingers. "Not too bad. It beats snake meat."

"Snake?" One of the former Plauditors dropped his jaw.

"Yeah. Long story. Hey, Jasper!"

Jasper met Xander with a bro hug and, releasing him, said, "Good to see ya, Xander. I knew you'd make it back in one piece."

Xander clapped Jasper on the back. "One piece, I am. Barely."

Wee must have heard voices. He, too, jogged over from where he'd spent the night.

Xander asked, "What's been happening since Ember and I left?"

Jasper grinned, his enthusiasm evident in his grab of Xander's shoulder. He seemed to have become the interim spokesperson for the group. "We're launched. We've gone out a couple people at a time. We're visiting homes, just like we planned, to provide fake services, then explaining our position. We give 'em a few pages of Serpio's journals that we copy here. All the warehouses are doing the same. We've only been out for a little over a day, but no problems yet."

"Thanks, Jasper. You've done a great job leading Phoenix." Xander's appreciation for his REM friend practically glowed off his body. "How's recruitment going? What happens when you tell people about Serpio?"

To Ember's surprise, Bixby spoke up. "A few citizens have reminded us that they heard Phoenix's original broadcast from the Plauditorium when Ember, Xander, and Will spoke. They've been confused since then, concerned that Phoenix was giving them false information and trying to cause chaos. But when we show them Serpio's own words from the journals, they listen. We've had to do some deep breathing with some of 'em. They get upset. But then they sign on."

Xander's head tilted back, and he raised his eyes to the rafters as if he were praising some unseen being. He then met Bixby's eyes. "And are you giving them something to ID themselves with as a member of Phoenix?"

Jasper answered, "The Phoenix hand gesture for loyalty, of course. Ember came up with that."

"My mom's really the one to take the credit. She taught me that whole language."

Talesa put her arm around Ember's shoulders. "But you remembered it, Ember. I'm so proud of you."

Jasper gave Talesa a toothy smile before resuming his explanation. "Banks in the east warehouse? He created an app for the Alt. It leaves an ultraviolet Phoenix tattoo on the wrist." Jasper grinned. "See? Here's mine." He moved his Alt aside, and there was an imprint. "Once recruited, each person gets the app. We send it to them right on the spot, along with the Morse code app."

Talesa spoke with force. "And you tell them, I hope, that this could mean their lives? We don't know how this will go."

Jasper answered, "Yeah. We tell 'em that, once they get the tattoo, they're committed. If they're showing hesitation at all and don't want to sign on, we warn them that their lives could still turn upside down. They could get caught in the middle. When we leave, we mark the wall by their door. The tattoo app works to mark our skin with a soft laser, but turned the other direction, it can burn other things. An upside-down Phoenix in black will be a 'tried and failed to recruit' signal."

"You'll help us get our tattoos right after the meeting," Xander asserted.

Ember did a fist pump. "So much progress since we've been gone!"

"Shouldn't be a surprise. You've been gone three days," Jasper said with an accusatory tone.

Xander bristled at Jasper's comment. "It was necessary. Three days to bring Talesa back safely. Not much to ask. But we have other news. I'm gonna let Ember's mom give you the lowdown."

"Everybody, center!" Wee called out, his loud voice ricocheting in the warehouse space.

One by one, REMs and Plauditors walked from different areas of the warehouse, joining in with high fives and "Heys!"

Talesa stood and addressed the crowd gathered there, her graceful posture and calm demeanor settling on the group like a cotton candy cloud. "I have some talents we can put to use. And there are other people in the city with similar ones." She explained the entire situation, including her own ability, glossing over Ember's time-warping power. "I know where everyone is, and I can communicate with them somewhat using my thoughts. But we have to meet with them, too. They'll need to understand all that's been going on and get special assignments."

The group babbled with exclamations and questions. Talesa couldn't begin to respond to the many questions all at once. "Please. I'll take one question at a time," Talesa begged.

Talesa answered a petite blond Plauditor in her mid-forties who asked, "What sort of abilities do they have?"

"They vary, so that's why we need to meet with each one. Some have heightened reflexes. Others have extreme strength. Some, like me, are telepathic. A few are slightly psychic where they'll sometimes get messages about their own futures, or the futures of those they love, through dreams or signs. One young man I know can bend metal with his mind. They're all a result of work done at Inventum. And look at Wee. He doesn't have ramped-up abilities, but look at how big he is!"

Wee jumped when Talesa said his name. And then he grinned. "Who says I don't got superpowers?" he kidded.

The group laughed, a few adding some verbal jabs.

"Why don't they use their powers already?" Jasper asked. "If I had special powers, I would!"

Talesa tilted her head thoughtfully. "Okay, imagine it. If they'd always done that, who would believe they didn't also have a way to manipulate their Alts? And they'd be hounded for their talents. Their powers could be abused. But that's the least part of the problem."

Xander stepped up on a nearby box. "Serpio would kill them. And he has been killing them. He can't tolerate anyone who might be a threat to him. Or superior to him." Xander sneered, his tone turning a hard metallic.

Ember felt Xander's vehemence to her core. "Yeah. He was going to hold me against my will and *use* me for my powers. I'm lucky he didn't choose to eliminate me. But he almost eliminated my mom." Ember walked closer, hammering a fist into her left palm. "That's why we fight. Serpio has to go down. We press on. The plan today … You do what you've been doing, going into homes. If it's working, that's ideal. But now, Xander and I are here to do it with you. Plus the hundred or so people in the city with mutations. Mom can tell us where they are, and Xander and I will go to them."

Wee suddenly came to life. "You guys can't be out there! If you're seen—holy Shazz! It would be suicide."

Xander winced before admitting, "It's not easy to hide you either, Wee." He punched Wee in the arm. "But hiding's not what we're here for. We can't make change by stayin' in this warehouse. I wouldn't"—he glanced at Ember—"and Ember wouldn't send you guys out and then hide ourselves. Not fair at all. If we're to lead this fight, we're in it."

Ember nodded vigorously. "True. We might die. All of us. But if we do, there will be others to take our places because we recruited."

Xander put his arm around Ember. "The only person who has to stay in the warehouse is Talesa. She's the most valuable because of what she knows about the people in the city. She needs to stay safe and send us out to specific places."

Talesa put up a hand in protest. "I can and should go out, too. I can talk to Inventum people better than anyone."

"Mom … maybe eventually. Let's get this going first. Then we'll see. Deal?" Ember fought to push down her panic. She wasn't about to lose her mom twice.

Talesa hesitated before she spoke, gazing out into space as if accessing a secret store in her mind. "Okay, but if I need to go, I don't want anyone stopping me."

Xander put his hand on Talesa's arm. "Sure. But only when it's the right time."

Talesa nodded. "Agreed." She extended her arm. "Now, is there a tattoo I can get around here?"

76

Ember's Venture

An hour or so later, Xander, Ember, and Talesa flashed their tattoos and practiced their Phoenix Loyalty hand gesture. Then, the group discussed strategies. Talesa would direct Xander and Ember to the whereabouts of several people that day. The rest of Phoenix at the West Warehouse would continue their occupational reach into the city.

For the remainder of the morning and the afternoon, Ember, Xander, and Talesa helped make journal copies, communicate with the three other warehouses by Morse Code, and debrief individuals who came and went in and out of the warehouse.

Part of the time, Ember fretted about discovery. Although Phoenix had stayed safe while she and Xander had been gone, her nerves wouldn't settle.

She asked a friendly female Plauditor, Jayne, about the warehouses' cameras, and she explained that Phoenix had placed a single piece of clothing over the cameras' lens.

"What if a Plauditor finds the failure?" Ember asked.

"Someone will—eventually. But first, it will be reported. Then, a troubleshooting team will look at it remotely. Without a fix, a work order's sent to a squad who goes out to the site to investigate in person. And if they do"—Jayne shrugged—"we'll have to take care of 'em."

Ember nodded, understanding Jayne's remark, but her heart twisted. They might have to kill people. Revolution was a bloody business.

Jasper assured her that once they'd first entered the warehouse with Ava's code, Phoenix had changed all the electronic locks from the inside.

Ember happily gathered together with Xander, Bixby, Jasper, Wee, and Talesa in the early afternoon. She realized how lucky they were to be all together again, safe for the time being.

Talesa started the meeting. "Are you ready to determine which person with mutations to contact first?"

"We'll need a healer if there is someone." Ember winced. She was already envisioning how the rebellion would cause harm to their people.

"Definitely. There is one. But is that who you want first?" Talesa looked from face to face.

"Can't we just find the one person who can take out Serpio?" Jasper asked, his leg vibrating as he sat on the floor.

"Don't tempt me," Xander said, his tone conveying a sharp anger. "I could just shoot him and get it over with."

Talesa let out a shallow gasp. "Without the citizens on your side, you'd be arrested by the Sciolists and tried by the Elite. That's a no. The people of the city need to be behind it."

"I wasn't serious." Xander winked, but Ember knew his heart. If he could, he would.

"Speaking of guns, we need weapons," Wee said, his forehead puckered. "We might eventually get strength in numbers, but it's not enough against Serpio. Who knows what he's got?"

"He doesn't have guns. If he did, he woulda used 'em by now." Bixby rested his chin in his hand and looked thoughtful.

"Wee's right, though. We need weapons if we want to succeed. So … Talesa? Who do ya know?" Xander's eyebrows waggled.

"Chester Arete's probably your guy. He works a day shift at the city's parts factory. Anything Tranquility needs to repair, he helps manufacture the pieces. With those parts, he can design and create different kinds of weapons, which is a natural talent—nothing extraordinary about it. But what he can do beyond that is to determine a person's weakness by simply being around them, similar to what Ember can do with emotions. Then, he can tailor a weapon to kill or defend against an opponent. For instance, what would be the weakness of a Sciolist?"

"Well, I sure don't know. Those guys are like living steel statues and creepy as hell." Wee gave a slight shiver.

"But Chester would know. And not just that. He can also use his body to produce an electric current. And not just a little small voltage surge, but one capable of doing damage. Put anything metal in his hands, and it becomes electric. Even a simple wire or a common tool."

"You think he'd make weapons for us?" Jasper's face lit up.

"First, I'll make contact with my telepathy to see if he's receptive. If he is, then we'll have to meet in person. This isn't something we can just Morse Code message about. He'll have to become one of us."

"Sounds like the best option unless there are people who can heavily influence people with words."

Talesa nodded. "You must read minds, too, Xander, to guess so well. One of the people I know can do that."

"Let's start with Chester." It seemed logical to get their weapons situation set up first. That alone would take a while, and they'd need to be armed. Two depleted shotguns were all they had, and they had no idea where to even get bullets. "Everyone agree?"

The group was unanimous.

"Who should we send to meet Chester?" Bixby's eyes were sparkling with hope.

"It should be Ember. It's dangerous, but I could convey to Chester that I'm sending my daughter. She has her own form of defense, too, if something goes wrong."

"I agree," Ember said. "With my Level One clothes, no one will pay attention to me. And with the Magistrate's fireworks going on, that would be the perfect time. Citizens and security will be at that event. A perfect distraction."

Xander's whole body jerked to attention. "You *can't* go. Way too dangerous."

The little group quarreled about their feelings until the very air was heated. Talesa and Ember were the only two electing to send Ember. The rest of the group raised their voices in protest until Ember thought she would scream.

"I'm *going*, Xander! I'm the best and only choice." Ember was not giving up. She was a fighter. Hadn't she proved that?

"You're not going alone, then. I'll go with you." Xander's aura flared a yellow-orange—resistance and worry.

"Not sure that's a good idea, love." Ember touched his arm. "I don't want to worry about you. It'll make it harder."

Talesa appeared to be staying out of the argument. Then she said brusquely, "Xander should go. If he's with you, it will look more normal—just a loving couple out for a stroll. There's even a place at the Cloud Nine Station that's secluded with hedges and foliage. Sort of a rendezvous for lovers. You can meet Chester there."

"Yeah. What she said." Xander beamed.

Ember sighed in frustration. She was hoping to do this alone. "Very well. We'll play the roles."

"Won't be hard," Xander said, a flirtatious smile quirking his lips.

"Perfect," Ember said. But her emotions took a dizzying loop. Where Talesa had suggested was where she'd had her breakup with Will. The painful memory made it a place she'd never choose to visit again.

~

BEFORE THEY WERE ready to leave, Ember took a moment with her mom.

She wrapped her arms around Talesa. "Bye, Mom. We'll see you when we get back."

"You sure I can't come with you?" Talesa said as she let go.

"No, Mom," Ember said, releasing her. "We'll manage."

"I know you'll manage. You've already done amazing things. And Xander'll be with you. And make sure you use your abilities."

"I will, and … I have. But Mom … I sometimes have trouble with my time-altering talent."

"What? Why?"

"I can't make the change happen without pulling emotions from other people. What if no one's around?"

"You have all the power you need."

"I don't understand."

"You only need to believe you can do it." Talesa patted Ember on the back.

"But then why wasn't I able to help you, Mom, when you were suffering and dying?"

"I suspect because you hadn't accepted who you are. You didn't believe in yourself. And because it was too late by the time you knew."

Ember embraced her mom again, this time with a different kind of thankfulness. Her mom always helped her put the pieces together. Her eyes teared up, the realization of what she'd almost completely lost coming front and center again.

"If I need it, I'll remember what you've said, Mom," she

said. Her heart swelled as she left her mom behind and went to find Xander.

～

Although it was a risk, Ember activated the app for a CommuteCar. It had been a little tricky, getting a Level One CommuteCar through her app. The other obstacle was to get the ride to a location without a GPS. With some help from a smart Plauditor, the crisis was averted.

Ember wished she could be as calm as Xander. His aura leaked only tiny pulses of orange, indicating nerves. "How can you be so calm?"

"We're facing danger, yeah. But we have to keep our wits about us and stay calm. We have to blend in. And I need to keep you safe. I can't do that if I'm strung out on adrenaline. And you—you have abilities to get us out of trouble." He reached for her hand, enclosing it in his with a squeeze.

"You have a lot of faith in me. More than I do in myself. I can't count on making the time power work. It seems to have a mind of its own."

"Yeah, you can. When you most need it, it's there. Look at all we've been through, how far we've come. Together, we're invincible." Xander smiled as he put his hands around her face and kissed her on the forehead.

Ember's Alt pinged with a surge in points. She held it up, smiling. "You're a great confidence builder. Thanks." Ember's nose wrinkled as she noticed a notification on her screen. "My Alt shows it's Appreciation Day for the Magistrate."

"No kidding? He'll probably be throwing himself a parade." Xander made a whirling gesture with his index finger.

"He usually does. Let's hope we've missed any festivities."

"It's nighttime. There will definitely be fireworks."

Within another few minutes, they arrived close to the

station. As she left the CommuteCar, Ember hoped that Chester would be on time.

Xander slipped his hand into hers. "C'mon. We stay close to the outer boundaries of the station and follow the hedge line to the spot. You're sure you know where this spot is?"

"Without a doubt. I've … been there."

Xander looked at her with a question in his eyes. "Okay. When we get close, we'll enter and wait."

Ember closed her eyes. "Put your arm around me, Xander. We're lovers, remember?"

"Nothing I'd ever forget," he said as his arm encircled her with a squeeze. "Let's do this."

77

Will's Memories

Will's mind had been bleary since the therapy room session. Serpio, though, had assured him that the brain fog would disappear, especially now that he was allowed to go home. The guest house stay was over.

Because there were massive gaps in his memory prior to the last few days, he'd reached out to Serpio, concerned that he wasn't fit to be a Plauditor after all. Serpio—always a benevolent confidant—reminded him that he had needed to take a short stress break from being a Plauditor a while ago. Apparently, his anxiety over the criminals at large had been putting his Alt points in danger. In compassionate concern, Serpio had had him on a mandatory vacation, a courtesy rarely extended to any citizen, much less a Plauditor.

But his time away was strangely dream-like. Even now, blurry images flashed through his head. As he tried to center himself to properly do his job, he remembered some sort of odd, hostile conflict in this very place. Confused, he involuntarily reached for his chest before dropping his hand to the table in front of him. And some horrible mental fragments of a trip to The Outside made him shiver. Nightmares for sure.

Random people floated through his mind like ghosts, sometimes with faces and sometimes not.

Will noted the time. Will had been sitting at his new Plauditor's station for three hours. He rubbed the arms of his chair in wonder and brushed a tiny speck of lint from his jacket. The chair in which he sat couldn't have felt more right. Just like when he first became a Plauditor, he was awestruck by the opportunity to serve.

In order to get his job back, he'd had to make some concessions after going to the therapy room. He'd had to undergo sensitive questioning by the Elite and be approved. Of course, Will had to take a new oath to be reinstated. That was okay. He understood the significance of pledging his loyalty and heart to the city. There could be no doubt of his dedication.

As he'd begun to do his job today, he became increasingly happier. The disorganization in his head improved. With all his concentration on the sector he was watching, he'd begun to feel like his old self—at least what he'd remembered was his old self. Nothing else was important but his service to the Magistrate.

All of the Plauditors here today, except for himself, had been night shift, and now, they had to work staggered double shifts. Will assured Serpio that he would be more than willing to do his share.

He couldn't help but steal a look at the Leaderboard at the front of the Plauditorium. In sparkling LED lights, he saw his name. His points were high—in third place for the morning. He grinned, feeling more satisfied and happier than he had in a long time. Back to where he felt at home. Back to where he could—and would—climb the ladder of success. His eyes trained themselves again on the screen in front of him, where he watched contented people go to and from the shopping center in the middle of the Orange Glen community.

The main door to the Plauditorium opened. He'd been

waiting in anticipation for this part of the morning. 7:50 a.m. Serpio entered right on time for the morning news announcements, heading directly to the broadcast room. Although Will was eager to do his job, his eyes and ears were eager to take in everything Serpio would say.

Will leaned back in his chair, his attention centered on the screen high on the wall of the Plauditorium where, minutes later, Serpio's face loomed large. Will noted a particular shine in the Magistrate's eyes.

"Good morning, my amazing Tranquility citizens. So happy to be addressing you today of all days. Great news. It is Magistrate Appreciation Day. Your warm thoughts are appreciated so very much. Thank you."

Will wilted slightly. How could he have forgotten? This was one of the biggest holidays of the year, and he had nothing to offer the Magistrate as a thank you. He wracked his brain, trying to think of something he could yet have delivered to Serpio. What could he give to someone who had everything? Flowers? A complimentary massage? An exotic pet? Nothing seemed good, especially with his limited resources. Something unique … a piece of jewelry maybe. Small but powerful.

His attention snapped back to the screen when he heard the word "fugitives." Will leaned in.

"REM fugitives remain on the loose. But do not fear. These people do not have the means or intent to harm you. We want them apprehended, of course, so that we can restore our city to its perfection. But we have everything under control. Our Sciolists are on high alert. We ask your assistance to report people you don't know who approach you for help or who make false accusations against me. If you see or hear of our Queen of Hearts, Ember Vinata, this is of the utmost importance. She is either a part of the rebellion or is being held against her will as the Plauditors are."

Queen of Hearts? Ember? That's an odd moniker for an enemy of the State. Will watched as Serpio's face softened when he mentioned her name. Almost as if he was fond of the girl. Weirdly fascinating.

Serpio took a deep breath and then smiled beatifically. "We will not allow fear to interfere with the happiness of our celebrations. We will not allow intimidation to mar a special day in our city. The parade will go on as scheduled on Main Street. This evening, fireworks will be ignited at Pleasure Park at nine. To ensure your safety and well-being, security forces will be in place."

When Will realized he wouldn't be attending any parades due to his schedule in the Plauditorium, he steeled himself against the disappointment.

Serpio seemed to read his mind as he continued. "It's easy to believe everything's going to be great when everything is going well. It's much harder to be optimistic when you're facing challenges in your life. But that is exactly when you need to apply your Tranquility strategies. Keeping a positive attitude is what gets you through. If something knocks you down, you must get up. If you dig deeply, you will discover your true strength. You *can* rise to the next level. That is all for now, dear Tranquilites. Have a peaceful and happy day."

The words resonated with Will. He found strength and optimism every day. And Serpio was truly being heroic in these difficult circumstances.

As WILL WATCHED the Magistrate's face fade from view, accompanied by Tranquility's anthem, a picture of Ember Vinata appeared on the screen. While he'd seen her photo being displayed before, this one was new. Again, it was a head-shot, but this time, the girl looked as if she was real enough to step into the room. Her eyes sparkled with joy, and her smile, cutely bashful, made Will feel a keen warmth spread through his chest. Her red hair flowed around her face like a fiery halo, anointing her with extra radiance.

He had an urgent desire to touch her hair, and before he knew it, he had stood up and reached out with his arm, as if he could do just that. He caught himself and cleared his throat before looking around to see if anyone had been watching. Sure enough, the guy at the adjacent desk raised his eyebrows and asked, "You okay?"

"Yeah. I thought there was some bug. No worries." Will fought the embarrassment before gazing back into his own screen as if his life depended on it.

It wasn't long before boredom set in. His thoughts drifted back to Ember's photograph. *She might as well be haunting me,* he thought. *But why? She's just a girl—and a renegade.*

He forced his thoughts to Serpio's Appreciation Day. The gift … And at that moment, he had an epiphany. A lapel pin —yeah! Serpio could wear it on his clothing and then would be able to tell everyone that Will had given it to him. The design … a Halcyon maybe? The bird symbolizing Tranquility. Then, he rethought it. Serpio should have something more regal. A crown came to mind. Yes … that was it! He'd have a small, gold crown made up at the jewelers. With a little luck, he could still get it made at the end of the day.

Yet the rest of the day, his thoughts were consumed with Ember's face, her eyes filling him with a disquieting lust. A lightning-quick second of memory followed where he felt a connection to this girl, as if she had been someone important to him. It was foolish, he knew. He'd never know a girl like that.

～

WILL FINISHED his shift and was eager to be free. He hoped that physically leaving the Plauditorium would rid him of the torment of his thoughts. The tease to his memory Ember's photograph caused was barely tolerable. He needed to hit the jeweler's. Then it would be a trip to City Hall to see the Magistrate. If need be, he'd leave his gift there.

As he flew out the door, a heady feeling of freedom made him almost dizzy. Being able to freely walk about the city was surreal. He hailed a CommuteCar and was at the jeweler's in his own community of Yellow Sunrise within minutes.

After the jeweler determined he had enough Alt points to purchase, he told Will to come back in two hours. *Great!* he thought. *I can still get this done before the end of the day, and Serpio will have his gift.*

Will glanced at his Alt. A couple of hours to kill. He set out, his independence a beautiful feeling. He left the shop, noting the smiling, laughing people walking the sidewalks on their way home. A sense of pride in Tranquility and the citizens made him break a grin himself. Putting tiny discs on his earlobes, he tapped the app on his Alt for music. Whistling and air drumming to a song on Tranquility Radio's Top Ten, he elevated his mood. As he walked, he realized with relief that his head seemed to be clearing more as evening approached.

A sharp flash of Ember's face suddenly pierced his mind. The invasion was so sharp his lungs resisted breath, like the wind had been knocked out of him by an unseen force. The image detonated any other thoughts. If he didn't know better, he'd wonder if his thoughts were being taken hostage by the girl herself. He blinked his eyes, trying to rid himself of the impression it was making. It was making him crazy. He began to run, as if he could flee from his own mind.

He broke out in a cold sweat, his breath suffocating in his lungs. Almost blindly, he ran through the streets. *Please go away, Ember.* He spoke it to himself before realizing he'd said it again out loud.

He ran until he'd entered a new neighborhood. This was Purple Vale. The upscale, orchid-painted homes and lush lawns screamed out higher-level Status. Even the streetlights, beginning to glow dully as the sun's rays ebbed, were more ornate than his own Level Twelve neighborhood. He stopped abruptly, another memory leaking in tiny droplets from his subconscious. *Ember used to live here.* He stood there panting, desperate and feeling helpless, unable to escape.

What? Why does that matter?

Maybe he'd developed some sort of delusions? Was that why Serpio insisted he take a stress break? Yet the further he walked into the neighborhood, the more he realized he was in pursuit of something. His mind was trying to make sense of a real-life confusion, a recollection buried deep inside.

He wandered through the streets, looking at each house on either side. One by one, he passed them by until he slowed, a double take harnessing his steps. There ... that house ... familiar. *Ember's?* Knowing his thoughts were completely irrational, he bounded the steps to the door anyway and rang the bell. When the door opened to a gentleman with a light beard in his thirties, Will threw his hand to his forehead. "Sorry ... sorry for bothering you. I—I have the wrong house."

The owner had to call after him. "No problem. Have a great day. Thanks for your service to the city!"

Will turned back the way he had come, his mind racing. He ran his fingers through his hair, almost yanking out the strands. Will chanted his mantra more than once before he was able to slow his steps to a normal pace. *I have the power to control my thoughts and feelings.*

A path just off the street wound through a park. Hesitating for only a second, he made his way down the trail. Wide curves took him down a hill to a landmark he recognized. The Birds Eye Pass Bridge. He slowed his pace, gazing up at the impressive geodesic structure lit with multicolored lights. This is where his life had really begun, where he'd saved a kid's life, risen to fame, and become a Plauditor. He gazed up at the bridge, his thoughts scattering like butterflies, and closed his eyes, letting the sounds of the city lull him. The rush of the Maglev as it went by, the wind ruffling the leaves on the trees, its whistle haunting in the night. A feeling of comfort allowed him to pull the butterflies back into a net in his mind.

Reliving his most heroic moment helped him get his thoughts back on track and into some solid memories—not the demon ones he'd battled today. He remembered instead how his adrenaline had been pumping. How his heart had been drumming out of his chest.

A stir of air feathered his hair and teased the leaves on the nearby foliage. His gaze settled on a blooming Duskduster bush, its white flowers bursting with perfume. He inhaled, instantly realizing that the scent held a memory. He put his hands to his head, another recollection almost falling into place.

The stairs to the top of the bridge were nearly a mile away. He paced for a full minute before the force of insistent thought crushed his resistance. *Go!*

He started walking in that direction and then broke into a run. He closed the gap to the stairs within six minutes, his body moving with an odd muscle memory. Breathless, he took the stairs two at a time until he reached the top. His lungs ached and forced him to halt. To his right was an area surrounded by Duskdusters. Although he was still a distance away, he wasn't giving up yet. Something inside was insisting he go there—a memory tugging at his brain.

The closer he got, a deep sadness struck him. The memory of a kiss flirted with his sanity, his spirit feeling split in two. He approached the bushes and reached out to pluck a flower, inhaling its scent, savoring it, hoping for answers. As he dropped the bloom from his hand, his gaze focused on gaps in the foliage. He knew the place—a small open quad, a mere six-by-six that he'd nicknamed Lovers' Lair. Parting the Duskdusters roughly, he peered in. But the space was empty, just as empty as his heart.

When inexplicable tears flooded his eyes, blurring his vision, the only thing he saw was inside his head. *Ember.*

A sharp pain struck the back of his head, an intense momentary sensation, much like a lightning bolt frying his brain. The pang struck swiftly and then left, and with it, the image of the girl.

It had been one huge mistake to come here. He needed to get away … *now.*

He tried to gather his wits about him as he turned to leave the scene, shaking his head.

Time to get back to reality—back to the jeweler. Exhausted, he made his way into the main depot to catch the Maglev and rounded the corner to the waiting area. In a last-ditch attempt to shake his ghosts, he turned around one last time to gaze at the place he'd left behind.

He blinked. Now he knew he was going crazy. There were two people heading toward the very place he'd just been, and one looked exactly like Ember. He pounded his forehead with his hand and looked again.

There was no doubt. This was not in his mind. The girl, Ember, was really there. For some reason, he knew her walk, her body, and the tilt of her head as if it was a part of him.

Heart pounding, he threw his head back for a moment, realizing this was the break he'd been hoping for.

Then, he pushed the emergency icon on his Alt. "Reporting a sighting of Ember Vinata. Please advise."

78

Will's Victory

A response came immediately: "Sciolists dispatched."

Will spoke into his Alt, his voice heavy and urgent. "A reminder to Sciolists. Ember is an Empath. She'll absolutely feel threatened and retreat unless you have the proper frame of mind. There can be *no aggression* —no malevolence. Be super calm—joyful. She'll never know what's coming."

He didn't know how to interpret the silence at the other end before a response came through. "Confirmed."

His remembering Ember's ability would ensure her capture. IIe smiled and almost laughed at his insight.

Behind the building, Will watched the two figures. Stopping for a moment, the beauty gave her companion a playful bop on the arm. They strolled along an inner curb, whispering and laughing. *They're crossing from the side of the station but staying close to the hedges.* They seemed headed for the tiny, secluded place from where he'd plucked the Duskduster flower minutes earlier.

The girl's male escort had his arm around her waist and pulled her close to him before they threaded their bodies through the foliage and stepped into Lover's Lair. Will's stomach twisted in a swirl of nausea. The thought crossed his mind … was he jealous? But that was insane. More possibly, the excitement of his discovery was turning him inside out. He checked his Alt. Definitely positive.

He needed to pace, to diffuse the adrenaline building up in his system, but he didn't dare take his eyes away long enough. Instead, he tapped his toe. The vibrations and some deep breathing helped him slow his heartbeat. Regardless, a dampness under his armpits and across his forehead wasn't something he could control.

He fought a rising urge to push his way into the spot where they hid. Arrest this girl himself—confirm his suspicion. Wouldn't Serpio be prouder of him if he did? But still, he hesitated, worried that he would embarrass himself if his suspicions were wrong. Or that he'd scare the couple away.

At last, Will saw a Sciolist coming from the west on foot, his electric lance in one hand. Will bolted out from behind the building to meet the Sciolist as he marched into the station.

"Hey!" Will called out, giving the Tranquility salute. He didn't want to attract attention, so he kept his voice controlled.

The Sciolist turned to Will. "Where's the fugitive?"

Will pointed to Lover's Lair. "She's in there. You expecting other Sciolists?"

"Yes. Any moment. And they're all mentally and physically prepared." The Sciolist's eyes swept the area and then he answered a call on his Alt. "Two minutes," he told Will.

"Good. They need to hurry."

"You're sure you saw Ember—*Ember Vinata*."

Will nodded emphatically. "I know. It seems impossible. And she's with someone else—a guy. They looked … cozy."

"Mmm. Just one person with her? Any weapons?"

"Weapons? No …" Will was beginning to doubt himself. Why would a fugitive be out without any defense in public?

Out of nowhere, three more Sciolists converged into the

station's waiting area. After giving the salute, all four Sciolists stepped away and briefly conferred.

"We'll be taking control now. You are excused," the first-to-scene Sciolist barked at Will.

"Wait—I can't even watch?" Will was beginning to feel irritated. This was *his* capture. He wanted the credit.

"You need to leave. We're clearing the area." Sure enough, two of the Sciolists were already instructing the few waiting passengers to exit the station. A nervous-looking guy approaching the waiting area was stopped, then hurried away.

"What about Serpio? Does he know?" Will felt glory slip through his fingers.

"If it is Ember, he'll be notified. Now, remove yourself. You'll be called later."

Called later. That's reassuring. "Okay … My name's Will—Will Verus. I'm a close confidant of—"

"We know who you are."

Will turned on his heel and walked away. But he wasn't leaving. Back behind the building, he waited and watched.

THE FOUR SCIOLISTS entered Lover's Lair from all sides, their yells overlapping.

"Stop!"

"You're under arrest!"

Will heard male shouts of "No! No, no, no!" And a female's voice, shrill and panicked: "Xander! Help! Shi—" Yells again, but not from Sciolists. "Can't you—?" Thrashing and shuffling shook the very roots of the bushes. *People are getting thrown around in there.* Then a moment of agonizing silence snuffed out the minutes.

When the Sciolists burst out of their seclusion with their captives in tow, Will's heart nearly exploded with excitement. He'd called it correctly.

The girl's hat was off her head, her brilliant, fiery hair flying in defiant strands around her. Her face, crumpled in misery and anger, was undoubtedly that of Ember Vinata. Her beauty alone confirmed it. The pictures he'd seen of the girl—even the one that haunted him all day—didn't do her justice. He felt himself react in a purely masculine way before closing his eyes and trying desperately to shake off the feeling. This was one reason he couldn't wait for the capture. He badly wanted—needed—to be near her. Soon, he would make sure he had that opportunity.

Two Sciolists flanked both Ember and the mystery guy. Will studied the male, who looked to be his own age, his black hair and dark gaze a devilish contrast to his Level One clothes. There was a familiarity about him, but nothing he could identify. The Sciolists secured their prisoners' hands behind their backs and thrust them toward the west end of the station, where Will could no longer analyze them.

He couldn't wait one more minute before making a call. "Serpio ... Happy Magistrate Appreciation Day ... Yes ... I've got the best gift of the day. We've captured Ember Vinata."

79

Ember's Failure

The second that Sciolists crashed their refuge, Ember and Xander tore off their Alts and smashed them with their feet on the concrete beneath them. It was the agreed-upon first defense for any compromised situation. The Alts would lead to a discovery of Phoenix if they were operational.

Although they'd destroyed their Alts, Ember's fear burned through her like a volcano. Every frayed nerve, every fractured thought, pushed her closer to an agonizing panic. Her breath went from shallow gasps one minute to enormous, heaving sobs the next.

How could she have been caught so unaware?

But she knew part of the answer. It was her fault. As she'd waited with Xander in the Maglev's garden space, she'd been focused on him. The kiss he'd given her right before they went into the hidden space had set her on fire. All she wanted was to kiss him until her mouth was bruised. And she did. They had broken apart only when Xander reminded her that the guy they were waiting for was coming soon.

Now she was caught, like a bug in a spider's web. She struggled with all her might against her captors, her fury at herself and the Sciolists growing at an exponential rate. She gathered her own emotions and pulled in Xander's, which were akin to a murderer's. Concentrate …

Pain pulsed into her wrists and traveled up her arms and into her body—electric shock from the cuffs. She felt as if every atom in her body was being shaken hard and fast. A burn spread into her torso while every muscle clenched so tightly that moving was impossible.

She couldn't think, couldn't fight. A chunk of time slipped away, but not because she'd engineered it. She wilted into oblivion.

When the surge quit, she felt raw, like the flesh had been stripped from her bones and steel wool had sanded down the organs inside.

They had reached the street. Two Sciolist vehicles were parked at the curb. Xander looked like he could start a fire with white, hot rage. His eyes were narrowed into a tight glare. He jerked and fought against them, as if sheer determination and strength could miraculously free him. Until they shoved a gag into his mouth, obscene curses flowed from his lips. To her horror, two Sciolists shoved him into one vehicle, and she was forced into the other.

$$\text{———————————}$$

80

Serpio's Conquest

"They're here, Magistrate."

The words electrifying his OmniCom vibrated from his ears and down Serpio's spine, sending him into a euphoric frenzy.

He'd waited far too long for this day. All the days, hours, he'd spent scheming, searching, and hoping had frustrated him beyond his limits. But now, Ember would be his once again. His heartbeat accelerated as he thought of being able to touch her. This time, he would possess her physically before beginning the effort to use her many talents.

Of course, she would be instrumental in finding the rest of the criminals at large and returning the Plauditors. The final victory!

Before leaving his home to meet his Sciolists at City Hall, he changed into clean clothes, selecting his tightest pair of pants. He scrutinized himself in the mirror, making sure his gold-toned tie was perfect and his jacket smooth. He combed his black hair away straight back from his face before brushing the sides down to where his hair barely grazed his shoulders. He was ready.

The way his mansion was attached to City Hall made his

walk to the holding cells quick. Serpio took the elevator down to where the building's hallway went to the left. Two interrogation rooms were around the corner. Ember would be in one, and her companion would be in the other.

He'd not yet called anyone in—not even an Elite representative. He wanted to savor the experience for himself first. He entered Ember's room, saluting the Sciolists and then pausing to glance at the two-sided mirror on the opposite wall, as if for reassurance that no one was yet watching.

Ember sat at a table. The chair across from Ember's would be his.

"The prisoner is secured?" Serpio asked as he sat down.

"Yes, sir," both Sciolists responded.

"You are dismissed. I'll take it from here," Serpio directed. He noted Ember had her arms pulled back and trussed behind her. The way she tugged her arms and thrashed her body in a ridiculous effort to get free made him almost sorry she was a prisoner. Almost. The gag was particularly pitifully controlling, making her eyes appear round and wild.

"Ember," Serpio said, the word velvety in his mouth. "I've missed you."

The girl squeezed her eyes shut for a long moment. To block him out? To contain her anger? Serpio didn't know. But he found any shape she made her face alluring. Even her anger. In fact, he coveted her fury. It made her seem wilder—more sensual.

"I'm going to take the gag off now, my dear. We need to talk." Serpio stood and walked around her to untie the cloth. As the cloth came away in his hands, he laced his fingers through her hair to feel its softness.

"Don't! Don't you touch me!" Ember snarled, her body pulling away.

The Magistrate stepped back and returned to the opposite side of the table to face her. A smile licked at his lips. "Ember, Ember ...we have more than enough time for that later, it's true. I'm not planning to keep you here as a prisoner at all. Nor will I be sending you to The Outside or ordering your execution, although the citizens may pressure me to do that if you're as dangerous as I think you are."

Ember spat, "You might as well kill me. I'm never going to submit to you. Or work for you. My loyalty is with my rebels."

Serpio raised his eyebrows in what he hoped was his most charming look of surprise. "Your rebels? They're *your* rebels? Hmmm. Your … friends. You really believe I won't be able to find them now? You'll happily tell me what I need to know."

"Why is that? Eliminating you is the most important goal in my life." Ember shook with unrestrained fervor.

"So you say. But … how about the boy next door?" Serpio tilted his head to the right. A slow smile perfectly framed his threat.

"Don't—you *can't* hurt him!" The wildness was back in her eyes.

"Ah, I see there is affection for him. Maybe more than that? I can harm him easily, without any permission from the Elite or anyone. Accidents happen during arrests. You *can* save your boyfriend, though." Serpio carefully scrutinized her reactions. Her eyes welled up, and a bright flush stained her cheeks. The boy in the adjacent room was someone extremely special to her. Excellent leverage.

"I … we … stand alone. We don't protect the other. We willingly give up our own safety for the greater good." The tears in Ember's already-red eyes spilled over.

"Really? You won't mind if I torture him a bit? Or worse? Your revolution is dead. It's pitiful. One way or another it will end sooner or later. 'Your' people are no match for Sciolists and our methods. You might as well at least save your boyfriend's life."

Ember jerked her chin up. "Go pound sand."

Serpio shrugged his shoulders. "Give up the rebels' location. I'm offering a chance to save your boyfriend as a courtesy because you are Queen of Hearts and you'll be mine either way. It's up to you."

"No. No, no, no!" Ember yelled. "You'll never break me. I won't betray the others! I—I won't!"

"I'll take that as a personal challenge. But perhaps the 'significant other' in the room behind us will be more receptive." Serpio already regretted having to leave Ember to see the other prisoner. He didn't know who the guy was, but he'd be a pawn nonetheless. He sighed and left his chair.

"By the way, your former boyfriend, Will Verus? He's the one who saw you and called in the responders. Let's see if your *other* boyfriend does a better job protecting you. I'll be back soon."

Ember's eyes narrowed into slits, and she gritted her teeth.

Her display of anger gave him goosebumps of pleasure. What a hot, sexy thing she was.

Serpio had to admit that the tip and capture of Ember were exceptional. Now, he had the added option of using Will against Ember. If he put them together, what fireworks would result? What information? A dazzling idea.

The Magistrate reflected on how he'd tested and doubted Will for so long, and now, the boy had given the ultimate proof of his loyalty. Will's handing over of Ember showed that he'd been loyal all along. Or had it been the final session in the therapy room that had finished the job?

He didn't mind if Will watched some of the questioning. In fact, he and Will could have quite the celebration together.

Once outside in the hallway, the Magistrate ordered the Sciolists to call for Will. Then, he directed them back into the room to be with Ember.

81

Serpio's Awareness

When Serpio opened the door to the other room, he couldn't stifle his gasp. Four Sciolists occupied the table, but he didn't have to wonder why. The man-child in the chair was none other than Xander Noble.

He stood for a brief moment in the doorway, his disbelief nearly choking him. Xander Noble was dead! But here he was, sitting as sassy as Serpio remembered in spite of the bonds and gag that kept him contained.

"Ah … Xander Noble. Back from the grave, I see." Serpio saluted the Sciolists before dismissing two of them. The others would remain, as this was no Ember. This was a powder keg.

Unlike Ember, Xander didn't thrash. Instead, he sat, eerily calm. But his defiance showed in his steely gaze and the flexing of the muscles in his arms. His teeth bit hard against the gag, his upper lip curled in an attempted sneer.

Serpio slithered into the chair across from his prisoner. "Xander Noble. Isn't this quite the surprise? The last person I expected."

Xander vehemently shook his head from side to side. Serpio laughed. The kid wasn't denying his identity, was he? No—just advertising an uncooperative attitude.

"I'm going to remove your gag, Xander. We have things to discuss." Serpio nodded to the Sciolist on Xander's right, who loosened the ties.

"I've got nothin' to say to you. I won't talk—with or without that thing."

"Now, Xander. You might find you have something to say after all."

"Only that you're an ass." Xander's eyes were dark as flint. "And that you couldn't kill me after all."

"There's always next time. I'm ready. Unless your girl-friend helps you out." Serpio's use of the word "girlfriend" both excited and angered the Magistrate.

"She won't break, not even for me." Xander's voice held an admirable conviction.

"You don't know what the terms are." Serpio sat back, his hand on his chin, projecting an in-control image.

"Doesn't matter. She knows I'll die for her and the cause."

"But Xander … the girl doesn't want you to die. She's over there begging me for your life." Serpio leaned in close to Xander's ear and whispered, "She's already offered herself to me to keep you alive."

At that, Xander jerked and thrashed. "That's a lie!"

Serpio walked away but turned back to say, "No. It isn't."

"You can't—you won't—"

"Have her? Yes, I will. Whether you live or not. No. Instead, I'm offering you and Ember other … compensations."

"I don't want your compensation. Just leave Ember alone. She's … *mine.*"

"Yours? You sound like Ember. She claims the rebellion is hers. That the people in it are hers. That's all. She didn't claim you were hers. Just that she wanted you alive and was willing to cooperate. Now, are you ready to make a concession for *her*? All I need is the location of the REMs and Plauditors."

"Or what? You'll kill me? Like I said, do it. I'm not playing traitor to save my life."

"If you give me locations, I'll send you to The Outside. No death."

"No." Xander's gaze could bore a hole into titanium.

"If you don't cooperate, you will die. I'll have Ember, but unless she cooperates, she'll be of no use to me. She'll have her own special fate."

"I know this. Ember's strong enough to hurt you. I've seen it. She doesn't need me to protect her."

"Very well. Let's see what happens when you two discuss it."

"Discuss it? You think Ember's gonna break—or I'm gonna break—just because we're in the same room? We've already said goodbye a hundred different ways." Xander jerked his chair forward to forcibly move the table. "She knows how I feel."

The smirk Serpio directed at Xander could have frozen the blistering terrain of The Outside. "Sciolists," Serpio ordered, "take Xander to the other room. Then leave."

It took two Sciolists and a third's backside forcefulness to get Xander off his chair.

Now it's time for the real show, Serpio mused. *Let's see what they do and say when they're together.* He chose a position behind the two-way mirror, making sure the speakers in the room were set to a higher volume and that recording was activated. He didn't want to miss a thing.

The Sciolists thrust Xander through the door to Ember's room.

"Xander!" Ember's strained vocalization of her beau's name told Serpio a story. She was desperate for him.

The guards seated Xander before following Serpio's mandate to release Xander's wrist cuffs. With the unbinding, Xander eyes widened in surprise. He jumped up, as if to fight against his captors, before changing his mind and running to Ember's side instead.

"Em! Oh … Em. Are you okay? You hurt?" Xander draped himself over her before pulling her to her feet. She fell against him, sobs seeming to erupt from her entire body. Xander examined her cuffs to see if he could release her hands from their bonds, then shook his head.

Grinning at the show, Serpio turned to see Will round the corner into the hallway. He returned Will's salute before he said, "Ah, Will, you're just in time. Look what you've done today, Plauditor. Not just one fugitive, but two."

Will approached the window, arms crossed. "Who? The other guy … he's …?"

"Notorious. You may remember him. Xander Noble? A REM."

Will gazed into the window where the couple was embracing. "I didn't recognize him earlier. Ember's wrapped up in him. I can't see his face yet."

"They're very attached to each other. They're lovers," Serpio whispered. He leaned in, as if wanting to join the embrace.

Will's barely audible gasp caused Serpio to glance Will's way. What was this?

The prisoners broke apart, Xander turning away before pacing the room.

Will didn't speak, but he shifted in place, his feet shuffling in an odd sidestep, almost as if he fought to regain his balance.

Xander stopped his pacing and sat down, pulling Ember into the chair next to his. He looked toward the mirror before dropping his voice to a murmur. "No matter what Serpio says he'll do to me, you can't offer him *anything*."

"I have to try! I can't let him kill you," Ember whispered.

"He says you offered yourself …" Xander said, under his breath.

"I didn't! But if I had to, to save you—"

"No, Ember! That would be like death to me anyway. Please don't! He won't spare me no matter what you do. Especially now that he knows about our relationship."

Will covered his eyes with his hand before dragging his hand down over his entire face in a gesture of what appeared to be disbelief.

Serpio shifted his attention to the boy next to him. *What is Will reacting to?* Serpio thought, his focus no longer on his captives. Could it be that he was jealous of the boy in the room? Why? Serpio had no doubts that Will even remembered his association with the girl. He'd made sure of that.

Will pressed his palms against the glass before curling his fingers in. "What's the reason they're both in there together?"

Serpio dropped his hand heavily on Will's shoulder. "To see if the relationship is as tight as I think it is. To see if, in a conversation, either one really refuses to help the other. To see if Xander will agree to having Ember cooperate to save his life." As each word fell from his mouth, Serpio felt Will's body begin to tremble underneath his hand.

"What's—what's going to happen to Ember?" Will kept his eyes on the girl but shrugged Serpio's hand off his shoulder.

Serpio held up a finger to his lips. "Shh … listen."

Xander leaned across to wipe tears off Ember's face before tenderly kissing her. "Promise me. You won't do anything rash. You should at least save yourself. *You can find a way, just like you always have.*" Xander gazed into her eyes as if he was trying to get inside her head.

Serpio sighed before turning to address his Plauditor. "Ah, Will. Look at that. So … cute. No, she won't be punished—not much anyway. She's too valuable. But him? One way or another, he'll be eliminated no matter what she says. I can't have Ember attached to anyone but me."

Will nodded and swallowed visibly. "She's someone you

desire. What man wouldn't?" He shifted his gaze to Xander, who'd stood up and was yelling at them through the glass.

"She's never going to give up, Serpio! Just come and get me!"

Will's eyes narrowed to hard slits. His hands, now down at his sides, clenched with anger. "*That guy …*"

Clicking his OmniCom, Serpio alerted his Sciolists. "Time to take Xander away. To the holding cell. Now." Within a minute, the guards entered, cuffed a writhing Xander, and removed him from the room to the sound of Ember's pitiful cries. He'd learned that Ember seemed more worried about Xander's fate than she let on. But he'd also learned something else. Will detested Xander. The hatred for the guy was unmistakable. Such emotion in a guy like Will, though … it went against all his reprogramming and all of Tranquility's Accords. Was there a monster hiding inside this young hero? His curiosity peaked. This was a novel occurrence. Again, it reinforced Will's loyalty to the city, but the intensity? He didn't need to be an Empath to know it was an emotion off the charts.

A thought entered Serpio's head. It would be interesting to see Xander and Will in a room together.

Will turned to Serpio. "I know it's an odd time, but I brought you something." Will dug in his pocket and pulled out a small package. "For you. For Magistrate Appreciation Day."

Serpio reached for the box. "Will! This is so very thoughtful. You know gifts make me very happy, especially from someone as special as you." The wrapping was gold, which Serpio removed before handing it to Will. "A crown? What a perfect gift." He extracted it from its container and pinned it on, immediately feeling almost as if the crown had been placed on his head. "You have gone above and beyond today, Will Verus. You can look forward also to a reward for the capture of these fugitives."

Will smiled but looked thoughtful. "Thank you, Magistrate. I'm glad to be of service, of course. I appreciate the reward, but as you know, I don't like being in the spotlight. If I could ask for one thing, though?"

"Of course." Serpio wanted to give Will at least a show of respect. "What are you hoping for?"

"I'd like just one minute. One minute in that room with Ember? Before she's taken to her holding cell."

Like earlier, Serpio caught a well-defined quiver in the young Plauditor's body. "I acknowledge you need closure," Serpio said carefully. "Is this because you have something to say to her? I'm happy to give her a message—because she knows you turned her in. If you go in, it will be … unpleasant."

"I know. I understand all that. I want to speak to her privately. If you could … if you could turn off the speakers and just let me have a moment? Just one minute. No Sciolists. It's not too much to ask, is it?" Will's jaw was set, and his green eyes held fire.

Serpio scrutinized Will's face and assessed his body language. Will's face appeared innocent, almost vulnerable. His body screamed the opposite. It carried a tenseness that a tightrope would envy. Mysterious. And too intriguing to deny.

"One minute." Serpio was already setting a timer on his OmniCom.

"No speakers."

"One minute, no speakers, no guards. Only because you proved yourself today."

Will nodded. "I'll be in and out. Thank you, Magistrate."

Serpio had no intention of turning off any speakers. In fact, this little scene would be one of the best entertainments of the day. A criminal facing her captor, who happened to be her former boyfriend. Too good. He watched Will as he entered the room.

Ember's face became an embodiment of her name. Serpio

had experienced Ember's dislike, but her hatred for Will was nearly palpable.

The fascinating piece, though, was not Ember, but Will. He walked into the room and stood there staring, as if he were starstruck, for the length of a quartet of heartbeats. Will gazed into Ember's eyes, as if memorizing their shape and sparkle.

Opening his mouth to speak, he hesitated, like his vocal cords had suddenly quit altogether. Then, he paced back and forth, agitatedly running his hands through his hair and across his face several times.

At last, he walked over to Ember's side a few inches away. "I'm—"

Ember interrupted. "You're a liar, a traitor, and a fool. I regret the day I ever met you."

Will swayed on his feet. His hands shook, and his eyes locked with hers. Then he gently touched her face with his hand, trailing his fingers down her cheek before touching her lips. His face flushed, and perspiration glistened on his forehead. Will's eyes were lit with a wonder seen on every child's face on Christmas morning.

Ember jerked her face away.

Will stepped back as if stung. "Ember, I—" Will held the words in his mouth, once again seemingly stopped by some invisible force or awkward shyness. Instead, he made a barely discernible bow and exited the room without looking back.

Serpio stood rooted to the floor in shock, his lips parted, his pulse racing. What he'd just seen had put everything in a whole new light. Will still had feelings for Ember. Feelings so strong—so overwhelming—that he couldn't even speak. And that was a very big problem.

82

Serpio's Lies

After the interrogations, Serpio spent the rest of the night sleeping in only short bursts. He had two problems on his mind. He could not keep Will around. And now, he had Xander—not only also a competitor for Ember's affections, but he was the worst criminal of them all.

By morning, however, he'd thought of the perfect—if not the most extraordinary—solution to both problems.

As soon as he was up, he sent a message to all Elite to attend a mandatory emergency meeting in an hour. The sense of urgency for a quick convene would work in his favor. He wanted the Elite to act quickly.

When he entered the room a half-hour later, he was happy to see Elite members already filing in and taking their places. What he had to present to them would be both thrilling and heavy at the same time.

At precisely 9:00 a.m., he gave the Tranquility salute and started the session.

"Members of the Elite, I've called for a special gathering today because I have some wonderful news. Two of our most notorious rebels have been apprehended and are in custody!"

An excited murmur fanned across the crowd.

"We now have Xander Noble and Ember Vinata." Serpio put up his hands to quiet the crowd as they reacted. "I was under the impression Xander had met an unfortunate accident some time ago. I'll be looking into why that information was incorrect." He stopped and stared at Ava for a moment. "But the misinformation doesn't make his apprehension any less amazing. Our Sciolists have done an excellent job trailing and detaining the suspects, and their work has paid off."

An Elite member dripping in gold finery stood and waited for acknowledgment. Serpio nodded his permission to speak. "Magistrate, where are the fugitives being held?"

"Xander Noble is in a holding cell. All his needs are being met. The girl is so much more fragile. Ember is in a guest house under lock and key with Sciolist guards for the present time. I assure you that we are doing everything we can for both of them to be comfortable and as happy as possible under the circumstances."

Feren stood to address Serpio, "Have you begun interrogations to discover where the other rebels are hiding? The information will be essential in restoring safety and order to the city."

Serpio put his hands in a prayer-like pose and pointed them back toward Feren. "My dear Feren. Of course. I have questioned each of them and given assurances for their safety." He stopped and sighed. "Unfortunately, neither of them is ready to give information, even with the promise of a sensitive, caring response from you. That's why we must discuss other options today. They may be choices we don't want to make, but our city is at risk until the rest of the rebels are apprehended."

One of Serpio's most trusted Elite rose to her feet.

"Yes, Ava. I *appreciate* what you have to say."

"Serpio, we must remember our humanity and our understanding. Perhaps by offering something they want, they'll be more amenable to sharing information."

"Ava ... thank you. If these were just true-blue Tranquility citizens, that would be no problem. But these are dangerous people. Ember Vinata is a young, innocent girl who has been drawn into a situation far beyond her years. The boy involved is attractive and has influenced her. The rebels want her because she has power. We cannot allow them to use and abuse her. I move that she be placed in the guest house for an extended period and then installed in my home for further protection and education, as she was before the rebellion occurred. If she isn't cooperative with information, at some point, with some genuine love and training, she could still be very useful and influential for the city. This would be one part of what you'll be voting on today."

Ava stood again, her brow wrinkled in concern. "Having Ember placed in your home is a long-term and perhaps dangerous option. However, I concur we would never, ever want to use force or send this young girl to The Outside. She could easily be rehabilitated. I would like the record to state that I would be willing to put her under my advisement."

Typical Ava, Serpio thought. *She's always looking for the best way to help.* He made a mental note to ask her about the accident with Xander.

Serpio applauded, his face set in a mask of appeasement. "I appreciate that offer, Ava. Could I get a quick second on the arrangement I suggested?"

Fifteen or so of the Elite stood.

"I suggest we take a vote on that arrangement, as I see we have more than one person who seconds the proposal." Serpio relaxed slightly. So far, the meeting was going better than he could imagine. "All in favor of the arrangement suggested, please stand."

The response was nearly unanimous, the Elite members looking around at one another and nodding.

"Very good. Ember will be treated with the utmost care. Now, I realize we have yet to discuss Xander. But first, I have some lesser news to share. I'm going to present this in the most positive way I can, but it is a disappointing situation. Prepare your hearts."

After allowing the Elite a moment to meditate, Serpio began to speak again with a soulful tone. "You're all acquainted with Will Verus. He's been before you for trial and then, at your determination, as a merciful act, taken under my wing. Since, as a body, we could not determine Will's loyalty to the city, I have tested him in multiple ways. In fact, with supervision, he assisted in the hunt for our missing Plauditors and the REMs. Although he discovered their escape route, he was not successful in his attempts to find the fugitives. I again gave him the benefit of the doubt. I was looking for his true colors at all times, and it appeared he had proved himself. A couple of days ago, I reinstalled him as a Plauditor, believing wholeheartedly that he'd earned his privileges back. Unfortunately, though, during the apprehension of Xander and Ember yesterday, Will alerted them both to our Sciolists' presence."

A series of gasps punctured the silence in the room. A grumbling chatter bounced among the Elite. Serpio observed the reaction carefully. Clearly, the Elite were confused and upset.

"Fortunately, our Sciolists were still able to apprehend both of these rebels. But Will could have jeopardized the entire operation. However, in the interests of compassion, Will is not in custody. Today's meeting will determine his fate."

Feren looked around at her Elite colleagues, then jumped to her feet. "My fellow Elites! Don't blame yourselves. We've done everything correctly."

Serpio nodded and wiped at his eyes with a handkerchief from his pocket. "Agreed, Feren. I can bring Will before you with a Sciolist to testify. But the evidence is solidly concrete. Will has been a double agent all along. Do we want to waste our time questioning the same person who lied to us before?"

A member in the third row held up her hand before rising

from her chair. Serpio gave her a nod. "All accused should come before the Elite. Will and Xander should be no different!"

Elite members rose to their feet. "A vote!" one called out. The others answered with the same words. "A vote! A vote!" A chant had begun.

Serpio smiled gently and raised his arm for calm. "A vote is in order. But also about whether we'll need to *act* differently this time."

Several Elite stood at once. Serpio chose the elder of the two, a man named Harris.

"They both need to be sent to The Outside immediately. We can no longer be merciful."

Serpio immediately jumped in, even over the murmurs in the chamber. He walked out from behind the podium, standing in front of the Elite close enough to touch those in the front row. "The Outside has always been reserved for significant crimes and for those who refuse emotional manage-ment. But Will is a special case. He and Xander Noble have both committed severe crimes against the state. Capital offenses. And they've been caught in the act. The Outside is not enough. Xander has survived The Outside and returned. Our city continues to suffer from the damage. Plauditors are still missing. REMs remain on the loose. The bombs, the lock-down of the Plauditorium, stealing from the library ... The list goes on. This is not mere emotional resistance. This is outrageous destruction and rebellion that we cannot permit ever again."

Feren left her seat to join Serpio in front. She paused before she pleaded for action. "This calls for drastic measures. We must restore our city to a calm, happy place. The treaso-nous acts of Will Verus and Xander Noble require a heavier hand. The lives and happiness of our citizens are at stake. If this rebellion continues, decent, innocent people could die.

These destructive tactics are exactly why we have the Accords —to prevent a slide into anarchy."

Serpio couldn't have asked for a better spokesperson in Feren. He added, "Feren is absolutely right. Rebellion leads to war. None of us wants to see the annihilation of the world like the Great War. One thing leads to another, and soon, it's too late."

A thirty-something female called out, "Tranquility must stand against unrest, or we're doomed to repeat history!"

Serpio walked to the podium and quietly tapped his knuckles on its surface. "I propose a solution to serve as a warning against future rebellion. We need an example of how intolerant we must be about insurgency."

Feren moved to Serpio's side and put her hand on his shoulder in a show of solidarity. "I agree. A message must be sent to all citizens about how ruinous this is to our way of life."

"Feren, if I may … I have an idea for the Elite to consider. Will has betrayed Tranquility a second time. Xander needs to be threatened to give us the information we need. Both should be punished. I propose … a face-off between Xander and Will." Serpio spoke softly, silkily. His words had to make an impact.

"A face-off? What are you imagining?" Feren moved closer to Serpio.

Serpio slowly paced in front of his audience. Explaining his vision required a precise language. "Will and Xander fight to the death in an arena. Will and Xander both have spears. Xander is the key example—the ultimate warning for sympathizers. He will die … at Will's hands."

A woman in a gold-sequined jacket stood. When she was recognized, she said, "This is a serious proposal. We don't want to be barbaric!"

Serpio tilted his head to the side to give the impression he was intently listening. "I know it's never been done before. But we have to make a public example of these people. Who knows how many others are on their side?" Serpio put his hand to his head in a gesture of despair. "If we don't act in a way that discourages sympathy with the revolutionaries, this will get out of hand before we know it."

Feren stepped forward and closely approached the Elite members, her eyes connecting first with the woman raising the objection and then at the others. "Yes ... a public display would discourage sympathizers. Not that any of our citizens would support such a group, but we need to make sure. If our citizens see the consequences of such disloyalty, it would be a good lesson for them."

Serpio wanted to hug Feren. She had practically sold his whole idea to the Elite in one speech! "Feren, that's a fine idea. I suggest something that the citizens should watch. The face-off should be a sporting event for entertainment and education. Will and Xander fight it out. The best man wins."

"What should we do with the winner afterward?" a younger blond Elite female asked. "We need to have a well-thought-out plan."

"I propose this. If Xander miraculously lives through it, we can still offer clemency for Xander *if* he gives us information. That goes for before or after the game commences. If he survives but withholds information, he'll get an additional handicap. He goes Outside completely tied. He would never survive it. Will, too, will go to The Outside if he wins, but without restrictions. Does that seem fair?" Serpio opened his palms to the group. He applied his most concerned expression.

Elite members bowed their heads and conversed quietly with the people around them before leaving their seats to confer with others. Feren finally approached Serpio. "The Elite is ready for a vote."

Serpio thanked Feren before addressing the group a final time. "This is such a sensitive situation. It requires so much soul searching that I believe privacy is in order. Please cast your vote by placing a card in the basket on your way out. I'll be personally tallying your responses and give you the results. If the majority is in favor, we'll schedule the face-off for tonight. Thank you all for your service and your ideas. Most of all, thank you for your compassion and foresight."

As the Elite filed out, dropping their votes in the basket, Serpio's attention was all on Ava. Once the competition in the arena was over, he'd have some digging to do.

83

Xander's Consequences

Xander didn't know how long he'd been sitting in the white, dimly lit cell staring at the walls. It didn't matter. Without a doubt, his hours were numbered.

He'd slept periodically during the night, exhaustion painting every cell of his body. He'd wake abruptly, his first thoughts hoping everything had been a dream, only to be crushed by disappointment. His next thoughts were always of Ember and how he'd probably never see her again. Despair was a bulldozer, pushing tears from his eyes to make room for more. He couldn't think of a time since he was a kid that he had really cried. Now, here he was. He wiped the tears away, grateful his hands were at least free.

Finally, he must have fallen asleep until the morning. An electronic whoosh and the clatter of a tray signified mealtime. Breakfast. Or was it lunch?

He ate ravenously. Although it smelled delicious, the food was bland, designed to be functional and nutritious. The food, though, would help keep his spirits up and his mind focused. He'd have to be sharp for any opportunity to escape.

His hopes were pinned on Ember being able to do something with her powers. Or maybe Phoenix would be missing them by now. Plans had to be brewing to get them out somehow.

Then, he thought of Will. No one had considered it worth the risk to extract Will from prison either. The revolution was too important to gamble on an escape plan, but now, with Talesa with them, would something be possible?

To his surprise, at that moment, the door opened. Two Sciolists entered his chamber, and the door shut behind them. Electronic cuffs were his fate again. He didn't fight, saving his strength for something that mattered.

"Let's go." One of the Sciolists barked the order.

"W—Where are we going?" Xander asked, knowing his question would likely be ignored.

A moment's hesitation marked time before an answer came. "To the Magistrate."

Xander nodded. This would maybe be his final walk.

XANDER SOON FOUND himself inside the Magistrate's pillared room—the room he remembered from both his banishment and his exit with Ember to The Outside. Serpio stood behind the massive, podium-like desk, his gold clothes trimmed with black today. Xander wondered if the black was for his benefit.

"Where's Ember?" The words were out of Xander's mouth before he could determine their wisdom.

"She's fine, Xander. No matter what, she'll be well taken care of." The Magistrate's insidious grin made Xander wince. "I'm offering you another chance to cooperate. Give me the location of your friends. If you do, you'll go out through that door." Serpio jerked his head in the direction of where the exit to The Outside was.

Before he was conscious of it, Xander lurched forward. It was too much to bear not to be able to kill this guy. "Even if I believed you—which I don't—you can rot in hell before I tell you anything."

"I didn't think you'd change your mind. I'm still hoping Ember will, though. In order to increase the stakes, I'm planning … a game."

Xander scowled, his eyebrows charging each other, head-to-head. "Ember doesn't play games."

"Ember's not playing. You are." Serpio chuckled before applauding softly. "You're the show. You and your friend, Will Verus."

Xander blinked, wondering what kind of trick this was. "Will's not my friend. He's your little bitch."

"Ah, so you truly aren't friends. I never knew for sure. That's a pity for Will, then. He's been loyal … to a point."

"What? Didn't he want to lick your feet?"

"I think he would. I think he'd do just about anything. What I can't fix is his unhealthy obsession with Ember." Serpio's speech seethed with contempt.

Xander let Serpio's words sink in. He could barely comprehend them. So, Will still had it bad? He almost felt sorry for the guy. "Will's facing this … game because he has feelings? But I shouldn't be surprised. Isn't that the ultimate violation around here?"

Serpio raised his voice. "Enough chatter! Tonight, you'll face off against Will in our outdoor coliseum. In a death match." Serpio looked like the cat who swallowed the canary.

A death match? What the—? What kind of game is that? "And what do I get if I win?" Xander challenged, his lip curled in disgust.

"You fight for your life. You get to live another day. If that's not enough, and if I like the performance, I'll give the winner some time with Ember. I would be watching, of course. It's a win for me either way." Serpio winked.

Xander spat on the table and cursed. "Disgusting."

"As you wish. Winning is still preferable to death. If you

win, the Elite has voted to send you to the Outside with certain … disadvantages."

"What's the point? A lethal injection works just as well."

"That's too good for you, Xander. With the competition, you're the poster child for the rebels! No one will join your cause after this demonstration."

Xander wanted to smack the self-satisfied expression off Serpio's face. Serpio must be desperate to launch a campaign like this. Xander smirked as he stood with his feet apart in a dominant stance, believing his message. "The rebellion will live whether I do or not."

Will's image came to mind. Xander loathed the guy. Traitor. Liar. He'd emotionally crucified Ember. But killing him? He didn't know if he could. When he thought he'd have to kill him or die himself, his stomach twisted. If Will was the aggressor, he'd have to act on pure instinct. This was what the Magistrate wanted … for him to go down in a blaze of glory. With the Magistrate's desire to see him dead, he'd have to prevail.

I'll fight, and I'll win. I'm ready.

Will's Test

The night of Ember's arrest, Will returned to his house. Ever since he'd been given permission to go home, he'd been joyful. Tonight, though, he stewed. Instead of getting Ember out of his head, he'd just about lost it when he was in the girl's presence. He'd been told she had powers. Was that it? Some black magic that was beguiling him?

He'd gone to bed sweaty, jacked up, and buzzing with longing. He woke more times than he could count, each time dreaming of the girl in a dozen different scenarios.

Not able to sleep, he got up and sat by the window, staring out of his yellow-walled apartment and thinking about the arrest. He swelled with pride as he considered his part in the operation. What were the chances? He must have been destined to find Ember.

Tonight, he'd easily secured his proper place as Serpio's right-hand man. He'd never seen Serpio so grateful. Will looked forward to seeing him again today. An appointment time came through his Alt to meet with Serpio at noon. Contemplating his most excellent future, he raided the kitchen for Jarnish and a very costly old-fashioned coffee. Some things were worth celebrating.

～

WILL WAITED for Serpio in Elite Chambers. That alone was special. He'd already been fortunate to have been there in the past, but today was all for him. He glanced at his Alt. His score was high, vibrating with a jump in points.

When Serpio walked in, Will was surprised to see him accompanied by beautiful Feren. *This must be bigger than I thought,* he reflected.

Feren walked to his side and put a hand on his arm. "I just wanted to offer you my best regards. I've always had high hopes for you." Then, she turned to Serpio. "I'll meet you later to work out details." With a parting Tranquility salute, she breezed out the door.

Will noticed that Serpio wore the lapel pin he'd given him the night before. It sparkled in the light, even against the similar gold of his jacket.

His heart seemed to turn over in his chest, skipping beats. He threw off the discomfort, instead throwing up his hand in the Tranquility salute as Serpio invited him to sit down in an Elite chair, taking his own more decorated chair himself.

"Will, so glad you could join me today."

"Thank you for inviting me." Will's heart kept beating erratically.

"It must have been difficult to see Ember and your former acquaintance, Xander, being captured yesterday."

Shazz, how did Serpio know how Ember made him feel? "It was … emotional seeing her, yeah. I don't remember the guy much." He shrugged and then frowned, the image of the male enveloping Ember in his arms setting off some internal alarm. In fact, it made him want to scream.

Serpio rendered an asymmetric smile. "That's understandable. The Elite gave your emotional state special consideration."

"Well … thanks. I don't really think that matters." Will pulled his head down into his shoulders.

Serpio stood and looked down at Will. "It matters a great deal. In fact, it's quite the defining factor. Your affection for Ember is a red flag. The Elite believe it impacted your judgment last night and will continue to."

"My—judgment?" Will searched his mind for what Serpio might be alluding to. He'd done everything correctly.

"Although you've worked very hard to prove yourself, we regrettably must ask for one more test."

Will pulled at his collar to open his shirt. He needed air. "One more … test? I've done everything!" He tried to smile, feeling instead of seeing his Alt points drop like a rockslide. "I —I captured your fugitives!"

Serpio folded his arms in front of his body. "That was an exceptional piece of work. But the Elite … they're still not totally convinced of your loyalty. I tried to explain that you've merely had some issues with memory. And you know I've been your biggest supporter." Serpio put his hand over his heart. "But the Elite need you to perform a very important job."

Will brightened. Not so much a test, but an important job! "Of course. I'll do whatever you and the Elite need me to do. You know that."

Serpio sat down again and drew his chair closer to Will's. "Our prisoner, Xander? We need to make him an example to the citizens of our city. We cannot and will not tolerate rebellion. Not from anyone." Serpio's eyes locked with his in an uncomfortable pairing. "Tonight, we'll be launching an entertainment spectacle for all Tranquility. You'll be the hero in training."

"Serpio, you know I'm no hero. But I'll be happy to help." Will began to wonder if this wasn't the best opportunity yet.

"It's a competition, Will. You'll face off in an arena against Xander Noble."

"Face … off? Like, in a fight?" Will kept trying to put a positive spin on this odd proposition.

"Yes. You'll have a spear—similar to the Stingers the Sciolists carry. Yours is called a Rayzer. It's longer, more lethal. Your job … is to kill Xander."

Will felt a wave of dizziness so strong he knew he violently shaken his head. "Kill? I'm to *kill* someone?"

"Quite an honor, Will. You'll not only get to prove yourself, but you'll take down Tranquility's most infamous criminal." Serpio's eyes shone with a light that Will often remembered his father had. The father that no longer loved him …

"What—what happens if I actually kill this guy?"

"You'll be beyond all future testing or accusations. Clear. Innocent! If you're successful, I'll give you a new position—a permanent place as my right hand. And, most of all, I'll give you a single opportunity to be with Ember."

"You'd do that? Let me be alone with the girl?" The thought made Will so excited he thought his Alt would explode. "I thought you had a claim on her for yourself."

"I do. But it would be the least I could do after you eliminate our most nefarious rebel."

Will felt heat prickle on his skin. "Don't know why, but I have a raging dislike for that guy myself. I get to clear my name, get a new position, and have time with Ember? I'm in."

85

Ember's Nightmare

The morning after her arrest, Ember jolted awake. Her nightmare had been familiar. Silhouettes faced off as blood ran down their bodies until it pooled on the ground. Rubbing the sleep from her eyes, she felt a wave of vertigo. When she was able to focus, dread clawed at her insides as she realized where she was. In the Magistrate's house. A déjà vu. This was the same bedroom she'd been given the last time Serpio took possession of her. Creamy gold walls and plush carpeting did nothing to soften her distress at being there.

She gazed down at herself. A nightgown? Or should she say "lingerie"? A short, filmy, gold A-line chemise with spaghetti straps dressed her torso, and a pair of satin boy shorts hugged her curves. When had her clothes changed? She didn't remember being brought here or undressed. Someone had to have medicated her at City Hall.

Although she knew it was futile, she climbed from the sheets and traipsed across the room to try the door. Locked. Serpio was taking no chances. She sat back on the bed, her mind racing. *I have to get out. I have to free Xander!* Her chest heaved with a breathless effort against the heavy pressure suffocating her insides.

A glance at the clock on the wall told her it was before curfew. The sun was up, but the sun's rays were only barely emerging, glowing against the partially opened curtains in the window.

She heard a knock on the door. Someone already knew she was awake. Cameras had to be picking up her every move. She shivered. The door opened with a deliberate, slow speed, like a yawn in the middle of sleep. With a calculated walk more predatory than a Greelox, her human nightmare entered the room. *Serpio!* Ember saw his aura, which was bright enough to cast shadows on the walls.

Ember remained seated on the bed. Then the realization of her vulnerable position dawned on her. Serpio had made it clear when she was in the holding cell what was on his mind. The last place she should be was on the bed.

She strode out into the room and stood facing him, her hands on her hips. "Here I am again—back in your stupid house. A prisoner. Watched every minute. I don't belong to you."

Serpio chuckled before leaning in. "You're quite different than the little girl I brought here a few weeks ago. You're fiery. It excites me. And neither of those *boys* you think you've loved will give you what you need. Only I can do that."

She felt buried in revulsion, frustration, and anger. She put her hands to his chest and gave him a shove, moving him but a few inches. "You'll never be what I need! I hate you."

A sensual smile leaked lazily onto his face. "You're incredibly ..." He shook his head. "... bewitching when you're angry."

She took a few steps back but couldn't avoid the way his passion poured over her like a bucket of paint, a slathering so opaque it was blinding. "Get over it."

"When everything is finished, we'll be a team—you'll take

your rightful place beside me. You'll finally learn what you can really be, what you were born to do. Once you learn to control that power, you'll be unstoppable. I will love you and cultivate that power." Serpio reached out, touched his fingers, dampened by excitement, to her face, and tilted her head up. She flinched and violently jerked her head away. When he responded with a low laugh, it made her want to claw his eyes out.

Ember took further steps backward until eight feet separated them. She folded her arms across her chest. "I'm not helping you with my abilities. Not cooperating. In *any* way. You make me sick."

Undisguised amusement flitted across Serpio's lips. He approached her like a lion stalked its prey. He settled for a stance a foot away, disregarding any boundaries of personal space. "Submit to me. Save your city and your friends. It will save you a lot of pain. If not, in the end, you'll be sorry you resisted."

Ember put her hands up in front of her. "I'll never be sorry for resisting you. I won't ever give you information. The rebels will take you down." The words flew out of Ember's mouth aggressively, as if each was a slap.

He leaned in further until she could feel his breath. "Instead of all these useless words, you should be thanking me for saving you. You're comfortable and valued here. You're a rebel. The Elite could have given you a far worse sentence— banishment at the very least. I convinced them that you're a mere innocent, that your power and your information are far too valuable to waste."

She strode across to the opposite side of the room. "Oh, well *thanks*. I'd rather die." Her emotions, mated with Serpio's, were an inferno.

Serpio followed her across the room to stand in front of her. He grabbed her hands and increasingly tightened his grip. His voice was rock-like, his brows raised and tight. "You won't have the privilege of dying. But because of you, others will die. Tonight, you'll see what your stubbornness is costing."

Ember tried to shake her hands from his. Impossible. She couldn't begin to control the tension in her own body, her jaw clenched, her shoulders taut. "Tonight? One day isn't going to change my mind!"

Serpio didn't take his eyes from hers. Then, he dipped his head, his eyes traveling to her lips, where they lit like a bee on a flower. "But, dear Ember, It will. Tonight, you'll be seated next to me at Amity Arena, where your two boys will be fighting it out."

Ember twisted from his grasp and backed away. *My two boys? Fighting it out?* Ember put her hand to the pulse under her neck. "What? What fight?"

"That's what I came to tell you in such a hurry. Every hour you resist is one hour closer to the face-off. Will and Xander will be in a duel to the death."

She could feel the blood drain from her face. "That's cruel and heartless, even for *you*. The Elite will never approve."

Serpio circled her like a vulture as she stood, helpless, whispering to her on all sides. "Oh, but they have. The fight is tonight." He stopped orbiting her, approaching her from behind. He put his hands on her shoulders. "Now, you could stop everything. All you need to do—only one small thing—is give us names and locations. Then it's all called off." Serpio snapped his fingers. "No fight. No spectacle."

Ember clenched her jaw and balled her fists, tightening her arms as she threw them into a stiff position at her sides. "I won't betray the rebels. And you're a liar. Why would I believe any promise you make me?"

Serpio reached out, putting his hands around her head to hold it in place. "Then you'll be responsible for the death of two people. Both of them are special to you. Who's *really* the heartless one?"

Ember turned her back on Serpio. Her rage and mournfulness were piloting her ship. She couldn't let Serpio see her pain. She fought off tears by blinking them away.

Serpio put his hands on her shoulders again and turned her around. His ruthless eyes pierced her heart. "Tonight. A servant will be by to help you dress and take you to the arena. Be ready."

"And what am I supposed to do all day until then?" Ember's throat dried her words into raspy heartbeats. She could smell her own fear.

His smile was as guiltless as a fairy Godmother's. "Whatever makes you *happy*, dear. Just don't bother the guard outside." He gradually turned, his eyes keeping a lock on hers as if they physically couldn't disconnect, no matter how hard he tried. Once broken, like the snap of a rubber band, Serpio exited without a backward glance.

IN TEARS, Ember looked out her window for most of the day. Xander would be fighting! *To kill or be killed.* Yet hadn't she known what was coming? Her dreams had been warning her off and on for weeks, and she'd chosen to put her head in the sand. Two figures fighting. The words "to the death" were burned into her consciousness like a bitter tattoo.

Every breath she took was a lesson in blame. She *could* stop this. She *should* stop this. She *should have already* stopped this. Why didn't she pay more attention to their surroundings when she was with Xander at Cloud Nine Station? It was irresponsible and selfish. The burden of guilt alone was enough to break her.

Why didn't she explore her dreams and think about what they meant? They were too puzzling. Two shadowy figures. She could never connect them to anything. But why, oh why, hadn't she at least told Xander?

And where was her mother? *Mom, please!* She kept waiting for some kind of mental message.

Two food trays were delivered, and she refused to eat. Couldn't eat, or she would vomit. Her stomach burned with acid and roiled with a nausea she'd previously never known.

As the hours passed, she wracked her brain for every possible solution to the horror of the arena. She knew she had enough power to turn back time if Xander were killed. There would be enough people around her; she could draw the strength. She closed her eyes imagining it, pulling up every trace of emotion she had. A buzz went through her veins, even at the thought of Xander in mortal danger. Her senses burned with readiness.

The time warp was the only solution, and it brought her comfort. The second Xander became injured, she'd act. She could save Xander like she had once saved Will.

The Will dilemma also weighed heavily on her. Would she exercise her power for Will? How could she stand by and watch him die, even if he was a traitor? She'd have to intervene. But how would she know the timing? The right moment to act? And how could she protect both of them at once?

So absorbed in thought, she'd not noticed the sun's rays bending behind the gentle hills outside and lengthening the shadows in her room. A knock on the door startled her.

A servant entered before Ember could say, "Come in."

"Hello, Ember. You're to get ready. Soap and towels are waiting." The petite woman, a Level Seven, pushed her physically toward the bathroom. "When you come out, I'll have your clothes ready."

Ember luxuriated under the hot water, but it didn't wash away her torment or her tears.

Maybe she could delay the competition if she refused to get dressed?

But no. The last thing she wanted was for the Magistrate himself to enter her room with guards and drag her out.

The servant, who introduced herself as Melly, helped her into a tight, satiny, sleeveless jumpsuit of gold. Regal, but revolting. The form-fitting top set off her breasts, and the low cut revealed enough skin on her chest that she constantly reached out in an attempt to close it. Then, Ember sat on a bench in front of a vanity, gritting her teeth, as Melly combed and curled her hair. The partial updo was finished with sparkling gold clips resembling butterflies.

When Melly began pulling vials of makeup from the drawers and dabbing brushes of color from them to her face, Ember grabbed Melly's hand to stop her motion and protested, "I can do my own makeup! Not like I've never done it before."

Melly's face crumpled. Ember had spoken to her sharply. It wasn't the poor girl's fault.

"Hey, I'm sorry. I know you're doing your job." Ember sighed. Then, she handed Melly a brush. "Paint away."

The girl giggled. "It's okay. I may surprise you."

Melly proved that she'd had training. By the time she was finished, Ember looked like a sophisticated version of herself, her cheekbones highlighted with golden rose and her eyes swept with a gilded green that sadly reminded her of Will's eyes.

"Here are your shoes," Melly said, pulling a pair of strappy, gold, high-heeled sandals from the wardrobe. "These are gorgeous," she gushed. "You must be so happy!"

Ember scowled before putting them on. The shoes seemed horrifically symbolic of her inability to run away.

She was ready. At least physically.

86

Ember's View

The first to arrive, Ember and the Magistrate settled into their seats.

Although she'd taken a shower and used the powders, perfumes, and deodorant she was instructed to, Ember was already sweating. Her agony made her palms sticky, and her chest glowed with the sheen of perspiration. The satin fabric of her clothing stuck to her body, creating a damp second skin that was uncomfortable and revealing. Her right knee took on a life of its own, jiggling in a nervous dance that made Serpio scowl. He placed his hand on her leg to quiet its vibration, enough of a revulsion to make Ember concentrate on keeping still.

She'd never been to Amity Arena, the site for sporting events. It had never held much interest for Ember. Built for the perfect view from every vantage point, the precisely pitched walls held rows of seats that nearly went straight up in a feat of advanced engineering that boggled her mind.

Sections were identified for Status. The section for Elite, where they sat, was the closest to the action, a mere fifteen yards from where the coliseum's floor dipped a few feet into a flat, round field about forty yards wide. Since Elite member-ship was significantly smaller than that of the other Status levels, the area around them held what looked like two hundred seats. It sat apart from all others in a slightly elevated box. Their seats were plush and overstuffed with beverage trays and individual speakers built into each chair's framework.

The seats around them were collecting members of the Elite. Of course, she'd never seen any of the people before until she recognized Ava. But she didn't dare allow herself to meet Ava's eyes. She wondered how Ava was enduring this and if she'd tried to stop it. Ava had done a lot for them, but this event had to be too big for Ava to stop on her own.

For each level, sections wrapped around the stadium, their chairs colored for Status, along with the matching concrete steps and bases for each row. The effect was a dazzling display of a circuitous rainbow.

But Ember had no appetite for the aesthetics. Her nerves were already lighting her up inside as she watched dozens of people filing in to take their seats. Many carried handmade signs with slogans: "End the rebellion." "Eliminate city waste." "Take heed of bitter deeds." "Who WILL win?" They babbled with greetings before a few cast bets on who would win the match. A few had perfected a cheer. "X Xander out! X Xander out!"

"Look, Ember," Serpio pointed around the interior. "This place will be full before you can say, 'Xander's going to die.'"

She didn't respond, keeping her eyes straight ahead on the empty venue before closing them completely in an attempt to block everything out. She couldn't block out her own dread, an insidious spider that burrowed into her gut., and could practically smell the audience's anticipation. By the time the arena was full of people, the emotional slam would be like being flattened by a giant steel vise.

She smiled to herself. *More feelings to pull together for a time warp.*

The citizens pulsed in by Status level, the higher levels first. When Ember opened her eyes, she was experiencing the heightened rush of happy, excited emotions from two Status levels filling the seats.

She turned to Serpio, her body already electrified from the emotional bloom. "Who got invites for this? And why would any peace-loving Trank want to be here?" Gazing around at the rapidly filling stadium, she gagged. The world couldn't be any more upside down.

"First come, first served for all Statuses. Whoever didn't win a bid for tickets will watch the broadcast from home or on the street."

Ember fought to keep the bile from rising into her throat. "You're *broadcasting* this?"

"Dear Ember. This is the most exciting and unusual event our city's ever had. It's also meant to be a lesson. Watching is required. Don't you understand? Xander and Will are the sacrificial lambs."

The rebellion. It's meant to be a warning against rising up. "You're *sick.* Just another way of using people. Like always. But this time, you've gone berserk! And why Will? He's been your spokesman—your beautiful puppet."

"Exactly. It can't be me, so it's got to be Will. Who else? He's loyal but also too … fascinated by things he can never have. He can prove himself, or not. Either way, fighting for his city, he'll be a hero, a title he'd lost for a while."

Ember sniffed to show her distaste. "He's no hero to me."

Serpio shrugged as if he was choosing between strawberry or chocolate. "We'll see what you think of him when he's fulfilled his task or gets killed himself."

Ember turned almost completely to face the Magistrate, her heart in her eyes and her pulse racing. "*Please,* Serpio. Just —just call this off. *You* can be a hero! You can show mercy!

The people of the city will go crazy celebrating your compassion."

Serpio eyes traveled down her body, tracing a line down her deep V back up to her lips. "You can be the hero, Ember. Just say the words I want to hear."

Ember was granite, steel, and iron. "I won't."

As each section filled, Ember vowed to herself to watch for the best opportunity to launch a time warp. *Believe in yourself, Ember. You can do this. You have to!* She flexed her hands as if to physically collect emotions from the air. But she didn't need to. She was absorbing hundreds of them at a time, so many that she thought she would burst from the overload.

An inner voice put her misery on hold. She sucked in a breath. *"Ember … we know your situation. We have plans."* A presence she knew was her mom's surrounded her. *"Stay aware."* Her breath caught in her throat, and she then let it go all at once.

She looked at Serpio, making sure he didn't hear it, too. But of course he didn't. The message was only for her.

"Excitement getting to you?" Serpio started to put his arm around her shoulders before realizing people would be watching and withdrawing it.

"Not excitement, no. I'm watching the people." She scooted as far away from Serpio as she could in her chair.

"Yes. But they're excited. I know you feel that." Serpio spoke to her, but his attention was on the people, raising his arm in salutes and giving short obligatory waves.

"When are we starting?" Ember stretched her feet out in front of her, weary of sitting in her seat.

Ember's mom's voice drifted into her mind again. *"Be ready to run."*

With her feet in the air, Ember reached down to unstrap her shoes. "These are ridiculous. They hurt! I'm taking them off."

Serpio placed his hand on her foot. "That is not your

choice. This event is not for bare feet. You're dressed for show. I forbid you to remove those." A Sciolist standing to her right glared at her before resuming his vigilant watch on the crowd.

Ember defiantly unbuckled her sandals. The Magistrate frowned, watching her, before he began to wave and smile again at the crowd.

Ember discarded the shoes under her chair. "Too bad. What are you going to do? Arrest me?"

Ember examined the arena. It was almost full. People were socializing and cheering, their voices a roaring confusion of highs and lows. Bodies—shifting, reaching, yelling, twisting, and jumping. The chatter of hundreds became a storm of sound.

Sciolists were posted throughout the stadium, an entire cadre of them to either side and behind their own seats. Ember took an opportunity to gather information. "Is every Sciolist in the city here?" She avoided Serpio's eyes, hoping he would think it only casual small talk.

"Twenty-five Sciolists in the city. Twenty-five here, inside and out. Security is tight." He trained his eyes on her, their blackness deep and foul. "You wouldn't get far if you ran, Ember. And if you did, I guarantee you that the pain my forces would inflict would incapacitate you."

Ember said sweetly. "How good of you to warn me."

Serpio jumped a little in his seat. His OmniCom had vibrated. "Get ready, Ember. The fight begins in one minute."

A screen lit up across from where they sat, and a hush fell on the crowd. A Level Fifteen announcer appeared. Garbed in a magenta suit and tie, he addressed the audience, his voice booming over the loudspeakers. "Ladies and gentlemen. Citizens of the great city of Tranquility. I am Adam Amplus, your host for tonight's unprecedented event."

A cheer went up through the crowd, although Ember felt both excitement and anxiety from the masses. She sat on the edge of her seat until Serpio gently pushed her back.

"Two highly famous individuals are in the arena tonight. Both of them are here as an illustration." The announcer paused and dropped his head for a moment before raising his eyes to the camera again. "This is a difficult lesson for us all. It is entertainment but also a warning. Our Elite and our Magistrate want nothing else than for you to be happy. These past weeks, a rebel group has ruined the peace and happiness of our city." A roar went up from the crowd, many of them shouting, "Peace, peace, peace!" "Because we cannot tolerate disloyalty and chaos, this is a powerful demonstration of what can happen if you rebel against the Accords. One of these individuals has committed crimes that require a fate much greater than Banishment. We cannot allow revolution. If you are caught as a sympathizer of this movement, you can be made an example of as well. Apprehending the rebels and containing the threat is our Magistrate's top priority. Now, I wish to introduce our Magistrate. Please give him the proper Tranquility salute and your support."

The announcer paused to allow Serpio to stand and wave to the crowd. The audience cheered and applauded, many casting him the Tranquility salute. Serpio pulled Ember to her feet before his hand opened toward her in a physical acknowledgment. The crowd applauded, although Ember had no smile for them.

Once Serpio and Ember were seated, the crowd began to stomp their feet in place. They were more than ready to get the show going.

When, Mom? The fight is starting! Ember knew her mom couldn't hear her, but she flung the thought outward anyway. Ember's desperation seemed to take on a persona of its own, clutching her throat and cutting off her air. It clawed at her heart, jerking every heartbeat into its own chest.

The announcer waited until the din quieted. "The rules of tonight's show … Each of these participants will have spears called Rayzers. Just like its name, the tip is razor-sharp. It is meant to kill, not to wound. This is to be a fight to the death. However long this takes—from minutes to hours—we will be here to its completion." A murmur swept through the crowd, a wave of shock that seemed more electric than the spears themselves. But the throng sat, transfixed, as if they were magnets to steel.

"Now, we introduce to you … an esteemed Plauditor who has *volunteered* to mete out justice—even at great peril to himself. Please welcome Will Verus!"

The mob came alive, standing to cheer wildly as Will entered the arena from an archway decorated with multi-colored bunting. Yellow bands around sections of the drapery accented Will's Status as Twelve.

Ember gasped as she fixed her eyes on Will. He looked so … vulnerable. Yet *strong*. His bare chest glistened in the spot-lights, underscoring his cavalier, unprotected exposure to his foe's wicked blade. The bulked muscles in his arms defined his strength, and his torso was tight and lean. Ember's blood thrummed in her veins.

From the waist down, jersey shorts hung to the top of his knees, bright as a fresh lemon, with two black stripes running down each side. His athletic shoes matched his shorts, even to the stripes along the sides.

She took her eyes off his body and stared at his face. Only a brief, crooked smile emerged as he turned around in a circle and raised his right arm with his weapon in it. Teeth flashed white. Color heightened on his cheekbones, Will's typical response to stressful or passionate situations. It marked the only emotion she could see outright, but she could feel his emotions, tight and electrified. Determination and apprehen-sion mingled with pride and defensiveness. His hair, tussled in an informal style so different from his normal no-hair-out-of-place look, moved with the breeze. When he brushed it back from his face, its ripple caught the stadium lights. The flaxen, blond strands glimmered as if they were sent from the sun. He was truly the Golden Boy.

Some catcalls rang out, more than a few female voices yelling out, "Marry me!" or "You're hot!" and "Woooo!" Ember dropped her eyes, her insides a mush of conflicting emotions. He was indeed so beautiful—and yet, his heart so black.

Serpio leaned over and whispered, "Any second thoughts yet?"

Ember shook her head mutely.

A Level Eight assistant ran out to the middle of the arena and pulled Will back toward the inner wall, where he gave him water and what looked like a pep talk. The guy patted Will's back, and Will nodded.

The announcer interrupted the crowd's cacophonous enthusiasm. "Ladies and gentlemen, our next player in this dangerous game is an infamous and unethical criminal—leader of the revolution … Xander Noble!"

A chorus of "boos" and chants of "X Xander out" pounded the air. Someone yelled out, "Karma's wicked!" to which laughter ensued.

As Xander emerged from the opposing entrance, Ember thought she might faint. She swayed in her seat, her head a gourd of feathers. Her vision blurred with tears as she took deep breaths to keep herself from hyperventilating. As her sight cleared, she watched him step into the arena as if he knew he was the sun and the moon combined. His proud posture marked his command of the situation. As he strode into the stadium's center, defiance oozed from every muscle and bone. His face never surrendered a smile, his lips pressed closed in solid determination. His glossy, dark hair was gelled back—an unusual look for Xander that Ember knew was allowing him perfect vision without distraction. Though she was too far away to see his eyes, Ember still caught the occasional flash of willfulness that demonstrated his dangerous spirit. She tried to capture his gaze, but Xander's eyes constantly shifted—darting around the crowd instead—before fixating a long moment on Will thirty yards away.

Shirtless like Will, his skin, like buffed marble, was deliciously tanned from being Outside. The clearly defined muscles in his chest and abs were sharply cut. Along his arms were taut ripples of muscle, each dip and swell marked. She wondered if his heart was pulsing as hard as her own.

Xander hadn't come out with a weapon in hand. His assistant, also a Level Eight like Will's, delivered his spear to him at that moment, showing Xander the tip at the top and how to electrify the shaft on the end.

So, Will had received his weapon earlier ... an advantage for him, Ember reflected, her anxiety rising up in a brutal surge. She turned to Serpio. "What's this? Did Will get special training?"

Serpio chuckled, his face alive with amusement. "That troubles you? Of course. Remember that the objective is Xander's death. Will had some time with his weapon beforehand. Not a lot ... just enough to make what he does effective."

Ember fumed. She got right into Serpio's face. "Not even a fair fight! You always surprise me with your level of sickness. And yet I should expect it."

"I always want you to be surprised, Ember. It adds to the fun of the moment. And later, I'll be ready to surprise you with all kinds of things." He put his hand on her knee, moving it up an inch at a time while keeping his eyes on the arena.

Ember pushed his hand away. "Maybe I'll surprise *you.*" She had plans up her sleeve that he couldn't possibly imagine. The time warp would come in handy if he got her into a situation she wouldn't tolerate. She only wished she had the power to make him explode into a million pieces.

When Xander retreated to his corner, the Tranquility

anthem began to play, and all the citizens held their arms up in the salute. As the notes faded out, the stadium lights intensified. The spotlight shone down into the middle of the arena, awaiting the two contestants. A spotlight for a kill.

87

Xander's Challenge

When his assistant gave the signal, Xander ran out into the center of the arena, keeping his eyes on Will. His opponent was in less of a hurry, jogging out to where he ultimately stood facing Xander, leaving them twenty feet apart. The mob whooped and hollered and stamped their feet.

The noise of the crowd was a clamor of animalistic sounds, screeches, and calls mixed with respectable applause and high-spirited cheering. A tangible excitement hummed through emotionally high-voltage air. The audience's buzz heightened Xander's emotions, pulling him into the exhilaration. He consciously chose to block out the noise, all his focus directed to the fight at hand. He tunneled his emotions into the tight space around him as if he could adjust the noise like you could adjust the vision on binoculars.

The two got in position, crossing their spears in the middle for the proper beginning stance. They stared each other down.

"Xander, you're gonna lose." Spoken through gritted teeth, Will's voice was tense as a tight spool.

Xander's body stiffened with the words, his eyes burning. "You … you traitor. Nothing lower than a turncoat." Xander spat on the ground between them. "I fight for justice and for Ember." He took a step forward.

A twinge of confusion crossed Will's face before an instantaneous recovery. "We have something in common, then. So do I." Will's words were laced with venom.

Xander brandished his weapon, testing its weight and maneuverability. The weapon felt heavy in his hands—heavier than its weight. The way it weighed him down had nothing to do with its mass. *Shit., I'm truly here. Fighting for my life. I detest this guy, but killing him …?* Could he? But he hated him. It was either Will or himself.

He moved his lance from one hand to the other, keeping his eyes on Will. The guy didn't even give Xander a nod of familiarity. It was almost as if Xander was a stranger to him. Odd. That was probably the only way Will could rationalize this job.

As he ran his hands along the Rayzer's shaft, he continued to measure Will up. Will wasn't calm. Xander had noted a slight tremble in Will's hands, but the set of his jaw and the gleam in his eyes spoke volumes. His body was stiff, almost to the point of inflexibility. Xander knew that posture was fear— he'd felt its effects himself. But he also knew fear could be fuel for success.

Xander wanted to appear unsure to his opponent; looking weak would catch him off guard. To a degree, he was unsure. But his own determination and invincible attitude hadn't failed him yet.

The bang of a flare shooting into the night signaled the start of the match.

Xander stood upright but leaned forward slightly in a protective stance. Sweat gathered on his forehead and upper lip. He held back … watching. Taking the defensive mode. His heart was in a battle all its own, galloping at full speed.

Will held his spear with both hands. He looked natural with it, as if it were a tool he used every day. Will moved closer; first a few slow steps, one at a time, and then a running charge toward Xander, the spear point out.

Xander dodged to the left, both of his hands tight on his weapon. He aimed his spear out in front of him and thrust it toward Will in several short jabs that missed. *Stay back!*

His hands dripped with sweat, his knuckles white as he clenched his weapon. He circled his opponent. Will turned in place to watch him, anticipating his moves by compassing in the opposite direction. *I can keep him caged in with this spiral. He'll be too busy to take a stab. He has to watch me.*

Xander stepped forward, his spear in a horizontal hold at waist level, but Will threw his lance vertically against Xander's spear. Xander managed to block with a high horizontal hold over his head. *Crack. Crack.* Xander narrowed his eyes in concentration, the sweat coating his hair, which was already no longer stiff.

Both rocked back for power, throwing their spears into an X-shaped clash. *Clunk.* Xander kept his footing, roaring, "Arrgh!" Will threw his head forward, a battle cry on his lips.

Will reared back and began to thrust, forcing Xander to step back two giant paces, assuming a cat-like warrior stance. He yelled and blocked Will's hit from the inside.

Will spun his Rayzer not once but twice and thrust again with fiery aggression. He squinted and frowned, his face rigid with concentration.

Xander gasped and fell back, feet flying. "No!" he spat. He spun his spear four times, a windmill of power, and charged forward.

Both jumped left before they crossed their lances, connecting with a thwack near the top of their spears.

But in the move, Will forced Xander's lance down to the ground. Trying to connect with Xander's head, he swung his spear in an arc. He growled as Xander ducked the swing, crouched like a tiger seeking prey.

His body leaning into a squat, Will swung again.

Xander jumped, avoiding the hit. He felt the power in his legs and knew he still had more than just defensive moves to offer. It was time to be the aggressor.

Xander hissed and tried to thrust into Will's face, but Will blocked it from the inside, pushing Xander's spear away from his body. He still held his Rayzer in his hands, but it was high. With Xander unprotected, Will threw his lance across Xander's chest, connecting.

Xander felt the blow blast across his torso, a force so strong he doubled over. He stumbled forward, and his own weapon dropped to the level of his knees. Not good. He tried and failed to shake off a spinning sensation in his brain.

Will ran in a few steps and jabbed the spear point into Xander's shoulder. He felt the sting and cried out as blood flowed from the wound and painted a trail down his arm. A deep cut—agony.

"Give up. Maybe you'll get a pass from Serpio," Will hissed.

"Piss off." The pain made him want to vomit, but he stood and regained his balance. *You're mine.*

Xander inhaled deeply, the oxygen reenergizing him. He rushed his opponent, turning sideways at a half run, his feet shifting one in front of the other. Xander struck downward at Will's feet, but the jabs missed as Will jumped in a jagged dance to escape the digs.

Until he sliced across Will's ankle. He watched Will cringe, his face crumpling and reddening with outrage and pain. A string of curses flowed from his lips.

Xander's eyebrows arched in surprise. He'd made a mark. But the curses were just as shocking. He'd never heard Will cross that line.

Will retreated a few yards but crouched, shifting back and forth with his feet. Blood leaked from the gash, the red color turning his yellow shoes orange.

"C'mon! Let's rumble! I've only begun," Xander growled,

his mouth quivering with fury. He bobbed the spear up and down in his hands, as if priming a pump.

"Try it." Will stepped forward. One, two, three. Then back. He stabbed at the air before activating the switch to electrify the end of the Rayzer. The tip lit and crackled.

Xander jumped back with both feet and grinned crookedly. "Making this hotter? I'm game." His voice was throaty and low.

Xander swept arcs with his staff, back and forth in wide semi-circles. He lunged forward and backward, rolling into an occasional thrust. He struck with both ends of his weapon, changing hands, in constant rotation. A smack to Will's side. Burned flesh—Xander smelled it.

"Ugh! You—" Will flew toward him, swinging blindly, intent on a retaliatory scorch that continually missed its mark.

Xander moved forward and back, each step a little closer, sweat running down his face in rivulets, pure adrenaline in liquid form. He drove himself forward, hitting his own spear against Will's in what resembled a match with swords. Smoke and vibration from the intersecting arcs buzzed audibly.

A thwack from Xander. Will returned a smash against Xander's staff. One hit and then another for what seemed like an endless clickety-clack, metal on metal. A buzz with each stroke. Their feet pulsed forward and back in rhythm with each hit. Xander's heavy counterstroke finally pushed Will off balance, and he tumbled backward to a sitting position on the ground, his spear barely still in his hands. Will turned over and sprung from the ground. Xander had no time to charge. Will had his weapon in position for a direct hit.

Xander backed up, his eyes on Will's hands, ready to dodge. The spear flew. *Missed!* The lance landed with a thud on the playing field some yards away. Will was suddenly without a weapon!

Xander circled Will and used the length of his weapon's

blunt end to hit Will's face. When Xander heard his staff connect, he winced. That was a blow.

Will tottered, off-balance, involuntarily recoiling. In a heartbeat's space, he touched his cheek, wiping away blood, before centering himself. Beads of sweat stood out on Will's head, his hair dripping with it. Already, his face bloomed with a lump that swelled second by second.

Xander prodded and then hammered Will's chest with the blunt end of the spear. Calculated thrusts pushed him further away from his weapon. *Got to get Will back on the ground.* He could inflict a fatal pierce. Xander pushed harder and faster.

Out of the corner of his eye, Xander caught movement. Will's assistant was running onto the field with another Rayzer! Xander, dumbfounded, watched as Will's helper handed off a new weapon with lightning speed. *So, that's how it is. Not even a fair fight.*

Will wasted no time. He turned his staff to the blunt end, using Xander's technique to retaliate. "I'm still standing!"

"Yeah. Not without … help," Xander managed to say, his upper body already bruising from Will's attacks. Xander could boast of exceptional balance, and he used it to his advantage. He toggled from one foot to the other, absorbing some strikes but avoiding others. A whoosh. Xander's weapon flew into a wide arc and made contact with Will's spear. *Thwack*. It was enough force that both his and Will's spears vibrated and burned with sparks.

"Ugh!" In a spin, Will swiftly and deftly turned his weapon to the sharp end. He jabbed it toward Xander. Faster. As Will stepped forward, he shortened the distance. He moved his hands along the shaft, shortening the length of it. Will advanced until the spear was merely a skinny foot from Xander's chest.

His heart in his throat, Xander spun to evade the approaching spear tip.

He slipped in stickiness below his feet, letting out a futile cry, before realizing it was blood. He scrambled but caught only air as he coasted onto the cement on his right side. He felt the corrosive shred of concrete against his limbs. The wind left him as he hit the ground. *Oooh … ow …* Curses streamed from his lips.

As Xander worked to sit up, Will closed the distance, towering over the rebel with the tip of his spear, ready to plunge it into Xander's chest.

88

Ember's Reality

"**H**oly Shazz! Xander!" Ember yelled, panic suffocating her lungs. "Get up! *Please*! Oh … oh no!"

With Xander on the ground, Ember was on her feet. *Xander, you can't die!* And by Will's hand? She was sick. A rush of fear and grief exploded in her chest.

Barooooooom! As if the thought triggered reality, an eruption shattered the space. A sudden thundering boom and then a whoosh, as if air was being let out of a giant tire. A burst of fire. Fractured, quivering concrete shrapnel flew through the air. Opposite of her on the far side of the arena was a smoking maelstrom.

A breach of the outer wall. If the explosion had blown into the center of the arena, both guys would have been killed.

"Xander!" Ember screamed without thinking, her voice smothered in the aftermath of confusion.

Shrieks and yells of a thousand frightened people cut like knives through flesh. A rush of human bodies jumped up and instinctively ran from their seats in panic. Undulating gray clouds billowed across the field where she'd just seen Will dominating Xander moments before.

A sheer veil of smoke hung over the battleground in front of her. She squinted her eyes to find Xander, fanning away wisps of smoke headed their way. *Please, Xander—run! Be alive!* She prepared herself for the grim possibility that Xander was already dead—killed by Will or even by the explosion.

This has to be Phoenix! Already on her feet, Ember got ready to run. *I have to get to Xander!* But the Sciolists beside her restrained her from breaking away. Instead, in a rude assault, they pushed her back into her seat and attended to both her and Serpio, asking if they were all right and checking for any immediate localized threat.

"Ember … You're … not hurt?" Serpio leaned in, capturing Ember's hand in his, the picture of concern. Serpio appeared untroubled over his own safety, instead breathing like a dragon, anger over the blast fueling every exhalation.

"Not hurt." She put her fist to her mouth and bit down to suppress the urge to scream.

Her chance of escaping had died. Her hope of rescuing Xander became a cinder. Unless … unless she could do something on her own. If Xander was critically injured, she would activate her time-altering ability. Already, she began to assess her own emotions and collect those around her. She'd be ready.

She balled her fists, her energy almost lifting her from her chair.

"Remain seated. You're safe," the Sciolist to her right said. "We're assessing the damage." He spoke into his Alt, murmuring something Ember couldn't hear.

Serpio yelled out orders to his bodyguards. "Make sure Will and Xander are being contained!"

But as the smoke dissipated, Ember spotted Will and Xander. Still in the arena. Both still standing.

89

Will's Revenge

"This is personal. Any last words?" Will pointed his spear to within an inch of Xander's chest.

Will's body was high on adrenaline and fury. Too bad he'd have to kill this guy. But Ember could be his … A flurry of panic invaded his chest, and his stomach was in knots. He gritted his teeth. He had a job to do.

What the—? Walls were rattling. Reverberations surged under Will's feet. Glass shattered. The mayhem ricocheted through his bones. When the explosion hit, he jumped, his heart slamming into his ribcage. He'd dropped his spear, the clatter disappearing like a whisper. He put his hands over his ears, but it didn't stop his skull from feeling off-kilter. As if caught in an unexpected blinding strobe, he couldn't stop blinking. Smoke settled on his body, his ears ringing from the turbulence behind him and thousands of screams. As if in a dream, the smoke hazed out the area where the audience sat. Dust settled in his eyes, and he tried to wipe it away, but it kept building. Will sensed rather than saw masses of the crowd moving in front of him.

His fight against Xander suddenly felt like an alien event in the midst of the explosion. But all Will could see at first was

Xander. The shock of the blast sent Xander into a rebound. He shot up from the ground before spinning in place and fanning the smoke with his hands. Xander's string of curses followed his retreat from Will to retrieve his spear. Xander held his weapon protectively against his body as his eyes searched the arena from where the blast occurred, then to the exits, and finally, to the stands. He paced almost a full minute before running toward the grandstands.

Will, too, struggled to see past their position in the arena. He stood, uncertain of what he should do next, and picked up his Rayzer.

The smoke drifted up into the amphitheater's upper levels, almost as if it was a fireworks display, only for effect. The stadium was a rabblement of disorder, the people still screaming, running around like trapped mice. He could see Sciolists trying to keep order, directing people this way or that to no avail. Bodies ran to the exits, pushing others out of the way. Footsteps thundered in a stampede of sound. Announcements over the loudspeaker were buried in the clamor. The sea of people undulated and swirled, roaring like a tidal wave ready to break.

He telescoped his vision, searching for Ember. Ember was out there, probably frightened and confused.

In the blink of an eye, Will located her. There she stood. The Magistrate shouted something unintelligible and then pulled Ember toward him. He took her face in his hands and pulled her closer. *His property.* Will's chest rose and fell, trying to breathe. He was suddenly dizzy, as if someone had punched a fist into his lungs and stolen every breath of air.

As if reality evolved into slow motion, the Magistrate stepped away from Ember, handing her over to Sciolists, who flanked her on both sides … Serpio turned to view the arena, most likely to make sure his contestants were still at each other's throats.

Will's brain pulsed with confusion. His hand went to his

forehead, sticky with sweat. He shook his head to clear what seemed to be a hundred million images bombarding his brain. A torrent of unfathomable grief flooded his veins. Something flickered. A memory resurfaced … then a primal urge to destroy. A cog in a wheel shifted. Ember … Xander …

His attention fell on Xander fighting his way through the crowd toward Ember, caught in a morass of hysterical bodies.

Will electrified his weapon. It crackled beneath his hands. He pivoted. Four decisive steps back. Six running leaps forward. He released his spear. It sailed through the air and hit dead on. Directly into his target—the chest of the Magistrate.

90

Ember's Awakening

Blood splattered onto Ember's arms. She gasped. "What … what—?" A scream threatened to slice through instant fog in her brain.

A Sciolist yelled, "Magistrate!" before elbowing past her to where Serpio had crumpled to the ground in a thick heap, hitting chairs on his way down, a spear clean through his body. Ember screamed but then stood paralyzed in disbelief. Her breath came in and out in short huffs. Hyperventilating, she rocked on her feet, grabbing onto her chair before she sank to the ground.

She tried to avert her eyes from the morbid scene but couldn't look away. Was this really happening? Was the blood in her dreams Serpio's?

Blood poured from Serpio's chest and gurgled on its way out of his body. Still vibrating with electricity, the weapon was searing his flesh and his inner organs. As she watched, the spear's electric current appeared to congeal the blood at the site of the wound.

Serpio gasped for breath. Rattling wheezes were spaced a thousand years apart. His shallow breaths were barely percep-tible. His eyes focused and then rolled back in his head in a dull, revolting flash of white. When Serpio finally struggled to speak, blood—not saliva, not words—drooled from his lips.

Ember held her hand to her mouth in a futile effort to keep from gagging.

Then letters of the alphabet piled up on each other, as if they were fighting for space in words from the lips of spectators. The sounds were a jumble of nonsense—syllables that didn't make sense at first. Dazed, Ember blinked and stared at the bystanders blankly until paragraphs and conversations emerged at last into intelligible statements.

"Serpio's hit!"

"Shazz! Who threw it?"

"It was Will! I swear! Saw it with my own eyes!"

"*Will?* He's one of us!"

Sciolists shoved her back out of the way. Shouts of "Medic!" echoed around her. Out of the corner of her eye, Ember saw Ava several rows up tussling to get through to Serpio's side.

"Let the Medic through!" resounded all around her. Sciolists laid Serpio out on the ground.

"He's not breathing!" A Sciolist had put his head on Serpio's chest. "Oh … hurry! Nothing!"

Another Sciolist had his wrist. "No pulse. Get help!"

Serpio … dying? Ember's eyes darted around her at the sheer pandemonium. People squashing and scrambling to get through made her body into a wall.

An obvious epiphany struck her. *Get away! Run! No one will miss me now.*

Xander! She panicked as she searched for him. She couldn't leave without him.

Ember pivoted to view the arena's fight zone. Her eyes scanned the space. No … No Xander. *Where is he?* She began to pant in alarm. *Xander?*

Instead, her desperate search efforts found Will a mere twenty feet away. Standing alone. In the spotlight. Her gaze locked with his as if the moon's gravitational pull captured the sun. She stepped into his eyes, an intense sea of green. All at once, she felt like she was drowning in their depths. Eyes—so clear, so … loving, and yet so resolute. The frozen tableau held her captive. He raised his right hand and signed: Loyalty. He followed the motion in slow, deliberate tempo all the way through to the final rest on his heart. His chest rose and fell with emotion. He trembled. And then a fragile smile swept her completely into his core. Her heart shattered, and the pieces melted into drops of lush guilt and forgiveness. Will held her gaze until she thought she would die from its impact. All love. All heroism.

She forced her way through the wall of groaning, panicked Tranquilites. With a sharp roughness, she shoved and shouldered her path down the aisle and breathlessly ran into the arena. The tears traveling quietly down her cheeks were fresh, falling into her gasping mouth. Her shoulders wouldn't stop shaking, and memories were bursting out of her skin. She threw her arms around Will in a zealous embrace, rocking back and forth. When he bent his head, gripped her face with his hands, and kissed her like he was pouring his soul into her, her world fractured into a million pieces.

91

Xander's Leadership

In less than ten minutes, Xander had processed so much that his emotions were pulverized. He could barely keep his head straight. He had just witnessed the unthinkable. All he knew was that, at the hands of Will, a miracle had happened.

He had to find Ember. Now.

But he'd missed her. Barely getting halfway up into the stands, Xander watched in dismay as Ember jigsawed her way down an aisle on the other side. Holy Shazz … The place was a shit storm.

"Ember!" But his words evaporated. Instead, he heard what sounded like a million voices uttering Will's name. He swung around to retrace his steps toward the center of the arena, his heart running circles in his chest. He drove himself forward.

He watched as Ember stepped onto the outer edge of the arena. Then, she ran, her body stopped by an airtight embrace in which she was lifted off the ground. A tight, braided rope suddenly constricted his heart.

What the—? His spine went rigid in surprise.

He watched in agony as Will took possession of Ember in

a kiss so deep it could suffocate a hundred breaths. And not just Ember's, but his. Something inside of him splintered into fragments. Every vertebra. Every bone. A mutilated skeleton with a bleeding heart.

As he burst from the crowd and dashed onto the field, he watched them separate.

The burn in his chest threatened to defeat him more than the life and death threat in that arena. But he had to get it together. They had to get out of there.

"Ember!" He reached her side and quickly hugged her. "You okay?"

"Yeah, yeah! You found me!" She put her hands on his arms and then noticed his shoulder. "You're … wounded. Still bleeding. Oh!"

Xander shook her off. "I'm fine." He turned to Will, who had taken a step back. Xander shook his head. "You—You're —What the hell? I thought I was done …"

Will shook his head. "I—I did what I had to."

Xander said, "Thank the stars! You good? Cuz we've gotta go! Now!"

Will nodded, his face serious. "Yeah! I'm with ya!"

"No doubt in my mind." Already moving, Xander seized Ember's hand and pulled her behind him. "Out through the blown wall."

The trio barreled across the field. Xander took the lead, the exertion causing blood to drip from his shoulder wound.

Dodging the broken glass and chunks of rubble, they burst through the opening made by the explosion and into the area outside, where they slowed.

"What now?" Ember tried to catch her breath.

To the sides and behind them, harried citizens were trailing from the arena, exiting in small groups, some still yelling, others silently wandering around to look for transportation.

"A CommuteCar!" Will ran to the first one he saw waiting in a line along the curb.

Xander ran his hands through his hair, his eyes wild. "No way. No Alts. None of us have 'em."

Will called out, "Gah! We're screwed!" His eyes swept the line of vehicles. "We could try breaking the glass—see if that'll work."

"Not a chance," Ember chided Will, "You know that."

A sound caught the wind. A siren.

Then another.

The three inhaled simultaneously.

"The Medics are coming!" Ember put her hands on the top of her head in a lock. "They'll see us! We can't be here!"

Xander gave a low laugh. "Perfect timing!"

"What? What the heck are you thinking?" Will looked at him as if he'd gone mad.

"C'mon." Xander motioned. He took off to a nearby ticket booth, and the others followed. *No one inside. Perfect.*

He kicked the door. "Get in. Duck down."

Xander knew he'd figured out their escape. They huddled down as the sirens grew nearer; then, they heard the squeal and crunch of MediCars pulling up outside the arena. *Fifty feet away,* he thought, peering up over the inner counter. He threw up three fingers and whispered, "Three cars."

Voices—calm, resolute, but hurried. Doors slid open and closed. The Medics were on fire. On their way to collect a dying Serpio.

Xander clocked a full minute of silence in his head. "C'mon! To the front MediCar!"

The group flew from the booth and sprinted like lightning to the ambulance, its lights still pulsing and its motor running.

"Get in the back—I'm front seat." Xander didn't even question his role. He had to be in charge.

At the sound of Ember and Will hitting the interior,

Xander pressed the dashboard buttons. "Emergency! Override program." He hoped this was how it was done.

"Override program," the MediCar replied.

"Elation Avenue!" Xander screamed. They'd arrive a half block from the warehouse.

"Speed?" the MediCar queried.

"Top speed!"

The MediCar raced off, jerking Xander side to side in the process.

"You're brilliant." Will's comment was unexpected.

"Survival, Will. That's what we do. And you—you—you're the …" Xander choked on the words, not able to get anything out.

Ember crawled on all fours until she was between the two guys. "You're both amazing." She reached for Xander's hand, squeezing it, before extending her other to Will. Xander couldn't see him, but he knew Will had Ember's hand in his.

A buzz erupted on the dashboard radio, followed by terse words. "The Magistrate will not need further med units." The voice stuttered, emotion cluttering the words before a silence took up a brief, ten-second space. "Time of death, 9:13 p.m. Alerting Kelasts … prepare for transport."

Xander blew out a blast of air. "*Dead!* I can hardly believe it! It's real! Phoenix succeeded today!"

"I'm free—we're free—of that monster!" Ember squeezed herself before a wobbly smile anointed her lips.

Xander felt Ember's emotions as if it was he who was the Empath.

"Where there's a will, there's a way." Will's lips formed a grim, straight line. He shut his eyes, and his fists closed before he opened both again. Then, he finally smiled, his eyes full of new light. "We should celebrate, but guys, the future's still a mystery. I know one thing, though. Whatever it is, we'll do it together."

Serpio's Candles

An hour later, candles and flowers already surrounded Serpio as he lay on a pallet draped in gold velvet in a quiet room designated for the dead.

No one was present.

Nothing stirred.

THE TIME HAD COME. Serpio opened his eyes and sat up.

SPECIAL GIFTS like Ember's were amazing. But they were nothing like his.

HE WAS IMMORTAL.

Before you go...

Thank you so much for reading *Facing Off*! I hope you enjoyed reading it as much as I enjoyed writing it. As an indie author, reviews mean **everything**. Not only do they let other readers know whether a book is worth investing in, reviews also give the author insight into what a reader loved (or didn't) about a story. **If you have a minute, please take the time to leave a review.** It doesn't need to be long, just say how you felt about *Facing Off*, the writing, the story, the characters, or anything. My everlasting gratitude if you do! And again, thank you so much for your support and following my series.

The story continues in
Bleeding Out
Book Three of The Tranquility Series

Keep reading for a preview chapter of *Bleeding Out*!

A sneak peak at Book Three,
Bleeding Out

CHAPTER 1: EMBER'S MESSAGE

The Magistrate is dead. The Magistrate is dead.

The words cycled through Ember's mind, keeping time with the wild heartbeat thrusting against her ribcage.

In a stolen MediCar barreling down the road, Ember's chest heaved as she tried to catch her breath. Less than ten minutes had passed since they'd raced out of Amity Arena, where Xander and Will had faced off against each other in a fight to the death ordered by the city of Tranquility's leader, the Magistrate. Now, not only were they fugitives, but Will was an assassin.

She grasped both boys' hands. Their emotions poured into her psyche, almost overwhelming her. Fear, yes. But also desire and love.

The rush drenched her. She abruptly dropped their hands and took a deep breath.

Xander's voice exploded. "Damn!"

Ember shrank back. "Sorry, I had to let go. I—" She felt his anger now instead of his ardor. The emotion rippled out like a lightning bolt connecting with a metal pole.

"No. Not that. Behind us! Sciolist vehicles. Two of 'em." Xander gritted his teeth from where he sat in the control seat.

In the aftermath of the chaos in Amity Arena, someone had finally realized they'd escaped and alerted the Sciolists, the city's police.

Multicolored homes, modern city structures, and floral borders whizzed by like a blurred abstract painting, but not fast enough.

A dozen shadows tossed darkness onto Ember's face, only broken occasionally by approaching red lights from their pursuers that flickered with demonic convulsions. She grabbed a blanket from the floor and held it tightly around her shoulders, hoping this was just another nightmare; but she knew it couldn't be.

"Any way to speed up?" From his position in the back, Will peered over Xander's shoulder.

Xander's gaze flickered across the front panel's minimal controls. "Yeah, looking … This is a MediCar. Should have some sort of hyperdrive for emergencies. Don't want to activate any sirens, though."

Will's face took on the pallor of white porcelain. "The wheels … they're totally up?"

"No way to know, but I think so. I'm not feeling any bumps. Are you?" Xander gave the few buttons on the dashboard a cursory glance.

"Can you find a higher speed?" Ember twisted in her back seat to look out the rear window. The Sciolist's distinctive red cars blazed behind them less than one hundred yards away. Terror ripped through her. *How are they so close?* They couldn't be caught! Not now. Not when they'd celebrated escaping just moments ago.

Her eyes settled on Xander in the front, his shoulders glistening with perspiration. She was sure sweat was running down his chest, too, still bare from his face-off in the arena.

Will also wore only shorts and shoes, his torso marked with bruises and his ankle crusted with dried blood.

"How'd they know we're in a MediCar?" Ember wondered, her frustration palpable.

Xander huffed. "The Medics aren't stupid. They know how many MediCars were called to the arena for the Magistrate's injury. And we're missing. So …"

"We're already at seventy miles per hour," Will noted as he pointed to the sparse dash instruments. "Can Sciolist vehicles go past seventy? If they don't, we'll leave them behind in no time."

Xander brushed long locks of his black hair from his forehead. "Yeah? We can't count on that. And we can't go to any of the warehouses. Too risky."

"The *warehouses*?" Will frowned and tilted his head.

Ember waved her hand dismissively. "Can't explain now, Will."

Will nodded before he moved further toward the rear of the vehicle, positioning his back to his friends. "I'll watch behind us."

Xander ran his hand back and forth under the dashboard. "I'm finding nothin'! There's no way to get this buggy goin' any faster." Xander brought his fist down hard on the middle console.

"Ouch. That hurt. Please, do not damage my interior," a female voice said from the center speaker.

Xander stared down at where he'd just slammed his fist. "What the—!"

Ember gasped. "Of course! We don't need a device. It's a voice command. MediCar, speed up!"

"Yeah!" Xander yelled.

But nothing changed. The car behind them sped up, but their MediCar didn't. The distance between them shortened, and the Sciolists' silhouettes were visible through the windshield of the car behind them. Panic rose in a wash of stomach acid into her throat. If Sciolists captured them now, Will would face murder charges for killing the Magistrate. She and Xander would be accessories, on top of their other crimes against the city—insurrection, kidnapping, escape …

Will's voice was like a drill, jerking Ember out of her thoughts. "Xander! You're in the navigator seat! Give the car commands!"

"Speed up!" Xander yelled at the top of his lungs. "One hundred miles an hour!"

"One hundred miles per hour. Are you sure this is your requirement?" the MediCar's sweet voice inquired.

"Yes. *Yes*! And—and turn right! Next street!" Xander gripped a foot-long metal bar riveted to the dashboard. "Hang on, Ember!"

As the car slid into the turn, Ember grabbed the back of Xander's seat with both hands but lost her grip and crashed against Will. Not unlike the race cars at the Fun Zone Ember remembered as her favorite ride, the meteoric velocity was a rush. This, though, was no fun zone. The hair on her arms stood up. Her knuckles blanched as the MediCar continued to gather speed. It ripped around the corner and through the red light. A massive yellow van crossing their path escaped destruction within inches of its taillights.

She screamed as the MediCar rolled to the outside of the curve before flying into a straight direction and careening down a broad avenue. Will's head jerked back with the surge, and he grabbed on to Ember's arm like a drowning man.

"Will—do you think we lost 'em?" Xander glanced into the side mirror and then at the camera on the dash.

"No Sciolists now. Few cars. It's almost curfew." Will grinned before his mouth shrank back to tight lips. In the dark, his face held shadows that disappeared when the next car drove by.

Having spent the last few hours in an adrenaline haze, Ember had lost track of time. The typical welcoming calm of curfew, marked by the moon's mid-position in the sky, was as evasive as blown bubbles in the wind. And if she didn't know the moon's surface was pocked with craters, she would have sworn it mocked them with its smile.

Instead, she noted each intermittent car that went by, wondering how everyone else could simply be going about their normal routine when their lives hung in the balance.

"MediCar, turn right at Nirvana Parkway." Xander's voice carried a newfound confidence.

"Xander, if we see no Sciolists, shouldn't we just keep on a straight course?" Will's question was laced with confusion. "Nirvana Parkway has tons of curves! A scenic route's not what we need." He dropped his hand from Ember's arm to wipe the sweat off his forehead.

Xander kept his eyes on the road, his tone as assertive as the street was straight. "I'm going to try a zigzag. A straight course is too easy to follow." He clipped his words toward the end of his response.

The car careened around another corner, and the motion gave Ember a sudden throbbing in her forehead. She'd never tolerated motion well.

Just ahead, a white neon streetlight revealed a crimson flash of paint. Oh no. A Sciolist vehicle crossing their path.

"Frikkin' Shazz!" Xander yelled, pounding the console again.

"Anger is a forbidden emotion," the MediCar was quick to respond. "Please, check your Alt points."

"Stupid car! Stop it," Xander groaned.

"They maybe—maybe didn't see us?" Ember breathed her words out in a rush.

"They're looking for us. Of *course* they saw us." Xander's words were wrapped in his characteristic sarcasm.

Ember shook her head. "Geez. Turn around, then."

"Not that easy," Xander complained as he scanned the

road ahead. "MediCar—make six alternating turns up ahead."

"Very well. Where is the emergency? I have no GPS coordinates," the vehicle's voice crooned.

Will held tightly to a stretcher separating him from Ember. "We'd better decide where we're gonna go, Xan. We can't drive around all night. Ideas? Ember?"

"Right. No warehouse ..." Xander ran his hands through his hair. "I got nothin'!"

"Ember, can you freeze time and get us out of here?" Will asked, training his questioning eyes on her face.

Ember laughed bitterly. "No. Even if I could generate the energy, it would only take me out of the time loop, and I can't do anything by myself to stop the Sciolists. There are too many."

Another sharp turn had them leaning to the right like warped statues before they shifted to the left with the next.

"Scrambling my brains here," Will complained in a serious drone.

"Where is the emergency?" the car persisted.

"Another Sciolist behind us!" Will's hand went to his forehead. "Pulled out from that alley! Gah!"

Dark fear weighed on Ember like an iron apron. What were they going to do? Should they pull over and take their chances on foot?

A voice pierced Ember's consciousness: *"Turn left!"* She shook her head and glanced around. Her skull throbbed. It didn't sound like the car talking.

"Turn left!" The second time, she knew. Sure enough, the voice was in her own head.

Her mother's voice! Talesa was using her special gift to communicate with her.

Ember pressed her fingers to smiling lips. "Xander—tell the car to turn left."

"What? Why? I've already told it six alternating turns ..."

"Xander! *Listen* to me. My mom's speaking to me—in here." She tapped her head. "Turn left at the next block!" She leaned forward and jammed her hands hard into Xander's shoulders.

"Yeah, yeah. Okay! Last turn was right, the next turn will be left anyway. Then what?" Xander's words pressed.

"Uh … your … *mom?*" Will's mouth opened a second time and then abruptly closed.

Ember shut her eyes. "Shhh." She concentrated, listened to her mother's voice in her head, and nodded. "That left is Bliss Avenue. Then go straight for three miles."

"Three miles? Ember, what if we can't shake the Sciolists?" Will's hand trembled slightly before he grabbed on to the stretcher again.

"They don't have the speed we do." Ember, her own fears suffocated by hope, reached over and patted Will's arm. "We're gonna follow my mom's directions."

Will frowned. "I didn't think you believed in ghosts …"

"Oh, Will. My mom's alive—sorry. So much to tell you."

Will blinked back at her, the rest of his face a stony mask.

As the MediCar approached Bliss Avenue, the Sciolist car behind them gained speed and matched their change of direction as if boosted by an unseen force. A booming voice on an exterior loudspeaker demanded they pull over.

"What the—! They're right behind us!" Will scooted closer to the back, almost smashing his face against the glass. "We've gotta turn—throw 'em off!"

Ember's eyes flared. "No! We stay on course."

Xander turned slightly in his seat to make quick eye contact with Ember. "I trust you—and your mom—but Will's right. By now, every Sciolist in the city knows our whereabouts. They'll converge at any moment. Then we'll be blocked in with no escape! Or they'll throw pylons up. That doesn't end well. I should know."

"Shhh!" Ember closed her eyes and tried to wall everything out. The emotions she received were Will's and Xander's, but also her mother's. And Talesa was calm. Ember could trust her. "She's telling us where to go. We need that."

Xander clenched his jaw and nodded. "MediCar, *emergency* speed. Three miles."

"Emergency speed is only for people who are dying. Are you confirming emergency speed?" The MediCar's dashboard lit up.

Xander extended his hand in a victory V. "Yes! Dying! Emergency speed. Three miles."

"Emergency speed. Three miles," the electronic voice validated.

"Perfect." Ember high-fived Xander before a sudden jerk. The MediCar's speed leaped, and the three renegades gasped. Ember held on to the side door, white-knuckled.

"How fast can this thing go?" Ember's eyebrows connected in a frown.

"We're at a hundred and twenty!" Xander threw his hands up before clenching the bar on the dashboard again.

"You guys seeing this?" Will gasped.

"What? I'm *feeling* it." An enormous grin slid across Xander's face as a vibration buzzed through the vehicle.

Will jabbed at the back window. "Hey … hey! Smoke! Our ride's literally smoking!"

"Oh, crap! What the—!" Xander's eyes widened. "We're gonna have a problem."

"You are approaching three miles. *Where* is the emergency?" the car pleasantly queried.

"Ember?" Xander demanded.

"Right turn on Purity Place."

On the dashboard, a yellow light suddenly flashed off and on with words accompanying it. "Warning. Functionality declining. Warning. Functionality—"

A loud pop interrupted the MediCar's alert, startling all of them. The puffs of smoke Will announced became a steady stream that billowed in waves from the back of the car.

"Shazz! Frikkin' Shazz!" Xander yelled.

"I can't see anything behind us with that thick smoke," Will groaned.

"MediCar, right turn. Purity Place." Xander's wide eyes darted back and forth.

The vehicle turned but dramatically slowed. A clicking sound accompanied a dragging sensation coming from underneath them.

"What's happening?" Will demanded.

"Heck if I know," Xander said.

"Energy is failing. Be advised. *Energy is failing.*" A red light pulsed on the dashboard. "The reactor capacitor is blown." The car's words were a death knell. The acidic smell of burning electronics filled the cab as the whine of the motor died down and silence replaced wind noise.

"This car is gonna be our doom! Why is it stopping?" Will's panicked words set Ember on edge.

Xander pumped a bright red knob to his right. "I'm trying everything …"

"That's not doing a damn thing, Xander. Stop it." Will clambered forward, his direct momentum adding an aggressive weight to his words. "The car's done! We need a plan. Now!"

"Okay, okay. I say we bail outta this car and take our chances on foot. Ember?"

"See that open door up ahead?" Ember pointed across the street.

"That garage?" Will asked.

"That's the one." Before the MediCar fully limped to a stop, Ember released the hydraulic latch on her side. "Get ready to jump ship. We're here."

A sneak peak at Book Three, Bleeding Out

Acknowledgements

Dear Readers~

This book has been a complete submersion into the agony and ecstasy of my beloved characters. While perseverating on finding just the right word continues to drive me crazy, I am loving the thrill of following my characters wherever they lead. I am immensely proud of this book and the journey I've taken with the people who now are more like my best friends: Ember, Will, Xander, and Wee.

I'd like to thank all the people who made this book possible: my family for their incredible unwavering support, brainstorming, and complete devotion to this project; to my amazing Escondido Writers Group who read and critique my work at each meeting and who keep me inspired; to Pete Peterson, who painstakingly reviewed my entire manuscript; to my Beta readers, Melissa Hadibi, Nate Lieberg, Diego Marquez, Karla Martinez, Emily Nava, Samantha Nguyen, Deanna Vuong, and Jeremiah Yolemi; to Trish Lucia and Laura Whitney who delivered my Beta readers; to my amazing cover artist, Natasha MacKenzie, who not only designed a breathtaking cover for *Rising Up*, my first novel, but outdid herself on this one; and to the readers and fans of *Rising Up*, who pushed me to continue this story about this society and its people.

And finally, to my Lord and Savior Jesus Christ, who's got me every step of the way.

About the Author

Tanya Ross loves frozen yogurt, golden retrievers, fat books, and quirky middle and high school kids. Her greatest joys are her family and her faith in Jesus Christ. When she's not writing, you can find her buried in social media to discover new friends and fellow authors.

Check out my website!

Discover more on my website and sign up for my newsletter at
https://www.tanyarossauthor.com

Book Club Questions

1. How did you feel when Will was captured at the very beginning of the book? Were you surprised?

2. Do you feel Ember is beginning to embrace who she is by the end of the book? Why or why not?

3. The million dollar question: Team Will, or Team Xander? Why?

4. Do you think Ember is a brave character? How much is she a feminist?

5. Do you feel Will did too much lying to protect his friends?

6. What comparisons can you draw between our world today and what these characters are facing?

7. What did you learn about the Cincinnati Subway?

8. If you had to live on The Outside or adhere to Tranquility's Accords, what choice would you make?

9. Is Xander a lovable character? Why or why not?

10. What was your favorite part of the book? Why?

www.ingramcontent.com/pod-product-compliance
Lightning Source LLC
Chambersburg PA
CBHW051549100726
47898CB00001B/24